Julian Symons made a reputation before the Second World War as the editor of *Twentieth Century Verse*, a magazine which published most of the young poets outside the immediate Auden circle. He has since become a celebrated writer of crime fiction and is also recognized as the greatest British expert on the genre. He has also written extensively about real-life crime in *A Reasonable Doubt* and *Crime and Detection from 1840*, and has written many articles on the historical background of both real and fictional crime. His survey of crime literature, *Bloody Murder*, was published in Penguin in 1985 and received the Mystery Writers of America Edgar Allan Poe Award. A new edition has been published recently. In 1976 he succeeded Agatha Christie as the President of the Detection Club, and was made a Grand Master of the Swedish Academy of Detection in 1977. He was created a Grand Master by the Mystery Writers of America in 1982. Mr Symons also has a separate reputation as a biographer and as a social and military historian. In 1975 he was made a Fellow of the Royal Society of Literature. His crime works include *The Plot Against Roger Rider*, *A Three Pipe Problem*, *The Detling Secret*, *The Tigers of Subtopia*, *The Name of Annabel Lee* and *The Criminal Comedy*, all published in Penguin, together with *The Julian Symons Omnibus*. Julian Symons has also edited *The Penguin Classic Crime Omnibus*. His most recent crime story is *Something Like a Love Affair*. In 1990 he received the CWA Cartier Diamond Dagger Award, probably the greatest accolade for a crime writer.

THE
BLACKHEATH
POISONINGS

A Victorian Murder Mystery
by Julian Symons

PENGUIN BOOKS

PENGUIN BOOKS
Published by the Penguin Group
Penguin Books USA Inc., 375 Hudson Street, New York, New York 10014, U.S.A.
Penguin Books Ltd, 27 Wrights Lane, London W8 5TZ, England
Penguin Books Australia Ltd, Ringwood, Victoria, Australia
Penguin Books Canada Ltd, 10 Alcorn Avenue, Toronto, Ontario, Canada M4V 3B2
Penguin Books (N.Z.) Ltd, 182–190 Wairau Road, Auckland 10, New Zealand

Penguin Books Ltd, Registered Offices: Harmondsworth, Middlesex, England

First published in Great Britain by
Collins Publishers 1978
First published in the United States of America by
Harper & Row, Publishers, Inc. 1978
Published in Penguin Books in the United States of America
by arrangement with Harper & Row Publishers, Inc.
Published in Penguin Books 1980
This edition published in Penguin Books 1993

10 9 8 7 6 5 4 3 2 1

LIBRARY OF CONGRESS CATALOGING IN PUBLICATION DATA
Symons, Julian, 1912–
The Blackheath poisonings.
I. Title.
[PZ3.S9927Bj]   1980]   [PR6037.Y5]   823'.9'12   79-24876
ISBN 0 14 02.3066 1

Printed in the United States of America
Set in Caledonia

CONTENTS

ACKNOWLEDGMENTS

My thanks are due to Mr. Malcolm Quantrill for providing the architecture of Albert House and Victoria Villa. If I have strayed at times from his original and more splendid accounts of these houses, it has been purely because of the needs of the story. Mr. David Leggatt kindly suggested possible sources of information about Blackheath in the nineties, and the Blackheath Local History Centre was immensely helpful in providing background material.

JULIAN SYMONS

THE BLACKHEATH POISONINGS

Prelude

THE extraordinary series of crimes popularly called the Blackheath Poisonings took place in the early 1890s, at a time when the Mortimer family had lived in that suburb on the edge of London for nearly half a century.

Charles Mortimer had in the 1830s founded the toy company that bore his name, importing toys shrewdly and successfully from Switzerland and Germany. A few years later, as the company prospered, he moved out from Fulham to Blackheath, which then counted almost as country but had a railway service that took travelers up to Charing Cross or Blackfriars in less than half an hour. Toys were Charles Mortimer's business, but his passions were for travel and for architecture, and in Blackheath he designed and had built for him not one but two houses. Albert House stood on the edge of the heath and was occupied by its designer, who lived there with his wife and four children, two sons and two daughters. Victoria Villa was built on Belmont Hill, no more than a mile away in the direction of Lewisham, and was bought by Charles's brother Ralph, who was a partner in the firm.

These were certainly remarkable houses. Charles Mortimer was a man of brief but passionate enthusiasms, and Albert House was the result of his youthful love for churches, particularly those in East Anglia. To have a house that looked like a church—what could be more Romantic? The entrance to Albert House was in the form of a lich gate, and the porch was embraced within the base of a stumpy buttressed tower. This tower was flanked by two stories that might have been the ends of aisles. It was open at the front and sides, and light carriages could be driven right in under the tower to the foot of the short flight of steps which reached up into the dark recess that framed the door. There was some local indignation when the house was completed because it was felt to be sacrilegious, but in time villagers became accustomed to it and even called it "the church."

Inside, the house was equally unusual. Its feature was the Great Hall, which ran most of the length and width of the house. In the Great Hall were carved stone columns reaching up to a boarded vault, increasing the likeness to a church. But church blended with cloister in the aisles that led off the Great Hall to the rest of the house, including the kitchen, pantries, stillroom, and servants' quarters and the breakfast room. The Great Hall itself had to serve as dining room, and because it was so dark (the light came from roundels set in the wooden vault), it was necessary always to have oil lamps burning. Indeed, the whole house was dark, including the library, which led off a gallery that ran around the hall, and the bedrooms, which also opened off the gallery. All had small lancet windows so that the house not only seemed dark and gloomy, but gave an impression of wintry coldness on the hottest summer day. Charles Mortimer was delighted with it. You felt, he said, the whole time as though you were in church.

He was equally pleased with Victoria Villa, which was the result of a visit to Italy. It was designed on a stunted

Palladian plan, and was an impressive model of inconvenience. An imposing colonnade curved concavely toward a pillared gateway, which gave entrance to a long, sweeping gallery. Behind the colonnade, to form a forecourt, sprouted two parallel wings, one containing the kitchens and the other the library.

The great curved gallery faced south across the gardens, and it evoked gasps of admiration from those who saw it for the first time. But just as in Albert House everything had been sacrificed to the Great Hall, so here the gallery's length meant that there was not much other accommodation. One end of it had to serve as the dining room, and you passed through this to reach the salon at the end of the gallery which jutted out into the western corner. The salon had been modeled on an ancient temple seen by Charles on his travels, and the dome stuck on top of it looked ridiculous within and an excrescence from outside. At the other end of the gallery were the breakfast room and the morning room, and again you had to go through one to reach the other. The bedrooms above spread out along the arc, all of them overlooking the garden. There were masses of windows and the house was gloriously light, but there was very little room to hang pictures or even to put ornaments. Ralph, a good-humored man, once called Victoria Villa a crescent-shaped white elephant, and the term "white elephant" stuck, although it was not used in Charles's hearing.

Charles Mortimer was proud of his houses, but Blackheath was unlucky to his family. Within a decade of the building of Albert House, his eldest son, Charles, had been thrown by his horse and had died of a fractured skull. Within another five years his son James had coughed away his life with galloping consumption, and his wife was dead too. She had succumbed to no obvious disease, but as it seemed because she lacked the will to live. From these blows, and in particular from the deaths of his handsome sons, Charles Mortimer never really recovered. He did not care much for his younger daughter, Louisa, who was very plain, but his older daughter, Harriet, resembled his fine sons in appearance. "You are my ewe lamb," he said to her, but although she acknowledged the necessity to remain with her father and care for him, she was far from being a ewe lamb. Her brothers had disliked Blackheath, feeling that it was too far from town, but Harriet loved it. She ran the house more efficiently than her mother had done and when she married, at the late age of thirty, it was on the understanding that Albert House should remain her home. By this time some small modifications had been made, including the replacement of some of the lancet slits by large rose windows, which increased the amount of light but looked extremely incongruous.

John Collard, Harriet's husband, was five years her junior. He was the mild, unassuming son of a barrister, who had for some years been reading for the bar. There were those who said he lacked a will of his own, while others said he wanted an easy life. Reading for the bar had taxed his inconsiderable mental resources, and he readily accepted the idea that he should enter the company as a junior partner. His presence there may not have been much help to his ailing father-in-law or to Ralph Mortimer, but it enabled Harriet to take an active role in the business. It was she who suggested that they should buy out Ralph, whose application to commerce had never been great, and whose children showed no interest. With her husband's acquiescence, she participated in the negotiations, which ended with Ralph's selling his shares to John Collard, and the renaming of the firm as Mortimer and Collard. The price paid was not excessive, and the negotiating solicitor was full of admiration for Harriet's business capacity. Harriet's interest in the firm became more marked after the death of her father at the age of seventy. He had suffered from a variety of illnesses, including gout and dropsy, and had been more or less bedridden for some time. She had superintended his care with her usual efficiency, making sure that he had special diets and was allowed nothing that might be bad for him.

"You've been a good daughter," he said a few weeks before the end. "But I wish . . ."

He paused so long that she said, "Yes?"

"I wish you'd let me die." As she told him not to be foolish, he went on. "What's the point of my being here? Can't see there's any; hasn't been for years. You run everything now."

She told young Dr. Porterfield that she thought her father was delirious, but the doctor found the old man perfectly sensible. Perhaps John Collard had much the same feeling as Charles Mortimer when during an influenza epidemic he slipped out of life as unobtrusively as he had lived it, or indeed as he had given Harriet three children, George, Charlotte and Beatrice. "Given" seemed the right word, for most of those who saw the family felt that the children were hers rather than his.

2

Ralph Mortimer had not shared his brother's liking for southeast London. He developed a strong objection to railway travel, on the ground that the number of people who occupied railway carriages in the course of a day made them dangerous to health. As he refused to use the railway, he found the district inconvenient for getting to town, and moved to St. John's Wood. Victoria Villa remained in the family, however, for Ralph sold it to a distant cousin named Peter Vandervent, a partner in a shipping firm. He was of Dutch origin, as suggested by his name, and the firm had a large and profitable trading connection with Holland. He made some minor changes in the villa, but Charles Mortimer's design defeated any attempt to do more. Considerable alteration to the gallery would have involved changing the whole interior structure of the house.

The occupants of the house and the villa, the church and the white elephant, were on friendly terms, and at the time of Peter Vandervent's death his son Roger was engaged to Beatrice Collard. Roger had been married before. His wife had died a few days after giving birth to their son, Paul. Roger had stayed at the villa, with a nanny and then a governess to look after the child, even though the house was obviously too big for him. Beatrice felt no reluctance in taking on a stepson, and they were married a decorous twelvemonth after Peter's death, in the middle 1880s, when Beatrice was in her twenty-second year. She was the youngest of the three children, and the only one to have inherited her mother's classical good looks. Both George and Charlotte had the puddingy unmade features of their father. Roger, on the other hand, had the dash and handsomeness conspicuously lacking in most of the Collards, and it is likely that even at the time of the engagement Harriet had it in mind that he would take a place in the firm. She had remained the ruling spirit in Mortimer and Collard after her husband's death, although her son George was nominally the senior partner. It was she who had seen that the English toy trade was developing, and had made arrangements for the warehouse to be turned into a factory producing a range of Mortimer and Collard toys. A couple of weeks after Beatrice's marriage, she spoke to George. It was Harriet's habit to be direct.

"It seems to me, George, that you find your work at the firm too great a burden."

George fidgeted with his pudgy fingers, picking at the cloth of the chair on which he sat. "I don't think so."

"Hexham tells me that he often finds it difficult to obtain decisions from you. Materials sometimes remain unordered for weeks."

"I don't know what he means. He could have spoken to me."

"He tells me that he has."

"I don't remember; I don't believe he did. It's those wretched clerks in the outer office. Hexham doesn't look after them properly."

"Hexham has been with the firm for thirty years. Nobody has said before that he is anything but conscientious."

"Oh, *conscientious,*" George said, as though this were anything but a virtue. "But he's hopelessly old-fashioned."

"I think you need help. I think you should offer your cousin Roger a partnership." There was silence. "I wish you would stop picking at that chair, George."

They were talking at one end of the Great Hall. George walked over to one of the rose windows and stood with his back to his mother, looking out. He jangled the coins in his pocket.

"Do you have anything against Roger?" Harriet asked.

"No, I've nothing against him. I like him. But he's been mixed up with one or two affairs that are supposed to have been a bit doubtful. You must know that."

It was true that Roger had refused to enter his father's shipping firm, preferring as he said to paddle his own canoe, and that he had paddled it sometimes in rough waters. He had been associated with the flotation of some Australian gold-field shares, and also with a firm that proposed to exploit the development of Paraguayan railways, among similar enterprises. Some of these stocks had shot up and down in the market like rockets, and if any fortunes had been made, it was for those who promoted them rather than for investors. Nobody, however, suggested that Roger had done anything dishonorable.

"You have to take risks to succeed in life." Harriet was capable of using this sort of platitude to devastating effect. "Perhaps you should have taken more risks, George. It is time you were married."

"Really, Mother."

"You are nearly twenty-eight years old."

George's face was flushed. "When I marry, who I marry, is a matter for me. I'm not prepared to let you rule my life as you did Father's. I won't let you interfere with my affairs."

Harriet was some inches shorter than her son, but she produced an impression of power. "I have no wish to interfere with your affairs, whatever they are. My concern is that the firm should continue to be run by our family, and that it should be run properly. When you have had an opportunity for reflection, we can talk about the matter again."

A fortnight later George offered his cousin a partnership in Mortimer and Collard. Perhaps Roger had expected something of the sort when he married Beatrice; perhaps his affairs in the City were not prospering. In any case, he accepted the offer without hesitation.

3

It was another four years before George Collard fulfilled his mother's wish and married Isabel Payne. She was the daughter of one of the firm's principal clients, a firm of wholesalers with a big warehouse in Clerkenwell, from which they sold to retail shops. The Payne family had some pretensions to gentility, or at least to a position in life that did not involve trade. Augustus Payne, Isabel's father, had been brought up in the style suitable for the son of a Lincolnshire landowner, with a fine country house called Langley Hall and a considerable estate. He had been sent to Winchester and then to Oxford. He had been in his second year at Christ Church when his father's sudden death revealed that there was little money in the bank, and that the house and estate were burdened with a network of loans and mortgages, some of them at exorbitant rates of interest. In the end the debts were paid by selling a lot of the land, but there was no money for Augustus, who was the youngest of the family. A fellow, as he said, had to do something. Augustus braced himself and went into trade, for which he turned out to have considerable aptitude. Now he had a fine house at Dulwich, and kept his carriage and pair.

Augustus was a bluff, sociable man, who did not forget that he was one of the Paynes of Langley Hall. People did not take liberties with Augustus Payne, or at least they did not do so twice. But still he had succeeded in life by keeping an eye firmly on the main chance, and he had five girls to get married. Although George Collard might not be the brightest spark in the world, he was the senior partner in an old established firm, and would presumably in time inherit most of his mother's money. Mrs. Payne gave occasional soirees to which eligible young gentlemen were invited, George among them. When he seemed distinctly taken with Isabel, he was asked more than once to dinner. The Paynes were a great family for round games, charades and poetry readings, and George was quite the life and soul of some of these family parties. He was particularly good at charades that involved dressing up, and gave splendid recitations of verses like "The Mistletoe Bough" and "The Old Arm-Chair":

> I love it! I love it! And who shall dare
> To chide me for loving that old arm-chair?

Sometimes Isabel accompanied him on the piano and sometimes, with hand placed on his breast and a pathetic tone in his voice, he seemed to be addressing her directly. But although George paid Isabel constant attention, he didn't actually say anything. It became clear to Augustus that he would have to be brought up to the mark. One evening after George, with Isabel at the piano, had given a spirited rendering of two or three ballads, he was asked into the study and given a glass of port.

"You're a pretty good hand at a song, George. Never heard a better; it's a treat to listen to you. And my word, doesn't my little girl enter into the spirit of it."

"Yes, Isabel is quite splendid at the piano."

"Seems to me you two get on pretty well."

"Isabel is delightful, quite delightful."

This, although enthusiastic enough, was hardly satisfactory. Augustus stood warming his backside at the fire.

"Thing is, a father's got obligations. Five girls to look after and all that. I can't do what I'd like for 'em all, but Isabel won't come to her husband with nothing. That may be the modern way, but it's not mine. And she's a pretty filly."

"Isabel is beautiful."

Augustus jibbed a little at that. "Beautiful" was not a word he used about women. "She's the best of the bunch for looks. And sweet-tempered—follows her mother in that."

George sipped reflectively at his port. Augustus found it necessary to be plain, even though the plainness did not leave him quite comfortable.

"Thing is, do you mean to speak to her? Because if you do there's no point in leaving it another six months, and if you don't I'd just as soon know."

George went on sipping, and playing with his fingers, lacing and unlacing them. Perhaps this was a nervous reaction, but it was infernally annoying.

"Well, man?"

"Isabel is beautiful."

Augustus found his irritation increased by this repetition of an irrelevant remark. What did beauty matter? The question was whether the fellow was going to come up to the mark. George went on.

"I had never thought—I know that I'm not a handsome man, I am not attractive—I don't think I can—"

Augustus felt inclined to laugh, but restrained himself. Was *that* all the man was worrying about?

"My dear feller, you're too modest. Women don't worry about looks, believe me. It's what a man's like that counts, his personality. You and Isabel get on—that's what matters."

"If you think she might . . ."

"I can't answer for her, can I? The thing to do is to pop the question."

Three days later Isabel told her mother that George had asked her to marry him.

"And what did you say?" Mary Payne asked.

"I told him I'd think about it." Isabel at twenty perhaps deserved George's adjective. She had small, elegant hands and feet, a flawless complexion of delicate pallor, and a good figure. She was a great reader and (so far as that was possible when her father did not care for the theater) a theatergoer. She was also prepared to talk about the latest book or play, even though she had neither read one nor seen the other. Mary Payne was never quite at ease with her daughter. She had a feeling that Isabel was always playing some part—the part of young lady about town (except of course that they lived out at Dulwich), or of a literary lady, or when they were playing charades, of an actress—and that her real personality had not been shown even to her parents. Mary was a straightforward woman, and asked what seemed to her the natural question.

"Do you love him?"

"Oh, as to that"—Isabel waved a slim hand and bent her lips in a faint smile—"as to that, I don't love anybody. I mean, I don't know that I ever shall love anybody."

"Oh, what nonsense, Isabel." And indeed her mother found the statement very great nonsense. You loved your husband just as you loved your children, as a matter of course. She admired Augustus more than any other man she had ever met, and the admiration sprang at least in part from the fact that he was her husband. To reassure herself, she added, "You don't mean it."

"Supposing nobody had thought of the idea of being in love, do you suppose it would ever have happened to people?" The question seemed to her mother vaguely irreverent, and she did not reply. "As to being admired, that's a different question; of course I like that. But I quite see that Papa wants to get his daughters off his hands, and that he would like me to get married. I suppose George Collard will do as well as anybody else. I shall tell him that my answer is yes."

It could not be said that the conversation left Mary Payne satisfied. "Isabel is a strange girl," she said to her husband in bed that night. "I'm not sure that I understand her."

"Nonsense, my dear. Young people have their fads and fancies."

"It isn't exactly fads and fancies. She seems to look at things so strangely."

"Just wait till she's got a couple of nippers running

around. Nothing like that to get silly ideas out of girls' heads."

His wife said nothing more. Much as she admired her husband, she saw that he did not understand what she meant.

"I'll tell you one thing," he said before he turned over to sleep. "Isabel will be able to manage him. Oh, won't she just! She'll turn him round her little finger."

So they were married at Dulwich. Isabel's sisters Clara and Violet were bridesmaids, her young brother Geoffrey was an usher, and Augustus, who always shone on such occasions, looked very impressive as he walked up the aisle with his daughter on his arm. Isabel also looked her best in a high-necked dress with a veil that fell almost to the level of her knees, through which she somehow managed to see. Her father said that she was stunning, George that she was like a princess in a fairy tale, and she accepted these tributes with the smile of one who knows that they are her due. Afterward there was a reception, with a big marquee put up in the garden, and the champagne flowing. Augustus made a stylish speech and Roger, who was best man, a funny one. George stumbled through a few words. Then the couple left for a honeymoon in Italy, Isabel having said that she wished more than anything to see the treasures of Venice and Florence.

When they returned they began married life at Victoria Villa. This unusual arrangement was prompted partly by the size of the house, which could comfortably accommodate another family. That was especially so because Roger and Beatrice had no children, Beatrice having twice miscarried. There were other reasons, however. One was that George and Roger hit it off very well. Roger, there was no doubt about it, took a lot of weight off George's shoulders at work. He got on well with everybody from the men in the workshops to the clients, knowing just when to exchange a joke and when to check a man from becoming familiar. There was also the fact that George had no money of his own. His relations with his mother had not improved, and before he married he had said more than once that he would move out of Albert House, which he called a dismal hole, and rent rooms. He had not done this, but had taken to spending more and more of his evenings in central London. He had become a member of two clubs, one named the Punch and Judy, which was used by people in the toy trade, and another club in the West End called the Gorgon. He sometimes returned slightly tipsy, after coming on the railway to Blackheath and then taking the growler up from the station. Harriet said nothing, but when Isabel had accepted him she told him that on his marriage he would receive the same sum as had been given to Beatrice. She paid no attention to George's protests about his rights.

"What rights are you speaking of? I know of none."

George flushed, moving uneasily from one leg to the other. "I know Father left everything to you, but as his heir—"

"Heir to what? There is this house and the business. If you applied yourself to the business and it made more profit you would receive more money. Even as things are, there should be quite enough for your needs. If you put your evenings to better use in the future, you will have no difficulty in supporting a wife."

"It was you who said I should get married."

"I said nothing about supporting you. I see no reason why you should have anything, but I am prepared to give you what your sister received. Charlotte, if she marries, can expect something similar."

With this money, added to what Augustus gave to his daughter, it would have been possible to have bought a house in Dulwich or Lewisham or Blackheath, or another of the southeastern suburbs, but Isabel said that she did not mind sharing a place. If one did not live in Belgravia or Mayfair, one might as well be anywhere. And as for sharing a house rather than owning one, what in the world did it matter?

So they went to the white elephant. At the time of the poisonings they had been there for rather more than a year. They, too, had as yet no children.

4

Harriet Collard had no faith in public philanthropy. She was opposed to the spread of free education, believing that it was a waste of public money to teach servant girls and laborers to read. She disapproved of welfare societies for the poor and of trade unions that tried to limit the number of working hours in a day. It was her tenet that God would help the poor, and that those who did not wish to work a twelve-hour day should make room for those who did. With the gift she had for making clichés sound like newly minted aphorisms, she observed that charity begins at home. She had, however, her private benevolences, which extended to an undergardener and odd-job man named James, whose wife, Pauline, had been a housemaid. She had always been sickly, and proved to be suffering from some mysterious blood ailment which deprived her of energy. The illness made her an invalid, and at last she died of it. Harriet had Dr. Porterfield attend on her as he would a member of the family, and after her death allowed James to stay on and take his wages, although he did little work and often reeled home from the four-ale bar in the village. Harriet's benevolence also resulted in an addition to the

household after her husband's death. Her enemies said
that she wanted another subject to rule.

The subject was Albert John Williams, son of Harriet's
younger sister, Louisa. It has been said that Louisa was
plain, and she could indeed have been called downright
ugly. It had been a relief to her father when she was
courted and briskly married by Major Williams, a half-
pay officer formerly of the Indian Army. It was understood that the major had plenty of money, and was rather
a catch for a toy merchant's daughter. He proved, however, to be intemperate, insolvent and intermittently un-
faithful, and her unhappy marriage ended when he went
off with a Spanish dancer to Venezuela, where he died
a couple of years later in some obscure uprising. Louisa,
who was already showing the family's consumptive tend-
ency, appealed to Harriet, who took her in together with
her young son, Albert John, the single fruit of her union
with the major. Louisa always expected that her husband
would return, asking for forgiveness, and when she
learned that the dancer had still been his companion
when he died, it hastened her own end.

The major had left no money, and Harriet undertook
the education of Albert John, who became known as Bertie. He was not sent to Eton or Winchester, because that
would not have been appropriate to his circumstances.
He went to the Blackheath Proprietary School nearby;
known as the Prop, it was regarded as the equal of any
day school in the country. There he got generally good,
although not enthusiastic, reports. "Certainly applies
himself, but I wish he didn't give quite so much of an
impression that butter would be likely to freeze in his
mouth," said one master. Bertie was not sent to university, which again would have been inappropriate, but
went straight into the business at the age of eighteen.
He had been there for three years at the time the events

of this story took place, and showed no particular talent for the work. He had become involved with the temperance movement and remained, as he had been at school, a vegetarian.

The dramatis personae of the affair have now been described. At Albert House there lived Harriet Collard, an imposing matron nearly sixty years old, her daughter Charlotte, who was not yet thirty but seemed destined to become an old maid, and Bertie Williams. About a mile away in Belmont Hill, which might be considered Lewisham rather than Blackheath, lived Roger Vandervent and his wife, Beatrice, with the seventeen-year-old Paul, who was Roger's son and Beatrice's stepson. In the same house lived George Collard and his Isabel. The family was a close one in the way of the time, in spite of the coolness between George and his mother. Twice a month the families at the villa came to Albert House for Sunday lunch, twice Harriet's household went to Victoria Villa.

In this family, during the space of a few months, three people died.

(1)

A Week in May

A DAY in May, a day warm as high summer. At Albert House wheels sounded on gravel, a level and confident voice was heard, Dr. Porterfield descended from his carriage beneath the tower to pay his fortnightly visit. The doctor was red-faced, and wore old-fashioned side whiskers. A thin gold chain extended across what he would have called his corporation. When he paid a visit he took a glass of Madeira if it was in the morning, a cup of tea if it was afternoon. First, however, he saw all the household, including the servants. The servants were lined up in the cavern of the Great Hall and he looked them over one by one rather as if they were animals, prescribing a bottle of tonic here and a purge there. Dr. Porterfield was strong on purges.

Later he saw Harriet in her bedroom, which was dark and somber, with thick red curtains and a great fourposter which had belonged to her father. She complained of pains around the heart. The doctor used his stethoscope, prodded gently a little here and there, pronounced it indigestion and prescribed a bismuth mixture. He then visited Charlotte and Bertie, visits on which, as always, he was accompanied by Harriet. Charlotte went unscathed, but Bertie's tongue was said to be a bad color.

"A few sulfur tablets may be a good thing. The blood becomes overheated in this weather."

"The food he eats is not nourishing," Harriet said. "Nothing but lettuce leaves—he might be a rabbit." And indeed Bertie, who was fair and pale, with pinkish eyes, had a slightly rabbitish appearance.

"Aunt Harriet, you know that I eat everything I feel to be nutritious. I simply abstain from eating the flesh of dead animals."

"Not enough red meat, too many cream cakes. Isn't that so, Doctor?"

Dr. Porterfield was a diplomat. "I am a believer— hum—in the value of good roast beef in building bone and muscle."

"And so am I," Harriet said emphatically. Then they went in to tea.

This was served in the lighter end of the Great Hall, where the sun cast strong circles of light through two rose windows. There were two kinds of cake, seed and fruit, a sponge sandwich filled with jam and cream, a variety of biscuits, bread and butter with strawberry or greengage jam. Harriet sat in her customary chair, which was upholstered in a woolwork pattern of various fruits. Jenny, who had been with her for only a short time, handed round plates with a slightly trembling hand.

"Bread and butter before cake," Harriet said to Bertie. His hand had been outstretched toward the cake tray, but he obediently took bread and butter. Miserable little squirt, the doctor thought, he'd do better standing up for himself sometimes. The doctor took fruit cake himself, and made conversation about a curious variety of cold that had afflicted many of his patients in the warm weather. She certainly rules the roost, he reflected, and always did, from the time she was a girl. If she'd married somebody with a bit more go than Collard—but then of course she would never have done that. A fine woman, but she couldn't be much fun to live with.

He watched Charlotte, who, having eaten some bread and butter, now took a piece of jam sponge. Charlotte was a short, dumpy woman, as plain as Harriet's sister Louisa had been, with the indeterminate Collard face, and mouse-brown hair. She was a clumsy eater, and now dropped a fragment of jammy sponge on her anonymous gray dress. Harriet refrained from speaking, refrained even from looking. Charlotte picked up the fragment, dabbed with her napkin. The doctor began to talk about the poetry recital at the Rink Hall that evening, which two of his daughters were attending, and asked whether Charlotte or Bertie was going. Bertie said that he was attending a temperance meeting. Charlotte merely shook her head.

"I'd lay a bet that young Paul will be going," the doctor said heartily. "I've never known a lad so keen about books."

"He should be looking after his schoolwork," Harriet said.

"Ah, but he's a dab hand at that too, if his father's to be believed." No comment was made on this. A few minutes later Dr. Porterfield took his leave.

Bertie had a room in the tower, reached by a circular staircase. He had just come down from it, ready for the South London Temperance Society meeting, and was at the head of the stairs, when Charlotte's door opened and she beckoned him in.

It was some time since he had entered her room, and he looked around with the eager curiosity that was part of his nature. It contained all the things that might have been expected in a lady's bedroom: a dressing table with knickknacks on it, an occasional table on which stood photographs of her mother and father together with others of Charlotte as a child looking awkward in pink muslin, of three children, and of family groups which included Bertie. The furnishings were like those of the other bedrooms: thick red curtains, a marble washstand, a dark-red Indian carpet. But there was about this room something, not exactly a smell or a perfume but a kind of womanly closeness, that made Bertie blink rapidly and almost sniff. Charlotte took hold of his wrist. Her hand was slightly moist.

"Bertie, I want you to do something for me."

"If I can, Charlotte. Of course."

"It will be no trouble. But can I trust you?"

Bertie blinked at her again, then looked down at the carpet. To another eye than Charlotte's his appearance, which was unmistakably that of some small furtive animal, whether rabbit, stoat or weasel, would not have induced trust. But she evidently saw nothing wrong, for, turning away from him to a small davenport which she opened and closed, she handed him a square, blue envelope.

"I want you to post this for me. If Mother found me going out for a few minutes she'd ask what I was doing and I couldn't explain—you know what I'm like. Turn it over, Bertie."

When he saw the superscription he understood. "So he's turned up again."

"He wrote to me. He's here; he wants us to meet. What shall I do?"

"Why not tell Aunt Harriet?"

"I can't do that. You know what she'd say. I wondered, Bertie . . ."

"Yes?"

"If I went to meet him one day, do you think I could

go out with you? You could say you were taking me to one of your meetings."

"And you'd go off to see him. Supposing you didn't come back at the right time?"

"I would; I'd be sure to. Please, Bertie."

He divined that this was what she had really called him in for, because she could certainly have found some excuse to post the letter herself. He said that he would think about it and on the way to the meeting, after posting the letter, which was addressed to Robert Dangerfield, Esq., he did. Charlotte had met Dangerfield three years earlier, at a charity dance. He was a man in his forties, a tea planter in Assam home on leave, and he made his interest plain. He came to Albert House several times, took Charlotte out to the theater, within a month proposed marriage. There had been family conclaves, from which Bertie was excluded—one of the things that he most resented was the fact that although he was a member of the family he was not treated as a Mortimer or a Collard. If he was to be kept out from such a family council, why should Roger, who also had no direct blood link, be there? Bertie did not forget such slights and deprivations. But he heard what happened, mostly from George, and it seemed that Dangerfield had been divorced. He had been the innocent party, it was true, but the circumstances were unpleasant. He had caught his wife *in flagrante delicto* with another man (Bertie had to search through books to find out what this meant), and there had been a shooting affray in which the other man was wounded in the shoulder. A charge of attempted murder was made against Dangerfield, and although he had been acquitted, the whole thing, as George said, made a bit of a stink.

"And then, you know, Mother isn't too keen on India anyway. I mean, your dad came from there, and he was a bad hat. Don't mean to hurt your feelings, Bertie, but he certainly was a bit of a goer." Bertie shook his head to show that his feelings were not hurt. He resented the father who had abandoned him, as well as the mother who had inconsiderately died and left him a poor relation.

"Do you know what Mother said?" George was very good at imitating women's voices, and now he caught Harriet's sharp but powerful imperiousness very well. "'Charlotte, you are twenty-seven, and I cannot prevent you from getting married. You can tell your suitor, however, that there will be no question of your taking any dowry with you. I think you may find that his ardor is reduced.' Can you imagine talking like that in this day and age?"

"What happened?"

"Charlotte said Mother had promised she'd get as much as Beatrice, and Mother said Beatrice had made a different kind of marriage." At that George fell silent, thinking perhaps about his own talk with his mother about money.

Whether Dangerfield found Charlotte unacceptable without her money, or whether Charlotte felt unable to disobey her mother, the result was that the tea planter had returned to Assam, and his name was no longer mentioned. And now he had turned up again, presumably on leave. Bertie thought about what might happen, and wondered how it could be turned to his advantage. That, indeed, was how he thought of everything.

He was in particularly good voice that night when they sang one of the Band of Hope songs:

> Oh, we're a youthful Band of Hope,
> All pledged strong drink to flee.
> Then let our watchword sound afar:
> "No drink, no drink for me."

Later an excellent speaker gave them the Malt Liquor Lecture, revealing that ale contained five percent alcohol, four percent barley, and ninety-one percent water. Was it not common sense to drink water? Bertie and his close friend Thompson agreed that it had been a very fine meeting.

2

On that same day in May, at just about the time when Charlotte was confiding in Bertie, Paul Vandervent sat at the bamboo table in his bedroom at the villa, writing a poem. Or rather, writing the first stanza of a poem:

> My lady's mantled marble cheek
>   Is delicate as ivory.
> Her eyes are like two pools of light
>   And blue as the eternal sea.

Was that descriptive of Isabel? Her eyes were blue undoubtedly, but was it perhaps overloading things to have a marble cheek that was like ivory? A second quatrain struggled to be born, but for the moment failed. Writing poems was for some reason much more difficult than writing English essays on subjects like "Things Seen in the Course of a Walk over the Heath" or political essays that asked him to "Discuss the Future of Great Britain as an Imperial Power." At all subjects that concerned ideas put down on paper he was acknowledged to excel, even though the ideas were sometimes held to be outrageous. His essay on the future of Great Britain had brought a visit to the headmaster's study.

"So," Mr. Bendall had said, "you think that the British Empire is doomed to extinction, do you, young man?"

"Not necessarily, sir."

"That is what your essay appears to say to your form master and myself."

"I suggested that it would collapse, sir, unless its subjects at home and abroad are treated more fairly, get better wages and have some voice in their own government."

"That is the language of street-corner socialists. What does your father think of such ideas?"

"We don't discuss them, sir. But I doubt if he would agree with me."

"I suppose not." Mr. Bendall's voice had been dry but not unfriendly. "You refused the chance of sitting for an Oxford scholarship, which you would have some prospect of obtaining. But of course it would still be possible for you to go to the university. What does your father say about that?"

"He would like it. But I don't want to go to Oxford; it would be a waste of time."

"Indeed? And how would you propose to use your time better?"

"I'd like to be a journalist."

"A penny-a-liner? Hardly a very high ambition."

"Or do some sort of social work. In any case, I don't feel I need any more education. I'd like to do some kind of job."

"You are an intelligent boy, Vandervent, but you have some strange ideas. I shall speak to your father. There is a strong strain of the old Adam in you."

The trouble is, Paul thought, that I only know what I don't want to do. I just don't want to be something boring like a civil servant or a doctor or a lawyer, I don't want to go into the army, and I certainly don't want to join the business. So what did that leave? Not much, as it seemed. He got up and looked at himself in the glass, which like the table was framed in bamboo. He strongly resembled his father, with curly dark hair and a thick growth of beard which he already had to shave every day. When I leave school, he thought, I shall grow a mustache. He wondered if Isabel would like it, decided that he must stop thinking about her, and went down to what had once been the salon and was now the drawing room.

The atmosphere of Victoria Villa was quite unlike that of Albert House. The drawing room there, or the part of the Great Hall used as a drawing room, was filled with an assortment of chairs, sofas and little tables crowded with ornaments and photographs. An embossed dark-green paper covered the walls, and the curtains were of the same color. Here there was more bamboo furniture, some of it curved to fit the circular walls, which were painted in light colors, soft greens and grays. The room had been done to Beatrice's taste, at a time when she had been greatly taken with Whistler and the aesthetic movement. She had such sudden passions, and at present was reconstructing the garden.

In the drawing room he found his father, Beatrice and Isabel. His father slapped him on the shoulder.

"Well, Paul, my lad, a terrible duty devolves on you."

Roger's dark hair was bright with some sort of oil, he had a dark beard and mustache, a ruddy complexion, and very white strong teeth. "You have to escort this fair damsel tonight on your own."

"I thought George was coming too."

"The scoundrel hath deserted her. Faced with the prospect of an evening with the muse he fled to his club. The fair damsel is in your sole charge, my boy. The responsibility is heavy."

He found it hard to contain the joy that leapt within him. "Mother, perhaps you would like to come."

"Thank you, Paul, but I've given up trying to understand poetry. The language is so very extravagant."

Isabel smiled faintly, and said in her low, musical voice, "Perhaps it would be better if you went on your own. I'm afraid that taking me is the most frightful bore for you."

A bore to take Isabel! He started to say something that would make her understand the contrary, but she cut him short and said that of course she would love to come. Then she went upstairs to make herself ready, Beatrice left them too, and he was alone with his father.

"Glad we've got five minutes. I wanted to have a word with you." His father looked at him, half smiling, half frowning. "You're pretty keen on poetry and all that rot, aren't you?"

"I like poetry, yes."

"I've been to see your head—what's his name—Bendix, Bendall. Says you're intelligent. That isn't surprising; you wouldn't be your father's son if you weren't." His teeth gleamed briefly. "What's this stuff about wanting to be a journalist?"

"I said I might be, that's all."

"You can put it out of your mind. I won't have it, you understand, won't have a son of mine being one of those grubby little fellows, smelling out secrets and taking pictures. It's ridiculous."

Paul Vandervent was much like his father in that a total rejection of his ideas always made him angry. He said, "How do you propose to stop me?"

Roger's frown deepened, but he laughed at the same time. "Now look here, my boy, you can't say I'm one of those fathers who says his word is law, am I?"

"No, I suppose not."

Roger cut and lighted a cigar, and stood puffing it. "I'd have liked you to go to a boarding school, Uppingham or Haileybury, but you wanted to live at home, so you went to the Prop. I'd have liked you to sit the Oxford exam, but you didn't want that. The head says you'd have got a scholarship."

"He told me I would have had a chance, that's all."

"He said you'd have been a cert; best English student they've had for years. But you've had your own way over all that, d'you agree? Don't bother; you can't deny it. But now you want to waste it all and I won't have it. There's money to send you to Oxford, and I'd still like you to go there."

"Dad." He did not know how to explain. "The world's changing; it's full of all sorts of new ideas."

"And you think there are no new ideas at Oxford?"

"Not many. I shouldn't be taught anything about—oh, Oscar Wilde, for instance, or George Bernard Shaw, or any of the new writers and artists."

"From what I hear of that fellow Wilde, he's just a poseur. Never heard of the other man. But if that's all—"

"I'd have to read the classics. Oxford belongs to the past."

"Just be good enough not to interrupt me. Now I'll tell you something. You say you want to leave school. Very well. And you don't want to go to Oxford. Very well. But I'll tell you what: if that's so then you go straight into the business—do I make myself clear?" His father's voice was raised; there could be no doubt of his anger. Paul felt a spirit of total rebelliousness rise in him.

"And if I don't want to do that?"

"Then by God, boy, you can clear off and fend for yourself, and you won't find that easy, I can tell you." No sooner were these words spoken than Roger seemed to regret them. "Now look, you have to earn a living, and this way's as good as another."

"Working with the Caterpillar—"

"The Caterpillar? Oh, yes, you mean Bertie. I know you don't see eye to eye with Bertie, but you wouldn't have much to do with him. I tell you what, Paul, I need you or someone like you. George doesn't take much interest, and that puts pretty well everything on my shoulders. Not but what I can bear it, but I could do with somebody young, someone I can trust." He dropped into a chair so emphatically that it shivered with the impact. "George spends too much time in his clubs; it doesn't do. And he's spending money too; I don't know how he gets through it. You could be a great help to me if you were in the firm."

When his father spoke like this, almost appealingly, Paul did not know what to say. He muttered that he knew nothing about the toy business.

"Nor did I when I went in. You'd soon learn."

The door opened and Isabel stood there. Roger's manner changed. "Ah, there you are. Off you go and listen to your poetry. Mind you enjoy it."

There was something about the conversation that disturbed Paul, something that seemed to have been left unsaid, but he forgot this when he looked at Isabel, who wore an ice-blue dress that set off the darker blue of her eyes.

If he had been on his own he would have walked down to the Rink Hall in the village, where the poetry recital was to take place, but of course with Isabel as his companion that was out of the question, even on such a balmy evening. Thomas, the red-nosed coachman, took them in the victoria, the hood down, the air cool and delicate. At the entrance they were met by long, thin Mr. Clutter, whose prominent Adam's apple bobbed up and down as he spoke, as though it had been attached to a piece of elastic. Mr. Clutter, an elderly bachelor, was secretary of the society. To Paul it seemed impossible that this dried-up old stick could have any true love for poetry. He was said to be an expert on the Lake poets, but then Paul had always found them rather dull, not at all up to Rossetti and Swinburne.

"Good evening, Mrs. Collard, delightful to see you. Evening, Paul. We have a feast this evening." He rubbed his hands together, a dry sound. "I'm told Miss O'Shaughnessy has quite a remarkable voice. And Mr. Devlin I expect you have heard before; a very fine baritone."

They passed beyond him and went down the hall to their seats, nodding to familiar figures: Mr. Ranger, the pop-eyed clergyman, with his wife and their three giggling daughters; old Colonel Munster, whose false teeth clattered as he said good evening, and Mrs. Munster, who looked at them over a pair of pince-nez in what seemed a condescending manner; Miss Plantin, the music teacher, who for three years had tried vainly to teach Paul the violin. What interest had they, or the local tradesmen who sat with their wives near the back of the hall, in poetry; what would they know about Oscar Wilde or Ernest Dowson? Paul looked forward to these meetings, but they were often a disappointment to him. Any feeling of possible disappointment was canceled, however, when as they sat down Isabel murmured to him, "Don't you think Mr. Clutter is like a stork? Can't you imagine him on one leg?"

No sooner was the remark made than he saw the felicity of it, Mr. Clutter a stork, Mr. Clutter on one leg with bobbing Adam's apple. He laughed, although with proper discretion. And now, bending toward him so that he felt the warmth of her almost touching arm, she asked, "Will it be an interesting program? You know I'm really quite ignorant about poetry."

The program said: "*English and Scotch Ballads.* A program of recitations and songs. With Irish songs by Miss Maureen O'Shaughnessy and Ballads sung by Mr. Michael Devlin."

"I don't know much about them, but they're mostly old songs and poems. I believe they're anonymous; they are what you might call popular songs."

"How interesting. Paul?"

"Yes?"

"You truly don't mind bringing me here tonight? With nobody else. I'm afraid it's such a bore for you."

A bore to be with her alone, to speak to her with nobody else there, to have her undivided attention—the preposterousness of such an idea overwhelmed him so that he found it impossible to say anything.

"I know nothing about art, yet I feel myself to be artistic, and you are the only person I can talk to about such things. You know I adore the theater, but George is not interested. At the last play we saw, Mr. Pinero's *Magistrate*, he fell asleep."

"Ahem! If I may have your attention, ladies and gentlemen." Mr. Michael Devlin was a red-faced, stout man with a fine carrying voice. "I shall begin our progam tonight with the old Scottish ballad 'Sir Patrick Spens,' the tale of a tragic death at sea. My friend Mr. Corby will be so kind as to accompany me on the piano." Mr. Devlin bowed deeply, Mr. Corby popped up from behind the piano to bow too, then popped down again. A bar or two was played, and then Mr. Devlin's voice resounded through the Rink Hall:

> "The King sits in Dunfermline toun
> Drinking the blood-red wine . . ."

When Mr. Devlin had finished he again bowed deeply, and retired, to be replaced by Miss O'Shaughnessy, who looked like a doll, with red patches on both cheeks and hair done in tight ringlets. In a light, trilling voice, Miss O'Shaughnessy said that she would begin with an Irish song of Mr. Moore's, very sad but very beautiful, called "I Wish I Was by That Dim Lake." Then came Mr. Tolliver, a junior version of Mr. Devlin, less portly, less red-faced, and with a slightly less powerful voice, to sing Mrs. Hemans's "Casabianca," which proved the hit of the evening so far. Mr. Devlin and Miss O'Shaughnessy topped it, however, with a spirited rendering of Calverley's "The Auld Wife Sat at Her Ivied Door," in which Miss O'Shaughnessy repeated the refrain "Butter and eggs and a pound of cheese" with such a rolling of eyes and wagging of forefinger that she seemed to add a new meaning with each verse.

Paul found himself, rather against his expectation, absorbed in the songs. No doubt they were crude compared to Rossetti's "Blessed Damozel," but the renderings were certainly spirited. In the second half of the program Mr. Tolliver and Miss O'Shaughnessy joined in the ballad of Lord Randal, the young man who returns from hunting suffering from a mysterious illness:

"O where have you been, Lord Randal, my son?
O where have you been, my handsome young man?"
"I have been to the wild wood; mother, make my bed soon,
For I'm weary with hunting, and fain would lie down."

What is the matter with Lord Randal? He dined with his sweetheart, ate eels boiled in broth, he is weary. And where are his bloodhounds? They swelled up and died, and he is weary. Then comes the last verse.

"O I fear you are poisoned, Lord Randal, my son!
O I fear you are poisoned, my handsome young man!"
"O yes! I am poisoned; mother, make my bed soon,
For I'm sick at the heart, and I fain would lie down."

Why did the sweetheart poison him? The ballad was frightening because there was no attempt at explanation. Paul felt a prickling at the back of his neck. While the ballad was being sung he was conscious that something strange had happened to his right hand. He looked down and saw that Isabel's hand, small and white, had been placed lightly upon his own. It seemed a magical accident, and he felt that if he moved to place one leg over another, or even to scratch his left leg with his left hand (to which he felt a strong, unaccountable inclination), the spell would be broken. He did not dare even to look sideways to see if she showed awareness of what she had done, but allowed the ungloved hand to lie upon his. Three of the fingers crossed his own but did not hold them, the other finger and the thumb lay upon the back of his hand.

He experienced a delirium of the senses that brought a choking feeling into his throat and made it difficult for him to understand the singers. During the last verse, however, the hand lying upon his jerked away as though moved by galvanic energy, then returned to grip his suddenly, fiercely. Fingers were laced with his, a nail jabbed almost painfully into his palm. The hand was withdrawn as the song ended, and it did not return again. Miss O'Shaughnessy was engaged now with an Irish song about a girl who waited years for the return of a youthful lover who had gone off to make his fortune. She accepted another suitor just before he returned, a rich man, to accuse her of faithlessness and to drown himself. Paul heard the words of this and other songs but could make nothing of them, for in his mind there remained the image of the hand placed over his, the warm quiescent tentacles that had moved to grip and for that single instant to jab.

Then it was over, the chairs were pushed back, and he could look at Isabel. She smiled at him but said nothing until they were in the carriage again. Thomas, his breath smelling of beer, was waiting among a dozen other carriages. There was clucking and shouting and then they were away, out into the village and up the hill. In the darkness she spoke, quite ordinary words.

"I'm glad I came with you tonight. I enjoyed it so much." He said that he had enjoyed it too. "Some of the songs are very sad, aren't they? I could have cried at one or two of them."

"I'm sorry."

"No, no—it's just that I was moved by them. I thought Miss O'Shaughnessy sang with wonderful feeling."

"Some of the poems are sad, it's true. Of course, there were comic songs as well." What an idiotic thing to say! And when he tried to make amends for the idiocy it came out as though he were a prosing schoolteacher. "Do you know 'The Blessed Damozel' by Rossetti? I think that is more beautiful than anything we heard tonight."

"Tell me a little of it."

" 'She had three lilies in her hand/And the stars in her hair were seven.' "

"You know so much." A sigh came across the carriage. "You are so young. And so romantic."

"I am not so young; I shall soon have left school."

"Dear Paul. You don't know what life is like. It can be very painful. It can make you very unhappy."

He did not know what to say. They swung into the drive, with Thomas, after his pints at the Railway Hotel, taking the turn more quickly than he should have. The carriage lurched a little, and he moved across it so that he felt the warmth of Isabel's body through her light coat. She was almost in his arms; their faces were close. He felt the faint touch of her lips upon his cheek. Then they had pulled up in the forecourt, he had gone round to hand her out, and she was saying something playful to Thomas about reckless driving. Watching her as she greeted Roger and Beatrice, he could not believe in the kiss.

Roger was in high spirits. "Do you know, it wasn't until you'd gone that Bee told me this evening was a jolly singsong. I thought it was one of those affairs where a fellow like me wouldn't understand half what was going on, everybody talking about the poet's soul, that kind of stuff."

"And what did you think I should have been doing at that kind of evening?" Isabel asked.

"You'd have been the beauty whose nature they were solemnly discussing, of course. And by Jove, if I'd thought that was the subject I'd have been there."

"There was nothing hard to understand, and if there had been, Paul would have explained it. George isn't back? Then I don't see why we should wait for him."

A cold supper had been laid out, and Roger and Beatrice had delayed eating until their return. This was something that could never have happened at Albert House, for Harriet was insistent upon punctuality at mealtimes. There was another difference. At Albert House meals were always served hot, and the food was well cooked. Any cook found to have been at the bottle—and lapses of this kind seemed to be an ingrained weakness of cooks—was instantly dismissed. Beatrice, however, had little interest in food, and as Harriet often disapprovingly said, let the cook serve up what she liked, when she liked, how she liked. The result was often extremely indifferent, something about which Roger occasionally complained. The question of what was eaten and drunk on this Saturday and Sunday was the subject of discussion later on, but at the time all that was thought by those around the supper table was that on this occasion the cook could hardly have been faulted, this being a cold collation.

There was a tongue, a piece of ham and a piece of roast beef, a sweet pickle and a hot pickle, a potato salad, a Russian salad and a green salad, and a rather odd-looking dish which turned out to be cold curried eggs. Roger carved and Jenkins, a general factotum who was also a butler, served. Jenkins was a small man in his early thirties, with a manner that combined slyness and servility.

Roger poured a red table wine that had been decanted, sipped it and made a face.

"This isn't the stuff we were drinking yesterday, Jenkins."

"I beg your pardon, sir. It is not the same bottle, of course, but it is the same wine."

"Doesn't taste like it; must be losing my palate. Pity George isn't here; he's got a better nose than I have."

At these words Paul was surprised to see a distinct sneer appear on Jenkins's face, a sneer wiped away as though with a sponge. At the same time the front door closed heavily and there was the sound of George's voice. A minute later he was in the room, breathless, apologetic, saying that he had been kept later than he had expected, asking whether the poetry evening had been enjoyable, sitting down at table.

George talked while he ate. He was a great eater, gobbling up food very fast as though he had a train to catch. He was particularly fond of rich desserts and sweets, and it was a family joke that any box of chocolates left around was likely to disappear, emerging again empty in a wastepaper basket. Now, speaking sometimes with his mouth full, he told them about a dynamite explosion that had taken place in London that evening. A bomb had, it seemed, exploded in the stalls of the Alhambra. It was thought to have been timed to go off during the performance, but in fact the detonation had occurred half an hour before people were in their seats. It was all in the last edition of the *Evening News*.

"Anarchists." Roger's face grew red. "The murdering villains should be expelled from the country."

"Or the Fenians." George wagged a finger. "What price Bee's beloved Fenians."

Beatrice had been in the past a great supporter of im-

portant but distant causes. She had been on the committee of the British Anti-Slavery Society, and had been
much concerned with the treatment of natives in the
Congo and the Sudan. Perhaps their problems had been
solved, for in the last few months she had been involved
with the idea of Home Rule in Ireland, although she had
recently given this up too. George was generally a good-
natured man, and it occurred to Paul that he must have
had a good deal to drink or he would not have made
such a remark.

Beatrice did not reply, but only looked at George with
a haughtiness very much like her mother's. Paul felt
bound to say something. "The Fenians don't do that, don't
blow people up."

"Oh, really?" A small piece of meat bobbed up and
down on George's lip. "Very interesting. We have it from
the horse's mouth that the poor Fenians are gentle folk
who wouldn't harm a soul. I'm sure the ladies and gentlemen who have mislaid their arms and legs will be pleased
to hear that."

"They just don't blow people up. They're working le-
gally, through Parliament, to try to get Home Rule."

There were households, like Harriet Collard's, in which
a boy of seventeen would have been sharply rebuked
for contradicting his elders, no matter whether what he
said was right or wrong. At Victoria Villa, however,
speech was free, and you were not expected to put a
padlock on your tongue because you were only half the
age of the person to whom you spoke. To support the
Fenians in conversation, however, was something that
not even Beatrice had done. It was asking for trouble
and sure enough trouble came, from Roger.

"What makes you so certain, my boy, that the Fenians
are all legal and simon pure?" He abandoned irony for

passion. "Fenians and anarchists, they're all tarred with the same brush—they want to blow everything up. They're damned villains, and a dose of the cat would do them no end of good."

Beatrice exclaimed at the swearing, although she did not seem greatly perturbed. Roger thrust his head forward at his son. "Well, sir?"

Paul saw his stepmother shake her head slightly. The truth was that he did not much care about the Fenians, or the anarchists either, but that strain of the old Adam noticed by Mr. Bendall made it impossible for him to resist reply. He took pains to speak as coolly as possible.

"I don't know what you would wish me to comment on, Father. To say that Fenians and anarchists are the same sort of people is not true. They don't want—"

"Do you understand what you're saying? I am a liar— *that* is what you are saying." Roger was very red. Cords stood out on his neck.

Paul regretted what he had said but, especially in Isabel's presence, was unable to prevent himself from going on. "If I'm not allowed to voice an opinion, that's the end of the argument. Or rather, there isn't any argument."

Roger started to say something, but his wife's voice cut short the words.

"We will not discuss this any further, if you please."

"*You* say that. It's because of those damned committees you're on that the boy's head is filled with all this nonsense."

"Thank you, Jenkins." Jenkins, who had been standing by the sideboard, opened and closed the door noiselessly. "Roger, I shall be glad if you will remember who is in the room when you are speaking."

"If a man can't say what he wants to in his own dining

room, things are coming to something."

"There is a time and a place. I am no longer a member of the Anglo-Irish Committee, and I have never talked to Paul about it."

Paul had noticed before that on the rare occasions when his stepmother asserted herself, his father calmed down remarkably. Now he said nothing more. The ladies retired to the gallery, leaving the men with the port. Paul went up to his room.

When he thought later on about the events of these days which took on the shape of nightmare for him, he placed the beginning of the nightmare as this little supper. It was not merely the bare possibility that the poisoner might have been at his business that evening, but that the tone of it all was so alien to the life of Victoria Villa. For the most part it was a relaxed and easy place, one where, as it had always seemed to him, two families lived happily together. People often came in, and then they played games, some with pencil and paper which needed tremendous concentration, others which were round games like hunt the slipper. They ended in helpless laughter from Beatrice because she had forgotten what she was supposed to be doing in a charade, or in some ludicrous joke from George. An era ended for Paul on that Saturday. Things were never to be the same again.

In his room that night, however, no foreboding touched him. The room itself always gave him pleasure, and so did the row of shelves on which he kept his tiny library, the Aldine poets and the moderns, Dante Gabriel Rossetti and his sister Christina, Sir William Watson, John Davidson. The events of the past half hour faded from his mind, leaving only the memory of the time spent with Isabel, the grip of her hand upon his and the touch of her lips. Another verse began to form in his mind:

> My lady's lips are cool as ice
> And yet they burn like molten fire

How did one end the quatrain? Wire, dire, expire, tire—there were plenty of rhymes, but he was not able to use any of them satisfactorily, and in the end went to bed.

3

The smell of food—of roast beef burned outside but a little bloody within, the slightly earthy smell of new potatoes, the somehow distinctly green smell of cabbage, the nostril-distending whiff of horseradish sauce and the acridness of mustard—the smells of that particular Sunday lunch at Albert House stayed with Paul forever. The smells complemented tastes but were somehow different from them, just as there was a distinct sweet smell to the trifle that followed, with its surrounding ices and jellies, which was not identical with the powerful sherry-laden taste experienced when taking a mouthful.

It was a Sunday to all appearances much like any other. Bertie had been with Harriet and Charlotte to All Saints Church on the heath, where according to Bertie (but what else would the Caterpillar say?) the sermon had been most elevating. The families at the villa went only occasionally to church, and on this Sunday nobody attended. Paul had decided that when he was called to the inevitable talk with his father he would apologize for the way he had spoken, but would stick to what he had said. After all, everybody knew that it was not Fenian policy to use explosives to kill innocent people, and why shouldn't you say so? But on Sunday morning nothing was said, Paul not called in, the squabble seemed forgotten.

And so to Sunday lunch, with experienced May and nervous Jenny waiting at table, and the conversation confined to local matters. It was Harriet's view that political and social affairs were the province of men and should not be discussed by ladies. A new tradesman offering open and closed carriages for hire had appeared in the Charlton Road, another butcher in the Old Dover Road, together with a baker and pastry cook. There were far too many bakers, in Harriet's view, and nobody ventured to disagree. A man had been attacked and robbed on the heath, and she said that this showed the idleness of the police force.

"They can't be everywhere. The heath's a big place," Roger said good-humoredly.

"The trouble is that they are not in the places where they are likely to catch criminals. There should be half a dozen constables patrolling the roads on the heath during the night." Again nobody cared to dispute this. "Another new dress," she said to Isabel in that tone of hers which always sounded censorious, even though that may not have been her intention.

"Do you like it?" The dress had leg-of-mutton sleeves and a wasp waist, and in color was in various shades of blue-green. This dress seemed to Paul to bring out the color of Isabel's eyes, which were perhaps rather green than blue.

"It is very up to date."

Roger coughed, and explained that some horseradish sauce had gone down the wrong way. Had he been stifling a laugh?

"Never did like the stuff," George said. The edge of his own plate was daubed with mustard. He was a great mustard man. He ate it with any meat except lamb, and now he spread mustard carefully over each piece of beef. Later, when questions were asked, Paul tried to remember who had eaten just what dishes. Isabel always ate little and rarely took potatoes, but had she done so on this Sunday? Had Beatrice and Charlotte used the condiments? Vegetarian Bertie of course had not eaten the beef, but had he taken all the vegetables? Certainly George ate heartily, including two helpings of trifle, and Beatrice also was a good trencherwoman. Beer was drunk by the men, water by the ladies. Recollection stretched no further.

It was another beautiful day, and after lunch they sat out on the lawn except for George, who retired upstairs to the library for what he called forty winks. Chairs with padded seats and backs had been brought out, and a mass of large cushions put upon a rug on the lawn. Harriet and Roger sat in two of the chairs talking, Beatrice and Isabel half sat and half lay among the cushions just out of earshot. As Paul approached the chairs from behind, he heard Harriet say, "I could not agree to that." Roger spoke rapidly in a low voice, and she repeated, "I certainly could not agree, not without some explanation."

Paul gave a warning cough. He noticed as he approached that his father's face lacked its usual ruddiness, and that Harriet's mouth was turned down in displeasure.

"I am going indoors to rest," she said, making this sound like a condemnation of those who were forcing her to such a course. Roger jumped up.

"Think I'll be off. Not feeling quite up to the mark. No need for you to come," he said to his wife. "I'll walk back and leave the carriage.

Paul thought of saying that he would walk back with his father, but decided against it. The day was fine, and perhaps if he stayed Isabel would talk to him. He sat in a chair, trying without success to think of lines that would complete the quatrain. Isabel did not speak to him, did not even look at him. She curled up on the cushions and closed her eyes.

After lunch Bertie also had retired, to his tower room. This had only lancet windows, and was extremely dark. The windows, which were in all four walls, provided lookout places from which it was possible to see everything that was going on. Bertie had a good view of Roger walking back toward the village, Isabel and Beatrice on the lawn, and Paul a few yards away from them. He had some feeling for Paul, who though worldly and irreligious, might yet be persuaded to see the light. As always after Sunday lunch Bertie read a few pages of the Bible, looking up occasionally at the texts around him on the walls. They said: *The best side of a public house is the outside,* and *Drinking habits bring a man to his bier,* and *Cold water will cure a purple nose.*

Then he decided to go to see Thompson, down in Lewisham. He was in the hall, about to open the front door, when Charlotte asked if she could come with him. As they walked out beneath the tower he said, "If you think Aunt Harriet will believe we're going out for a walk together, I'm afraid you're mistaken."

"She's in her room, lying down."

"But you will find that she knows we've gone out together. She knows everything. Are you going to see Dangerfield?"

"Why shouldn't I see him?"

He blinked rapidly. Sunlight always hurt his weak eyes. "I didn't say that you shouldn't. But it is wrong to try to deceive Aunt Harriet."

"Perhaps I'll tell her myself," Charlotte said unconvincingly.

"I hope so. Where are you meeting him?"

"At the entrance to Greenwich Park. Will you walk with me to the gate?"

They crossed the heath, leaving Blackheath Vale on their right. Children were flying kites, boats were being sailed on the pond by the Hare and Billet, couples strolled in their Sunday best.

"We shall walk through the park, talk and have tea there. It is harmless enough surely; even mother could not complain, or not with reason. But she does not need reason; she hates me."

Supposing—the thought came inevitably into Bertie's mind—supposing he were to tell Aunt Harriet that Charlotte had said those words: would she be pleased, as she sometimes was, or would she give him one of those glances that frightened him even though they were unaccompanied by speech? He could never be sure of her reaction, which was a pity. Charlotte went on, as though talking to herself.

"If Robert asks me again, I shall marry him. I have made up my mind. There are not likely to be many men in the market. You know that Mother has refused to give me what she gave Beatrice. She wants to keep me by her, somebody to order about, an old maid."

"You should not disregard her wishes. You should ask for help from the Lord."

"I did that before, but no help came. If that is blasphemous, I cannot help it."

They reached the gate and there was Dangerfield, standing just inside. Bronzed, lean and upright, he was still a strikingly handsome man. Now he took Charlotte's hand and held it for a perceptible space of time, bowing low so that for a moment he seemed about to kiss it. Then he reasserted his ramrod straightness.

"Bertie saw me over here."

"Good heavens, of course. Bertie, I'd never have known you. My word, what a difference time makes—how you've grown."

Within Bertie a well of anger bubbled up at the indignity of being addressed in such a way by a man who had nearly been in prison, a man who was not really respectable. He blinked quickly and muttered something, but at that moment he made up his mind to tell Aunt Harriet about these two.

4

Paul had been keeping a journal for two years. He did not make daily entries, but recorded things, sometimes at length, when they interested him. He wrote in it on that Sunday evening:

Father is ill. I have just been up to see him (8 o'clock). He says he feels very cold and that he can't keep anything down. Told Beatrice he should see a doctor. She said it was just a chill, and that she'd call Dr. Porterfield in the morning if he was no better. Extraordinary, how calmly we can hear the illnesses of other people. It seemed to me he was in quite a lot of pain, but perhaps she is right. He certainly said that he had a chill, and it may be working itself out.

What made the weekend unusual, even unique, was that evening spent with Isabel. I can remember every moment of it, every word she said, each gesture. When I looked at her as she listened to the poetry recital, the beauty of her profile was such that I thought I would faint.

I could go on driveling like this for pages. A note to myself: Paul Vandervent, stop it. Another note: Remember that she is Uncle George's wife.

Why did she say that she was unhappy? Why say it at that moment, and to me? If I stand back and look at Isabel with detachment (something I can do with other people easily enough, but in her case the effort is immense), there is something strange about her. It is as though she went through all the prescribed actions of life here automatically, or like a somnambulist, while concerned all the time with some other life of her own. She takes no interest in household affairs (I'm sure Beatrice would be pleased to have some of them taken off her hands) and although she is always polite to George, it is the sort of politeness one would offer to a stranger. What interests her? She likes the house, this wonderful folly, our lovely white elephant, but doesn't really appreciate how remarkable it is. She reads a lot of books, but most of them are slushy novels. When she said that she knew little about poetry, that is perfectly true. If she went to the Rink Hall, perhaps it is just because she was bored. Yet I feel sure that fires burn below that calm surface. What would she say if I told her I was in love with her? Remind me that I am at school, no doubt. True, but not for long. The last fragment of this last term and then—finish.

Monday morning. Father is ill, and to me mysteriously so, although nobody else thinks that. I shall put down what happened.

Last night I had given up writing in this journal, and replayed a game of chess between Morphy and Zukertort, admiring again Morphy's genius for the unexpected. I had gone to bed, but not to sleep. Some of the moves occupied my mind completely. I saw the chessboard in my mind, with all the pieces in their places, and tried to work out how Zukertort's use of the French Defense might have been improved. This was mixed up with thoughts of Isabel, who seemed to be on the other side

*of the chessboard. She was wearing a green frilly night-
dress in which I once saw her for a moment when her
bedroom door had been left open. I thought how extraordinary it was for her to sit there in my room playing
chess against me in a nightdress. She spoke and smiled,
but the words were lost in a hammering that was going
on. I woke, although it seemed to me, as I say, that I
had not been asleep, and heard knocking. When I opened
the door Isabel was there. She was wearing the green
nightdress, although it was covered by a dressing gown.*

*I must have stared at her—I had through the next hours
a feeling of unreality enhanced by her appearance in
what I suppose I must call my dream—for she spoke my
name rather sharply. She said that Beatrice wanted me,
and that Father was worse.*

*As I went along the corridor I heard George talking
downstairs. Isabel said he was speaking to Jenkins, who
would send for Dr. Porterfield.*

*"But—" I could not think what I wanted to say, then
it came to me. "But we have the telephone." It had been
installed a few months ago, so that there was instant
communication between the house and the office.*

*"Dr. Porterfield doesn't." I saw that she was flushed,
even excited, her eyes sparkling. It was as though a sleeping princess had been brought to life. At the door of
the bedroom I hesitated, with a presentiment that something dreadful lay inside.*

*Within the room my first sensation was one of relief.
In the soft light thrown by the gas mantle above the
bed I saw Father lying, head back on the pillow, apparently at peace. Beatrice sat beside him and her face, when
she turned to me, was calm. He's better, I thought, asleep;
how stupid of them to wake me up. Then I smelled sickness in the air and Father moved restlessly, groaned a*

little. Beatrice got up, tiptoed toward me with finger to lip. One of the maids, Hilda, took her place beside the bed.

We stood in a corner of the room, whispering. "Roger has pains and he keeps vomiting."

"What can I do?"

"I don't know. Nothing. He asked for you a few minutes ago, but now he seems to be resting."

At this moment Father cried out, "Oh. Oh," and reared up in bed. Hilda held a chamber pot in front of him and he retched violently into it, though almost without result. Then he sank back groaning. I know now what people mean when they say that eyes are glassy, for his really did look like bits of glass, unseeing and without depth, when I bent over him and said that I was here. His hand wandered about the eiderdown, then found mine and gripped it. I said something about not going away. Beatrice wiped his face with a damp flannel.

"Paul," he said in his normal voice. "It's Paul." His eyes were closed, as though looking at the people in the room was too painful.

"I'm here, Father."

"Can't understand what's happened. It must be something—" He did not complete the sentence, but said, "Who's here?"

"Mother and Isabel. George has sent for the doctor. He'll give you something when he comes."

"You're a good boy." His eyes opened again just for a moment. "I want you to promise"—there was a long pause before he went on in a loud voice—"not to have anything to do with those damned Fenians." Before I could say that I had nothing to do with them, he cried out again, jerked up in bed as though pulled by a string, and with his eyes tightly closed, retched a little bile into the pot.

(48)

I don't know how long it was before the doctor came, but the time seemed never-ending. The scene in the bedroom was awful, although if I ask myself why, it is not easy to find the answer. Partly, perhaps, it is because Father has always been a strong man, one accustomed to being obeyed, and to see him fighting against pain and jerked about like a fish seemed against nature. And then I felt guilt at the things I had said on Saturday night. They had nothing to do with his illness, but still they were an additional cause of distress. But more than this, in the bedroom I felt that I was intruding upon secrets I did not wish to know. The great double bed bore the imprint of more than one body. It was natural that Beatrice should share the room and the bed, for she was Father's wife, yet I did not want to see the evidences of the life that they shared, her clothing on a chair and her slippers beside the bed.

And something else too. Isabel did not stay long in the bedroom, but while she was there I found that I was watching for the flashes of whiteness occasionally revealed in arm or leg, and I even found myself constructing a fantasy in which she knocked on my door, and stood there with her cheeks flushed as they were in the bedroom, and a slight inviting smile on her lips. Such thoughts disgusted me, but I still felt them.

By the time the doctor arrived, Father was better. At least he was quiet, and did not seem in pain. His eyes retained their glassy look, but he was conscious of all that went on. He seemed to have difficulty in speaking, and we all talked in low voices. Beatrice sat beside the bed with some contraption on her head like an inverted tea cozy, which was meant, I suppose, to keep her hair in place. I found myself wondering whether she could possibly have slept in it. I sat on the other side of the bed; Isabel flitted in and out gracefully, sometimes whis-

*pering a few words to Beatrice. Hilda came to clean up
the sickness, rubbing at the carpet. She took away the
chamber pot, emptied it and brought it back. I found
my eyes beginning to close. The time was nearly two
o'clock.*

*All this changed with Dr. Porterfield's entry. He has
a naturally loud voice, and what I suppose would be
called a bedside manner. No doubt he had dressed hurriedly, but this was not apparent. He is the kind of man
who inspires confidence in other people because he is
always sure that he is right. When he took Father's pulse,
lifted his eyelid, sounded his heart, prodded about in
the region of his stomach, and then stood back stroking
his chin, we all waited for some pronouncement rather
as though what he said would actually provide a cure.*

*"We have been eating something that has very much
disagreed with us." Those were his words and they did
bring relief, although it is hard to know why. "It's possible that what we ate has worked itself out of the system.
If that is so, then all we shall need is something gentle,
something to settle the stomach. You have no pain now,
Mr. Vandervent?"*

*"Hardly any at all," Father whispered. "Much better.
Just that my throat is sore."*

*"Very natural after so much retching. What about food,
now? What have you eaten?"*

"Lunch at Albert House."

*"Roger felt unwell in the afternoon and came home."
George spoke for the first time since he had brought the
doctor. "You remember, Bee, you said you thought it
might be a chill."*

*"Yes, I see. Did the abdominal pains come on after
lunch?"*

*"No. This afternoon I felt not very well, but nothing—
nothing to what I felt later."*

"Unwell but with no sickness. And what have you eaten since then?"

"A ham sandwich. Glass of beer. Drop of whisky."

"And the retching started at about seven o'clock, I think you said."

Father did not reply. His eyes were closed again, as if keeping them open was too great an effort. It was Beatrice who said, "Yes, at almost exactly seven o'clock. It seemed to get better and then came on again. I am sorry to have called you, but it was really very—very severe."

"You were perfectly right. But I hope the worst is over." He took Beatrice by the arm and led her out of the room. Isabel and George followed. Father opened his eyes.

"Paul." I bent over him. "That man's a damned pompous old fool. We have been eating something. Doesn't know what he's talking about." It was odd to hear such words spoken in whispers. Then he whispered, "Look after your mother. Beatrice. Be a good son to her."

The words alarmed me. "It's only something you've eaten; you'll be better in the morning."

"Those pains, you can't imagine them. Like a great crab tearing at my stomach. Will you go in the business?"

I wondered if he was delirious. "Father, I'm still at school."

"I want you to go in the business. Talked about it yesterday."

"Yes."

"That's what I want, Paul. You've got a head on your shoulders. George, you know, George is not much. No more is Bertie. I'm not sure—" I waited for him to finish the sentence, but he did not do so, and when I asked what he meant he seemed not to understand, and was off on another tack. "I've not been a good father. Nor husband. You get on with Beatrice, don't you?"

"Yes."

"That's good," he said, *and patted my hand.*

A moment later Beatrice returned. Dr. Porterfield had gone, but would call again in the morning. In the meantime Father was to have nothing more than arrowroot or a little beef tea. Hilda and the underhousemaid Doris would sit by the bed until morning, although the doctor thought Father would sleep now. Beatrice was having a bed made up in the dressing room.

With that we all went to bed. It was a warm night, but I was shivering. I fell asleep at once, but woke soon after six and wrote all this. Now off to school, which seems absurd. School now that I'm leaving it is simply tiresome.

5

Harriet, like Dr. Porterfield, would have nothing to do with that newfangled invention the telephone. The doctor said quite frankly that he did not want to be bothered with a lot of calls from hypochondriacs, but Harriet professed herself unable to manage the instrument. The problem of when to stop speaking and to start listening was one that she seemed to find it quite impossible to solve, and after some attempts to speak into the listening end (the voice came through that end, as she said, and obviously you should reply through the same hole) she gave up the idea of installing the machine. It was half-past ten on Monday morning when a note was brought to her from Beatrice.

Dearest Mamma,

Roger has some sort of stomach upset, a rather violent one. The doctor says it is something he ate. He seems a good deal better this morning, and is asking to see you.

I wouldn't bother you, except that he has asked me three or four times to send for you.

Beatrice

Harriet's routine of life was fixed, and she did not like it to be disturbed. In the morning she attended to household affairs and wrote letters, in the afternoon she betook herself to one of the committees on local affairs of which she was a member, or rested. On this occasion, however, she was at the villa within an hour. She found Roger looking greenish, although he said he was better. He complained of feeling cold.

"They say it's warm in here, but I'm frozen. Is it warm?"

"Quite warm." She looked with disfavor at the curved windows which followed the line of the gallery below. "There is too much light. It is bad for your eyes." To this Roger made no reply. "At least the windows are closed. I thought Beatrice favored that nonsense about fresh air."

"I had them closed, I felt so cold. My feet—there's no feeling in them."

"You should have a hot-water bottle." Harriet had little sympathy for the ill. She always suspected them of malingering.

"I don't think it would do any good. It's not that kind of cold."

"Then you must wait for the doctor. Why did you want to see me?" Roger stretched out a hand, took a glass from the table beside the bed, sipped. She asked sharply what it was.

"Arrowroot mixture. Tastes disgusting, but seems to ease my throat." He put back the glass. "About the business."

Harriet's skirts rustled. There was an undertone of an-

ger in her voice. "We talked about this yesterday. What
you suggest is impossible. What would become of
George?"

"He could be given a pension." He sat up and spoke
with more energy than he had yet managed. "He's really
useless."

"You have said that before. But he is generally liked."

"People like talking to him, he's good company. But
when customers find that he hasn't dealt with their orders—"

"That is why we arranged that he should move to the
other side of the business and deal with ordering from
our suppliers."

"He's hopeless at that as well."

"You have taken some time to discover it," she said
dryly. "Cannot Bertie help him?"

"Not much better, too indecisive." Roger sank back
again. "You like Bertie, don't you? But you shouldn't trust
him."

"If I am to believe you, there is only one reliable person
in Mortimer and Collard," she said, not unkindly. "I can
only repeat what I said before, Roger, that I should need
proof of what you are saying. You should give me credit
for knowing George's character. He is my son."

"Supposing—" he began, and stopped. "George should
never have married Isabel."

"You have no right to say that. I shall not listen to
such talk. When you are well again we can speak about
the business, but I will not listen to personal gossip." She
placed a kiss on his hot, dry forehead. "You will feel better
tomorrow. If a new arrangement is necessary, there can
be no hurry about it."

Beatrice met her downstairs. "How did you find him,
Mamma?"

"Well enough to talk a great deal of nonsense."

"If you could have seen him last night. He was in such pain."

"I think his mind may be wandering a little." She saw her daughter's look of alarm. "Perhaps not, but like many people who are ill, he has fancies."

"You mean that what he wanted to see you about—"

"Was between the two of us. And now I must go. I have a number of things to occupy me at home."

Dr. Porterfield, calling half an hour later, was upon the whole pleased with his patient.

"We have a much better color. The pulse is stronger. Yes, I think we are on the road to recovery."

"What do you think it was, Doctor?" Beatrice asked.

"My dear Beatrice, there can be no doubt of the cause." The doctor had known Beatrice all her life and used her Christian name, although he did not take the same freedom with Roger. He now patted the stomach which swelled like a balloon under his frock coat. "We have eaten something that very much disagreed with us."

"I see."

"Something has been eaten that is not fresh. As a result the digestive system is offended, rebels, gets rid of the intruder. Once he is expelled we are better."

"I am not better." Roger might have been a dummy for all the attention paid to him by wife or doctor. "My feet are cold. What I could do with is a decent tot of whisky."

The two of them, talking near the door, ignored him. "What shall I do, then?"

"For the moment continue with the liquids—arrowroot or beef tea, whichever is preferred. I shall pay another call early this evening. Then perhaps a coddled egg or custard—"

"God damn it." There was a thud, almost a crash. They turned to see Roger glaring at them from the carpet.

"Roger, what are you doing? What do you want?"

"What do you think I want?" The two of them helped him over to the commode. Then Beatrice withdrew, and it was the doctor who gave a shaky Roger his arm back to bed. "I don't know what you mean by saying I'm better when I can hardly stand."

"Nevertheless—*nevertheless*—our pulse rate has improved, our color is better, the sickness has gone."

"I still *feel* sick."

"Naturally. It is the course of the illness."

"And how long is it going on for?"

"Today you must stay in bed. Tomorrow—well, let us see how you feel this evening."

Before leaving, Dr. Porterfield inspected the contents of the commode, shook his head slightly as though he were reading a fortune in tea leaves, and said to Beatrice that they were not out of the woods yet. Then he left, to dispense wisdom elsewhere.

Beatrice spent most of the afternoon in the garden. After the Parnell scandal and the collapse of support in Britain for the Irish home rule movement (support of home rule seemed uncomfortably like condoning adultery), she had given up interest in social questions. But she was a woman who always needed some interest outside household affairs, and she had found it recently in the garden. Charles Mortimer's original garden based on Italian models, with lots of statuary dotted about, had long since been replaced by an orthodox English garden, and it was with just this that Beatrice had become discontented. She had been converted to the view that the usual English garden with its flower beds laid out in a geometrical design, and its gravel paths that meandered around various evergreens, was dull and repetitive. A garden, she had read in William Robinson's *The English Flower Garden*, should not be "daubed like a colored advertisement," nor should it be filled with laurel and privet hedges. On the contrary, it should be natural, with flowers growing where nature had seeded them, and one plant drifting into the next. There must be control, obviously, but it should not develop into those strict regimental lines of geraniums and calceolarias that were so common. She became, as always, passionate in her reforming zeal. "They are weeds," she would say to Beddoes, the head gardener. "We must have them up."

"What, ma'am, you mean them flowers?" Beddoes would look sadly at the lines of yellow calceolarias and blue lobelias, or the bed of mignonette. "You want me to take *them* up?"

She confirmed that this was what she meant and Beddoes, shaking his head, did what he was told. The result was not altogether a success, or at least not in the short term. The weeds were exterminated, grass was sown and flowers appeared in it, but the Robinson precepts could not be fulfilled in a month or even in a year, and there were times when she looked on her handiwork with dismay. She had moments of hesitancy about getting rid of the gravel walks and left two or three of them, but they did not blend well with the new style.

On this fine afternoon she put on gardening gloves and boots, and an old hat of Roger's, and went out to supervise Beddoes in the work of making the terraces on the slope leading down to Lee Green into a single smooth lawn. The terraces had been made in the style fashionable forty years earlier, with formal flower beds and steep grassy banks, and she found Beddoes with two assistants digging away with spade, pitchfork and crowbar, building up in some places, breaking down brick and stone terraces in others. He leaned gloomily on his spade. "This was what you wanted, was it, ma'am?"

The effect was undoubtedly one of devastation. It was

fortunate that this part of the garden was concealed from the villa by a tall hedge. "It will be all right, Beddoes; not this year, perhaps, but next. What is Charlie doing?"

"Using weed-killer, ma'am. You said you wanted a new path making over there. Got to make sure nothing comes through, kill off the phlox as used be there. That's what you wanted."

She said a little uncertainly that it was. One could not have phlox growing in the middle of a path, or she supposed not, although of course what was natural should be encouraged.

"Mr. Roger and Mr. George was down the other day, asked what was going on. I said it was what you wanted. Mr. Roger said he'd never seen anything like it." Beddoes paused, with a characteristic champing of the jaws, to let this sink in. "Young Paul, he was asking too."

She got a hoe from the garden shed, which was in a little enclosure beyond the main area of devastation, and went back to the main garden. She hoed some of the remaining beds in a half-hearted way, and wondered whether Beddoes should be replaced. No doubt he knew his job, but it was plain that his heart was not in the work he was doing. It was strange, she thought, how set in their ways people were, how reluctant to accept and try to understand new ideas.

This had never been her own way—she had always been willing and even eager to look for new ideas, although she soon tired of them. As she hoed she allowed her thoughts to drift into a make-believe world where the two children who had been conceived but not born were alive, and playing in the garden. Gerald and Geraldine were so inquisitive they were into everything. "Beddoes," she said, "Beddoes, be sure to keep the weed-killer where little Gerald can't get at it." Two tears rolled down her cheeks. You must try again, Dr. Porterfield had said.

She became aware of somebody standing beside her. It was Jenkins, deferential as always, but with something in his soft voice that gave it a note of mockery.

"Cook is asking how many will be dining this evening, madam."

"Just the family as usual. Not Mr. Vandervent, of course. Dr. Porterfield says he must have nothing but liquids for the next day."

"Mr. George will be in to dinner?"

She said rather sharply that so far as she knew he would. There was nothing that one could object to in the man's words, yet something about the tone was almost insolent.

"Hilda says that Mr. Vandervent is feeling a little stronger."

Was there again an undercurrent of something disagreeable? She decided that her imagination was playing tricks. Back in the house, she washed her hands and went toward the gallery. She passed Hilda, scurrying along head down, as though she wanted to avoid notice.

"Jenkins says that Mr. Vandervent is feeling a little stronger. Is there anything he needs?" In a whisper Hilda said that there was not. She was not a bad-looking girl, Beatrice thought, although her nose was too long and her eyes too close together. "Tell cook to make some beef tea, and then take it up to him." The girl hesitated. "Well?"

"The master said—I don't think he wants anything like that."

"Just do as I tell you." Hilda looked so scared that Beatrice said more gently, "He may drink it if it is there. Dr. Porterfield said that he should have it."

In the gallery she found Isabel, with a sketch pad in front of her. Only in the last few weeks had Beatrice appreciated how idle her sister-in-law was. When it was first suggested that they should share the house, she had welcomed the idea in the belief that Isabel would take over some of the household duties. Indeed, she had been a little concerned that she might lose her own place as mistress of the house. It soon became clear, however, that Isabel took no interest in what food was ordered, whether the cook was extravagant or whether Jenkins ran things efficiently. Nor had Beatrice been able to rouse her to any enthusiasm for Anglo-Irish affairs or for the reformation of the garden. It was difficult to know what she did find interesting. She read the newspapers thoroughly, especially reviews of the latest plays, which seemed to Beatrice ridiculous since George did not take her to the theater. She was endlessly concerned with her clothes and her appearance, and once or twice a week would stir herself to go up to London by train. Sometimes she went over to Dulwich to see her family. Otherwise she rarely rose before ten-thirty, and then might lie on a sofa until lunchtime reading one of the novels she ordered from Mudie's library. She spent much of the early evening in preparing for dinner up in her room.

On the other hand, she was easy to get on with, made few demands, was almost always good-tempered, and accepted eagerly any suggestion for entertainment, either outside the house or at home. Beatrice occasionally found her sister-in-law looking at her with an air of sympathy or even of pity that was puzzling and slightly annoying.

Now she stood behind Isabel and looked at the drawing, which showed a corner of the garden not yet changed according to the Robinson plan. There was a bed of tulips and a small lawn, sketched with a gentleness and delicacy that lacked character. Isabel looked up, smiling.

"I'm afraid it is not very good. You know, I should like to be an artist, but—"

"You could take lessons. All artists have to be trained."

"I could do that, I suppose, but it would be no good. I can learn things quickly, but only so far. After that I can't understand or I lose interest. Isn't it strange?"

Beatrice became aware that somebody had entered the gallery. It was Paul. Now, as Isabel tore the page from the pad and was about to crumple it, he said, "Please may I have it?"

She gave him the drawing. Beatrice, watching her stepson, thought that Isabel should be careful. The boy was infatuated with her in a mooncalf way, and she did not discourage him as she should have. Perhaps she should ask Roger to speak to his son—but then she remembered that Roger was ill. At that moment Paul asked about his father.

"He is feeling better. The doctor was pleased with him."

"May I go up to see him?"

"I think not just now, Paul. I should like him to get some sleep. Did you have a good day?"

"School days are all the same, boring. Thank goodness I'm leaving."

Paul, Beatrice thought, was a problem. No doubt he was intelligent, but he was also alarmingly obstinate, as that argument on Saturday night had shown. Of course, she thought as he did about the Fenians, but he shouldn't have gone on in that way. He was not in her view a likable boy, although she supposed that he might be called handsome. He was certainly nothing like what Gerald and Geraldine would have been.

It occurred to her that she should speak to cook about dinner, and she was on her way to the kitchen when Jenkins came running down the staircase which curved back over the entrance, a staircase which in spite of its inconvenience had been Charles Mortimer's pride and joy. He was unusually agitated.

"Could you come at once, madam. Mr. Vandervent has had another attack."

She found Roger bent over a chamber pot, retching. In the pot there was a little green-yellow bile. He looked at her despairingly, then sank back on the bed. When she spoke to him he did not answer. She told Jenkins to send for the doctor at once, and spoke to Roger again. He whispered something inaudible. When she bent over him she heard the words: "Throat. Can't breathe. And my feet—cramp in my feet."

"The doctor will be here soon."

But it was half an hour before he came, and then it was not Dr. Porterfield but his partner, a pale-faced, heavily bearded young man named Hassall, who was said by some people to be very clever. Now he felt Roger's pulse and then pulled up his nightshirt and pressed his stomach. Beatrice turned away her face because she did not care to see her husband's naked stomach, but she heard the questions. "Does this hurt? And that? And that?" Sometimes the answer was no more than a groan, sometimes a whispered "Yes." When Hassall had finished, Roger said, "Cold, Doctor, so cold."

"His hands and feet are icy," the doctor said to Beatrice in a reproving tone. Then he turned back. "What have you eaten recently?"

Roger shook his head. Beatrice said, "He has eaten nothing."

"Or drunk?"

Roger made a gesture toward the arrowroot and the cup of beef tea beside it, which was still almost full. Dr. Hassall looked at them both, picked them up, smelled and tasted. "Nothing else?"

Roger's eyes were closed. He made no reply. "He has had nothing else," Beatrice said. "Dr. Porterfield said he might have these."

"Of course." In the dressing room he said, "I must tell you that your husband is very ill. He is suffering from some acute form of gastric poisoning."

"But when Dr. Porterfield saw him this morning he seemed so much better, and he's had nothing since then."

"Sometimes such attacks recur," he said without conviction. "Dr. Porterfield is out on a visit. I left a message for him to come as soon as possible. In the meantime I will remain."

"Is there nothing at all we can do?"

"Hot-water bottles for the feet. A compress for the stomach may help to relieve the pain. I could inject morphia, but I have to send for it and I fear—"

He did not say what he feared, but she responded quickly. "Perhaps it would be better to wait. My husband is Dr. Porterfield's patient."

In the glance he gave her there was perhaps something ironical, but he made no comment, merely bowing slightly and returning to the bedroom. She ordered the bottles and compresses to be sent up. As she did so George came in. She told him the news and he went upstairs. When he came down again he seemed shaken.

"I say, the old fellow does look ghastly." They were all in the great gallery now, and he came across and patted Beatrice's shoulder. "Never mind, old Roger's tough. I wish Porterfield were here, though. Don't take much to that Hassall chap sitting there with a long face."

There followed a space of time that Beatrice could neither remember nor gauge. She could not have said whether it was minutes or hours before Dr. Porterfield arrived, full of a cheerfulness that vanished when he saw the patient, nor at what time dinner was served or whether it was served at all. One or two moments stood out. One was when she listened to the doctors talking about giving Roger a sleeping cachet, which Dr. Porterfield thought he might be able to keep down, while Dr. Hassall appeared to think that it would be of no use whether he kept it down or not. Then there was a struggle to administer the cachet, with Dr. Hassall holding Roger's arms and Dr. Porterfield forcing his mouth open and saying soothingly, as one might to a dog, "Good fellow, good fellow, just swallow now, that's all." At that instant Paul came, stared, and spoke to her fiercely.

"What are they doing to Father? How can you let them do that?"

She was starting to explain when the sick man freed himself from the grip on his arms and lurched forward and upward in the bed with a great cry, expelling the cachet from his mouth. Dr. Porterfield gave a cry too, examined his finger and said unbelievingly, "I have been bitten. He has bitten me."

"I fear it is useless," said Dr. Hassall.

"Father." Paul approached Roger, knelt beside the bed. "Speak to me, say something."

Roger's eyes remained closed, but he put out a groping hand. The boy held it for some moments, then cried out, "Cold, it's cold. Father is dead."

Dr. Porterfield came over and murmured that his father's hands and feet were cold because of his illness. Paul burst into tears, and ran from the room.

That was a time she remembered. Then there was a moment when she was reminded, by Isabel of all people, that word had not been sent to Albert House. The coachman was dispatched at once with an urgent message, but the failure to tell her mother seemed terrible to Beatrice. Harriet had seen Roger that very morning, and Beatrice felt that she would be found blameworthy, even though telling her mother could not have helped Roger. This thought stayed with her, and was pervasive even during the third scene, when Dr. Hassall came to the gallery and asked if they would all go upstairs. They did so, to be met at the door by a head-shaking Dr. Porterfield.

"My dear Beatrice." He took her hands. "Oh, my dear Beatrice."

She felt as though she had a high temperature. The shapes of the room seemed to shimmer as though seen in a heat haze. "How is Roger?" she said questioningly. She approached the bed and there he lay, looking peaceful. "Why, he's asleep."

The doctor patted her small hands with his large ones. She noticed that one finger was bandaged and thought, that's where Roger bit him.

Dr. Hassall said, "Mrs. Vandervent, there was nothing we could do for your husband. He is dead."

For a moment she was unable to understand. Then she recalled a choking cry—was it Paul's or George's or her own?—and then the shimmering of the room grew greater so that it truly shivered before her. Somebody said, "Look out, there," then Dr. Porterfield's voice seemed to be repeating, "My dear Beatrice . . . my dear Beatrice . . ." and after that she knew nothing.

From Paul Vandervent's journal

Tuesday. I am sitting at the desk beside the window in my room. If I look out I see the garden, and it seems just the same as it was yesterday. On the desk I have propped a photograph of Father. He is smiling and looks as though he is about to speak. But the reality no longer exists. I shall never hear his voice again, I shall never play chess with him, he will never bring home the firm's new toys as he did when I was a child, pretending that he had brought them for me when he really wanted to play with them himself. I remember a railway track

with an engine that blew out real smoke when you put
a little pellet in the funnel. He loved that.

I cannot understand it. I write in this journal to keep
myself from thinking about the terrible reality of his
body lying cold in that room. There is nothing else for
me to do. Because of his death I am not going to school,
but I am thought to be too young to help with what
are called the details. All that is in the hands of George,
as I suppose it must be. The funeral will be on Saturday
if the doctors give their consent. At present they are uncertain about the cause of death.

This first became apparent when Stepgrand arrived,
flanked by Aunt Charlotte and the Caterpillar. I write
Stepgrand although I call her Grandmother, for really
she is my step grandmother as Beatrice is my step mother
and Charlotte my step aunt. I always think of her as
Stepgrand. I am deeply conscious that there is no direct
link between their blood and mine. I watch all their actions critically, I cannot help it, and it seemed to me
that Stepgrand's chief emotion was indignation because
she had not been called in time to arrive before Father's
death. She said that she thought it extraordinary that
she had not been told earlier.

"I did not think of it, everything happened so quickly,"
Beatrice said.

"I should have thought that somebody could have
found time to tell me."

George murmured something. Isabel said that she
ought to have thought of it.

Stepgrand had placed herself on a sofa, and the rest
of us were arranged around her more or less in a half
circle. The blinds had been drawn, but there is so much
window space in the gallery and the blinds are such
flimsy affairs that light still came through. She frowned
at that, but said nothing. Stepgrand likes darkness.

"What I find incomprehensible is that when I saw Roger this morning he said he was better."

"That's what Dr. Porterfield said, isn't that so, Beatrice?" George asked. Beatrice nodded.

"Then he must have eaten or drunk something which made him worse. What was it?" There was no answer. "What did Roger have to eat or drink after I saw him? Beatrice, I am speaking to you."

It was as though Beatrice had been asleep. She said now, with a start, "Nothing; he had nothing."

"That is ridiculous."

"A little arrowroot mixture, beef tea. Nothing solid."

George had been sitting a little uneasily, as he often does, fidgeting with his fingers, bending them over as if he were counting them. "That's the devil of it, begging your pardon. The doctors can't quite account for it."

"The doctors?" Stepgrand said.

"Young chap named Hassall came round too, Porterfield's partner. They were going back to look at their textbooks and so on, talking about a post-mortem. Opening up the body; a bit distasteful. Sorry, Beatrice, shouldn't have mentioned it, but thought I'd better let Mother know how things are."

Stepgrand looked from one to the other of us, then said deliberately, "It will not help us to starve. I take it cook can provide something to eat. Isabel, perhaps you will see to it."

Isabel looked startled, then rang the bell and gave instructions to Jenkins. She was very pale and looked upset, which of course was natural. I don't know whether Stepgrand had it in mind to ease the tense feeling in the room, but the meal had that effect. During it we relaxed and spoke to each other naturally, as we had not done for hours. Only one small incident marked the meal. Hilda was serving with Jenkins, and as she was putting *one dish in front of Beatrice she suddenly started to cry.*

"Oh, the poor master. I am so sorry, ma'am, I am so very sorry."

Jenkins took the dish she was holding and told her to pull herself together, but Beatrice intervened.

"Thank you, Hilda. It is a sad time for us all, but we must be brave." Hilda was actually on her knees. "Now you had better go to your room. Dr. Porterfield is sending round some pills to help me sleep. I will give you one of them."

"Oh, ma'am, you're so kind." And with those words Hilda left us.

Why do I write all this down? Partly to occupy myself, to avoid thinking about that still body on the bed, partly because I read somewhere that a writer should always put things down on paper. He should commit what happens to memory, the book said, but also make notes, anywhere and at any time, about what he sees and hears. But there is something more. At some time when I went into Father's bedroom I saw something that was not right, that was out of place. I have tried to recall it, to fix the things in the room as though they were in a photograph, but I cannot do it. Whatever I saw was, I feel, on the bedside table, for it was on the bed and the table that my attention was concentrated. What stood there? The cup of beef tea, the glass of arrowroot, a napkin to wipe Father's mouth, nothing more. So was there something out of place on the bed? I cannot remember.

This morning they have been making arrangements for the dressmaker to come and measure Beatrice for her widow's weeds, and Isabel for a black dress. Of course, such outward signs mean nothing. Will Uncle George mourn deeply? I don't believe he has any deep feelings. Will Isabel truly mourn? Why should she? Or Charlotte?

*And the Caterpillar—I suppose he will whine about fa-
ther going to a better world than this.*

*As for me, I feel an ache inside like a bruise. I shall
not forget, I shall never forget. I truly loved him, and
cannot bear to think of that silly argument on Saturday
evening. Was it only Saturday evening? I can hardly
believe it. It is my first experience of death.*

On Tuesday afternoon Harriet sent a note to Dr. Porterfield, asking if he would be good enough to call upon
her. He came at six o'clock and was shown into the library.
A decanter of sherry stood on a little side table, and at
her instruction he poured a glass for each of them. Perhaps he knew what they were going to discuss, and it
may be that he felt it should be faced at once.

"A most distressing affair. Everything which should
have been done was done, my dear Mrs. Collard, I assure
you of that."

"I do not doubt it. I wish I could have seen you last
night, but I was not told in time."

"It was"—he searched for a word—"distressing."

"What did he die of? I suppose it was food poisoning."

The doctor sipped his sherry to allow time for reflection. "I think—hum—undoubtedly. But—there is a but."

"That was your diagnosis when you first saw him. And
I have never known you wrong."

The doctor's stomach swelled a little, no doubt with
pride. "But, as I was saying, there are—hum—baffling
features. Baffling, undoubtedly."

"Are you saying that your diagnosis was mistaken?"

"By no means. But both myself and my partner, Dr.
Hassall—"

"He is very young, I believe."

"He is young, certainly."

"And so of course lacks the experience which gives us so much confidence in you. I remember as clearly as yesterday when you attended my dear father; he would have nobody else. His trust in you was complete. So is mine."

She looked up at a painting of Charles Mortimer, who even in the gloom of the library appeared bluffly benevolent. Dr. Porterfield looked at it too, and said that he had been a fine man.

"For many years we have thought of you as a friend of the family. I am quite certain that you would not wish to do anything that caused us distress. Roger was unwell here on Sunday at luncheon. That was the first sign of his illness. Then it developed, as I understand from you, and rapidly became worse, so that it was impossible to save him. Was not that the course of the illness?"

"In general terms, undoubtedly."

"It is a pity that you did not foresee the crisis when you saw him yesterday morning, and that you were out in the afternoon." The doctor made protesting sounds. "Naturally I realize that other patients make calls on your time. I only regret that poor Roger should have been attended by so inexperienced a practitioner as Dr. Hassall."

"Dr. Hassall is very well qualified." Harriet did not reply to this, nor did she look at him. There was an oil lamp beside her chair, and in its light her profile was carved as though in metal. For some reason this refusal to look at him disturbed the doctor. He said almost apologetically, "Hassall feels strongly, you see, about those baffling features. He was better, and then suddenly became much worse. It is . . . baffling."

"But such fluctuations are not unknown?"

"By no means. But Hassall says—"

"I don't give a fig for what Dr. Hassall says. He is young

and no doubt ignorant. It is *your* opinion that I value."
Now she did look full at him, and the dark intensity of
her gaze was such that he lowered his eyes. "I will speak
plainly. My family has lived here for almost half a century.
The scandal and gossip caused by an inquest would grieve
us all deeply. To enter a witness box and speak of the
last hours of the person dearest to you in the world—
can you imagine what that would mean for Beatrice?
And then to have the personal details of one's life revealed in public . . . I appeal to you as an old friend
not to expose us to this."

Dr. Porterfield's jowls shook, his stomach swelled. "If
only he had not suffered that relapse."

"I have nothing more to say. I wished to make sure
that you fully understood my feelings. If they are ignored,
then I shall know that I was mistaken in thinking of you
as a friend."

"Do not think that, please do not think that for a moment, my dear Mrs. Collard. I believe myself that Hassall
is worrying unduly, and if I can persuade him otherwise
I shall do so."

"*Persuade* him?" Harriet managed to get infinite scorn
into the word.

"With you young men it's theory, nothing but theory,"
Dr. Porterfield said. "I've known the Collard family for
more years than I like to think about, and I tell you that
what you suggest is out of the question."

"I am not suggesting anything." They were in Porterfield's large consulting room, which, with its comfortable
chairs and its examination table hidden away behind
screens, might have been the smoking room in a gentleman's house. The impression was enhanced because both
doctors were in fact smoking, Porterfield a meerschaum
and Hassall a Turkish Abdullah cigarette. "I am saying

(71)

that I am doubtful about the cause of death, and that a post-mortem would clear up the doubt."

"Hassall, I really must ask you not to drop ash on the carpet. I have mentioned it before."

"I'm sorry."

"I do not know quite what you mean by doubts. They seem to imply that something is wrong."

"Oh, really, it is too much." The young man jumped up and began to walk about the room. "You were there at midday—"

"A little earlier."

"Very well. You find the patient well on the road to recovery. Those are your own words. A few hours later he is plainly dying. I thought you agreed that the circumstances were such that it would be unwise to sign a death certificate. You remember what Taylor says?" He went to the shelves, took down the thick blue volume, found the page. Porterfield continued to puff at his meerschaum. " 'If there be any doubt that the cause of death was natural'—*any* doubt, mark you—'the most unsatisfactory course is to ignore scruples, and to sign a certificate on the simple disease, and to make no reference—' "

"You need not continue. I read Taylor in medical school."

"Very well, then. What did old Mrs. Collard say to make you change your mind? That's the thing."

Porterfield puffed away until a cloud of smoke surrounded him, and wreathed in it, he looked with his round head and round stomach like an image of Buddha. Here, at home and in private, he was no longer unctuous and a little subservient, but a figure of authority. "You are young, Hassall, you have a lot to learn."

"In the way of the world, no doubt."

"Perhaps in the way of the world. The Collards are people of consequence in Blackheath. A scandal that in-

volves them—and a post-mortem is scandalous in itself—
will be something they deeply resent. They and their
friends will not forget the doctor who refused to give a
death certificate."

"What on earth has that to do with it?" Hassall almost
shouted. He put out his cigarette.

"If it should prove that the death was natural, then
the doctor who had been so disobliging—to a family
whom he knew very well, mind you—could expect to
lose a large part of his practice. Half at least, shall we
say? It is no use shaking your head like that; I have seen
it happen. And it would be the better half that went—
the carriage trade, as vulgar people call it. Those left
would be artisans, tailors, grocers. Such a physician would
be well advised to move, but I am too old to move. He
would have no need of a partner, I can tell you that."

"You are exaggerating."

"Not at all. People want reassurance from their doctors.
They don't want to be told that they eat or drink too
much, that they have an incurable growth, or that they
will be dead in twelve months from consumption. They
want us to say that they look a little better, that acute
constipation may be causing the pain, to recommend an
ointment for their rheumatism or their gout, to give them
a tonic mixture when what we should be saying is that
they ought to eat and drink less and take more exercise.
In fact, they pay us to tell them what they want to hear,
and to cure a few imaginary illnesses. They do not want
to be told uncomfortable truths."

Hassall was staring. "I have never heard you talk like
this. So cynically."

"A doctor who remains an idealist after he is forty must
be a fool. But I remember Taylor."

"Do you mean there is no doubt?"

"I don't say that. In many cases where death comes

suddenly there is something puzzling. If there were a substantial doubt in my mind I should not grant a certificate. As it is, I shall. The burden is mine, my young friend; I was Roger Vandervent's doctor. You understand that?"

"Yes."

"Do you have anything more to say?"

Hassall shook his head. He stood behind Porterfield as the doctor filled in the certificate in his fine copperplate hand. Opposite "Cause of Death" he wrote: "Gastric fever."

6

Letter from Charlotte Collard to Robert Dangerfield

Sunday afternoon

Dearest Robert,

I do hope you got the note I sent on Friday to tell you the tragic news, and to say that I did not think I should be able to meet you at the Observatory today. Yesterday was poor Roger's funeral, as I told you, and Mother would think it so strange if I went out today without some special reason. Of course, I have the best reason in the world, which is to see you, but I cannot tell her that. Oh, Robert, I am so unhappy that I cannot see you today. I look out of the window and think that we might be together in the park as we were last Sunday, and that you would hold my hand and tell me you loved me, as you did then. Please say that you forgive me. I shall come down early to look for a letter from you on Tuesday morning.

The funeral was quite a grand affair. There were more than twenty coaches. Isabel's father, Mr. Payne, was there, of course, with his wife and the rest of the family. He is a very fine-looking man. There was nobody from Roger's side except a sister of his first wife, Patricia. I must say I saw no particular reason why she should have come, as I don't think she knew Roger well. However, some people like funerals. And then there were quite a lot of people who knew him in business. They all paid tribute to Roger, one or two going so far as to say they didn't know what would happen to the firm without him. Some of them were rather coarse. One man said to me, "Mr. Vandervent, he was a real live wire if there ever was one." He told me he was a toy dealer. He was certainly not a gentleman. I suppose Roger had to meet such people.

Apart from that, everything went off very nicely. We went back to the villa after the service and I must say that nobody, not even Mamma, could have found fault with the arrangements made there for refreshments and that sort of thing. Poor Beatrice is dreadfully upset, her eyes were red from crying, but she bore up bravely. Dr. Porterfield has given her a tonic, which she says is doing good. He spoke to me, the doctor I mean, and told me that there is a tremendous amount of what he called gastric trouble about, which starts with sickness and then can turn to fever, as it did with poor Roger. He asked how Mother was bearing up, and I told him she seemed unaffected, although of course she was sorry. After all, Roger was not actually a Collard.

And now that I am writing about Mother, I must confess that I haven't yet spoken to her. *Don't* be angry, Robert, *please*. I meant to speak, but then this terrible and unexpected death of Roger's made it too difficult for the time being. There was some question about the death certificate, I don't know exactly what and it's all right now anyway, but I know Mother was upset, and when she is upset she is always particularly sharp with me. But I shall speak as soon as the time seems to be right, oh, I shall. Are we to meet next Saturday in the park? Saturday is often easier than Sunday. Dearest Robert, I long for a letter.

Charlotte

Letter from Robert Dangerfield to Charlotte Collard

Park Lodge Hotel, Kensington
Monday

My very dear Charlotte,

Your letter delighted but saddened me. Delighted because I'm pleased to have a letter in your very own hand—I don't possess many of them—and saddened (I might use another word if I did not love you) because it shows the irresolution that is your basic weakness. You certainly need somebody to look after your affairs!

But I am beginning with my usual bluntness, when I didn't intend to. I meant to start by saying that it was wonderful—astonishing—beyond belief to see your dear face again, looking to my eyes more beautiful with your maturity. I long as you do, or you flatter me by saying, to look at that face every day and to lose myself in the deep pools of your eyes. You see you are turning a tea planter into a poet! I should say an ex-tea planter. For I have just received news that the firm in which I was a partner has been sold, and the purchaser of course has his own manager, who will be taking over my job. Do you remember that I told you I suspected dirty work somewhere? Well, I was perfectly right. As I told you, we needed some extra capital, which I hoped to raise over here, but Matheson, my so-called partner, has worked this trick on me while I was away. The devil of it is that he owns most of the shares, and I can do nothing to stop him. There will be money coming to me, but much of it will be swallowed up by debts. As I told you, we have had two wretched seasons.

This is no reason for depression. Quite the contrary, the blood of the Dangerfields is up, and I shan't be sorry to have said good-bye to that liver-grilling Indian climate. My future lies over here, as I suspected when I came on leave, and with God's help and with you beside me, it will be a bright one. But that means that you must speak to your mother, and soon. She may breathe smoke, but after all she is not a dragon, and you must tell her that she has no right to refuse you the same settlement that she made on your sister. Will your brother and sister not support you in this?

You will think that I'm being uncommon business-like, but can you be surprised that business occupies me at present? It is not that I fail to understand the blow you have suffered in the tragic death of your brother-in-law. Please give my deepest sympathy to your sister in her sad loss, if she would care to have sympathy from me. But as you say yourself, beloved Charlotte, the man was not of your own blood but only related by marriage, and I hope that what I say now won't make me seem in your eyes callous or unfeeling. I say in your eyes, because that is all I care about. If I stand well with you, what should I care for the rest of the world?

What I have to say is this. Your family firm has lost one who was, it seems, a respected and energetic man of business. Well, here is another respected and energetic man of business (if I may blow my own

trumpet enough to say so). It is true that a tea plantation is not a toy firm, but the problems of business
are not so different but that my knowledge can be
applied. . . .

But there I give up, my love, for what do you know,
what need you know, of business? Nothing, I hope.
Forgive me for dwelling so long on such matters
when what I long to do is to clasp you in my arms.
But with this news from India my problems are urgent, and I cannot be idle. I must settle something
soon or be away looking for my fortune elsewhere.
This, you know, will not be what I wish, but what
hateful necessity compels.

We will meet on Saturday, dearest, at the park gate.
I shall be there at three o'clock, and I shall hope
you bring good news. But the best news of all will
be the sight of you.

Your Robbie

From Paul Vandervent's journal

*Sunday evening.   Yesterday we put my father into the
ground. Many mourners, most of whom did not care
whether he was alive or dead, a long service with the
vicar talking about our brother who had been a pillar
of the community (he went to church only as a social
obligation), the walk through the graveyard with the sun
bright overhead, and then the box lowered into the
ground, earth thrown on it, heads bowed, amens echoing
like the baas of sheep. It was graciously permitted that
Father should take his place in the family vault, even
though he was not a Mortimer by birth. There had been
some discussion over this, and it was settled that the favor
should be permitted. The talk at the family conclave,
as George called it, made me so angry that I could not
speak.*

Nor did I talk much after the funeral, when they all crowded into the gallery, ate and drank and said what a fine fellow he had been, meaning very little of it, and what a beautiful house it was, when they were laughing up their sleeves at its oddity. I stood by a window and watched and noted. How many of them truly missed Father, felt anything like the ache inside me? Not George, guzzling away, talking cheerfully to the loud businessmen who came, I suppose, because they were his customers or he was theirs. Not Isabel, I think, though she was pale. Not Stepgrand, not Charlotte, and certainly not the Caterpillar, whom I heard talking about the evil of drink while he stuffed himself. He may not eat meat, but he makes up for it by eating twice as much of everything else, particularly anything sweet. Yesterday he ate trifle, ice cream pudding and some sort of mousse.

I spoke to only two people. One was Isabel, who seemed almost as much out of place as I. She stood by herself, hardly eating or drinking, looking very pale. I said I hated what was going on, and she asked if I found it false.

"False, yes. If they cared for Father they could not eat and drink and laugh. The whole thing is a masquerade, a sort of game."

"You are so young." She put her hand on mine for a second. Did she remember that night a week ago when her hand had positively sought mine and gripped it? "If people don't feel sorrow, why should they show it? Nothing can bring Roger back."

"If they feel nothing they shouldn't be here; it's hypocrisy." At this I was brought up short by awareness of somebody at my elbow. It was the Caterpillar, saying what a fine address the vicar had given, and asking whether Isabel would like something to eat. I don't understand how she can have smiled at him, but I suppose she would have said that is what people do. I moved

*away, and so got into my second conversation. That was
with Dr. Porterfield, who was standing by the fireplace,
a chicken leg in one hand and a glass of wine in the
other.*

"Dr. Porterfield," I said. "What did my father really
die of?"

He stared at me, took a bite at the chicken leg, put it
aside and wiped his mouth. He has little piggy eyes, and
a great stomach that juts out so that you can never get
very near him. "Gastric fever."

"That's not quite what I meant. It was something he
ate. What could it have been?"

"It could also have been something he drank."

"I can't think of anything he ate or drank that other
people didn't take too."

He took out a toothpick. "That means little. You can
cut two slices from the same leg of pork. One is well
cooked, and the person who eats it comes to no harm.
The second is nearer the bone, is underdone and infected,
and that sets up food poisoning."

"We didn't eat pork last weekend. There is no r in
the month."

"I am well aware of that, my boy. I used it as a—
hum—example, nothing more. Your father ate or drank
something that disagreed violently with his physical system, and he died of it. Does that satisfy you?"

I thought a moment. "No."

"Then you must remain—hum—unsatisfied, I fear. My
dear Mrs. Ranger, how are you? I thought Charles's address was splendid." And he moved away to speak to
the vicar's wife.

Tonight, up in my room, I say again in this journal
that there was something strange about Father's death.
Why was he struck down, and nobody else? And when
he was so much better, why did he become ill again?

Why can I not remember what it was I noted in the bedroom? I want to ask all sorts of questions, but who would give me the right answers?

I wrote another verse of the poem about Isabel:

> My lady's pallor is extreme,
> She gazes at some distant star
> As though, caught in a cloud-clapped dream,
> She lives within that avatar.

Then I lacked the will to go on with it.

(2)

The Months Between

THE FACT of a man's death seems to those most closely linked with him—wife, friends, business associates—enormously important. Those who have loved him feel that their lives must be totally changed, people who worked with him think that the gap he left is almost unfillable, friends despair of finding anybody who knew as much about whatever may have been their spheres of joint interest—the topography of East Sussex, say, or the order of precedence at a dinner table. Yet a few months later everything is going on as though he had never existed, except that when his name is mentioned people speak of him in a reverential tone, as though death had transformed a sinner into a saint. At least, that is what happened in the case of Roger Vandervent as June moved into July, and July melted into August. During the months between Roger's death and the events of September, several things happened which bear upon this narrative.

It was on the first Saturday in June, a hot, clear day, that Charlotte met Robert Dangerfield again. She wore a blue-and-white-striped dress and carried a matching parasol. Robert's gray suit was formal, his hat elegant and a little dashing. They walked down the main path to the Observatory. Charlotte stood on the line that marks Greenwich Mean Time, clapped her hands and said that she was at the center of the world. Robert watched her indulgently, a smile curving the thin lips below the waxed mustache. Later they sat and talked on a bench overlooking the Queen's House and the dark ribbon of the river.

"Mamma will never do it, Robert. She will never consent to your taking Roger's place."

"Hang it, I don't mean immediately. I should need to get to know the ropes, of course."

"It is no good thinking of it."

"How can you tell if you won't speak to the old dragon? I know I said she isn't a dragon, but from the way in which you talk, I must be mistaken. She's the genuine article, able to burn up unwanted suitors with a blast of brimstone. Come, Charlotte, she has behaved badly to you, and you know it. She has cheated you of your inheritance. It is you who have a right to be angry, not she."

She dug the point of her parasol into the gravel. "You see, I am such a coward. Perhaps if you wrote to her—"

"It would be useless. The ice must be broken, and it is you who have to break it. If I wrote to her she would tear up the letter; if I called she would not be at home. You must make her believe that our lives are linked. Then she will receive me."

"That is the truth, that our lives are linked?"

"Of course it is."

She said timidly, "Since it is the truth, couldn't we get married and then live together somewhere—very quietly, of course, because I know that we should be poor. We should be together and you would get some kind of job, because with your experience there must be jobs. If Mamma helped us that would be a blessing, but we should not depend on it."

"You dear sweet goose, what should we live on? And where? Do you want me to take you to some dismal hovel in a filthy street, some stew where the sluttish women would laugh at your ladylike ways? My sweet, because I love you I could not do it."

She went on prodding at the gravel. Her voice was low. "But, Robbie, surely we should not have to live in that kind of place. You said you would have some money coming."

"A trifle. It will be eaten up by debts. I have commitments which as a man of honor I must meet. And let me be frank—it is no use deceiving ourselves. I have been used to some creature comforts; you have been gently brought up. To see you soiling your hands with housework, to know that I could not provide for you to live as you should, would be unbearable. A man on his own can rough it, but to ask sacrifices of the woman he loves—no, I could not do it. I would rather go away forever."

On the following evening Charlotte spoke to her mother.

2

A few days later Roger's position in the firm was the subject of a discussion that took place in the Great Hall at Albert House. It might have been called a board meeting, except that no board meeting of Mortimer and Collard had ever taken place; or a family gathering, except that Augustus Payne was there, and Augustus was not a member of the family. George was present and Beatrice, and so was Bertie Williams. The meeting took place in the dining end of the hall, around the great mahogany table that would have seated thirty people. Oil lamps burned at this end of the room, leaving the other end almost in darkness. If anybody had doubted that it was to be a business meeting, such doubts were dispelled by Harriet's first words.

"I have called you together to discuss what should be done in the firm now that poor Roger is gone. He was an excellent man of business. I relied upon his advice, and he will be difficult to replace, or so it seems to me. But I have called you together to find out your opinions. George."

"Yes, Mamma?"

"You are my son. It is right that you should speak first."

George looked startled. "I agree entirely—oh, yes, absolutely—with what you've said. Roger had a wonderful grasp of detail, got on well with everybody. Replacing him—I don't know how we can do it."

"That is all you have to say?"

"Suppose I could take on some of his work pro tem, although my hands are pretty full. Hexham, now, is a very good fellow; wouldn't you say he was a good fellow, Augustus?"

"As works manager, yes. Excellent at his job. As a replacement for Roger, a chap dealing with clients, I just don't know what they'd think. Trouble is, the feller's not a gentleman. Doesn't pretend to be, mind, but people wouldn't take to dealing with him, in my view." He coughed. "Tell the truth, my dear Mrs. Collard, not sure why I'm here."

"I think you may soon understand. Bertie."

"Oh, Aunt Harriet, I don't pretend to know about these problems. My position in the firm is very humble, and I doubt if my opinion is of any value."

"What do you think of Hexham?"

"He is a decent, temperate man, and he keeps the men to their work. But as a replacement for cousin Roger . . ." He shook his head.

"Very well." The little woman in black at the end of the table looked from one to the other of them. With the exception of Augustus, who regarded her with a blend of respect and amusement, she dominated them all. "Beatrice. Did Roger ever say anything to you about changes that he had in mind?"

Beatrice had been staring at the floor. "No. But surely, Mamma, it is to you that he would have spoken about any possible changes."

"He did." With grim satisfaction she looked from one to the other of them. "I just wanted to make sure he had not spoken to any of you. He said that you had been hopeless with the customers, George, and that now you were on the other side of the business you were extremely slack in ordering material. He suggested that you should be asked to retire. And, Bertie, he said that you were not reliable."

George's pudgy face was flushed. He stood up, then sat down again. "I don't know what to say; it's outrageous, ridiculous. I mean, it was Roger who wanted to take over dealing with customers, and since he wanted to do it I didn't stand in his way, but I never had any trouble, none at all. Of course, some of them are rough diamonds. Roger used to jolly them along a little."

"What have you to say, Bertie?"

"Only that my work has always been done conscientiously. Roger liked to keep important things in his own hands. My position is humble, as I said, and I sometimes thought that Roger wished it to be. But it would not be proper for me to speak ill of one who has passed over."

"Mr. Payne, had my son-in-law said anything of this to you?" Augustus shook his head. "But perhaps it may make you change your mind about Hexham?"

" 'Fraid not. People would feel they were being fobbed off, talking to an inferior. Wouldn't do, believe me."

"I do believe you."

"Aunt Harriet." It was Bertie's voice, quiet as usual, but warm with admiration. "You have an idea of your own, I can tell it."

"It seems that nobody has a suggestion for Roger's replacement. Perhaps Hexham could do the detailed work, George, while you see customers." George looked doubtful. "What do you think of that as an idea, Mr. Payne?"

"Not very much."

"Again, neither do I. Your knowledge of the trade is a long one. Is there any hope that you might be persuaded to an amalgamation of your firm with Mortimer and Collard?"

Augustus shook his head. "Thought you might have something like that in mind, but again I have to say, won't do. You're manufacturers and you've got firms who make toys exclusively for you. We're wholesalers. Two don't mix. And we sell toys from all over the place, not just yours. You'd want us to sell your lines, give up others. No, it wouldn't do."

"Was that your idea, Aunt Harriet?"

"Don't interrupt, Bertie." Harriet did not care for her effects being anticipated. "It seems to me that we have now considered and rejected some obvious possibilities. I have two ideas, both based on my wish, which we all share, that Mortimer and Collard should remain a family concern. The first concerns Paul. Beatrice tells me that he is determined to finish his education, and not to go on to Oxford. I suggest that he should join the firm. Beatrice, what do you say?"

"I should be very pleased. It is what Roger wanted. But I don't know if he would accept—boys have odd ideas nowadays—and I am afraid I have no influence over him."

"I will speak to Paul." She looked round the table.

George muttered that it was an excellent idea, Augustus said he seemed a bright lad. Then Bertie spoke.

"He knows nothing about the business."

"And so of course he will have to learn."

"What will he be doing?"

"George will see that he gains a thorough knowledge of all kinds of work. Then we can consider."

"I can see a difficulty, although I hardly like to mention it," Bertie said. You will, Augustus thought, you'll mention it, you treacherous little tyke. "I have heard Paul express ideas that might almost be called socialistic. I hope he will not try to force such ideas on our good conscientious workers."

"If he does, he must be told that such things will not be tolerated."

Bertie subsided into sulky silence. George asked about the other idea. Harriet looked from one to the other of them, then said, "Bertie, be so good as to ring the bell."

The old girl's enjoying herself, Augustus thought admiringly as Bertie used the bell pull. I don't know who ran the business when Roger was alive, but I know who's running it now. And he thought also, as she was asking the maid to show the gentleman in, that it was a pity he'd married Isabel to such a poor tool as George.

The man who entered, a tall, bronzed figure with a soldierly bearing supported by his waxed mustaches, was unknown to Augustus Payne but, he saw, not to the other people in the room. Harriet, however, introduced him.

"This is Mr. Robert Dangerfield. You have met George and Beatrice. And I think you know my nephew Bertie Williams. This is Mr. Augustus Payne, Isabel's father." Dangerfield advanced, took Augustus's hand in a firm grip, nodded to Bertie, and then stood at his ease until invited to sit down, when he placed himself bolt upright on the edge of a chair and folded his arms.

"Mr. Dangerfield has recently returned from India, and is now intending to settle in this country. I think I'm right in saying that he has considerable business experience. It is my suggestion that he should join the firm. That is my idea, Bertie."

The rest of them stared at Dangerfield as though he were on display in an exhibition. Nobody spoke. Without quite knowing what was going on, Augustus realized that the man's appearance was a shock. Partly to fill the awkward silence, and partly out of sympathy for the fellow (it could not be easy to sit there like a stuffed dummy while everybody gaped at you), he asked a question.

"Do you have any experience in the toy trade, Mr. Dangerfield?"

Dangerfield's voice was deep, his words bitten off with military precision. "I have twenty-five years' experience of the Indian tea trade in every aspect."

"But the toy trade?"

"I know nothing of it. I suppose, though, that one business is much like another in its essentials."

Silence again. Then George spoke. "What post did you have in mind, Mamma?"

"Mr. Dangerfield understands that he will have to familiarize himself with the particular problems of our business." Dangerfield's head nodded once, then he resumed his about-to-be-photographed immobility. "He will be under your authority, and you will give him the benefit of your experience. Now that Roger has passed on, no doubt your duties will become rather wider. Bertie, I suggest that you should take over the invoicing and accounting, for which George will no longer have time."

The old girl's damnably clever, Augustus thought, as he saw Bertie noticeably brighten up. She gets George out of a job that he no doubt does badly, gives a sop to Bertie, and gets her own way about this stuffed dummy of an Indian tea planter all at once. She's the best man in the family, and that's a fact. Whether the Indian tea planter was up to the job remained to be seen, but he would have laid a bet Harriet was prepared for that. And even as he put this question mentally it was answered, as George asked exactly what Dangerfield's position would be.

"That is to be decided. Perhaps he might be called the assistant general manager. It is only the matter of a name, after all. He has in any case agreed that our arrangement should be at first for six months. I am sure that we shall then want to make the position permanent, and we shall all hope that he has the same feeling." She doesn't ask whether they agree, Augustus thought. Take it for granted, that's the way. She's not only the best man in the family, she's the best businessman too, or at least she is now her son-in-law's gone.

"You said something about it remaining a family concern," Beatrice said. Harriet stopped her before she could continue, and asked Bertie to ring the bell again. Obviously Charlotte must have been waiting outside, for the door from the entrance hall opened almost at once. Even in the dim light she could be seen to be blushing as she came in.

"Mr. Dangerfield has asked my permission to marry Charlotte, and I see no reason for withholding it. So you will see that when Robert joins us, we shall remain a family concern."

Now everything became movement, as if a tableau of statuary came to life. Robert Dangerfield uncrossed his arms, got up, kissed his future bride, his future mother-in-law and his future sister-in-law, shook hands with George and Bertie and Augustus. Two maids brought in champagne, corks popped, glasses were filled and raised. Bertie drank soda water. Augustus, viewing it all

with a friendly but ironical eye, thought that it had been
well managed. He thought also that Dangerfield looked
a fellow with a good solid bottom to him, but that you
never knew. He remembered a man with just such a
convincing solidity who had nearly sold him some worthless gold shares the year before.

3

From Paul Vandervent's journal

*June 12. A red-letter day, or is it a black-letter day, in
my life. Yesterday, with much to-doing about the importance of the occasion, Beatrice told me that Stepgrand
wanted to see me. Off then after ridiculous and as it
seemed unending school, that will have ended forever
in a couple of weeks, to Albert House. I never approach
that grim mock-Gothic pile without a lowering of spirit.
Those spires like forks on which the devil toasts the un-
wary, the tower where the Caterpillar sits spinning mischief, the damp graveyardish smell that meets you inside
on the hottest day—all of these make me shiver
internally.*

*I must say for Stepgrand that she doesn't beat about
the bush. Apparently there was a family conclave yesterday, to which I wasn't asked because of my youth. Very
necessary since father almost ran the firm on his own,
so far as I can gather. It seems that Charlotte is to be
married to her former suitor, Mr. Dangerfield. Stepgrand
disapproved a few years ago, but agrees to the match
now. Mr. D. is also to take up a place in the firm. So
far as I could gather, he and Uncle George will do together what father did on his own. But what about me?
The conclave—or Stepgrand—proposes that I should join*

up and learn the business. *That isn't how it was put, but when I asked a few questions it became clear that's what it amounts to.*

I think she expected me to say yes at once, and she certainly wasn't pleased when I said I'd think about it. But with Stepgrand you never know, and although she tapped impatiently with her ivory-topped pencil, I think she wasn't really angry, not even when I mentioned money. As I had expected, I should be paid not much more than pocket money for the first year. When I said I didn't like this, she answered sharply that she would have thought I should be pleased to follow in Father's footsteps.

"I should be," I said, "if I thought that I might ever occupy the position he held, but so far as I can see, I should be some kind of clerk for ten years or so, at everybody's beck and call. That wouldn't do for me. In much less than ten years I want to be my own master."

She gave a grim smile. "You have to start somewhere. Why not in the family firm? I should have thought it might have weighed with you that it was what your father wanted."

"It does." I hesitated and then said, "There's another thing. You know that I believe every man should be his own master, not just me."

"That is nonsense. Some will always be masters and some will be men." I was going to quote something from Oscar Wilde's "The Soul of Man Under Socialism," when she said, "If I found that you had been talking in that way to the men, that would be an end of your employment. Your father would not have tolerated it, and—" I am sure she was about to say "neither will I," but she substituted George's name.

So that's it. When I got home Beatrice asked what I had decided. I said that I had not made up my mind.

June 13.

The Prop most tedious. This morning the Latin master said, "No doubt you think we have nothing more to teach you, Vandervent." I replied that I had already finished the translation from Horace he had given us. Floored him.

Later made up my mind. I shall go in the firm. I was moved by thoughts of Father, as that old fox of a Stepgrand had calculated. Wrote her a letter, which Beatrice said was the proper thing. Other reactions what might have been expected. Beatrice said she was pleased, but seemed not very interested and why should she be? George slapped my shoulder, said he was glad I was coming into the old firm. And Isabel? She smiled sweetly, and said that she hoped I should not stop writing poems. I have the feeling that she avoids me now.

June 14.

I have remembered what it was I saw in the bedroom! But the result is—well, is nothing, I suppose, although it must be called mysterious.

My recollection came from the attempt to see what was on that little table beside the bed, to fix it in my mind as if it were a photograph. I had tried this before without success, but now suddenly I saw it. There, nearest to Father, was the glass of milky arrowroot mixture, almost full. Beyond it, a little further from him, the cup, white with a blue line round it, containing the beef tea. A napkin was beside it. And nearer to Father, between the arrowroot and the beef tea, was the clearly defined print of a damp glass. I had noticed this on Monday evening, a few hours before he died.

At some time, then, another glass had been on that table. What was in it, and who had taken it away? And now that I had remembered, what could I do about it?

I spoke first to Beatrice, asking if Father had had anything else at all to drink on that evening. She said he had not, and did not seem to understand what I was talking about. But it had been Hilda who was beside the bed during most of the day, not Beatrice, so I spoke next to her. She began to cry, and said she had not meant to do anything wrong. I asked her what she meant.

"You see, the master, he said it would do him good, make him stronger."

"What would?"

"He kept it in that cupboard under the washstand. He said it would do him good, but nobody must know, so I washed up the glass and put it away."

"But what did he keep there?"

"Why, the whisky. Oh, Mr. Paul, you won't say anything to the mistress, will you?"

Then she told me. I remembered Beatrice had mentioned Father saying something about wanting a good tot of whisky. He had told Hilda to pour it for him from the bottle he kept in the cupboard, and she had done so. Then he drank a little arrowroot because, he had said, the doctor mustn't smell whisky on his breath, and he told her to wash up the glass and said she was a good girl. She did what he told her, and put back the bottle. She hadn't dared to say anything about it afterward, because she would have had to admit that she had disobeyed orders.

The story didn't seem to amount to much, except that father had been feeling much better. But then there was something that made it look rather different. I thought that I would look in the cupboard and see if there was something wrong with the whisky. Father's room had been kept locked since his death, and Beatrice had moved

*into another bedroom. I knew where the key was,
down in Jenkins's pantry. I got it, unlocked the door and
went in.*

*There was something upsetting about the fact that
everything was the same. Father's silver hairbrushes were
on the dressing table, his razor and shaving brush on
the washstand, there were photographs of him at school
and as a young man. It was all the same, and he might
have been just about to come in. But he would never
come in again.*

*I unlocked the cupboard beneath the washstand and
looked in. There was nothing inside, nothing whatever. There should have been not only the whisky, but
a bottle of brandy and one of port which Hilda said
he kept there. Who had taken them? Jenkins was an obvious possibility, but when I spoke to him he said that
he knew nothing about any drink in the cupboard. He
looked sly when he said it, but then he always looks
sly. Who else? Well, anybody might have taken the keys
from the pantry as I had done, for they were clearly
labeled. I don't see what more I can do about this, but
it strengthens my feeling that there was something
strange about Father's death.*

4

On a June afternoon three weeks after Roger's death,
Isabel took the train up to London. She sat alone in the
coach marked "For Ladies Only," and carried with her
George Newnes's publication *The Strand Magazine*. She
turned the pages and glanced at the plentiful illustrations
which, together with the stories by a writer named Doyle,
were supposed to be the secret of the magazine's success.
She read nothing, however, but looked out the window

at the fields of Lewisham, the dockland cranes visible at New Cross, and then the grimy brick of the dismal approaches to London Bridge. At the Charing Cross terminus she walked out of the station across the road to Adelaide Street, and moved from there unhesitatingly among the narrow streets and alleys at the back of the Strand. Her walk was that of somebody who knows her way. Her face had the blankness of a mask. She carried on her arm a capacious old-fashioned black reticule.

Near to Long Acre, at the edge of Covent Garden, she stopped at a tall, narrow house and took a bunch of keys from the reticule. The house was one of an undistinguished pair which had somehow survived among the surrounding jumble of small shops, stationers, shoe repairers, cheap butchers, greengrocers selling slightly spoiled goods from the market. She opened the door, closed it quietly, and went up the uncarpeted stairs. There was a curious smell in the house, a combination of dirt and dust. She did not touch the banister rail, knowing the mark it would leave on her white gloves.

The house was divided into numbered apartments, two to a floor, with on each half landing a window done in several colors of glass. On the second floor she stopped, and used another key to let herself into the apartment numbered 3. Inside there was a tiny hall which led to a living room and a bedroom. It was all dark, the hall because it had no source of light from outside, the rooms because the curtains were partly drawn. She did not pull them back, but lit the gas and then stood looking about her, not letting her gaze linger on the big double bed and the dressing table, but moving purposefully to pick up a comb and brush, nail scissors, a scent spray, a small ivory-backed mirror with "I" engraved on it. She put these into the reticule, and moved to the sitting room. There were two letters on the center table with its brown velveteen cloth, both addressed to A. Wilson, and she tore these open. They were bills, one of them for the rent of the apartment. The letter she had expected to find was not among them.

She looked for it in the hall, then returned to the sitting room and went again into the bedroom. She searched, thoroughly but without haste. She did not find the letter. She left the bills on the table, locked the door again and went down the stairs. On the ground floor she tapped on the unnumbered door nearest the entrance.

The man who opened it wore dirty trousers tied up with string, and a frayed vest. He smelled of drink, and when he spoke half a dozen rotten teeth were visible, so that some of his words came out in a lisp. He recognized her.

"Mr. Wilthon you want, he'th not here. Ith he coming?"

"I don't think he will be here today."

"He'th owing rent. Can't keep his roomth unleth he pays. If he doesn't want them—"

Isabel's blank mask was paler than usual. She said in a low voice, "I think you have a letter addressed to him. In a blue envelope."

The small pouched eyes looked at her keenly. "Upstairth, the letterth."

"This would have been another letter, rather different in appearance. If you kept it yourself I should be glad to have it."

"Oh, no. Oh, no." He moved back suspiciously. "You're thaying I took it. That'th a lie. Any letterth for him are in hith room, and my bill'th there too. Are you going to pay it?"

"Mr. Wilson will pay it. Do you have the letter?"

"If I had it, why thould I give it to you? You're not Mr. Wilthon."

"You know me; I am a friend of his. If you happen to

have the letter down here and can find it, I would pay you something for your trouble."

His lips moved in and out. "I give Mr. Wilthon another week. If he doethn't pay by then, I let the roomth to someone else."

"About the letter . . ."

"Don't know about any letter. Never seen it."

He retreated. The door was shut in her face.

On the way back to Charing Cross she threw the comb and brush, the scent spray and the nail scissors into a street dustbin. After a moment's hesitation she threw in the hand mirror too.

When she had returned to the villa she sent for Hilda. The girl came into her bedroom, head slightly lowered as usual.

"Hilda, you remember that I have sometimes asked you to take letters to the post for me."

"Yes, ma'am."

"And you have always taken them straight to the post and put them in the box?"

"Yes, ma'am."

"Look at me, Hilda." The girl raised her head reluctantly. Both women were pale, but Isabel's pallor was that of ivory while Hilda was white as milk. "A letter I wrote has not arrived. Are you quite sure that you posted everything? Perhaps one was dropped, perhaps you gave it to somebody else, who promised to post it. If that happened I should like to know."

Hilda sniffed. "All the letters you gave me I put in the post."

"You are quite sure? If I found out that you were not speaking the truth I should be angry."

The girl repeated what she had said. She did not say it convincingly, but then she habitually mumbled as though there were something wrong about speech, so that if you swallowed your words you might not be found guilty of having spoken them. Isabel let her go, and determined to put the whole thing out of her mind. She was good at forgetting or ignoring unpleasant things, and this held no more than the possibility of unpleasantness. Within a few minutes she was immersed in *The Strand Magazine*.

5

There was no question of Beatrice's having to sell the villa after Roger's death, but her financial position was a little obscure even to the family lawyer, Mr. Cleverly. A quite considerable stockholding came to her, but it seemed all to be invested in shares that it would be inadvisable to sell even though they did not produce a large sum in dividends. Ready money had come through Roger's position as a partner in the firm, but although he held a few shares he had been paid as a working partner, and Harriet had made it clear that there was no question of anything being paid to Beatrice simply because she was Roger's widow. Perhaps it might eventually be necessary to sell some of the stocks, although Mr. Cleverly shook his head at the prospect. In the meantime things went on very much as they were.

She felt, however, that this was not as it should be. Roger's death ought to make a difference to her own life; she should be doing—what was it she should be doing? She desired a radical change in her way of living, without knowing what it might be or how it could be brought about. There was a change obviously, in the sense that she no longer shared the big double bed with Roger. All her things had been moved to a room at the end of the wing that curved like a scimitar out into the garden.

This room had been intended as the nursery, and when she lay down at night she found her thoughts invaded by the two children who had never existed. They also entered her dreams, sturdy, chubby little Gerald and his younger sister, Geraldine, a wistful elfin creature with amusing old-fashioned ways. The room had windows looking out on three sides, and she wandered from one to the other of them on warm nights, staring down into the dark garden.

Perhaps she should spend more time in the garden, really immerse herself in it? The great Robinson's advice was that the gardener should be taken into one's confidence, and that the best results would be achieved when there was complete cooperation between the planner of the new garden and the executive hand that carried out the grand design. The trouble was that Beddoes, so far from understanding the grand design, seemed to think that she was moved by mere caprice. It was true that she had sometimes changed her mind about the placing of particular flowers or the elimination of a shrub. She might have been prepared to acknowledge that she had tried to do too much too quickly, but with Beddoes it was impossible to discuss such things. She stood with him one afternoon looking down at the recently sown grass which next year should be a velvety lawn. Beddoes, however, expressed his doubts about this. Taking away the terraces, he said, meant that the lawn would drain right down to the bottom.

"It must be watered frequently at the top—is that what you mean?"

"We can water all right, ma'am; it's the soil. Needs feeding."

"Then let us feed it." This vision of the hungry earth was new to her.

"By rights she needed feeding before sowing, specially at the top there."

"You mean the grass won't come through?"

"Don't say that. Just won't be what she might, that's all."

Why had he not said this before? It was useless to ask, but she was about to say something when she became aware of a disturbance at the bottom of the garden. Voices were raised in altercation, and at a nod from Beddoes one of the undergardeners began to run down the slope, avoiding the newly sown grass. When she asked what was wrong, Beddoes scratched his chin and said it was Joe Brown.

"Joe Brown?" Then she remembered the name as that of a man who had been employed in the garden. He had often been late and had used atrocious language, so that in the end Roger had dismissed him.

"Joe gets down in the Railway Hotel and has hisself a few drinks, then comes up here, makes a nuisance of hisself. I'll see to him."

"*I* will see to him, thank you, Beddoes."

At the bottom of the garden there were a number of sheds, a couple of greenhouses, and a gate that led through to Lee High Road. Just beside one of the sheds a man was shouting something at two of the gardener's boys. One of them spoke to the man as she approached and he turned to her, taking off his cap with what seemed meant as insulting mock politeness.

"What are you doing? You have no right to come here. You have been dismissed."

"Begging your pardon, but I didn't know the ground was so precious I'd be doing harm just by treading on it."

One of the boys gave a quickly checked snigger. Beddoes said, "Get off now, Joe. You've taken more than you should."

The man took no notice, but spoke to Beatrice. "Get rid of a man for being half an hour late and using words that never hurt nobody, but there's worse things than that and nobody says nothing."

"What are you talking about?"

"It's what they say at the Railway."

"What do they say?"

The man muttered, then spoke loudly. "They say Mr. Roger, he died awful quick. Some of 'em say he took poison." -

There was silence. She felt herself trembling. "This is private property. If I find you here again I shall call the police."

The man took a step forward and, again with an effort, she stopped herself from moving back. "You got no call to be so hard with me. Nobody can say Joe Brown don't do his work, and Mr. Roger he got rid of me just for a few words as weren't meant for no one else to hear. Never spoke to me or gave me a chance to say anything for meself, just got rid o' me like that. If he took poison I ain't sorry."

She cried out to Beddoes that he should send for the police, but the gardener had already stepped forward, and helped by one of the boys, had turned Joe Brown around and started to march him out the gate.

The incident disturbed her, and it seemed that her interest in the garden declined from that moment. She had always been impatient to see quick results from anything she did, and her absorption with Robinson and in planning the future shape of the garden seemed simply to fade away. She had a friend who spent a great deal of time helping the East End poor through some charitable organization, and Beatrice accompanied her on two visits to Whitechapel, but the place depressed her and it seemed to her that the people did not really want to be helped. More and more, at night, she found herself thinking of what she called in her own mind the missing children.

6

From Paul Vandervent's journal

July 18. Monday. The beginning of my third week at work. Already it is a sort of routine. Out of the house each morning with Uncle George, then the walk down to Blackheath station, with Uncle G. making some remark about it being just the thing for stirring up the blood, the Caterpillar waiting at the station, where we stand in a particular spot so that we may take our seats in a particular carriage (the fourth first-class carriage in the sixth coach of the train). The train comes in, we settle into our seats, papers are opened. End of conversation until we get out at Charing Cross. Then Uncle G. says something like "Another day begins," or "Double, double, toil and trouble, eh?" and we are at the big frontage which says in faded letters "Mortimer and Collard." The premises are within a few minutes' walk of the station.

They are in a narrow street and they are gloomy, like I suppose most of their kind. There are two big warehouses in which the toys are stored, and another which is used for packing goods and sending them out. Then there is a workshop with various antiquated-looking machines for making toys, and a separate department where they are colored. On the two floors above are the offices, most of them poky little rooms with dirty windows. There are three or four people in most of these rooms. The two big offices were used by Father and Uncle George, but even these are drably furnished. Father's room has samples of the firm's goods displayed in showcases, a big desk with drawers, and two comfortable chairs for customers. Uncle George's room is similar but smaller. There has been a question about who should have Father's room, Uncle G. or Dangerfield. Obviously it should be Uncle G., but Dangerfield laid claim to it because he said he would be dealing with most of the clients. Uncle G. is so easygoing he didn't seem to mind, but Stepgrand put her foot down. I don't think she trusts Dangerfield, and she's obviously keeping a careful eye on him. So he shares an office with the head clerk, and in the meantime Father's office is empty. I looked in there last week and there were his things on the desk as he'd left them, including the pen and inkstand I gave him last Christmas. I shall never forgive myself for that last argument with him. What was the point of it? None.

As for me, I am meant to be getting an idea of how to order supplies, how to invoice customers, when to ask for payment, and so on. I share a little room with the Caterpillar among all the bills and invoices, with files all around the walls. Could there be a worse fate? He watches me out of his little red-rimmed eyes when he thinks I'm not looking, picks his nose occasionally, sometimes talks about it being a privilege to work in an old family firm with a wonderful tradition. Ugh!

7

"Six o'clock." Paul shut the ledger with a thump.

Bertie consulted the silver half hunter that had been given him by Harriet. "I'm afraid you are a clock watcher."

"I only mentioned the time."

"The time is something we should never consider when there is work to do. A watched clock never reaches the hour."

"But still it's six o'clock. I've finished. What are you doing?"

"These invoices should be sent out."

"Do you want any help?"

Bertie gave a sweet, sad smile. "It would take too long to explain the details, but I am grateful for the offer. Of course, you are still only learning; it can hardly be expected that you will have mastered everything."

Paul looked at him, but said nothing. Five minutes later he had packed up his books and said good night. The other office workers left very soon afterward. Hexham, the workshop foreman, came up.

"We're just finished, Mr. Bertie. You're working late."

"There is a great deal to do. Young Paul." He shook his head a little.

"Seems a bright lad. Sharp, Mr. Roger always said."

"He is clever, no doubt, but I am afraid the will to work is not there. However, these are early days. We must not judge hastily."

"Will you lock up down below, Mr. Bertie?"

Bertie said that he would. When he had made sure that he was alone in the place, he closed his account books, put aside the invoices, got the office keys from where they hung down below, and went along to what had been Roger Vandervent's office. The office itself was open, but the drawers on the left-hand side of the desk were locked. Bertie proposed to open them and see what was inside.

He could not have said exactly what made him want to do this. His nature was such that a locked drawer, like a sealed letter, was an offense to him. He delighted in the discovery of secrets even when they related to things in which he had no interest. He had no particular expectation of finding anything important inside the locked drawers. It was simply that if he opened them he would have knowledge not possessed by other people, and at some time and in some way the knowledge might be used to his advantage. For a moment, as he sat down at the desk, he imagined himself in Roger's position, exercising power in the firm. What would he do? There would be much less idleness and joking down below, no doubt of that. Hexham might have been a good man once, but he was much too easy. And there was idleness up here too, idleness and drinking. There had been afternoons when Roger Vandervent came back with a customer who was staggering under the furious liquid taken into his stomach. Their voices would be loud, they laughed inanely. With the demon of drink inside him, the man would place an order, and Roger would come in later waving it under their noses. . . .

He shuddered at such thoughts, and tried the keys in the top desk drawer. To his annoyance none of them fitted. Perhaps Roger had kept the key with others on a chain, but still the desk was not necessarily inaccessible. He tried a trick that he had seen done by a teacher at the Prop when a classroom door had been locked and no key was available. Bertie's reactions to such things were quick and his memory retentive, and he had not forgotten how, with a waggish injunction to the boys not to tell anybody of his burglarious skills, Mr. Meach had deftly inserted a knife in the gap between door and frame and turned back the lock. Bertie had asked for and eventually been given a similar pocket knife, with three blades of which one was long, thin and flexible, but he had had little occasion to use it, although he had once opened the door of a summerhouse. Now he took out the pocket knife, inserted the thin blade in the space between drawer and desk, worked it up, over and around, and heard a decisive click. The top drawer opened, and it controlled the two others, as he found when he pulled them. The scratch made on the edge of the desk was hardly perceptible, and he would be able to close the drawers again without trouble. What had he found?

The top drawer was a disappointment. A packet of cigarettes with flint and tinder, three pipes and a crocheted cigar case, embroidered and with tassels, with the initial "RV" on it. No doubt it had been made by Beatrice.

The second drawer contained papers. These looked promising, but also proved disappointing. There was nothing even faintly scandalous about them, except for an exchange of letters between Roger and a man named Standing, one of their biggest customers, agreeing that Standing should get two and a half percent commission on any order given to Mortimer and Collard. This was deplorable, the kind of arrangement that Bertie would stop immediately if he managed the firm, but it was not really interesting.

He opened the third and bottom drawer, and gazed unbelievingly at what he saw. The drawer contained a woman's corset, her gloves, and a strange cuplike device.

He stared at these things, then took them out in a gingerly way. He had never handled a corset in his life, and felt this one with a mixture of excitement and distaste. It was a large garment, shaped so that it narrowed at the waist and with laces at the back to tighten it, yellow in color and decorated with dark-blue rosettes. So women put this round their bodies, laced it up, and appeared with a figure that was not their own, unnatural. The things that one read in the papers about wasp waists and tight lacing really involved this kind of armor. Bertie had never kissed a woman except in a dutiful family way. He thought now of Isabel tightening the laces of this corset, and then rebuked himself for the impurity of such feelings. He picked up the gloves, which were of fine white kid, and slipped one on his arm, which surprisingly it fitted comfortably enough. The other article was a shaped piece of material containing two cups. Behind each of these was a slit and into these slits there had been pushed soft pads. It took him a little while to realize that the device was meant to fit over the bosom, and that the thick pads would push it out. This bosom protector, or whatever it should be called, was torn at the top. Just beside the tear was a dark patch as big as a half crown, a patch that looked like blood. He remembered that a few days before his death Roger had appeared with what he had said was a cut on the back of his hand, a cut that had looked (or was memory playing tricks?) more like the marks of fingernails.

What woman did these things belong to, and what had been her connection with Roger? Above all, what were they doing in the desk drawer? It was plain that they should not be allowed to remain there, and it was with a feeling of virtue that he found some brown paper, wrapped it around them, and closed the desk again, leaving it unlocked.

He showed the things to Harriet that evening after dinner. A few weeks earlier, after escorting Charlotte to the park, he had told her of Robert Dangerfield's return, explaining that he felt this to be his duty. The result had not been what he expected. Aunt Harriet had thanked him, but she seemed not to have rebuked Charlotte for her secrecy, and later had actually welcomed Dangerfield and given him a place in the firm. Since then she had asked him twice how Dangerfield was settling down. He had replied cautiously, for it would not do to show enmity to the man. Now she listened to him with composure as he told her how he had found these things while looking in Roger's desk for some missing invoices.

"You say they were in an unlocked drawer."

"Yes." He could not say anything else.

"Why did you expect to find the invoices in Roger's desk?"

He had not been prepared for such a question. "I—I had no idea where they were; I just thought they might be there."

"And have you now found them?"

"Yes; they were in my office after all. Paul had put them with some other papers. He is always moving things round, I am afraid."

She looked at the articles of clothing, but did not touch them. "Why do you bring these things to me?"

"I thought—" Why had he brought them to her? He could not have said exactly why, except that he felt anything discreditable to other people must somehow be to his own eventual benefit. "I thought they might be the cause of scandal. And I was not sure what this one is, the one with the cups."

"It is called a bust improver. You were not responsible for the tear in it?" He said no. "You may leave them with me, Bertie. Thank you."

He felt afterward that he could perhaps have used the things in some more profitable way. When he left the room she was looking at them with an odd expression.

8

The letter came on a Monday morning. It was brought up to Isabel with breakfast, which she always took in her room. It was addressed in a straggly hand to Mrs.

Collard, and the postmark was Camberwell. The envelope and paper were of the kind that could be bought at any cheap stationer's. The letter was written in the same straggly hand, and it said:

> If you want your letter back put five pounds into an envelope and send to Jack Jones, 123 Rexile Road, S.E.5. I think the police might like to see the letter but I will give it back for five pounds.

She considered what to do while she dressed with her usual leisurely care. By the time she was ready to face the day, she had decided to pay the money. When she shopped she had things charged to her account, but she had a little store of money, some forty pounds, that she kept for an unspecified emergency. She took a five-pound note from this, put it in an envelope folded in a plain sheet of paper, addressed it as the letter requested, and later in the morning went out and posted it herself. It never occurred to her to wonder how the letter had passed into the hands of Jack Jones. Nor did she doubt that it would be sent back to her.

9

Robert Dangerfield had moved out of the Kensington hotel into rooms, but they were in Kensington and not Blackheath because, as he said to Charlotte, he did not want to wear out his welcome by being always on the doorstep. He came over on Saturdays and Sundays, and once during the week for dinner. Harriet had given her consent to a marriage early in the new year, and although this was not soon enough for Charlotte, Robert seemed content.

"It is such a long time to wait," she said. "And there is really no need for it."

"Mark of respect for Roger. And then it gives her time to see how I'm settling down. I'm on six months' trial, y'know. May not be a dragon, your mother, but she sees further into a brick wall than most."

"Oh, but talking about six months was surely a matter of form. It was to soothe George's feelings."

"Perhaps. He's moving into Roger's office next week, and I take over his. Stupid arrangement because I'm dealing with customers and it's the best office. Obvious I should have it. However, that's the way your mother wants it so that's the way it's to be."

"Did George ask specifically for the other office?"

"Don't think he cared either way. Can't understand him, to tell you the truth; just doesn't seem interested in the business. Not likely to give me any trouble." He coughed slightly, regretting the phrase, and stroked his mustache. "There's another thing. Has she said anything about your settlement?"

Charlotte stared at him. "Since she has agreed to our marriage, she must be meaning to give me what she gave to Beatrice."

"You haven't spoken to her."

"No. Surely it's you who should speak to her, Robbie. If you feel it's necessary."

"It's devilish awkward." Then he saw the expression on her face—they were alone in the Great Hall after dinner, Harriet having gone to bed and Bertie being up in his tower—and took her hands. "My dearest Charlotte, you don't think I care about it except for you." She said nothing. "You won't be marrying a man with money, I've told you that, just a battered old tea planter who hasn't made much of a go of things. When we get married I don't want us to live in rooms, so if we're to have somewhere decent, your mother's money is important. For the time being, that is, until I'm pulling down a decent salary. She's a skinflint, you know, the old lady; not giving me half what she should. Do you understand?"

"I suppose so." He pulled her to her feet and kissed her. "But still you had better talk to her yourself."

He did so one Sunday after family lunch. They talked in the library. If he looked in one direction Harriet fixed him with her steely gaze; if he looked in another, Charles Mortimer seemed to be looking down at him. He was not comfortable, but still he said what he had to say. When he had done she paused before answering. A shaft of sunlight shone through the window on her silver hair.

"When last you courted Charlotte, I was opposed to the suit because of some uncertainty about your previous marriage. This time I have agreed. I have shown faith in you by giving you a position in the firm. But—I will speak frankly, I always do—I still have a feeling that your interest in Charlotte may be based on what she brings with her when she marries." He began to protest. "Please let me finish. At the end of the year your position in the firm will either be established, or we shall agree to part company. If the first of these things has happened, then Charlotte will receive what I gave to George and to Beatrice. If not, then I shall have to consider the position again."

The old she-devil, Dangerfield thought, she certainly knows how to keep a man on tenterhooks. He managed a laugh and said that he would have to make sure that she would want him to stay after the six months.

She smiled. "That is well said, Robert. From what I hear, you have settled down successfully."

"Thank you. There is one more thing, if I may be as frank with you as you have been with me. Our financial arrangement is—well, let me say it is not liberal."

"It will be changed when the six months are up."

"But in the meantime things are extremely difficult. I have debts—"

"They are none of my affair," she said sharply.

"Of course not. But if it was possible to make an arrangement by which after three months—"

"It would not be possible. You made an agreement knowing what you were doing, or at least I suppose so. When six months have gone by we shall make another agreement, and you will be free to accept or refuse what I suggest. There is no more to be said."

Inwardly he raged. Outwardly, what could he say but that he accepted her decision?

10

Beatrice took up lawn tennis. Roger had been an enthusiast for the game, which he had learned to play at the houses of friends. He had had a court made just out of sight of the house. It had been prepared according to the best advice, thoroughly drained and made perfectly level. Beddoes, who had superintended the work, regarded the court with disfavor, but still he did what he was told. Roger had been delighted, but he had played only a few games before his death. When George said one day that he had thought of making up a tennis party, and asked whether Beatrice would object to such an activity so soon after the tragedy, she realized suddenly that what she wanted more than anything else was to learn to play the game. It would prove somehow that she was independent of Roger, who had never particularly wanted her to play, and it would also be a rebellion against the hypocrisy of mourning.

"Why shouldn't you? Roger planned the court; he would have wanted it to be used."

"My feeling exactly."

"We are living in a new age now, and it is absurd to behave as we did when I was a girl. I shall play too."

"You will? But won't people think it's—well, you know—a bit much?"

"I don't care what they think. I hate these clothes." She looked down at her widow's weeds. "They are meaningless, out of date. I have worn them for more than two months, and that's long enough. I shall not wear them again. And I shall learn to play tennis."

"By Jove, old girl, you do have spirit. What will Mamma say?"

"Mamma can say what she likes. I don't care."

"And about the tennis . . ."

"You can arrange the party."

So George got up the party, which consisted of the family and half a dozen other people including the Ranger girls, and it was agreed to be a very jolly affair. Beatrice was surprised to discover that she had a natural aptitude for the game. She used an underhand service—bearing in mind the view of the famous Miss Dod that for almost all ladies an overhand service was a great waste of strength—and she played only doubles. At the same time she was by no means one of those ladies who simply stayed on the back line and let their male partners do all the work. She went to the service line, which all the experts said was the best doubles position, and actually learned to volley, something that few ladies attempted. She wore a dress that hung from the shoulder, with loose sleeves and a wide skirt to give freedom of movement. Even so, of course, she had like all ladies to leave it to her partner to turn and run back if an opponent was unsporting enough to lob. She practiced every day with some of the Ranger girls and Dr. Porterfield's daughters, and as always when her enthusiasm was aroused read everything she could find about the game. Her interest in the Robinsonian garden vanished completely.

Among the other members of the family both George

and Paul were good players, George employing a particularly cunning horizontal service. A game of tennis on Saturday afternoon became a regular thing. Dangerfield played in a flashy but indifferent manner when he took part, and Isabel and Charlotte participated only to make up a four when nobody else could be found to do so. Bertie played no games but occasionally came to watch, bringing with him Thompson, his friend in the temperance movement, who played a very careful game conducted entirely from the base line. Young Dr. Hassall and his wife also took part, but in August the doctor moved to another practice in Kent.

Harriet knew of the parties, and must have known also that Beatrice took part in them, but she said nothing, nor did she comment on the subdued dark dresses that Beatrice wore instead of widow's weeds. One day, however, she asked her daughter to come to see her, and when she arrived produced the articles of clothing given her by Bertie.

"I presume that these do not belong to you."

"Hardly, Mamma." She picked up the yellow corset. "This is for somebody much larger than I am; I should have thought you would have seen that. And the gloves and that—that affair are certainly not mine." She had a bust that did not need improvement.

"You have no idea who they might belong to? They were found in a drawer of Roger's office desk."

Beatrice looked at her, lips tightly closed. Mother and daughter looked remarkably alike at that moment. "Mamma, what are you suggesting?"

"Nothing. I made a statement."

"I don't understand. This thing has a tear in it. And that looks like a spot of blood. What would Roger have been doing with such things in his office?"

"That is what I am asking."

"I said I have no idea."

"There is nothing you want to tell me, nothing you are keeping back?"

"Mamma, it seems to me that you are suggesting something to Roger's discredit. If you mean that he could have had a liaison with some disgusting woman of the town, the idea is unthinkable."

"I did not say that; I have no such thoughts. I mean to find out who these things belong to, and why Roger had them."

"And if I don't wish you to find out?"

"I do not like mysteries, and in particular I do not like mysteries that seem to have some connection with the firm."

"The firm! Do you ever think about anything else?"

"It has educated and provided for you. It is necessary that somebody should think about it."

"What do you propose to do?"

Harriet said that she would consider what was to be done. As a result a man named Edwards came to Albert House. Harriet had seen his advertisement in the daily paper ("Confidential Investigation for the Gentry, Secrecy Observed") and Mr. Edwards, concealing his surprise both at the extraordinary appearance of the house, which he described afterward to his wife as being like a blooming monastery, and at the nature of the assignment, took away the articles of clothing. There was a maker's name inside the corset and also inside the bust improver, but as he said, it would be a tough job to trace anything from that. He would do his best, but he did not guarantee results.

On the same day in August Harriet saw Dr. Porterfield and told him that she was suffering from pains and palpitations around the heart. He sounded her, said that he thought it was indigestion, and prescribed a mixture. If the discomfort persisted they would try something else.

She took the opportunity of saying that she had heard of Dr. Hassall's departure, and that she thought he had been wise to move and gain experience elsewhere. Dr. Porterfield agreed that she might be right, although Hassall was a very able fellow. He had been replaced by a much older doctor named Grant, who was thoroughly reliable. The mixture, which was reddish, had a thick sediment and tasted unpleasant, something of which Harriet rather approved. She drank the bottle and said it seemed to ease the pain a little. She had a second bottle, and a third. She took three doses a day, at lunch, dinner and bedtime.

11

Paul had an hour free in the middle of the day, unlike the men on the machines, who were given no more than fifteen minutes in which to eat the bread with a scraping of fat which for most of them made up the midday meal. At first he spent much of the hour talking to them, but they were disappointingly unresponsive. When he said that they ought to have more time free at midday they stared at him, and one asked what they would do if they had it. Then George said he had been told that Paul was talking to the men.

"Won't do, young Paul, they don't like it. Leave them alone and they won't interfere with you. Agreed?"

"I've only been chatting with them. Surely there can be no harm in that."

"That isn't what I heard. I was told you were trying to talk them into some kind of socialism. That won't do."

"It's nonsense! I haven't done anything of the kind."

"Glad to hear it. But give it up anyway. Masters and men don't mix."

Paul had not much doubt that Bertie had informed

on him. It was a trial to share the same office. They sat opposite each other on high stools, so that when Paul raised his eyes from the ledgers with which he was occupied it was, very often, to find Bertie watching him. Bertie was coming out in spots. Whether as a result of his vegetarian diet or for some other reason, a virulent red spot appeared one day on his nose, to be succeeded by others on his chin and an unpleasant crust like a cold sore at one side of his mouth. When Paul asked how long he would have to stay in this accounts office, George said that it was no use trying to run before he could walk. As soon as he was familiar with the way the business was run they would find something else for him to do.

The free hour at midday, when he could get away from Bertie, was very welcome. Occasionally he went down the Strand and had an eightpenny or shilling meal at a chophouse, but on fine days he would buy a roll and a piece of cheese and eat it in Embankment Gardens. Then he would walk along the river to Blackfriars, returning up Fleet Street, where he looked wistfully at the newspaper offices, out of which men he imagined to be reporters occasionally swaggered, men with cigars in the sides of their mouths, and hats stuck on the back of their heads. Or he would walk around the Lowther Arcade, which led off the Strand, listening to the cheapjack salesmen trying to lure gulls into putting down a small deposit on a guaranteed Italian marble inkstand or a table said to be genuine Sheraton. From there he sometimes wandered in the direction of the Haymarket, the center of prostitution, which was quiet at this time of day, with pavements deserted and shutters drawn.

One day he bought a mutton pie at a baker's, walked as far as Leicester Square, and sat there eating among the grass and flowers, meditating on what life would be like if he had managed to get a job on a paper. He emerged from a daydream in which a cigar-smoking editor clapped him on the shoulder and said he was the smartest young reporter on the paper, to see Uncle George walking across the square in the direction of Charing Cross. He had an odd walk, bustling and jerky, so that you would not have been surprised if he had toppled over. Paul's view was from the back, but there could surely not be two men with Uncle George's walk, wearing the suit in an unusually vivid shade of blue that he had on that day. It was surprising that he had not greeted Paul, but perhaps he was in a hurry. As Paul watched, Uncle George reached the other side of the square and hesitated for a moment, as though uncertain where he was going. At the same time a pigeon, who had been walking around Paul in a stealthy manner, looking for crumbs, hopped on his knee. Paul's attention was momentarily distracted, and when he looked up again Uncle George had disappeared.

Of course he had not disappeared; that was ridiculous. But he was not walking left toward Charing Cross nor right in the direction of Haymarket. He must have gone into one of the buildings near which he had been standing. Where had Uncle George gone? If indeed it was Uncle George, something about which Paul felt less sure now that the man had vanished. He crossed the square to the point where, as nearly as he remembered, the man had stood. Directly in front of him was a button and lace shop named Merriment. Next door to it in one direction was Morton and Able, Tailorings, and on the other side was a cigar store called the Caravanserai. The man in the bright-blue suit, whether or not it was George, had gone into one of them.

By now Paul's blood was up. Perhaps Uncle George was being fitted for a new suit? But Mr. Morton, or perhaps Mr. Abel, said that nobody had entered the shop in the last few minutes. Merriment's button and lace shop was small and dark, and at first seemed to have nobody in it at all. Then a little old woman appeared who shook her head to every question, without seeming to know what Paul was talking about. That left the Caravanserai. He pushed open the door and entered. A tall, dark-complexioned man wearing a fez stood behind the counter. Half a dozen customers, most of them young, sat around the store on leather couches, smoking, drinking coffee and reading the newspapers, which hung in a rack on the wall. There was a fragrant smell of cigars, and blue smoke hanging on the air. None of the men was wearing a blue suit. The man in the fez asked politely whether he would care for coffee, and said that he could recommend some fine new Havanas that had just come in. Paul stammered something and walked back to the office. When, later in the day, he told Uncle George that he had seen him in Leicester Square, he was met by a blank look. George had been up to Holborn at lunchtime, he said, nowhere near Leicester Square. So it had just been a man whose back view and blue suit had deceived Paul. Even so, what had happened to him?

12

From Paul Vandervent's journal

Saturday, September 10. Two weeks now since I have written in this diary. Longer than that since I looked at the poem about Isabel. Is it the effect of working day after day at a tedious job, shut up in that dismal office with the Caterpillar, that has destroyed the desire for poetry? Was the poetry bad in itself? Very likely. Or has there been a change in Isabel, has she become less

*friendly? Sometimes in these past weeks I have thought
so. Today all that was changed.*

*This afternoon we got up a tennis match, a doubles,
George and Beatrice against Isabel and myself. A bigger
party had been planned, but in the end there were just
the four of us. Isabel had been pressed into playing because Dangerfield had taken Charlotte off to some show
in Hyde Park. We were not badly matched. I suppose
I'm better than George, because although he gets a lot
of twist on his horizontal service, it can never really com-
pare with an overarm service in strength. On the other
hand, Beatrice is certainly a better player than Isabel,
who generally retreats to one side of the court and leaves
it to her partner to take all the play. Even though it
was only a family game, we were all togged up for it,
which I suppose was a bit ridiculous, although the result
was that Isabel looked more lovely than usual in a white
silk blouse and a skirt that was at least a couple of inches
off the ground. She had a little dark-blue jockey cap
perched on her head. Beatrice looked less decorative, but
her play was more practical. She even sometimes took
off her white gloves to serve, and her service was quite
hard for a lady—Isabel's is the gentlest pat over the net.*

*All this is by the way. I'll come to the point. We were
losing by three games to two when I had to play a shot
that brought me close to Isabel. She took a step back,
tottered and almost fell. I put an arm out to support
her, and as I did so become aware of a strong smell of
gin. I am thought to be too young to drink spirits, although I have tried them on my own, but I know the
smell of gin. I could hardly believe that she had been
drinking in the middle of the afternoon, yet there really
was no doubt about it.*

*"I think I must rest," she said. "I am so tired." As she
walked over to a chair she swayed a little, and said it*

was a touch of the sun. George and Beatrice came over and said it was hot, which was true, and that we had been playing strenuously, which was not. Neither of them seemed surprised when Isabel said that she would go indoors and lie down, and it occurred to me that they must both know that at times she is given to drink.

A blessing that the Caterpillar was not there. We should have had a sermon.

After tea I went up to my room and tried without success to write more of the poem. Instead I found myself thinking about my stepmother, and about her marriage to father. I had never thought of father's age, I suppose because he was so quick and energetic that he always seemed young. It had been a shock when the preacher had said that he died "in the thirty-ninth year of his age." I had never thought, either, of Beatrice as much younger than father, but of course she was, at least ten years younger and perhaps more. It must have been difficult for her to accept a stepson who regarded her simply as the woman father married, a kind of housekeeper. It was when we played tennis that I realized Beatrice was still a young woman, that many men would find her attractive, that she would probably marry again. I realized, too, that I liked her independence, and a certain wildness about her, things I had never thought of when father was alive. I thought of her then chiefly as somebody who took him away from me—I was twelve when they married, and it seemed to me that we had always got on perfectly well without any woman around the house except somebody to keep house. I wondered for the first time about the two of them, how they had got on together, whether they had been happy.

These thoughts were interrupted by a tap on the door. Isabel was there, her face paler than usual. She said she wished to ask me something, but once inside the room

*seemed not to know what to say. She looked at the rows
of books I call my library and admired the ivory chess-
men. I said that Father had given them to me, and she
turned her head away. Seen like this, with profile turned
to me and hair coiled at the back of her long, beautiful
neck, she looked like a painting by Rossetti. Then she
said, "I have come to ask your help. I have nobody else
I can turn to. And you are clever, although you are so
young." I said something, I don't know what. I knew
for the first time what is meant by saying that the heart
leapt into the throat. I gulped, and found it hard to
breathe.*

*"I have written some foolish letters. There is nothing
wrong in them, but if George saw them he would be
upset. Do you understand? Oh, you are so young," she
cried out, almost with irritation, as though it was my
fault.*

"I understand."

*"Somebody has got hold of them, I don't know how.
He is asking for money."*

*"Do you mean that you need money to get them back?
I am afraid—"*

*"No, no; of course I should not come to you for money.
At first the man—I suppose it is a man—said he had
one letter, and I sent him money to buy it back. But he
did not send it, and now it seems he has others. He asks
for money every week. I cannot go on paying it."*

*"You should be bold. Tell him to do what he likes;
you won't pay anything more."*

*She did not look at me as she said, "I could not let
George be upset in that way."*

*"I don't see how I can help you. Have you met the
man? No, of course you can't have met him."*

*"I write to an address, that is all. I wondered if—no,
it is too much to ask of you."*

I said, "I will do anything for you, you must know that. Do you want me to go and see him?"

"You are such a romantic boy, Paul. You must not have foolish notions about me."

"But is that what you want? Of course I will do it. I will go there and give him a thrashing." This looks uncommonly foolish as I put it down, and I can only say that it did not seem so when I spoke. And yes, that was what she wanted. She gave me a piece of paper on which she had written the man's address: Jack Jones, 123 Rexile Road, Camberwell. I said I would go that night.

"There is one more thing," she said. "If you get the letters back, please do not look at them. It is not that there is anything wrong about them, but there are things I would not wish you to see."

How could she think that I would read her letters? I said simply that I would go at once. She smiled at that, the first time she had done so. Then she pressed my hand and was gone.

I was filled with eagerness to do something for Isabel, and it was not until I was on the omnibus going to Camberwell that I thought about what I was doing. I did not exactly wonder what might be in the letters, and to be truthful I suppose I avoided the thought. But it did seem to me that the interview with the man Jones might not be as simple as I had felt when I was with her. Suppose he said that he did not know what I was talking about, or just told me to mind my own business? Suppose he was the leader of a gang of thugs? Well, I should just have to wait until I saw him.

It was a cold evening, drizzling with rain, and I sat inside the omnibus, which was stuffy and had a smell about it which may have come from the wet straw on the floor or from a bearded Irish peddler of tapes and cottons who wore a filthy old coat marked with grease spots, and dirty, tattered trousers. I had never been to Camberwell before, and the conductor did not know of Rexile Road. A lively discussion started among the passengers as to exactly where it was, in which the tape and cotton seller joined, and it was agreed that I should be put down at Camberwell Green. So I got down there, asked directions, and learned that Rexile Road was not far away, a turning off Grove Lane.

Camberwell, or this part of it, is a mean area. The green itself was full of people, and there were stalls selling cheapjack goods, stalls offering jellied eels and hot saveloys, but once away from these, Camberwell Road was dismal. Grove Lane, into which I turned, was a little better, but Rexile Road was a street of mean little houses recently put up by contract builders, and run-down shops. It was badly lighted, with very few lamp standards, and boys or vandals had knocked out the mantles from some of these. What should I find when I reached my goal? I thought I was prepared for anything, but still I was in for a surprise. Number 123 was a shop. The name on the fascia was not Jones but Paxton. I peered into the dimly lighted window, while deciding what to do. It held an assortment of things, bootlaces and writing paper and a number of patent medicines like Holmby's Gout and Rheumatism Lotion, which was advertised by a cardboard poster showing a man bent over and walking by means of a stick on one side, and the same man upright and alert on the other.

A ping sounded as I entered the shop. A man came from an inner room and asked what he could do for me. He was perhaps forty years old, his head was bare as a billiard ball, and stuck into a corner of his mouth was an old-fashioned clay pipe.

"Are you Mr. Jones?"

"That I'm not. My name's Paxton, Elias Paxton."

"Does Mr. Jones live here? Perhaps he's a lodger."

"I've got a lodger, but his name isn't Jones."

"I was told Mr. Jones lived here."

"Then you was told wrong."

"Now look here," I said. "A friend of mine has been sending letters here to Mr. Jones, and I know he has received them. It's no use your telling me another story, because I know that for a fact."

"And look you here, young feller. You never said anything about letters. You asked if Mr. Jones lived here, which he doesn't. Asked if I was Mr. Jones, which I ain't. You ain't asked, nor I ain't said, nothing about letters." He took the pipe out of his mouth, grinned at me with satisfaction, and put it back."

"Well, then," I said, rather at a loss.

"Well, then. It may be Mr. Jones has his letters addressed here for a consideration, like others. I ain't saying he does and I ain't saying he doesn't; no more am I saying whether he collects 'em or whether he don't. What I do say"—and here he took out the pipe again and jabbed me with it quite hard in the chest—"is that it's none of your business. So you just hop it, vamoose, skedaddle, stop poking your nose into what's none of your business. Do I make myself clear?"

I made what I'm bound to admit was an undignified exit.

Sunday, September 11

Have resumed in better spirits. Spent some wakeful hours in the night trying to make a plan of campaign, starting from the point of view that the visit hadn't been a dead loss because at least I'd found out something. I talked to Isabel this morning.

"The man has his letters addressed to this shop, and then collects them. You said you hear from him every week. Is it always the same day?"

"Yes. His letters come on Thursday morning."

"And you answer on that day?" She said that she did. "This week don't answer until Saturday. Send your letter by the morning post. It should reach Camberwell by midday. I shall wait near the shop until he collects it."

"How will you know it is the man?"

"I shall stay nearby, and when anybody goes in the shop I shall walk past and look inside to see if a letter is handed over. I'll buy some envelopes with a very distinctive color so that I can recognize them."

I was excited by what seemed to me a brilliant plan. When Isabel asked what I should do when I found Jones, I was a little disconcerted. My ideas had gone no further than identifying him. But we agreed that the most sensible thing to do was follow him and find out where he lived. I can't wait for the chance to do that. But most of all I want to confront him.

Tuesday, September 13
Today bought in the Strand paper and envelopes of an odious deep purple. Unmistakable.

Thursday, September 15
Spoke to Isabel. She had received the letter, showed it to me. No more than a few lines saying that the writer looked forward to receiving a remittance. Remittance was misspelled, with only one t, and the writing did not look that of an educated man. I repeated that she should not write until Saturday morning, and said that she should not send money. She replied that she had to send it. When I asked why, she would say nothing more. At the same time she told me that the store of money she possessed was running low, and that she could not ask George for more.

Friday, September 16 At dinner this evening Isabel came down with the hazy look that I now know means *that she has been drinking. Later when the port was passed round she kept refilling her glass. George in the end said that she had had enough. She abused him, saying that she was shut up here like a prisoner, and that he never took her out. Then she turned to me.*

"Paul is the only one of your whole family who ever reads a poem or has any true appreciation of a picture, or . . ." Then she forgot what she wanted to say. It was embarrassing.

George was gentle with her. "You had better go upstairs," he said. "Come along now—I'll see you to your room."

She got up a little unsteadily and said that she did not want help. Then she looked at me, and for a moment I feared that she was going to ask me to take her upstairs, but happily she went alone. Afterward neither Uncle George nor Beatrice said anything about what had happened, but looking across the table I saw his features set in such an expression of misery as I have never known on his face. The villa was a happy place when father was alive. Now everything seems to be changed.

Later, in my room, I became overwhelmed by a feeling of despair, a sense that my life was falling apart, and a presentiment of something awful about to happen. I began a poem:

> *The light of life is spent. There was a time*
> *For laughter and for singing and for love.*
> *But now all that is past, and I must move*
> *Through nightmare horrors that defeat all rhyme.*
> *And in this world, paler than any ghost,*
> *I see your shadow move among the lost.*

I could get no further. I put it with other fragments into the file marked "Poems."

Saturday, September 17—Evening   I must put down all the events of this extraordinary day. In the morning saw

*Isabel, who said that she had written the letter and asked
me to put it in the post. She had posted the earlier ones
herself. She was very pale, her eyes a little bloodshot,
her manner almost cold. Posted the letter, then went for
a walk across the heath and into Greenwich Park,
looked down on the Queen's House and the river,
my head full of gloomy thoughts. The letters showed
that a secret existed in Isabel's life. Why did I not
insist on knowing what it was? Why not confirm
or deny my dreadful suspicion that the letters had
been written to a lover? But I knew that I should
not do this, and at the same time I began to feel
that I had been absurdly sanguine about spotting
the man at the shop in Rexile Road. I had thought that
with the letter being delayed, he would be anxious to
collect it as soon as possible, but this might not be the
case. Supposing he left it until next week, or it was
handed over in such a way that I could not see the envelope, or the pipe-smoking Paxton spotted me and ordered
me to clear off? The more I considered such possibilities,
the more hopeless my mission seemed. But I will not continue with an account of these doubts, because as will
be seen, they proved irrelevant.*

*By this time I had decided to walk to Camberwell,
and you must imagine these thoughts as taking place
while I was going down Blackheath Hill and entering
the dingy purlieus of New Cross. I reached Grove Lane
before midday, turned into Rexile Road, walked past Paxton's shop with the barest glance inside, and stationed
myself on the next street corner, strolling up and down
and trying to look as though I was waiting for somebody.
Within a few minutes I saw the postman go into the
shop and hand over some letters. By my reckoning, Isabel's would be among them, or would have come by an
earlier post.*

In my waiting I had an unexpected piece of luck. There

were stalls in the road on this Saturday morning, selling
greengrocery, cat's meat, fish that smelled very high. And
there were hawkers with trays, containing all kinds of
household goods. Among all these I was not conspicuous.
People went into the shop, mostly women and small boys.
I ignored them, but when a man entered I contrived to
be standing by the window advertising Holmby's Gout
and Rheumatism Lotion. Most of the men bought shag
tobacco. One collected a letter, but it was not in a purple
envelope. A clock nearby chimed one o'clock, and reminded me that I had been in the street for nearly an
hour.

By the time the clock had struck three, I was hot and
hungry and ready to believe that my idea had been useless. Then, with a feeling of total incredulity, I saw coming from the direction of Grove Lane a feminine figure
I recognized. She had not seen me and I quietly crossed
the road, to stand beside the fish stall opposite. I was
so excited that I did not notice the smell.

It was Hilda. She was wearing a blouse and skirt, the
blouse with leg-of-mutton sleeves, and a pillbox hat.
There was no likelihood that she would see me, for she
was scurrying along head down as usual. I knew that she
would be going into Paxton's shop, yet could hardly
believe it when she did. Looking through the window,
I saw her speak to Paxton, who that afternoon was not
smoking his pipe. He took out a book and she wrote in
it, no doubt acknowledging receipt of the letter. When
she had signed, he produced from beneath the counter
the purple envelope. Hilda did not look at it, but opened
her bag and put the letter inside. I just had time to move
away from the shop when she came out, scuttling back
the way she had come. I let her get to the junction with
Grove Lane before catching up with her and putting a
hand on her shoulder.

It quivered beneath my touch. She turned, and I saw terror on her face, the first time I have seen it on the face of any human being. What she said, however, was commonplace enough. "Oh, Mr. Paul, you did give me a fright."

"Hilda, you and I must have a talk."

"A talk," she repeated, as though she had never heard the word before.

I had seen a tea shop near the green, and I led her to it now. The cakes in the window looked flyblown and decrepit, and inside it was dark, but there was nobody else in it at this time in the afternoon, and the elderly waitress took our order and then left us alone. When I asked whether Hilda wanted anything to eat she shook her head.

"You know what we have to talk about." I felt like one of the teachers at the Prop giving a wigging to a badly behaved pupil. "That letter in your bag."

"Oh, Mr. Paul," she whispered. "Oh, Mr. Paul."

"You know who wrote the letter." She nodded. "I want you to tell me who asked you to collect it."

"I can't."

"Then I shall have to tell the police. You have been a party to blackmail."

"Don't say that. Oh, my God, he never told me that."

"Who never told you?"

She said nothing. The waitress brought the tea. Hilda poured it with a trembling hand while I repeated the question.

"He made me do it. I never wanted to, but he said there would be no 'arm. Mr. Paul, you won't say anything about this, will you?"

"You must tell me everything. Have you been collecting the letters?"

"Yes."

"Who made you do it?"

"Please, Mr. Paul, don't make me tell you." Tears began to roll down her cheeks. She fumbled in her bag, produced a handkerchief, dabbed at her face. I felt embarrassed by the tears, which seemed to put me in the wrong, but knew that I must go on. I saw the letter in her bag, asked for it, and she gave it to me.

"How many times have you collected letters?"

"I don't know, five or six. I thought I might be able to get them from the box in the hall, but Mrs. Collard, she posted them herself."

"Why did you do it, Hilda? You must have known it was wrong." She sniffed. "Who made you do it?" She sniffed again. My embarrassment was replaced by anger. "Very well, it will have to be the police."

She gave a wail loud enough to be heard by the waitress, who looked across at us. In her agitation Hilda lost all her aspirates.

" 'E'll do me an injury, I know 'e will. 'E said it would be all right, there'd be no trouble, she'd pay up and the money'd go to what 'e called our fund, that's what Charlie said."

"Charlie?"

"Mr. Jenkins. Him and me are going together, going to be married. So when Charlie found the letters—"

"Where did he find them?"

"He didn't tell me, said it'd be better if I didn't know." She gave me a swift glance, in which there was something sly. "You don't know much about it, do you?"

"I shall find out, I can tell you that." I leaned over the table, gripped her arm tightly. She gave a little cry. The waitress came over.

"We won't 'ave anything of that sort hif you please. If there's nothing else, perhaps you'd like to pay for your tea and leave."

I paid and we went out. Hilda adjusted her hat. She had regained some of her composure. "Anything more you want to know you'll have to speak to Mr. Jenkins. I'm not saying anything else, and I shan't, not if you was to take me into a police station this minute."

"I shall ask him, you may be sure. And I shall advise Mrs. Collard to go to the police."

Again she gave me that sly glance. "I should talk to her first."

I left her waiting for an omnibus and walked back to Blackheath, trying to decide what to do. I must tell Isabel before tackling Jenkins, but other questions burned in my mind. What did the letters contain, who were they written to, how had Jenkins got hold of them? Then I thought that problems like these did not greatly matter. I had found out who the blackmailer was, and it would be simple enough for Isabel—or for me acting on her behalf—to get back the letters by threatening Jenkins with the police.

I returned feeling pleased with myself. When I walked up the drive, however, and went in under the colonnade, Jenkins was there in the hall. He had obviously been hanging about, waiting for my return. He asked if he could speak to me.

"Why, Jenkins? I have nothing to say to you."

"If you'll excuse me, I think you might be interested in what I have to say to you."

"Very well." I led the way through the gallery to the circular drawing room at the end of it. I saw, too late, that I should have returned as soon as possible. By letting Hilda come back before me I had lost the element of surprise. Now Jenkins stood before me, with his eyes darting about as usual, but seemingly at his ease. He licked his lips and then spoke.

"I'm sorry you've let yourself act as a spy, Mr. Paul,

in what's none of your business. However, that's neither here nor there. I just wanted to warn you against doing anything you'd be sorry for."

The impertinence of this was more than I could stand. "How dare you speak to me like that? You're a blackmailer, Jenkins, and I'll see you end up in jail. If you think adopting this tone is going to get you out of trouble you're very much mistaken."

"That's just what I mean. Hard words don't break bones, but if you go to the police you'll get no thanks, I can tell you. I don't mind coming to an arrangement, but—"

I had to restrain myself from striking him. "Get out. Get out of this house."

"With respect, that's not for you to say. You just speak to Mrs. Collard before you say things like that." With a mocking sketch of a bow, he left me.

Ten minutes later I was with Isabel. She and George had been invited out to dinner at her father's house, and one of the maids was helping her to get ready. She joined me in the drawing room, looking radiant. I had noticed before that any social occasion stimulated her. When I produced the envelope she exclaimed with pleasure, but as I went on to tell her about Jenkins her expression changed. When I spoke of going to the police she stopped me.

"You must not do that, Paul. Anything but that."

I stared at her. "What did you want, then—what did you expect?"

"I don't know. I just wanted the letters back. I hoped you might be able to arrange it for me. It was foolish to ask you, you are so young."

I was stung by that. "Young or not, I know enough to understand that if you go to the police there'll be no publicity, Jenkins will be sent to prison and you will get the letters. How many are there?"

"I'm not sure. That is, I'm not sure how many he has. I must talk to him."

"Talk to him? But, Isabel, he is loathsome. He cannot stay in this house; it would be intolerable."

"Dear Paul." She was carrying a fan and now she tapped my cheek with it. "I am grateful to you, indeed I am. You have done wonders. But now you must let me speak to Jenkins. He must leave here, I quite agree; it is simply that I must talk to him first. Now here is George. We must go." She came close to me, touched my cheek with her lips and whispered, "Thank you." Then Uncle George appeared in the doorway, wearing dinner jacket and black tie.

"Come along, Isabel, mustn't keep your noble father waiting. I must say you look lovely, m'dear, pretty as a picture. What's the matter, Paul? You look as if you'd found sixpence and lost half a crown."

I said it was nothing. I wondered how Isabel could look so serene. When they had gone, I suddenly became aware that I had had nothing to eat since breakfast. Had supper with Beatrice, who talked all the time about tennis. Then up to my room, where I wrote all this.

13

Earlier on this day Harriet had received a letter in the post. It was a report from the detective named Edwards. She read it with surprise. Afterward she took out the yellow corset, the gloves and the bust improver from the locked cupboard where she kept them, and looked at them carefully. Then she put them back in the cupboard and tore up the letter.

(3)

A Week in September

BROWN Windsor soup, haddock with a thick creamy sauce, Welsh lamb with roast potatoes, green beans, red currant jelly, mint sauce, then a dessert of trifle and jellies with cream—that was Sunday lunch at Albert House. Most of those present might have seemed, to a detached observer, occupied with other things. Harriet was watchful at the head of the table, but apart from a comment on Isabel's small appetite, she spoke little. She ate well, although she complained of indigestion, and took a dose of medicine after the meal. Isabel was quiet. George, napkin tucked under his neck, ate greedily but was not his usual boisterous self. Paul said little and ate little too. He avoided looking at Isabel. Bertie also was silent, casting occasional glances at George and at Dangerfield, as though he expected some scathing remark from them, to which he was prepared to respond. Beatrice began to talk about a tennis tournament she was arranging for the following Saturday, to which she had invited a Mr. Lambert, a solicitor who lived locally and had actually played in that year's Wimbledon championship. She may have been intending to annoy her mother by flaunting this account of her tennis activities, but Harriet said nothing, and Beatrice's remarks were received with so little interest that she abandoned them.

Of the company only Dangerfield and Charlotte seemed in normal spirits. Dangerfield, indeed, was in a positively good humor. The dishes had been cleared away, and they were taking coffee, when he tapped gently with his spoon upon the saucer, slightly twirled his mustaches and stood up.

"Ahem. If I may have your attention for a few moments, I have an announcement to make." With a roguish expression which seemed the precursor of a wink that never came, he continued. "Wednesday is a day of particular importance. It is—ahem—"

"Aunt Harriet's birthday."

That, of course, was Bertie. The incipient wink was replaced by a positive frown, quickly wiped off.

"Precisely. Charlotte and I thought it should be marked in some way, and I have—ahem—reserved a box at the theater on Wednesday evening." He was interrupted by a belch as sharp, and as briskly cut off, as though it had been a rifle shot. Nobody looked at Harriet, from whose mouth the sound had emerged, nobody showed awareness that anything at all had happened, except that on Paul's mouth a smile struggled for expression. "The box will accommodate us all, and I very much hope that you will be our guests on Wednesday evening."

They all waited for Harriet to speak, but she said nothing. Isabel said, "But isn't that a perfectly charming idea. We would love to come, wouldn't we, George?" George made an assenting sound. "What is the play?"

"*Lady Windermere's Fan,* at the St. James's. It is one of the hits of the season."

Now they all looked toward Harriet. She rose from the table. "I feel unwell. I shall lie down. Charlotte, send for Dr. Porterfield."

She moved into the gloom at the end of the Great Hall and ascended the stairs. The other women went with her. Dangerfield looked a little upset. "I say, do you suppose she really doesn't like the idea? Charlotte said she'd enjoy it."

George chuckled. "Don't worry. I've never known Mamma to receive a gift gladly. She's pleased to have them, all the same. Wonderful idea, my dear fellow, wish I'd thought of it myself. As a matter of fact, she's been so sticky about presents in the last two or three years that we don't give them now. But you'll find she'll come round."

"It's my belief that Aunt Harriet said nothing because she was feeling unwell," Bertie said in his nasal voice. "I am sure she would not be unappreciative. She has always welcomed the little gifts I have given her on such occasions."

"What were they, temperance tracts?"

Bertie gave Paul a forgiving smile, although the red pustules on his cheeks showed a little more prominently. "Some very fine work is produced by the movement, showing in visual form the evils of drink and the blessings of temperance. I gave her a print of *The Drunkard Redeemed* by Mr. Desmond Craikie, R.A., which greatly impressed her."

"Would she consider the theater sinful?" Dangerfield asked. "Charlotte said she hadn't been for years, but used to like it."

"What about you, Bertie?" Paul asked. "Is going to the theater a sin?"

"I am not opposed to any form of seemly gaiety, but our Lord told us to beware of painted images. I would never presume to judge others, but I should not myself feel it right to look on such a piece of make-believe."

"You don't want to come, Bertie?" Dangerfield said. "That's all right. But I hope I haven't put my foot in it with Harriet, and I hope there's nothing really wrong with her."

About that Dr. Porterfield was reassuring. It was a stomach upset, nothing more, and it came from eating injudiciously.

"At the age your dear mother has reached, the digestion is not what it was. She should be eating lightly, rather small meals, no heavy puddings or rich foods. But today at lunch, haddock in a cream sauce, a trifle with more cream added to it . . ." He shook his head. "You see the result."

"What is the medicine doing for her?" Beatrice asked.

"It is partly an aid to digestion, partly a tonic. It will help, but it cannot perform miracles."

"Do you think she should see a specialist?"

"At present, I should say no. There is always the possibility of an ulcer, but that would cause pain rather than the discomfort she feels. My view is that it is really a question of diet. I have given her a good talking to"— he shook his head smilingly to show his awareness of the difficulty of doing that—"and I hope she will pay attention to it. She is feeling much better now, although she should stay in bed for the rest of the day."

And in fact by teatime Harriet seemed almost recovered, although she did not get up. She gave what might be called an audience to her children, and Dangerfield as well, in her room. In the fourposter bed she looked tiny, but her color was good and her manner alert. She dismissed the doctor's views as stuff and nonsense.

"He said I should eat fruit, as though that did anything but give you colic. My father never ate a pear or an apple in his life. And salads—stuff that's good for nothing but rabbits."

"But, Mamma, what do you think caused the pains?" Charlotte asked.

"Getting older, the illness you can't cure. I said as much

to Porterfield, and he more or less admitted it. But I've no intention of giving up the business, so don't think it." She did not look at anybody in particular when she said this. "Robert, I didn't thank you for the invitation to the theater. It is ten years since I've been to a play."

"Then you'll come?"

"Of course I shall come. Why ever did you think I wouldn't?"

2

That evening Paul tried, and failed, to see Isabel alone. When they returned she was in conversation with Beatrice about next Saturday's tennis tournament, then they had supper, and immediately afterward she complained of a headache and went to her room. Hilda was not in evidence but Jenkins was still there, hovering around at supper and behaving as though nothing had happened. To his astonishment and disgust, Paul found that he felt awkward in the man's presence. What on earth was Isabel playing at? His frustration was such that he went upstairs and knocked on her bedroom door. He got no reply, perhaps because she was asleep or perhaps because she refused to answer. On Monday morning he would have gone to work before she came downstairs, but he determined that he would insist on seeing her in the evening.

He would not have been reassured if he had heard the conversation that took place between husband and wife when George came to bed. He had just taken off his collar with a sigh of relief—it was nearly three inches high and was distinctly uncomfortable for his short neck—when she spoke. She was not in bed but lying on a chaise longue in a pretty blue and pink zephyr dressing gown, frilled around the neck. She had been reading a magazine, which she put down.

"George, please listen and don't turn round. And don't start to ask questions."

"Very well, m'dear."

"I want you to let me have five hundred pounds."

George's fingers had been busy with shirt buttons, but now he stopped. He did not look around, but he could see Isabel reflected in the glass. "What in the name of the Almighty do you want with five hundred pounds?"

"I said you were not to ask questions."

"All right, then, here's an answer. It's impossible. Can't be did."

"Supposing I gave you a reason."

"An excellent idea." He turned, a not very presentable figure with shirt unbuttoned and braces dangling.

"It is money I must have for a family purpose. I can't tell you more than that."

"To do with your father, d'you mean? He seemed pretty cheerful to me the other night. Or is it one of your sisters?"

"I can't tell you anything more."

"Doesn't matter, not worth your thinking up a story, don't bother. I told you, can't be did."

"What do you mean?"

"Just haven't got the ready, that's all. You need it so badly, you'll have to ask your father. After all, you say it's a family affair."

"You must have money. We don't even live in our own house."

"Perfectly true. But those little bills you run up with a dressmaker here and a milliner there, do you know how much they add up to?"

"Are you saying that I should never have any new clothes?"

"Not at all, m'dear. I'm saying clothes cost money, and yours seem to cost a fortune. I'm saying Mother's uncommon tight-fisted, especially since Dangerfield came into the business. So what with one thing and another, there's nothing to spare, and whatever little trouble you've got yourself into you'll have to get out of without five hundred pounds from me."

"You don't know what you're saying." Her voice was very quiet, hardly above a whisper.

"I know very well the state of our account at the bank. There's no use in talking about it any more. I'm coming to bed."

3

Monday and Tuesday seemed to Paul, when he thought about them afterward, among the strangest days he had lived through. He went up in the train to Charing Cross each morning, returned in the evening. On both days he expected, or half expected, that Jenkins and Hilda would be gone. But that did not happen. He caught only a glimpse of Hilda, who scurried away as soon as she saw him, but Jenkins was there with his mock servility hiding a sneer. And the most maddening thing was that Isabel quite obviously avoided Paul. On Monday she went to Dulwich for the day, returned late and went straight to her room. On Tuesday she was busy with Beatrice, arranging details of Saturday's tournament.

"I have put Mr. Lambert to partner Isabel. Do you think that's a good idea, Paul?" He said that he did. "And I want you to play with Lottie Ranger. Poor Lottie; if only she didn't hit so wildly. Do you know that the last time she played, three balls were lost? But she tries hard; she deserves a good partner."

Isabel asked what Mr. Lambert looked like. Tall and dark, Beatrice said, and very much up in the latest thing, especially in the world of art.

"He sounds delightful," Isabel said. "Between the

points he will be able to tell me all about this year's Royal Academy. But I shall have to reveal my ignorance, which will be perfectly dismal." At that moment George came into the room. "I shall tell him that my husband is a monster who keeps me locked up. He must be the true knight who will rescue me and carry me off to an exhibition."

George made some inane comment, to which Isabel responded with a further inanity. Was this silly giggling creature the Isabel who had gone with Paul to the poetry recital?

"George, who do you wish to play with?" Beatrice asked. "I think if I put you with Mrs. Winter, she's very steady. How about that?" Mrs. Winter was Dr. Porterfield's elder daughter, and her husband was something in the post office.

"Oh, indeed, very steady. She holds out her racket and hopes that the ball will hit it. Yes, of course, Bee, do as you like. I have to go over to see Mamma. I don't know what she wants, business affairs, but she said she'd give me a bite to eat, so I shan't be in to dinner."

"I will come with you," Isabel said.

George's doughy features showed a hesitancy not at all unusual. "Well, I don't know if that would be a good thing."

"Oh, please, George. You know that Harriet is always saying I don't care for going to Albert House, so she'll be surprised. Isabel has mended her ways, she'll say; she is a suitable wife for George after all."

"You'll be bored when we go off to talk business."

"Not at all. I shall talk to Charlotte about Robert and their wedding. Or perhaps Robert will be there, in which case he can tell me about Assam and how he used to rule over a thousand natives. That will be fascinating. Do please let me come."

George laughed and said all right, and they went off

together. As she passed Paul he caught the smell of drink. He spent the rest of the evening helping Beatrice with the tournament, arranging couples and order of play. Then he went up to his room, and wrote another verse of the poem:

> There was a time I would have hoped to be
> Your lover, but I know that time is past,
> And all my thoughts must now be fixed at last
> Upon the irresponsive cruel sea
> Of life that tears the two of us apart.
> Yet still within the waves I hear your heart.

4

On Wednesday George, Paul and Dangerfield all left the office early. Bertie was ready to come with them, but Dangerfield stopped him.

"No need for you to come with us. You're not joining in this sinful entertainment." Bertie looked venomous for a moment, and then said that of course he was perfectly right, and that in any case there was a great deal of work to be done.

George and Paul changed into evening dress at the villa, Dangerfield went to Albert House. There Charlotte greeted him, unusually animated. "Oh, Robbie, I'm so looking forward to this evening."

"So am I. How's the old lady?"

"She's been getting ready since early afternoon."

"Is she better?"

"Oh, quite well again. It was only a stomach upset. Robert, it was such a clever idea of yours."

"My dearest Charlotte, I'm a clever fellow."

"But can we afford it? And going out to supper afterwards as well."

He tapped his nose. He had, she had noticed before, some very coarse habits. "Have you heard the old saying about a sprat to catch a mackerel?"

At about six o'clock the party from the villa came in the brougham, and they drove to the theater in this and the Collard landau. Harriet, of course, went in the landau, with Charlotte, Dangerfield and—because the landau was much roomier than the brougham—Paul. Harriet sat upright in the place of honor, on the right-hand side of the carriage, with Dangerfield equally upright opposite her. She had an expression of disapproval which, as Paul knew from past experience, did not mean that she was not enjoying herself. From across the carriage she inspected his dress lounge, with its roll collar covered with black velvet instead of a dress coat's silk.

"You should be wearing a proper jacket." Paul had been told by the tailor that the dress lounge was the modern thing and had almost replaced evening dress. "But it suits you. You look like your father." Clop-clop went the horses. Paul thought about Isabel. Harriet addressed her prospective son-in-law.

"This was a thoughtful idea of yours, Robert." Dangerfield inclined his head. He was, of course, wearing evening dress, although the jacket looked rather worn, perhaps from much use in Assam. "It is to be hoped that the play is not too rubbishy. I cannot bear a rubbishy play."

"The man who wrote it, Oscar Wilde, has a reputation as a wit."

"I have seen some of his work in *Woman's World.* It was trivial but not rubbishy."

"Oscar Wilde is a poet," Paul said. "And a socialist." Harriet forbore to comment.

Clop-clop up the Old Kent Road, clop-clop across Westminster Bridge, and they were nearing the theater. In

St. James's Square there was a confusion of carriages, much calling and even shouting between drivers, but at last they turned into King Street and were there. As they entered the foyer and stood waiting for the other carriage, Paul could not restrain a feeling of excitement. He had not been to the theater more than half a dozen times in his life, and the last occasion had been a visit to a farce called *Mr. Ogilby's Stockings* two years earlier. He had gone with his father and stepmother, and he remembered with shame how priggishly superior he had felt at his father's uproarious laughter over Mr. Ogilby's predicament at having left his stockings (quite innocently, of course) in a lady's boudoir.

He just had time to look around and see with relief that dress lounges were quite the order of the day, especially among young men, when the rest of the party arrived and Dangerfield was leading the way to their box. He placed himself between Harriet and Charlotte. Paul was next to Stepgrand, with Isabel on his left. George and Beatrice sat a little behind them. Above them a great chandelier sparkled, and around the walls the new electric lamps gave a harsher, brighter glow than gaslight. Harriet looked at the program through a lorgnette, then turned the glass on Paul and said, "And what is your opinion of business life, young man?"

The question was so unexpected that for a moment he was lost for a reply. Then he said that he was beginning to master it.

"I hear good reports of you." So that must have been the subject of her conversation with George the previous night. "I am told you have new ideas. They are welcome, providing one is certain that they are superior to the old ones." There seemed nothing he could say. "Thank you, I am quite comfortable," she said to Dangerfield.

Then Isabel spoke to him. "Do you know much about Mr. Wilde's work, Paul?"

"I have read quite a lot of it. His poems are very beautiful. There is one verse I remember particularly:

> "I can write no stately proem
> As a prelude to my lay.
> From a poet to a poem
> I would dare to say."

She turned her head and looked directly at him. "You must not—" she began to say, and then the lights went out and the curtain rose to show Lord Windermere's morning room with its elegant bureau on the right covered with books and papers, its sofa and tea table, and the window opening onto the terrace. A ripple of applause came from the audience as they took it all in while Lily Hanbury as Lady Windermere arranged roses in a blue bowl, and told the butler that she was at home to anybody who called. The caller was the cynical Lord Darlington, and soon the applause had changed to laughter as Lady Windermere told him that he was better than other men although he pretended to be worse, and he replied: "We all have our little vanities, Lady Windermere."

Was that funny? Paul rather thought it was, and he thought some of the other dialogue amusing in a brittle way, but as the play developed through the revelation that the apparently wicked Mrs. Erlynne was Lady Windermere's mother and was prepared to sacrifice herself to save her daughter from disgrace, he found himself even more caught up in the melodrama. When, in the last act, Lady Windermere said to her husband: "There is the same world for all of us, and good and evil, sin and innocence, go through it hand in hand," he felt that in some way this applied to Isabel. What secret was she hiding? Did it belong like Mrs. Erlynne's to the past?

Then the play was over, the curtain came down to immense applause and was raised again as George Alexander, Marion Terry and the rest of the cast stood there smiling. The applause died away a little, but swelled again as a bulky figure in evening dress and wearing a green carnation in his buttonhole appeared from the wings and raised a hand.

"Ladies and gentlemen, I said on the first night that I was glad you admired my play almost as much as I do. I am delighted that you still do so. I compliment you upon your good taste, and the cast upon their perfect performance."

He bowed and retired. Dangerfield said, "That's the Wilde fellow. Did you ever see such infernal impertinence?"

Isabel said she thought the intervention really rather amusing, George that the man was obviously a cad. Harriet said nothing about the play until, a few minutes later, they had ordered oysters followed by fillets of sole and lobster at Scott's. "That was a very fine house they lived in. Where was it, in Carlton House Terrace? It must have been very expensive to keep up. And then with those demands from Mrs. Erlynne . . ." She shook her head.

"But, Mamma," Beatrice said, "it was only a play."

"I know it was a play, you foolish girl. But plays must be like life, or what is the point of watching them?"

They were all silenced. The oysters were eaten, with some jokes about there being an *r* in the month, and suggestions by a waggish waiter that he had been down that very day to Whitstable and had brought them back on the train. The sole was acclaimed excellent and the lobster, which came piping hot in the shell, delicious. The late-summer raspberries that followed slipped down easily enough. Harriet had said that she did not want to receive any presents, but her health was drunk in champagne.

On the drive back, Beatrice went in the landau, so

that Paul was with George and Isabel in the brougham.
Isabel was in ecstasies about the wit of the play and the
brilliance of the acting, and said that she would like to
go to the theater every night. "I should like to be a drama
critic, the first lady drama critic in the country. I should
write only about plays that were witty or profound, or
in which there were wonderful actors like Miss Terry
tonight. What do you think of that?"

"I think you're talking great nonsense." Gaslight
through the carriage showed George's face set in a plump
mask of gloom.

"You're grumpy. Paul, what do you think?"

"I should read everything you wrote before I looked
at any of the other critics."

"Now you're like Lord Darlington, saying things you
don't mean. I adored Lord Darlington."

When they got back to Albert House a light was shining
in Bertie's tower room, and another gleamed in the entrance. Otherwise it stood in forbidding darkness. They
all went in for a few minutes and chatted about the play.
Glasses of port were drunk, although Harriet took only
her medicine, which she said had a nasty taste. Dangerfield was staying over because of the difficulty in getting
back to Kensington, but the residents of the villa said
good night. The evening was over.

5

Dr. Porterfield was not an easy man to wake. Doctors
do not always follow the advice they give to their patients,
and it was his habit to eat cheese on toast every night
before going to bed, accompanying it with a drink of
rum and milk into which a few drops of laudanum had
been blended. Upon this unusual mixture he slept

soundly, snoring so powerfully that his wife had long ago declared for separate rooms. On this night she had to shake him soundly before he groaned, shuddered, blinked and stared at her.

"It's the coachman from Albert House. Mrs. Collard's been taken ill."

The doctor heaved himself out of bed. Seen in his nightshirt, lacking teeth and the corset which kept his stomach reasonably confined, he looked much older than when fully clothed, and also a little uncertain of his movements. While Mrs. Porterfield helped him to dress, and knelt to put on his boots, he kept up a running fire of comment on the inconsiderateness of patients and the stupidity of their eating habits. By the time he had asked the coachman what was wrong, and had been told that Mr. Dangerfield had said he should go and fetch the doctor quick because Mrs. Collard was very ill, he was his usual solemn and imposing self. And he was if possible more impressive as he stood by Harriet's bedside, feeling her pulse, gold watch in the other hand. Harriet's features seemed to have fallen in and her nose to have sharpened, so that she resembled a bird. She had vomited into the pot beside the bed. "I have been poisoned, Doctor," she said.

The doctor had heard about the fish supper. He said something about a bad oyster.

"I tell you I have been poisoned." She closed her eyes as though the effort of speech had been too much for her.

Dr. Porterfield stood looking down at the tiny figure in the bed. Then he took Charlotte's hand and led her to the little dressing room. Dangerfield was waiting there. Both he and Charlotte were in their night clothes.

"I should like to get a second opinion, but I fear there is no time. Charlotte, you must be brave."

"You mean that Mamma is— Oh, it's not possible." She burst into tears.

"She must have eaten an oyster that was virulently infected. She is suffering from acute ptomaine poisoning."

"D'you mean to say there's nothing to be done?" Dangerfield asked incredulously. "Dammit, Doctor, there must be something."

"You can pray, sir, and I hope that your prayers may be efficacious. In the meantime your brother and sister should be told. I shall return to my patient, and give her what comfort I can."

"It's possible, surely, that she'll pull through?" Dangerfield said.

"Anything is possible. But her age is against her. I cannot encourage you to hope."

As he turned away he became aware of Bertie, standing just at the door of the dressing room, his red-rimmed eyes watering as he dabbed them with a handkerchief. "Has Aunt Harriet passed away?" he asked.

A certain air of eagerness about Bertie made the doctor respond brusquely. "She is very ill."

Bertie came into the bedroom and stood looking down. "It is a judgment," he said, and turned away.

Dr. Porterfield did not leave his patient. It was his duty, he said, to make her as comfortable as possible. He was there to greet George and Isabel, Beatrice and Paul, when they came from the villa, driven up Belmont Hill and through the village in the thin light of early dawn. They stood around the bed, looking at the still figure in it, until Beatrice burst into a storm of weeping and was led away.

A little later Harriet recovered consciousness for a few minutes. Only the doctor and the maids were with her, but George and Isabel came in from the dressing room. She took George's hand and whispered, "My children,

where are they?" The maid ran out to call Charlotte and
Beatrice, but by the time they reached the bedroom Harriet had lapsed again into unconsciousness. Dr. Porterfield
inspected his patient at frequent intervals, and just after
six-thirty in the morning he folded her hands over her
breast and drew up the sheet over her face. They were
all in the room except Beatrice, who was lying down,
and Bertie, who had returned to his tower. Charlotte
buried her head in her hands, and Robert tried to comfort
her. Isabel stood looking down impassively, then almost
ran out of the room. George, who had been twisting his
fingers, murmured something apologetic and went out
after her. Paul looked at the body's outline beneath the
sheet.

"I don't believe it," he said.

"I beg your pardon." Dr. Porterfield was startled.

"You say it was an oyster. I don't believe it. Her death
is just like Father's."

"You are very young, and you know nothing of medicine. Any similarities are superficial. You would know
this if you had seen other deaths from food poisoning."

"But her feet were cold, and—"

"I cannot discuss the matter with you," the doctor said
abruptly. But he did talk about it later to George and
Dangerfield, choosing his words with care.

"There are superficial resemblances between your
mother's death and that of your cousin Roger," he said
to George. "But they are no more than that. Your cousin's
death did have some puzzling features. Your mother's
is more straightforward. She had a history of digestive
trouble, and ate very injudiciously. Not that this affected
the issue greatly, except that it made her more sensitive
to any kind of gastric upset. It is possible that if she had
been a younger woman with a good digestive system she
might have pulled through. But something she ate, either

the oyster or the lobster, had evidently been virulently contaminated."

"We all ate oysters," Dangerfield said.

"Yes, but there need be only a single bad one in a dozen." He shook a head heavy with knowledge. "If you had seen as many deaths as I have from ptomaine poisoning caused by eating tinned food that had been half eaten and then left lying where flies could reach it—"

"But this was not tinned food."

"Obviously not," Dr. Porterfield said a little impatiently. "But the result is the same. I have seen similar cases too often to be mistaken."

"It was her birthday party, and I arranged it. I shall never forgive myself."

"How could you possibly have known? But it is indeed a tragedy, and I feel it myself. I have known your mother, George, since the time when she was a young girl and I was a young doctor. A remarkable woman. She will be a great loss to the community."

This was the general view. The local paper, the *Blackheath Guide*, printed a two-column obituary headed "A Prominent Blackheath Family," and more than thirty carriages followed the coffin to All Saints churchyard. She had died early on Thursday morning, and was buried on Monday. In the following days the wheels that were to bring legal processes into action began to turn.

6

The first links in the chain that placed Isabel Collard in the dock on a charge of murder were forged, quite against his intention, by Paul. In the days after Harriet's death he found it no easier to speak to Isabel than he had before. She spent some time at her father's house in Dulwich, which was natural enough, and was much with Beatrice, which also was natural, but quite clearly she avoided seeing him alone. In the meantime Jenkins remained, moving about with his usual mock servility, saying "Mr. Paul" in a manner whose deference was just short of insulting. One evening Paul could stand it no longer. They had finished dinner, it had been cleared away, and Jenkins was padding across the hall to the servants' quarters. Paul called him and he came, with that characteristic half smile, half sneer on his face. The long gallery was empty and they talked there. This time Paul was determined to come to a conclusion. He tried, however, to keep calm.

"Jenkins, I am sorry to find you still here."

"As I said before, Mr. Paul, I am not employed by you but by Mrs. Vandervent. While I continue to give satisfaction I am happy to stay."

"If she knew the things I could tell her about you—"

"That would hardly be wise. It would be very distressing for Mrs. Collard. And now if there's nothing else you require I will leave you, Mr. Paul." He began to sidle out of the room. It was too much for Paul.

"You damned filthy blackmailer, I'm going to the police. I shall go tomorrow."

Jenkins was visibly shocked. His head jerked back, his tongue shot out, licked his lips, was withdrawn. Paul was reminded of a cobra he had once seen spend its venom on the glass in the zoo. The man's words, however, were mild.

"I shouldn't do that, Mr. Paul. Nobody would thank you for it; you'd even be sorry yourself."

Paul stood close to him. He never knew afterward what restrained him from knocking the man down, except an ingrained feeling—which as a socialist he of course deplored—that a gentleman did not raise his hand in anger to a servant. "Jenkins, I mean this. You are to leave this house in twenty-four hours, and take Hilda with you. I don't care what excuse you make. If you are here tomorrow evening I shall go to the police and report you as a blackmailer."

Jenkins gave him one long look. Then he turned, with his usual sketch of a bow, and went out.

Paul returned home alone on the following day, since George had said he had a number of things to clear up, and might not be home for dinner. There seemed to be nobody about. No meal was laid at the dining end of the gallery, there was nobody in the drawing room. In the garden he found Beddoes, who said that he had not seen Mrs. Vandervent that afternoon. Back in the house, he rang the bell. An underhousemaid named Beth appeared. He asked where Jenkins was.

"Beg pardon, sir, Jenkins is gone. He went this morning sudden, said something about family matters. The mistress was that upset. And he took Hilda with him. Scared she was, but she's gone."

His heart leapt with the sense of victory. "Where's Mrs. Vandervent now?"

"Gone to Albert House, sir. She seemed in rather a state."

A voice at the door said, "Thank you, Beth, that will do." It was Isabel. He rose to meet her with a smile.

"Isabel, you've been avoiding me." She did not deny it. "I've done it, I've got rid of him."

"You fool." He was horrified that she should call him that. He saw now that her eyes were red from crying, and he smelled drink on her breath. "How I wish I had never asked you to find out about the letters. I was so stupid, stupid, stupid." She struck her forehead with her fist.

"I don't understand. Tell me what happened." She stood there saying nothing, and in his anxiety to know, he took her by the shoulders, an action she misinterpreted, for she broke away crying that he must not do that. He said again, "Tell me what happened."

"You threatened Jenkins, didn't you? Said you'd go to the police. What do you think he did? Went to the police himself."

"Jenkins."

"He went to them, gave them my letters, said he'd just found them. Hilda backed him up, of course. I had been paying him a little money each week to try to keep him quiet. He would have done nothing." Paul did not know what to say. "Do you know what sort of letters they were?"

A feeling of dread oppressed him, an awareness that he was about to be told something terrible.

"They were love letters."

He had known this, of course he had understood that the letters must have been written to a lover, but he knew that there was more, that he had not heard the worst. She looked at him as though he were an object, not a person. Her voice was a little slurred with drink; the words ran into each other. "I had no need to write them, do you know that, I wrote them for my own pleasure, I wanted to write about it, do you understand what I mean, silly boy, how can you understand, you don't know who they were written to, do you, *do you?"*

He said that he did not, although in truth he did. The knowledge had been with him, unadmitted or rejected, since she had told him that the letters existed. It had ached within him so painfully that he was almost glad when, with her features distorted and the corners of her mouth damp with saliva, she spoke the words.

"They were written to your father."

7

Inspector Charles Davis of R Division of the Metropolitan Police, covering Greenwich, Woolwich, Lewisham, and taking in Blackheath, was an image of what, in most eyes, a policeman should be. He kept his uniform clean and well brushed, made sure his men did the same, and was a master at taking drill. The majority of the men lived in the section house at Greenwich, but he and his wife had rented a little cottage in Lewisham when he was made inspector and his wages went up from a sergeant's two pounds a week to very nearly double that. The inspector had several stations to look after, but he had a particular feeling for the one at the bottom of Blackheath Hill, partly because he had been in charge of it himself as sergeant, and partly because of its closeness to the heath. He liked Blackheath, feeling that it was a place where the nobs lived and that it was a mark of distinction to look after it. And Blackheath was also a place where, in spite of what was said about the dangers of the heath at night, there was not much serious crime. Of course, there had been the murder of the servant girl at Kidbrooke, but that had been twenty years ago, when Charlie was a constable, and anyway Kidbrooke was not Blackheath. The chief trouble was with drunkenness at the pubs in the village, especially the Railway Hotel and the Three Tuns. Then there was the occasional burglary—hadn't his namesake Charlie Peace been caught in the end when attempting a burglary in Blackheath?—but in general it was a peaceful place.

Charlie Davis would regale cronies of an evening with

tales of the flyboys he had caught at Blackheath Fair, the sharpers who played the monkey-and-wheel trick, with a monkey picking out a numbered ball to decide a lottery (the ball was dropped back before the mugs saw the number), the pitch-and-toss man and the three-card trick merchants. But all that was a while back, and he was concerned now most often with a smart turnout at the daily parade before the men went out on patrol. He always looked smart himself, with boots well shined, trousers freshly pressed under the bed, and buttons bright enough to dazzle you on a sunny day, and he saw that the men looked that way too. All this was familiar police work to Charlie Davis. Nothing in his experience had prepared him for the letters brought in to Sergeant Miles at Greenwich police station by the man Jenkins, and shown by Miles to him. They shocked and puzzled him, and he did not know what to do about them. He used the telephone, which had been installed in the station a couple of years earlier, and spoke to Superintendent Titmus, head of R Division, who was stationed at Lee Green.

"Letters? That's an odd thing," the superintendent said, without mentioning the nature of the oddity. "You'd better bring them down yourself, Charlie. This calls for a conference."

A conference was serious. It meant that the super knew something related to the letters that Charlie Davis didn't. Half an hour after the telephone conversation, they sat in Titmus's office, which was almost as bare as the inspector's own, although there was an armchair for visitors. Charlie ignored it, and sat in a wooden chair while Titmus read the letters. The two men were very different in appearance. Charlie Davis, with square face, short-cropped hair and handlebar mustache, looked like a true British bulldog, while Titmus, long-nosed and lean-faced, and with as small a mustache as regulations allowed, had the air of some more aristocratic animal, perhaps a borzoi. There were ten letters in all, some of several sheets, written in a large, flowing hand on blue writing paper. The superintendent read them with no comment other than a couple of whistles. When he had finished he said, "Hot stuff." The statement was obviously true, and Davis did not comment on it. "This man Jenkins—what exactly was his story?"

"Said he had heard rumors about Mr. Vandervent's death, that it was not a natural one. Said housemaid Hilda Mount had discovered letters when clearing out cupboard in bedroom, brought them to him. He thought they should be in hands of police."

"Relax, Charlie; you're not giving evidence in court. Have a gasper." The inspector took the offered cigarette and lighted it. "What sort of impression did you get of Jenkins?"

"Very shifty. More to the story than he was telling, I haven't a doubt. The girl's under his thumb, but I should say she was frightened out of her wits. They say they left their jobs at the villa of their own accord because Jenkins felt he couldn't stay after bringing us the letters, but I beg leave to doubt it."

"Do you know the family? I know the name, of course, but that's all."

"I knew Mrs. Collard—the old lady who's just passed away—quite well. She was always on at us to have more policemen patrolling the heath at night. And the family, son and two daughters, I know them all to pass the time of day. The son and daughter live at Victoria Villa, that glass-house place in Belmont Hill."

"And it was George's wife who wrote these, and they were written to Beatrice's husband. There's the making of a fine scandal."

"Exactly so, sir."

"But nothing to do with us, not our concern, unless there's some basis for the story that Mr. Vandervent's death wasn't natural. How about that?"

"I've heard rumors, nothing more. You hear things down at the Railway, people saying he died extremely sudden. Which is true."

"That's just smoke, but what about fire?" Davis did not reply. "Is there any fire? You'd better look at this. It came this morning."

The letter was from an address in Kent. It was quite short.

To the Superintendent of Police, Greenwich District

Sir:

I was both distressed and disturbed to read this morning in the *Blackheath Guide,* which is sent me by a friend in the area, of Mrs. Collard's death, and in particular of the circumstances in which it occurred. These seem to me remarkably similar to those in which Mr. Roger Vandervent died less than four months ago.

I was not myself Mr. Vandervent's physician, but I attended him in the last onset of his illness. I thought at the time that a post-mortem should have been conducted to determine the cause of death. It was my opinion that some of the characteristics of his illness suggested the possibility of some mineral poison. Dr. Porterfield, who was in charge of the case, did not agree.

Now that Mrs. Collard has also died suddenly, let me urge how desirable it is that a post-mortem examination should be made, if only to decide the cause of death beyond doubt. I would write to Dr. Porterfield myself, but I fear that he would not welcome my intervention.

Yours faithfully,
Harold Hassall,
M.D.

"Do you know this Dr. Hassall?"

"I've spoken to him. Young chap, Dr. Porterfield's junior partner, but left a few months ago, soon after Mr. Vandervent died. You don't think—"

"That's just the point, Charlie. I do think. I think there's a strong whiff of stinking fish."

"Dr. Porterfield, though, he's been in Blackheath since he was a youngster. He's very much respected."

"Oh—ah, I'm sure they're all very much respected."

If there was one thing about the superintendent that Charlie Davis didn't care for, it was that he sometimes didn't speak about professional men as he should. A doctor was not, of course, exactly gentry, but still he was a figure you naturally looked up to, and with Dr. Porterfield, who had seen the Davis children through chicken pox and scarlet fever— But awareness of the awful things that the superintendent was suggesting broke in on these thoughts. In a slight daze he heard that the superintendent would himself see Dr. Porterfield, and would arrange to see Mrs. Collard. Davis would be in charge of an investigation to cover all the local chemists and see what poisons had been purchased and signed for that year, and he was also to make inquiries about what poisons might have been available at the two residences. To poke his nose into the affairs of people who had been placed in a more fortunate position in life than his own was not what Charlie Davis regarded as proper police work, and the conference confirmed his feeling that the superintendent was a bit of a radical.

8

"Yes, of course I remember Roger Vandervent. He was my patient."

"And you were perfectly satisfied that his death was caused by gastric fever?"

"Obviously I was satisfied, or I shouldn't have signed the—ahem—certificate. Don't beat about the bush, Superintendent. What exactly is it that you want to know?" Dr. Porterfield puffed at his meerschaum and enveloped himself in a cloud of blue, so that his face was seen softened as in a kind of mist.

"You had a partner named Dr. Hassall at that time. Was he equally satisfied?"

"Is that the way the wind blows? Now, Mr. Titmus, don't mistake me. Hassall is a smart young chap, but he's sometimes just a little too smart for his own good, you understand?" Titmus nodded. "He was—I don't know what you'd call it—too modern for some of my patients, so he left me and set up on his own, somewhere out in the country. I was sorry to lose him, because he was clever." The doctor's corporation heaved as he coughed. He wiped his eyes.

"And was Dr. Hassall satisfied?"

Porterfield went on wiping his eyes, then blew his nose resoundingly. He's giving himself time, Titmus thought. I can still smell that fish. Smoke blurred the face again. Through it the doctor said, "That's something I disremember. I'll ask you again, Superintendent, what is it you want to know?"

Why not tell him? Titmus thought. Although he was annoyed that he had to speak through the blue haze. "It's been suggested that Mr. Vandervent might have taken poison. And that his death was similar to Mrs. Collard's."

Puff-puff. The air of the consulting room was heavy with smoke. "You've got this from Hassall."

"It has been suggested that a post-mortem on Mrs. Collard would clear up any doubt in her case."

"Are you asking me to authorize one—is that what you're here for?"

"I am saying that it would clear up any doubt."

"What doubt?" Now Porterfield got up, knocked out his pipe and confronted Titmus squarely. "My position is that I have signed a certificate that Mrs. Collard died from acute food poisoning. I had been treating her for digestive trouble for some time. Dr. Hassall knew nothing about her case, you know nothing about it. As far as I am concerned, these tales are no more than tittle-tattle. If you have any evidence of what you are suggesting, bring it to me and I will consider it. In default of it, no, sir, I will *not* authorize the exhumation of my old friend Harriet Collard. You must proceed as you think fit, but you will do so without my help. Good day to you, Inspector."

Titmus, who did not lack humor, acknowledged that his demotion was a nice parting shot.

He saw Isabel Collard in the early evening of the same day, in the drawing room of Victoria Villa. He had heard a good deal about the place, but the reality exceeded his expectations. He was impressed by the entrance colonnade, overwhelmed by the great length of the gallery, but less impressed by the drawing room. It was furnished with a lot of bamboo furniture, and there were Japanese prints—or they might have been original pictures, for all Titmus knew—on the walls. The feeling of awe engendered, however, didn't last. The superintendent believed that the rich lived one kind of life and the poor another, and also that the upper classes were no better than they should be. The villa confirmed the impression made by the letters. He felt a natural curiosity about the person who had written them.

The room was empty and he stood for a moment or two looking at the pictures, whistling under his breath, which was one of his bad habits when alone. Then a sound, nothing so abrupt as a cough, made him turn. She stood in the middle of the room, a slight, elegant figure. My word, you're a looker, he thought, and then as he approached to take the limp hand this thought was supplemented by awareness that she had been drinking, and then by a feeling that she was uncommonly cool for somebody who must know that she was in for a nasty interview. She invited him to sit down, and then there was a pause, deliberate on his part because he wanted her to speak first.

"Well, Superintendent." Her eyebrows were raised a little. "You have my letters." He agreed that he had. "And you have brought them back?"

"They're not with me, Mrs. Collard. There are some questions I should like you to answer."

"Questions? But really—" She broke off and began again. "These are personal and private letters, as you will know if you have read them. They were stolen from the person to whom I wrote them. I fail to see what possible questions can arise."

You're a cool one, my word you are, Titmus thought. You're so cool you'd put out the flames in hell. But still, let's see if we can't warm you up a bit. "There is the question of whether you wish to prefer charges against this man Jenkins. When we spoke on the telephone you said he'd asked you for money. That'd be blackmail; we'd charge him with that."

"I think you must have misunderstood me. The telephone is a treacherous instrument."

"So he didn't ask for money?" She shook her head. "Then why did he bring the letters to the police?"

"You can hardly expect me to answer questions about his behavior. He had been dismissed, and I supposed this was a kind of revenge."

"Why was he dismissed? And the maid, Hilda—was she dismissed with him?"

"I couldn't tell you. I don't concern myself with domestic affairs."

He felt a dislike of Mrs. Collard developing, and with it a determination to break down her defenses. All right, he thought, we've been gentle so far; now let's play a little rough. "These are very unusual letters, Mrs. Collard. And they were written to your brother-in-law, the late Mr. Vandervent. A woman who wrote letters like that to anybody, but especially to her brother-in-law, would do anything to get them back. The only reason a man like Jenkins would keep them would be to ask for money. Would you want your husband to see them?"

"You are being impertinent." She rose, and he saw that her defenses were far from being broken. She was as cool as ever, and drink had certainly not dulled her wits. "I do not care to answer any more questions. I want my letters, and if they are not returned I shall have to seek legal assistance to get them back."

He got up too, and he was saying something about her attitude being unwise, when the door opened. A young man put his head inside, said that he was sorry, and was withdrawing when Titmus stopped him.

"Just a minute, please. You'll be Mr. Paul Vandervent."

"That's right."

"Superintendent Titmus of the Metropolitan Police. I should very much like the chance of a few words, if you can spare the time."

"Is it about Jenkins?" He was a dark, curly-haired youth with an ingenuous, open face. He looked now at Isabel Collard.

"Partly, sir. And in part about your father's death." Titmus looked at Isabel when he said this, and could detect no change in her expression. She went now to the door. When she reached it she spoke the young man's name.

"Yes?" he said eagerly.

"The police have refused to return my letters. This . . . gentleman has asked insulting questions which I have refused to answer. Please don't say anything unwise, Paul."

"Isabel." He jumped up, but she had gone. Why, Titmus thought, the boy's in love with her, or thinks he is. And sure enough, he said that he was not going to talk about the matter, and made for the door. The superintendent spoke when he had his hand on the knob.

"The object of my questions is to decide the truth about rumors that your father's death was not a natural one."

Paul turned and came back. "That is what I have been afraid of."

"Do you have some reasons?"

"There are things I should tell you. But I will not talk about Mrs. Collard."

Titmus could feel his long nose quivering, as it always did when he believed himself to be on the scent of something. He said that his only interest in Mrs. Collard's affairs was in the connection they might have with Mr. Vandervent's death, then he settled back in one of the bamboo chairs and prepared to listen. By the time they finished, an hour later, he had heard not only about the bottle of whisky that had disappeared, but the whole story about Paul's attempt to recover the letters and the departure of Jenkins.

9

"What's got to be done has got to be done." It was with this piece of ancient wisdom that Charlie Davis always consoled himself when faced with something disagreeable. This business of poking around in chemists' shops was not what he thought of as police work, but still it had to be done. He sent P. C. Phillips around to talk to the gardener at Albert House, and Sergeant Miles to look at the poison registers. He had a slight acquaintance with Beddoes at the villa, and had a chat with him in person. Having a chat was not so simple. How did you chat with somebody and ask, just casual like, whether they had any poison on the premises?

He meditated for some time on the best way of doing it, and as a result dropped in at the public bar of the Railway Hotel, which he knew Beddoes used. He found the gardener there, bought him a pint, and said it was a bad business about Mrs. Collard. Beddoes agreed. And sad too, coming so soon after Mr. Vandervent's death. Beddoes looked hard into his tankard, drank deep, and said that was right. Charlie Davis was rather stumped by this incommunicativeness. He was thinking that a straightforward approach might have been better after all, when he caught the eye of a man glaring at him through one of the glass partitions that separated the public bar from the snug. The eye was bloodshot.

"When you going to do something, eh?" the man said.

"Do something about what?"

The face disappeared, and materialized again beside him a moment later. The man wore dirty nankeen trousers and a shirt open at the throat. He had a cap set sideways on his head.

"It 'appened at the glass house and now it's 'appened at the church, so when are you going to wake up? That's what I'd like to know."

The church? Charlie remembered that the locals used this name for Albert House. Beddoes intervened.

"Now, Joe, least said soonest mended."

"I likes that. Oh, yes, I certainly likes that. It's all very well for you, Jim Beddoes; you got a job you want to keep. But everybody 'cept the bluebottles knows what's what."

Beddoes began to say something, but Charlie stopped him. "Let him talk. First of all, what's your name?"

"Joe Brown. And I've lived around here all me life and never lost a job before they got rid of me. Just like that." He snapped his fingers. "The Dutchman, I mean. And for nothing."

"You'd been drinking," Beddoes said. "That's all there was to it, Joe—you'd been drinking."

"And what of it? I'm a better man drunk than you are sober."

"And you used some language, don't forget that."

Charlie thought it was time he took charge. "I want to know what you mean by the police doing something. About what?"

Joe Brown thrust his jaw forward. "About the Dutchman. And now old Mrs. Collard. Everyone knows they was poisoned."

There was at this moment silence in the bar, so that the last word came out loud and clear. The heads of half a dozen customers were turned to them. Harris, the landlord, stopped polishing a glass, put it down, went away out of sight. Beddoes began to speak, but the inspector stopped him.

"What makes you say that?"

"Stands to reason. Wasn't nothing wrong with the Dutchman, was there? And he just snuffed out like that. And Mrs. Collard, she wasn't ill either, from what I've heard—just here one day, gone the next. Ain't natural, is it?" He looked round and was rewarded by a murmur of agreement.

"You said something about poison. Have you got any proof of that?"

"Plenty there, isn't there? Plenty of weed-killer. And didn't she tell you to get some more, Jim—get another kind, she said, ain't that so?"

Beddoes reluctantly agreed. "Mrs. Vandervent was making changes in the garden, and a good deal of weed-killer was needed. Some of it wasn't very successful, and she asked me to try a different kind which she'd read about in the paper."

"Said it was more *refined*. I was there, I heard her."

"You know the doctor was satisfied?"

"He would be, wouldn't he? Friend of the family." The sneer that he got into this was tremendous. "All stick together, don't they? And the bluebottles like you, they just look the other way."

The inspector warned Joe Brown not to let his tongue flap around so much in his head, but he went away thoughtful. There was weed-killer easily available, and obviously a good many people agreed with Joe that it might have been used. Then on the following day Sergeant Miles made his discovery in the poison register.

Davis had chosen Miles for the job because he was a much better hand at book learning than his colleagues. All of them could read and write—though you couldn't have said that of every bobby when Charlie Davis had entered the force a quarter of a century earlier—but not many of them did if they could help it. Miles, on the contrary, always had his head in a book or a paper. He was a smart-looking, well-set-up young fellow, and his reports were clear and concise. He had tried the Blackheath chemists first, without success. Then he spread his inquiries to Lee Green and Lewisham on one side and Greenwich on the other, and it was in Greenwich that he struck lucky.

"Funny little place, sir, in a side street off Romney Road. Funny fellow keeps it too, name of Morley. However, his poisons book's all in order, and there's this entry in it for arsenic. I couldn't take the book, of course, but I copied it out." And he showed the inspector what he had put down in his notebook in a neat copperplate hand. "Arsenic, 3 oz. For Domestic Use. Mrs. Collard. 18th May."

"Does he remember what she was like?"

"He does, sir, but I think you'd better talk to him yourself about that."

Before doing so, however, the inspector told the superintendent, and Titmus decided to come along with him. The shop was old-fashioned, with a bow front and small leaded panes in the windows. Inside, it was dark and had a strong medical smell. Mr. Morley was tall, thin, and a talker. He wore a black eye patch, and explained that he had lost an eye long ago in the Ashanti campaign.

"I was assistant to the divisional surgeon, gentlemen; been in the army since I was a boy. Loved the life, never thought I'd leave it. But one of those Kaffirs came at me with his spear, and though I dodged I wasn't quite quick enough." He indicated a scar which furrowed the side of his forehead from the eye. "I'm lucky to be alive, but I lost one of my peepers. Tried a glass one, but I could never get on with it. It meant the end of army life for me, so I set up shop here. It's kept me going, though I miss the open-air life and the excitement. You gentlemen will understand what I mean. But you don't want to hear me gassing about what's past and gone. Here's what you want to see."

He produced from under the counter a small black-covered book, and they saw the entry that had been copied by Miles. It was the only one for that day, and it came at the bottom of a page. Though it had been hurriedly scrawled, the name "Collard" was plain enough.

"All shipshape and Bristol fashion, I hope, gentlemen?"

"It seems to be," Titmus said. "Do you remember anything about the purchaser?"

"Undoubtedly, sir. This was a lady, fairly tall, wearing— well, now, you won't expect an old bachelor to talk like a dressmaker, but it was some kind of coat and skirt rather tight around here." He indicated his hips. "That's the latest fashion, I daresay. Color was some sort of blue, and she had one of those hats on that comes to a point at the top."

"Sugarloaf crown," said Titmus, whose wife had bought one a couple of weeks earlier.

"Ay, very likely. Then she had white shoes, doeskin. I noticed them because I was apprenticed to a cobbler before I went in the army, so I look at shoes. Very smart, these were. She was well turned out altogether; don't have many like her coming in my little shop."

"I can see you're an observant man. And now the most important thing: would you recognize her again?"

Morley shook his head. "She wore a veil. Never lifted it, so I didn't see her face."

"You can't remember anything at all of what she looked like?"

"I'd like to help, sir, but Jacob Morley don't invent, nobody ever said he did. Captain Cranston, that was our divisional surgeon I mentioned already, he would say you could trust Morley to tell you what was so, not a word more and not a word less. That's Jacob Morley, always was, and it's no use asking him to invent because he won't do it."

"Nobody's asking you to," Titmus said tartly. "What

about her voice? She must have spoken to you, said what she wanted the arsenic for."

"You're right, sir, she did just that," the chemist said in a congratulatory manner. "Don't ask me for the precise words now, because I couldn't give them. But the gist of it was that she needed it for domestic uses. She didn't specify what they were, and why should I ask? I had no reason to believe anything different, had I? No reason now, for that matter." He looked from one to the other of them inquiringly, blinking away like a one-eyed owl.

"Just so," Davis said. "No reason to think anything at all, Mr. Morley. These are inquiries we're making, that's all, and we'd be glad if you'd say nothing about them."

"Mum's the word, sir. Nobody ever said Jack Morley couldn't keep his own counsel. I remember Captain Cranston said—"

Titmus had listened to these exchanges impatiently, and now cut them short. "What about the voice? Was she what you'd call a lady?"

"Happy to be able to reply in the affirmative. The voice was low, rather quiet, but yes, it was a lady. It was not, shall we say, one of the lower classes. Again I have to say that it was not the kind of voice I hear very often."

"Any particular accent?" Titmus asked unwisely.

"Upon the matter of accents, sir, I have no expert knowledge and shall have to ask to be excused from answering."

They got nothing more from the chemist, except that the lady might have been anything between twenty-five and forty. Afterward they discussed what they had learned. Titmus attached more importance than Charlie Davis to the entry in the poison register.

"There's no way around it, Charlie," he said. "Mrs. Collard, or somebody using her name, bought arsenic down in Greenwich less than a week before Vandervent died.

For domestic purposes, she said, but what could they have been when there's two sorts of weed-killer for the garden, and I don't doubt rat poison in the house? And why go two or three miles to Greenwich to get it, instead of buying it in Blackheath? Just tell me the answer to that."

Davis could not tell him. He simply felt that it was impossible that a family like the Collards should have been mixed up in such discreditable matters. When Titmus suggested that the inspector should read those letters again, the offer was refused. Davis had been truly horrified by the letters, but as he said, they had in them no suggestion of any sin but adultery. The whole thing, he suggested, was based on gossip.

Titmus listened to him, his long nose trembling occasionally. Then he nodded, but not in agreement.

"Only one way to stop gossip, and that's to find out the truth. I shall ask for an exhumation order."

"On old Mrs. Collard?"

"On both of them."

10
From Paul Vandervent's journal

Tuesday, September 27. I have written nothing in this journal since Stepgrand died, but I must do so now. I sit in my room looking out at the wilderness Beatrice has made from this part of the garden, and wonder at the horror that has embraced our lives. It spreads wings over us all like some gigantic harpy, so that we live permanently in what seems a Greenland night. Today I learned that the police have obtained an exhumation order. They will dig Father's body out of the ground and open it to see whether he died what is called a natural death. And Stepgrand's too, but I don't care so much about that.

The thought of Father, decayed in the coffin but I suppose still recognizable, being exposed to the surgeons, the bright instruments cutting into dead flesh—I cannot bear it. They say that the nails grow long after the body is dead. Will his be long as a mandarin's? Will they say that while they are about it they may as well trim his nails? I cannot endure the feeling that it was in part my words that moved the police to action. How could I do anything else but speak to them? Yet if I had known the effect of my words, I might have kept silence.

This is miserable stuff, and I am ashamed of myself for writing it. Let me try to put down some details— not so much of what has happened, for nothing in particular has happened, as of the way in which we now behave to each other. Life has changed so totally that we might be different people from those we were only a few weeks ago.

Isabel. She still avoids me, perhaps she hates me. If I enter a room she leaves it; if we have to be in the same room together as at mealtimes, she does not speak to me. One day I found her alone, and began to say that I was sorry for what had happened. She answered that I had made things as bad as they could be, and she would be pleased if I did not meddle any further in her affairs. I think she was half drunk, but that does not mean she was saying anything but what she intended.

Beatrice and George. Incredible as it seems, I think neither of them knows the truth about Isabel and Father. If they knew, would they not be bound to show it in some way? But our lives have been so much changed by Stepgrand's death that I cannot be sure. I sometimes think that Beatrice is no longer entirely sane. Stepgrand died on a Thursday, and of course the tennis tournament Beatrice had arranged for the Saturday following could not take place. Yet she was extraordinarily reluctant to give it up. I was there when George spoke to her about it on Friday morning in the gallery. At first she seemed not to hear, then said vaguely, "Oh, do you think so?"

It takes something to surprise Uncle George, but he was taken aback. "Of course you can't go on with it, Bee. Mother died yesterday."

"Yes, I know. But you see . . ." She was looking out from one of the long windows, and her voice faded away as though she had forgotten what she wanted to say. Then she went on: "I feel so sorry for the court."

"Bee, you're overwrought. You should go and lie down."

She looked at him in astonishment. "Why should I lie down? I am not ill."

"Now look here, old girl, you lie down and have a nap." George put an arm round her shoulder, patted it in his half-hearted way.

"I must go to see Charlotte. There are things we should do."

"Dangerfield can look after that sort of thing. He takes care of everything now, runs things as though he were still on his tea plantation or whatever it was. But I'll have a natter with him."

"You really think I must stop the tournament? I was so looking forward to it."

I've always thought of Uncle George as a good-natured man, but he was as near to exasperation as I've ever seen him. He said very mildly that he and I would see to it all, she needn't worry about it. When she had gone out he spoke to me.

"Paul, your mother's feeling the strain, you can see that. I'm going to get the doctor to have a look at her. That business about the tennis—you'll see to that, won't *you? They wouldn't come anyway, but we should send notes all the same. Or call them up, if that's easier."* I said I would look after it.

It was a sunny day, and the light came in through every side of the room, bathing Uncle George in it. When Isabel stood in this gallery with the rays of such a light glowing round her, I had thought of her as the Blessed Damozel. Seeing George there now, pudgy, awkward, rather like a dummy in his black clothes, I wondered how she could ever have married him. Then I remembered that she had been my father's lover. At that moment it occurred to me that my uncle and my stepmother remained ignorant of this.

Later that day Porterfield came up, saw Beatrice, and prescribed a sedative for her. She said nothing more about the tennis, seemed to have forgotten it. I wrote notes to everybody.

Dangerfield and the Caterpillar. On the Sunday after Stepgrand died we went to the church for lunch as usual, except for Isabel, who was visiting her family. It is extraordinary that we do so many things as usual when the whole of life has changed. Nobody took Stepgrand's place at the head of the great table, and the meal was eaten mostly in silence. Then the Caterpillar, on his second helping of apple pie, which he had loaded with cream from the big silver jug, said, "What's being done about the firm?"

Nobody replied for a minute. Then Uncle George said that we could think about that later.

The Caterpillar blinked. "Things can't just be left. I went to the office on Friday. I thought it my duty; the men expect it."

It was Charlotte, of all people, who rebuked him. "Your aunt will not be buried until Monday, Bertie."

He was not abashed. The Caterpillar is really an arma-
dillo or an alligator, his scaly skin is so thick. "Somebody has to be there. And he came in on Friday." He
made a gesture, without quite pointing, at Dangerfield.

"Did you, Robert?"

"For a short time. It's as Bertie says, my dear, somebody
has to tell the men what's happening. Nobody would
have appreciated that more than Harriet. Business must
go on and orders have to be dealt with, even though
there has been a death in the family."

George's voice was shrill as he said, "You mean I
haven't been there—that's what you're getting at."

Dangerfield gave a slight cough. "Nothing personal
meant. Only son and all that, quite different for
you."

"You'll find our workers aren't like your damn coolies."
George got up from the table, his hands trembling.
"Damn disgraceful," he said as he went out in the direction of the library. Dangerfield tugged at his mustache
and said he must apologize for George's language, but
it struck me that he wasn't displeased. I thought the Caterpillar looked happy too, although that may have been
the result of the amount of food he had consumed. Was
there an unholy league between them? Sitting in that
great cloister of a dining hall, it was possible to imagine
anything. Of course I had not been up to the office either.
It occurred to me later on that perhaps the Caterpillar
felt gleeful about that.

On the Monday, Stepgrand was buried. I felt little emotion, although I liked and admired her. I think emotion
had been drained away from me, first by Father's death
and then by the discovery about Isabel. Shall I ever recover from that?

Another verse of my poem:

You were the sun, I was your satellite.
The bright illumination of your face
Once seemed to me the image of all grace,
But now my images are of the night.
When I was serious you only played.
Faith, love and dream, they all have been betrayed.

Can I ever admit to myself that Isabel regarded me as no more than a schoolboy with whom it amused her to flirt? And that afterward she merely used me to try to get back her letters? Why do I find that I can forgive my father, but that I cannot pardon her?

And what is the point of doing this stupid job, which I took only to please Father's memory? Shall I leave home, do some kind of social work in the East End, try to improve the lot of the working people? I am not sure if I have the nerve for this, or even truly desire it.

On Tuesday Mr. Cleverly, who has been the family solicitor for years, read Stepgrand's will. We assembled in the Great Hall. It was not a bright day, and even with all the lights on the atmosphere was sepulchral. Mr. Cleverly, a man with a voice like soapy lather, read out the last will and testament of Harriet Jean Collard, which had been made in June, soon after Father's death.

There were small bequests to the servants—twenty pounds here, thirty there, and fifty to William the coachman. A hundred went to Dr. Porterfield, for his care of the family over the years. There was five hundred pounds for Bertie, which was five hundred more than he deserved, and the same amount for me. Then the rest of the estate was to be divided equally among her three children, George, Beatrice and Charlotte, with an extraordinary provision about Albert House. The language here was splendidly typical of Stepgrand, and I'll try to quote it from memory as it came through Cleverly's soapsuds.

"I was brought up in Albert House, have lived in it throughout my life, and it will always remain dear to me. I recognize that my feelings may not be shared by my children, but it is nevertheless my wish that some member of my family should continue to live in it. The house is the principal asset I have to dispose of. If, therefore, any of my children should agree to live in Albert House for fifteen years after my death, I bequeath it to them absolutely. In the event, which I consider unlikely, that two of them wish to live there, they will each inherit a half share of it." If none of them wanted to live at Albert House it was to be sold. In that case half of the money was to go to the children in equal proportions, and the other half to the Distressed Gentlewomen's Association. The remainder of the estate was to be divided equally among her three children.

There was more, but that was the gist of it. When Cleverly had finished, somebody let out a sigh. Then Dangerfield spoke. He had not been mentioned, and so I suppose felt free to ask questions.

"Can you give us some idea of the estate's total value?"

The solicitor almost chuckled, and it was as though the soapsuds were coming out as bubbles. *"That depends to some extent on the valuation of the house. Mrs. Collard was convinced that it was worth a great deal, and she may have been right. On the other hand, it is not everybody who would care for it. Considerable alteration would be needed to bring it into line with modern views about comfort."*

"And the rest of the estate?"

"Mrs. Collard had some government stocks, which she was unwilling to dispose of. She had some railway shares. There are also her shares in the business, the value of which depends on the family intentions regarding its continuation. If the business were sold, then the proceeds

(179)

might be considerable. If it is to be carried on, however, Mrs. Collard's shares would be divided equally among her children, so that no money would change hands. Unless, that is, you decided to take in another partner, in which case shares might be sold to him at a mutually agreed price."

"So the business shares are worth nothing?"

"Unless you all agree to sell them to an outsider, and find one willing to purchase, that is so."

"And the other stocks and shares you spoke of?"

"It is hard to say. Perhaps between ten and twenty thousand pounds."

"She was not a rich woman," Dangerfield said. In the dim light it was not possible to see his expression.

Mr. Cleverly bubblingly agreed. "Mrs. Collard was comfortable, and of course in her lifetime she had an income from the firm. But she was not rich." Nobody else spoke. "I tried to discourage her from the conditions she made about this house, but she insisted on them. There is no hurry at all to make a decision, but perhaps when you have all had a chance to consider the position, you will let me know your feelings. Perhaps I should emphasize again that if the house is sold, only half of the proceeds will be divided among the three children."

Good-bye, Mr. Cleverly. It seemed to me that the contents of the will shook up Dangerfield, that he had expected there to be something like a hundred thousand pounds in money and shares. Nothing was said directly about the will after Cleverly left, except by the ineffable Caterpillar, who told us that he wouldn't mind living at Albert House. "It has been my home from early childhood, and I am much attached to it," he said in his unctuous way. I couldn't forbear saying that he wasn't being given the chance to make a decision, and he replied that

*he only wanted to show how happy he personally would
be to help carry out his aunt's wishes.*

*And for myself, what did I think or feel? Nothing that
I could put down on paper. Five hundred pounds is more
money than I have possessed at any time in my life,
more than most of the workers in the firm will earn in
five years (the average wage except for skilled men is
between a pound and thirty shillings a week), but I have
no idea what I might do with it. There seems to be a
mist at present between me and the world; it is as though
I had been given enough laudanum to dull the senses
but not to induce unconsciousness. I go about my affairs
at the firm in a waking dream, thinking: This cannot
go on.*

*Then a couple of days after the reading of the will,
the police came to the villa. By unlucky chance I entered
the room when they were speaking to Isabel. Perhaps
this did not matter much anyway, for they would have
spoken to me sooner or later, but this too seemed part
of the life that was turning from dream to nightmare.*

*And today the exhumation. When I think of what is
happening as I write these words, I cannot bear it. Light
pours everywhere into the villa, and the light is as harsh
and pitiless as the darkness of Albert House is dangerous
and obscure. I draw the curtains in my room and lie
down upon the bed, but there is no escaping from this
light.*

11

The exhumation took place on a Tuesday. Forty-eight
hours later, just before midday, Superintendent Titmus
was driven up to Victoria Villa in the police hansom.
Inspector Davis accompanied him. As they pulled up at
the entrance colonnade Titmus shook his head.

"I don't like this kind of place, Charlie. Something wrong with it, it's not natural." He thought this over. "Not normal, if you see what I mean. And Albert House, that's worse."

The inspector rang the bell, and asked the maid who answered it if they might speak to her mistress. Both men looked solemn as they stood waiting. When Beatrice came to meet them, Titmus gave his subordinate a furious glance. She looked from one to the other inquiringly.

Titmus spoke. "Superintendent Titmus and Inspector Davis, ma'am. You're Mrs. Vandervent?"

"Yes. You have come to tell me the result of the—the exhumation, I suppose."

"Could we speak more privately, Mrs. Vandervent?"

Beatrice led the way into the gallery, waved a hand at the great space around, and said, "Is this sufficiently private?" She sat down and looked at them expectantly.

Titmus said stiffly, "I am sorry to inform you that the medical hexperts"—he coughed, and corrected himself—"experts have come to the conclusion that the deaths of both your husband and your mother were caused by the hadministration of poison." He left the second unnecessary aspirate uncorrected. Beatrice put a hand to her mouth, but did not speak. He continued without a pause. "It was in fact Mrs. Collard that we wished to see."

Beatrice went to the bell pull, told the parlormaid to see whether Mrs. Collard was in her room, and to ask her to come down to the gallery, and then resumed her seat. "Do you—" she began. Titmus held up a hand to stop her.

"I cannot answer questions, I am afraid, ma'am."

"Won't you sit down, Superintendent. And Inspector."

"Thank you, but we prefer to stand."

When Isabel entered the room they all turned to her. She was perfectly composed, although her face was paler than usual. Titmus cleared his throat. "Your name is Isabel Collard."

"Isabel Mary Collard, yes."

"Isabel Mary Collard, I have here a warrant for your arrest, on the charge that on or about the twenty-second of May you were responsible for the administration of poison in the form of arsenic to Roger John Vandervent, thus causing his death. I have to ask you to accompany me, and to warn you that anything you say may be taken down and given in evidence."

Davis waved the warrant. Isabel did not look at it. She spoke in a ringing tone. "I have to tell you, Superintendent, that you are totally mistaken. Beatrice, you will tell George."

"Yes, of course. But this is ridiculous. It is some awful mistake."

Titmus gave the sketch of a bow. "We have our duty. Perhaps you would like your maid to pack some things, Mrs. Collard."

"But you'll be coming back? She'll be coming back?" Beatrice cried appealingly.

"No, ma'am," the superintendent said. "Mrs. Collard will not be coming back."

(4)

The Trial

CHARLIE DAVIS had done few more disagreeable things during his life as a policeman than supervision of the searches that had to be carried out at Albert House and Victoria Villa. "Had to be" was the right phrase, because Charlie felt it wrong that they should be pushing their noses into the affairs of the gentry. Asking questions about them was bad enough, but opening drawers and looking through private papers was worse. And the job was not made any more comfortable by the fact that two of the men in the detective department of R Division were involved in the searches. These men, Watts and Grey, were of course not in uniform, and it always seemed to the inspector that a man in civvies looked sloppy. And then, although they were no more than sergeants, they put on airs and had little jokes between themselves. He got the impression that some of these jokes were at his expense, as though he were just an old fogy.

The main object of their search was arsenic, or something from which arsenic could have been derived, and this proved to be plentifully available. Both of the detectives were short—it was doubtful whether they would have reached the minimum height for a uniformed man, five feet nine inches—both had red faces, and they were both named Bill, or at least that was what they called each other. They found a tin of weed-killer in the garden equipment at the villa, another at Albert House, and a tin of rat-killer in one of the cellars there, or as Bill Watts facetiously called them, the dungeons. Watts later on asked Bessie, the cook at the villa, whether they were much troubled by rats, something she considered as a personal slur.

"Why should we be, then? When I keep everything clean in the kitchen?"

"Generally get rats around. Course you can get rid of 'em with poison. You mean to tell me you've never put down rat poison?"

"I couldn't say, I'm sure. You'd have to ask one of the men."

The coachman when questioned agreed that they'd had rats around the stables and that poison had been put down for them, but said it had been a good while back. Watts nodded, as though satisfied. "A good while back, Bill, you heard him say that?"

"I did, Bill."

"Then just you look at this tin. Looks pretty brand new, eh? Not a trace of rust on it. I don't reckon that was bought more than a couple of weeks back, what do you say?"

"I'd say so too, Bill."

They were excited also by some flypapers that they found in a drawer of the villa kitchen. There were three packets of them, which seemed a lot, but what was the reason for excitement? The Bills explained.

"These 'ere flypapers is just exactly what was used in the Maybrick case. Remember that, Inspector?" Charlie Davis had some vague recollection of it. "Full of arsenic, flypapers are. This Mrs. Maybrick, she soaked 'em and got the arsenic out, then popped it in her husband's drink. Meat extract, wasn't it, Bill?"

"Meat extract it was. Course, she was American."

At Albert House they saw Miss Collard, who came into the study when they were going through her mother's papers. She stared at them and walked out again. The inspector himself took a hand in looking at these papers, and it was he who found an account from the A-1 Detective Agency, Jas. H. Edwards, Prop. He saw this with surprise, for he knew this Edwards, who had been a bobby at another station in R Division, a great talker and boaster. Edwards had often said that he reckoned there was more money to be made outside the force than working in it, a kind of talk which Charlie Davis did not approve. You weren't in the force for what you could make out of it.

The inspector went with the two detectives when they talked to Jenkins, the former butler, and Hilda, the parlormaid, at their lodgings in Deptford. It was plain enough that Jenkins was a wrong un, but when Davis put to him the story told by young Paul Vandervent about having blackmailed Isabel Collard, he denied it flatly, and neither the inspector nor the two Bills could make him budge. The girl, however, was another matter. She admitted going to collect the payments and said that Jenkins had made her do it. When they confronted the man with this, though, he shrugged.

"That's what she says, is it? Well." He paused, then went on. "If Mrs. Collard had had her fun, why shouldn't she pay for it?"

Davis could not restrain himself. "You're admitting it, then, that you're a filthy blackmailer?"

"I'm admitting nothing. What Hilda did was on her own. I knew nothing about it. I walked into the station, didn't I, walked in to give information the way a man's supposed to if he thinks there's something wrong."

"You'd been sacked first."

"And who by, might I ask? That young puppy—you think I'd pay any attention to him? If I was to be sacked, it'd be Mrs. Vandervent who did it, nobody else. I found those letters the way I said, I went to the police, and this is the thanks I get."

They got nothing more out of him. He had seen nothing before Mr. Vandervent's death to suggest that anything was wrong between the two families, he had never seen any sign of unusual affection between Mr. Vandervent and Mrs. Collard. All of them got on extremely well together. Hilda told them nothing more regarding the bottle of whisky, and apart from her story about collecting the money, confirmed everything Jenkins had said. The inspector thought she had been coached by Jenkins, but the detectives were less sure.

"Oh, I dunno, I thought she told 'er tale pretty well," one Bill said. "Mind you, some counsel'd give 'er a real roasting in the box. Old Russell, for example. I shouldn't like to be 'er after old Russell 'ad been at 'er, would you, Bill?"

"I—should—not," the other Bill said emphatically. "That Russell's hot stuff."

"Jenkins, now, he's a fly one, very fly. Got 'is 'ead screwed on the right way, knows how many beans make five."

"And which side his bread's buttered, wouldn't you say, Bill?"

"And which side his bread's buttered, that's for sure."

On the following day the inspector went to see Edwards, who had a little office in the city, near Cannon Street. Davis had made an appointment by telephone to save the chance of the detective's being out, and had not stated his business. Edwards was a big, aggressive man, with a large red nose, and hair that seemed to bristle straight upward out of his scalp. He was smoking a cigar and offered the inspector one, an offer Davis did not accept.

"How are you keeping, Charlie? And how are the boys down in Greenwich? I've been meaning to look in at the section house, but do you know, I just haven't had the time." He waved a hand at his desk, which was certainly thickly covered with papers. Davis said he was glad things were going well.

"Everything's A-1." Edwards beamed as he made this reference to the name of his agency. "And now can I make a guess at what brings you here? A certain inquiry re Mrs. Collard of Albert House—would that be it? I thought so. When I read that the young Mrs. Collard had been charged, I said to myself I shouldn't be surprised if there are questions asked about that inquiry."

"If you thought you had useful information, it was your duty to inform the police."

Edwards laughed heartily. "Always were a stickler for doing things by the book, weren't you, Charlie? But if you're in the position of yours truly, you have to think about protecting your client."

"In this case your client is dead."

"I grant you that, but does it alter the case? We could argue the toss over that for an hour or two, I daresay. But tell me, Charlie, what is it you want to know?"

The interview so far had been gall and wormwood to Charlie Davis. They had not been on first-name terms when Edwards was in the force, and he had thought nothing of the man. To have him using this familiar tone, and suggesting that he had a right to withhold information, was intolerable.

"I want to know exactly what you did for Mrs. Collard, and I want to know it now. If you think you've got a right to keep things back you can come down to the station and talk to the superintendent."

"Now then, now then." Edwards took the cigar out of his mouth, apparently astonished. "Is that a way to talk to an old friend? Have I said I wouldn't cooperate—haven't I asked what you want to know?"

"I've told you what I want. This is a criminal case, Edwards, and if you hold anything back you'll be in trouble."

"I tell you what." The inquiry agent went to the cupboard behind him, which was filled with old lawbooks. "These look all right, clients like to see 'em, but I can't say I have much call to open them. Just bought 'em by the yard for the look of the thing. But I do take a few of 'em out sometimes, because I keep something important behind them." He took out half a dozen volumes to reveal a bottle of whisky. "I find I talk better with a glass in my hand. Clears the mind, as they say. You'll have a noggin, Charlie, for old times' sake."

It did not seem wise to refuse. Edwards took two dirty glasses from a drawer, put large tots of whisky into them. "To the old days and may they never come back. Now, you want to know about Mrs. Collard's little commission. Right then, I'll tell you.

"It was a few weeks ago she got in touch, wrote to say she'd seen my name in the paper. I went to see her and she gave me certain feminine garments, to wit: a bright-yellow corset in good-quality satin, a pair of white gloves, also of good quality, and an article known as a bust improver. The corset and gloves had the name of a West End shop inside, Bakers of Bond Street, where presumably they had been bought. Mrs. Collard wanted to know who had bought them. I can see from your face that you're surprised, and so was I. If it had been some clients, I don't mind telling you I'd have said no, but

Mrs. Collard, well, she had a way with her. You knew her, I expect, and you'll agree that she was a real lady of the old-fashioned sort. If she wanted to know who'd bought those things, she had a reason, and a good one."

"So you said yes."

"I said yes, though I told her not to expect too much. A corset and gloves, they're sold every day, aren't they? And naturally I tried to get some idea of why she wanted to find out who bought them. But Mrs. Collard—well, the look she gave me would have frozen the appendages off a brass monkey, if you'll pardon the expression. 'I'm paying you to obtain information, Mr. Edwards,' she said. 'What use I make of it is my affair.' It turned out easier than I expected. And it'll surprise you." He took a slug of whisky. Davis stayed silent, waiting to be surprised. "They remembered selling those garments, and why? They'd been bought by a man."

The inspector did not show surprise, although he felt it. It was unusual for a man to buy such garments, and Charlie Davis certainly wouldn't have bought them for his wife. On the other hand, he knew there were some men who did that kind of thing. He asked if the man had given a name.

"He did better. He had them sent to his office, and do you know what the name and address was? Mr. George Collard at Mortimer and Collard. The old lady's own son. What about that? And I'll tell you something else. These weren't a present for the wife. The gent had a bit of fluff in an apartment, and they were a gift for her. How do I know? They're not the kind of things you buy for the wife, are they now?"

"Did you tell Mrs. Collard this?"

"Not in person. I sent in a report as requested, saying what I'd learned. I returned the articles. I had a note in reply asking me to send in my account. I did so, and received payment. End of story. What do you make of that?"

What Charlie Davis made of it was that he would have to speak to George Collard, and ask him some unpleasant questions. Why couldn't people in the upper classes behave themselves? They had money, their lives were easy, they didn't have a working day like his which lasted for sixteen hours. It was their duty to set an example to the rest of the country, and for them to go messing about with women who weren't their wives was nothing short of a disgrace. He said so to the superintendent. Titmus was not impressed.

"Don't you see, Charlie lad, it's because they've got time on their hands that they do these things. If Mrs. Collard had been doing a job of work every day, or had half a dozen children to look after, she'd never have got into mischief."

"And with her brother-in-law. Living in the same house. It's disgusting."

"Right you are, Charlie. Those letters are certainly hot stuff. They'll go against her. Mind you, when you say it was in the same house, there's no proof of that. They went to this place he'd rented for their little spot of you know what." Some of the letters were in their envelopes, and the rooms near Charing Cross had been traced.

"But that's no excuse for Collard buying this stuff. He seems to have been doing the same thing."

"When one kicks over the traces, the other often does the same," Titmus said sagely. "But I tell you what, Charlie. I can see this is getting you down. I'll talk to Collard myself. In the meantime these are the garments in question, are they? I must say, they're a bit of all right." Titmus tried the corset around his own slim waist. "He certainly likes girls with a bit of body to 'em. I wonder how that thing came to be torn; that's something I must ask him."

The superintendent saw George Collard on the following day. He went to the man's place of business, feeling that this was a matter he might be ready to discuss more freely away from home. Collard seemed a bit jittery, but that was not surprising in the circumstances. Titmus had decided on a direct approach. He had the clothes in a brown paper parcel, which he unpacked and put on the desk between them. George Collard put his face in his hands.

"Mr. Collard, I've been given to understand that you purchased these articles from Messrs. Bakers in Bond Street. Can you confirm that?"

"Yes," came from behind the hands.

"Right, sir. Now, I'm not saying that this has anything to do with the matter concerning your wife, but I should like an explanation. In particular, I should like to know why your mother employed an inquiry agent to discover who had bought them."

Collard took away his hands, blew his nose, wiped his eyes. Titmus thought his distress seemed genuine. "I've done wrong," he said. "I should have come to you before, but this can't have anything to do with Roger's death, so I thought—"

"Best let me be the judge of that, sir. Tell the truth and shame the devil."

"True, true. But what I have to say is painful." Collard wiped his eyes again, put away the handkerchief. "Almost since the beginning of our marriage my wife and I—well, we have rarely shared the marriage bed, although of course I knew nothing of what was going on between her and Roger. But I am aware, Superintendent, that I am physically not an attractive man. I thought before we married that I was not a proper husband for Isabel, and I was right. I was quickly given to understand that she did not find my advances congenial, and I ceased

to make them. If I had been a different sort of person—
But we cannot be different from what we are."

"Very true, sir."

"Of course, if I had had any idea that Isabel was—well,
I don't know what I should have done. Nothing, perhaps.
I am not a practical or decisive person, as my mother
knew. It was Roger who ran the firm, and now that he
has gone it is in Dangerfield's hands. I see that this was
bound to be so, although I wish it were otherwise."

Titmus nodded, but this was still not quite the matter
in hand. He made a gesture toward the corset, which
lay between them. Collard was silent for a moment or
two.

"Since I was denied by my wife I sought . . . release,
perhaps you might call it, in other directions. These articles were to be a present for a lady of my acquaintance.
I foolishly left them in the office after I had bought them,
and the parcel, I suppose, was open. I went out for a
couple of hours, and when I returned they had disappeared. I searched for them, but as you may imagine, I
could hardly ask questions."

"They were found in Mr. Vandervent's desk."

"So I understand."

"You do not know why he took them? Or how the
tear came in that—that article, and the blood on it?"

"No."

"Have you anything further to tell me about these
articles?"

George Collard hesitated. "Yes. Somebody had given
them to my mother, and she had found out that I had
bought them. She asked me who they had been bought
for, and why. I refused to tell her."

"How long was this before her death?"

"A few days. But, Superintendent, I appeal to you. This
can have nothing to do with Roger's death. If such a

story is told in court it will ruin me. I don't mind so much about that, but it may damage Isabel too. Surely— surely it can be kept out of court."

"That's not for me to say, sir, although for myself, I don't see why it should be mentioned. There is one more thing, though. The name of the lady."

"The name of—Oh, no, really, it would be too shameful."

"I'm afraid we must have it, sir."

"Very well. But you'll find—Oh, well, I suppose it must be." He wrote down a name and address and handed it over to Titmus.

The name was Florence le Duc, the address one in St. John's Wood. Bill Watts went to see the lady. Within ten minutes she had admitted that her name was Flossie, that she came from the East End, and that she occasionally received gentlemen friends. The detective described George Collard and she agreed that he came to see her, and sometimes brought little presents. "He wants to see me looking nice, dear," she said. "You know how gentlemen are."

When Titmus heard that the presents had been intended for a prostitute, he was moved to pity. "Poor devil," he said to Charlie Davis. "He pays for it, and gives her things as well. You know something? I feel sorry for men like that."

Charlie did not reply. In his eyes it was one more example of bad behavior among people who should have known better.

2

It was a cold day in October, with a thin rain falling, when a landau drew up outside number 10 New Court,

Lincoln's Inn, and four passengers got out, all of them male. They climbed two flights of narrow uncarpeted stairs, and opened a door into a small anteroom. A clerk with a pen behind his ear pushed his head through a hatch and said, "You'll be . . . ?"

Augustus Payne, who was looking more impressive than usual in a long astrakhan fur coat, said, "We are here to see Sir Charles Russell."

"Sir Charles, yes. If you'll just . . ." He withdrew his head, closed the hatch, opened a door beside it, and led the way down a passage so dark that they had to fumble along it, and so narrow that two people could not have passed each other. At the end of this passage was another door. The clerk opened this, said, "If you'll sit down, gentlemen, Sir Charles won't . . ." and disappeared.

The room was lit only by two hissing gas jets, one of them with a broken mantle. Beneath one of the lights sat Mr. Humperdinck, the solicitor who had been engaged by Augustus for Isabel's defense. Augustus had taken charge of all such matters as soon as he heard of his daughter's arrest.

Mr. Humperdinck was a small, rosy man with a ready smile and a habit of rubbing his nose with one finger. Augustus made the introductions. "Mr. George Collard, my daughter's husband—I think you've met. Then this is Mr. Dangerfield, who is engaged to marry Miss Charlotte Collard, and young Paul Vandervent, Roger's son."

"Rather a big party."

Augustus raised his eyebrows. "George naturally has an interest, and Dangerfield is here as representing Miss Collard. Paul—well, he has been concerned in one or two aspects of the affair, and it was thought Sir Charles might like to talk to him."

"Ye-es," the solicitor said doubtfully. "You've heard, I expect, that Sir Charles is a little idiosyncratic. I hesitate

THE BLACKHEATH POISONINGS

to mention it, Mr. Payne, but one of his particular aversions is to fur coats. A colleague of mine once went in to him wearing a fur coat, and Sir Charles asked him to take it off."

Augustus removed the coat. "I will do as you say. But I hope Sir Charles's advocacy is better than his manners."

"There is nobody to touch him. You may count yourselves lucky that he has taken the case."

They knew this, or at least they knew of Russell's fame. Now in his early sixties, he was the most famous barrister at the bar. He had become a national figure a few years earlier when he had destroyed Pigott, the forger of the letters purported to have been written by Parnell, in a few hours of devastating cross-examination. His power, his irascibility, the way in which he could dominate a jury, had become legendary. He was a man of strong passions, which included support of home rule for Ireland, the country in which he had been born. It was said that he disliked all solicitors.

They waited a few minutes more before the clerk reappeared, led them down another corridor, a little less dark and a little less narrow, opened a door, said, "Mr. Humperdinck, Sir Charles, and . . ." and retired.

This was a big room with a great cluttered desk in the middle of it. The man at the desk had strong features, a square face and a large, powerful boxlike mouth. His eyes were large too, and seemed strangely luminous, as though (Paul felt) he were using them to look inside you and discern your thoughts. He half rose from his chair, barely nodded to Humperdinck, sat down again, looked from one to the other of them. When he spoke, his voice was harsh and strong, not musical.

"There are a great many of you. I was under the impression that this was a consultation, Humperdinck, not a committee."

The solicitor said deferentially, "These gentlemen all have a close connection with the unhappy affair."

"The poisoning, you mean. Why not say so?"

Humperdinck rubbed his nose. "Just so. And—"

"And you'll be young Vandervent, who tracked down the letters. That was like something out of Lecoq. Do you know who Lecoq is, Humperdinck? I see you don't. He comes in books written by a Frenchman, finds out who committed crimes by measuring footprints, works out what people are thinking by the way they look at things in the street, that sort of stuff. I don't read many novels, but these are very clever. I wish I were as clever, but I'm not; I can only judge by expressions on faces, and I can see you're not pleased with me. You're young Vandervent. You, sir, what's your name?"

"I am Augustus Payne, Mrs. Collard's father."

"And you other gentlemen?" They were introduced. Russell glared at them from beneath thick brows. "You're thinking I'm a bully. Well, you may be right, but I don't bully in court, gentlemen, not unless it's necessary. I like to be direct, that's all. There are too many of you here, as Humperdinck should know. Humperdinck does know it, but didn't like to tell you. Humperdinck's a fool. But here you are, and here, I suppose, you may as well stay. What have you got to tell me? Don't look surprised; I'm here to learn from you today, for you to tell me what you think and know. They say I never read a brief." He slapped a hand on the papers in front of him. "Sometimes that's true, sometimes not. I have devils who get these things up for me, give me the heart of a case. But I'll tell you what it is about these poisonings. I use the plural, although the police have only proceeded on the one charge because that's all they can do by law. They've picked Vandervent's death because they feel their case is better in relation to him, but you and I know, and the jury will know, that Harriet Collard was poisoned too. And I'll tell you what it is: at present I don't see my way clear, don't see it at all. So talk to me, gentlemen, and I hope I shall be wiser when you've done so. You now, Mr. Payne, tell me about your daughter, what kind of woman she is."

Augustus coughed, and began to talk about Isabel. He was followed by George, Dangerfield, then Paul. While they talked, Russell rose, scratched his back with an ivory tickler from the mantelpiece, walked about the room. Sometimes he asked questions, and as Paul realized after a time, some were questions designed to reveal the relationship between Isabel and her husband, and some were aimed at discovering her state of mind. When it was Paul's turn, Russell questioned him closely about Isabel's possible reason for choosing him as the person to employ in a detective role. When he said that he supposed she thought he could be relied on and that there was nobody else to turn to, the barrister looked at him sharply but did not comment. In all, this session took a little more than an hour, and although the questions had been calmly asked and innocuously phrased, every one of them felt as if he had been subjected to a searching physical examination. At the end Russell returned to his desk, very deliberately took snuff. Thus encouraged, Augustus took some too.

"Forgive me for walking about," Russell said. "I like to keep on the move. I notice you get your snuff at Fribourg and Treyer, Mr. Payne. We share the same taste; best house in London. Well, gentlemen, you'll expect me to say something, and I will. In some parts the case against Mrs. Collard is weak, in others it is strong. The weakness is lack of any motive. I see no good reason why this lady should have wished Mr. Vandervent dead. She does not appear to have gained in any way. But there is evidence that she bought poison—"

"Preposterous," Augustus said. "Inconceivable."

"Mr. Payne, I listened while you spoke. Please give me the same courtesy. I say that there is evidence of her buying poison. And there are the letters. Have any of you seen the letters? I see that you have not. The prosecution are going to use the letters—they are at the heart of the case—and I must know more about them. I must know why they were written at all, when she was living in the same house—" He checked himself. "I beg your pardon. I must not forget how painful this is, particularly for you, Mr. Collard. Humperdinck, you should have had better sense than to let Mr. Collard come here." Humperdinck stroked nose with finger, said nothing. "In general I think it foolish that counsel should seek an interview with a client accused upon such a charge as this. But cases are particular, not general. I shall talk to Mrs. Collard. Humperdinck, you will arrange it. If you speak to Wilkinson on the way out, he will tell you when I am free."

It was Dangerfield who, as they got up to go, asked the question which was perhaps in all their minds. "Sir Charles, what are the chances?"

It seemed for a moment that the man behind the desk had not heard. Then the heavy brows came down, almost concealing the eyes, the savage mouth closed tight in disapproval. "I am not in the habit of giving odds in such matters as though I were on a racecourse. Good day to you, gentlemen."

3

Among the things about which Charles Russell felt passionately was the idea that law was above all individuals, and must be administered with strict fairness irrespective of the worth of the people concerned. The law, he thought, should never bend, and the contempt he felt for all solicitors and many of his fellow barristers was because he found them too flexible. In his twenties he had written to his future mother-in-law that successful barristers in Ireland had obtained their positions because of the flexibility of their opinions, "and so a profession which once reckoned *great* men in its ranks and stood marked for its independence would now be more fitly characterized for its servility." There was nothing yielding about Charles Russell, and for this reason some thought him a poor lawyer, blind to every aspect of a case except the one he wished to see. Yet it was part of his strength that he never gave way. To shake hands with him was like gripping a bar of iron, and when he accepted a case his commitment to the cause of his client was total.

In this particular case of the Crown versus Isabel Collard, Russell had no doubt that he was defending a wicked and immoral woman. He had married when he was twenty-five, and had never looked at another woman. He was as disgusted by Mrs. Collard's conduct as Charlie Davis could possibly have been, but disgust was not to the point. No doubt she was immoral, but it was his duty to make sure that her immorality did not sway a jury trying her on a charge of murder. To talk to her might help toward this end. But there was another reason for talking to her. In spite of his disapproval, Russell would not have been human—and he was emphatically that— if he had not felt curiosity about this woman. He had seen a photograph, but he knew that these are often deceptive, and he was prepared for the sort of boldness, the flirtatiously challenging air, that he especially disliked in women.

But the woman brought in by the warder to the interview room at Brixton Prison did not look like that at all. She was meek in manner, almost demure. Her look was candid, and if she often stared down at the ground rather than meet his gaze, that did not displease him, for it was his opinion that the most audacious criminals were prepared always to outstare you. There was a table between them, the woman warder stood by the door leading to the cells, little Humperdinck sat beside the entrance. Russell paid no attention to either of them, or to his surroundings. His attention was concentrated upon the woman.

"Madam, my name is Charles Russell, and I have been engaged to appear on your behalf at your trial."

"I know that, Sir Charles. My father and my husband have told me. They have said that I am lucky you agreed to accept the brief."

"You do not think so?"

The shadow of a smile touched her face. "I think that I am unlucky to need your services."

"Just so. You know that we shall be concerned in court only with Mr. Vandervent's death. Since you had no part in it yourself, you will understand that somebody else closely connected with the family is likely to be responsible. Do you have any idea who this might be?"

"None."

"So far as you are aware, nobody had reason to wish him dead?"

"Nobody."

"Do you know how poison might have been given him, or did you have any reason to think it might have been administered?"

"No."

"It will be part of the prosecution case that you bought a supply of arsenic from a chemist in Greenwich named Morley. There is a signature in his poisons book which purports to be yours. Did you in fact make such a purchase?"

"No. I have never been into the shop, and do not know where it is."

"Can you think of any reason why somebody should have forged your name—because that is what it comes to, doesn't it, that somebody signed your name in deliberate malice?"

The elegant shoulders were shrugged. "I cannot think of a reason. Obviously there must be somebody who hates me."

"But you do not know who it might be?"

"No."

These were answers that he had expected. He now approached the delicate, or as he felt it, degrading part of the case. "You had had intimate relations with your brother-in-law Roger Vandervent."

She did not reply for a moment. "I was in love with him."

"How long had this relationship existed?"

"For some months; perhaps six."

"And how often had intimacy occurred?"

"I would not call it by that word." He forced back the scornful things he felt like saying, but his look must have been eloquent. "I do not know; I did not count the times."

Was there irony in the reply? He decided to ignore it. "Did it ever take place at your home, your joint home, Victoria Villa?"

"Once, at the beginning. Then Roger said it was too dangerous, we must make another arrangement."

Again he restrained himself, but something of what he felt must have sounded in the rumble of his voice, for behind him little Humperdinck stirred uneasily. "And so that you could continue this relationship, Roger Vandervent took rooms in—" He looked at his notes, but the solicitor filled it in for him by saying, "Bedfordbury."

"Yes."

"How often did you meet there?"

Her reply was barely audible. "Sometimes once a week, sometimes twice. Never more often. There was a period when we did not meet there for three weeks."

"And when you had this apartment in Bedfordbury, intimacy ceased altogether at the villa?"

"I have said so already." She had been staring at the table, but now she looked up at him, her face still composed and her voice even. "Sir Charles, I do not understand why you are asking such questions. You sound like counsel for the prosecution rather than the defense."

At least she has spirit, Russell thought. She is a slut, but behind that demure look she is a fighter. He thrust his head forward, and spoke in the harsh voice that had terrified many witnesses. "Then I will tell you, madam. There are two reasons for my questions. One is that if Roger Vandervent's wife or your husband knew of this relationship, it would provide a possible motive for the crime." She gave a little gasp, but said nothing. "From what you say, however, it is not likely that they knew. The other is that I am looking for an explanation of the letters you wrote. You saw this man every day, you were intimate with him once a week, yet you wrote from your home in Blackheath to the apartment he had rented letters that I forbear to characterize. Why did you do it? I have asked myself, but I can find no answer. If you think me brutal in asking such questions, believe me that is nothing to what will be made of them by Treasury Counsel. The verdict may rest upon these letters. If I am to combat what is said about them, I must understand why they were written."

She pondered over this, and for the first time showed

some emotion, taking a handkerchief from her sleeve and touching forehead and lips with it. Her voice, too, had a vibration in it that had not been there before.

"I am not sure that I can explain it to you, Sir Charles, but I will try. I hope you are blessed with a happy marriage. I have not been, and neither was Roger, although for different reasons. Neither of our families had children. Beatrice had had two miscarriages, and was fearful of another. I do not think they were intimate, as you call it, very often. And my own marriage has never been happy. I think George is a natural bachelor."

"Something similar could be said of many marriages. They may not be ideal, yet the partners remain faithful."

"Oh, you are talking like some out-of-date textbook," she cried. "We are not textbook examples, but people. Roger was a passionate man, Sir Charles. Perhaps you can accept that. And I—I, too, am a passionate woman. I had needs and desires that were not fulfilled by George. Roger and I were bound to love each other. I knew it as soon as I had been in the house with him for a month. He knew it too. We fought against it without success. Don't tell me that I should have left and gone to live somewhere else; that would just be more copybook morality."

"I will tell you nothing, madam. I am here to learn." The tone of this fairly made Humperdinck shiver, but Isabel Collard seemed unaware of it. She leaned across the table with arm outstretched as though in appeal, so that the wardress momentarily shifted in nervous alertness. Then Isabel sat back in her chair.

"I am not ashamed of writing the letters." She waited expectantly, but Russell merely inclined his head. "You ask why they were written. I was in that house—have you seen it? It is beautiful in a way, I suppose, but it is a kind of glass barracks, where there is no privacy, one is always on display. I saw Roger every day, yet I could never speak to him about anything except the weather or business or some other rubbish. So to express what I could not say in that house I wrote the letters. I sent them in the post, and they were waiting when we met. Sometimes he would open them when I arrived and read them aloud. He said that they were the most wonderful letters a woman had ever written to a man. But of course I meant them to be destroyed; I never thought he would keep them."

"They describe in part your pleasure in the intimacies you encouraged. He read them to you, and you performed the actions described in them. Is that correct?"

"Correct—oh, perhaps it is *correct*, but it is utterly wrong. You make it sound cold-blooded. We were in love with each other."

Russell's shoulders gave a great heave and Humperdinck, seeing this from the back as he had often seen it in court, when that heave of the shoulders had preceded the destruction of a witness, feared again a terrible outbreak of anger. But the words that came were mild.

"I am here to understand, not to judge. Judgment will be made in another place. Roger Vandervent preserved the letters, and then you were blackmailed and paid what was asked."

"Yes, but I could not go on doing so. I had to ask George for money and he refused it."

"So you got Paul Vandervent to act as a kind of detective."

"Yes. That was foolish, and wrong. He has a sort of calf love for me, and I played on it. He reminded me of his father; I think that is why I did it."

"Very well. Now you have answered the second part of my question, but not the first. Are you sure that neither Mrs. Vandervent nor your husband showed that they knew of your relationship with Roger Vandervent?"

"No. Neither by what they said nor by anything they did. I am sure that they knew nothing of what you call our relationship."

For a moment it seemed that Russell would say something more, but he merely rose, made a half bow and turned to go. For the first time, her voice rose in alarm.

"I hope my frankness has not influenced you against me. You won't give up my defense?"

He turned, and spoke in his deepest, harshest voice. "I never abandon anything. I have accepted the task of defending you, and I shall fight for your acquittal. Your solicitor will tell you that when I have decided to fight I usually win."

With that they left her. As the prison gate closed behind them, Russell turned and looked back. His features were somber.

"If ever a woman deserved to be in prison, Humperdinck, it is that one. She should be horsewhipped for her behavior. It is fortunate that she cannot take the stand and talk as she did to me, or she would destroy herself.* But, Humperdinck, I would be ready to swear that the woman, loathsome as she is, did not commit the crime of which she is accused."

4

In the weeks following Isabel's arrest Paul gave up his journal, and abandoned writing poems. He performed the routine actions of life mechanically, rising in the

---

* Russell was referring to the fact that at this time an accused person was not allowed to enter the witness box to give evidence on his or her behalf. The law was changed in this respect by the Criminal Evidence Act of 1898.

morning, shaving, eating breakfast, going up in the train
and doing what was necessary at work. It seemed to him,
however, that the figure who carried out the duties be-
longing to Paul Vandervent was no more than a mirror
image of the person also bearing that name who, in an
immeasurably distant time, had taken Isabel to the poetry
recital and had talked to his father about the future. That
Paul Vandervent no longer existed, and it was another
person who answered to his name.

Life at the villa was strange. Both George and Beatrice
were now aware that they had been betrayed by their
marriage partners. George seemed to Paul little affected,
although he realized that he might know his uncle as
little as he had known his father. Outwardly he was the
same Uncle George, a little clumsier in his movements,
more inclined to weave his pudgy fingers together, more
absent-minded than ever at work. Weekly visits to Isabel
were permitted, and George went faithfully each week.
He had asked once if Paul would care to go, but Paul
had refused. Isabel and his love for her belonged to that
dead time of which he could not bear to be reminded.

Beatrice's reaction was different, and remarkable. She
filled the villa with more people than had come there
in her husband's lifetime. There could be no more tennis
tournaments now that autumn was moving into winter,
but there were musical evenings and card games, like
commerce and speculation, limited loo and double
crambo, as well as more serious evenings, with three or
four couples playing partner whist. George participated
occasionally in the musical evenings, but Paul absented
himself from it all, taking long walks on the heath as
far as the Green Man, where he might have a pint or
two of bitter, or walking up to the closed gates of the
park and then making a circuit of the heath. A replacement for Jenkins had been engaged, a man named Hales,

and there was a new parlormaid as well. Beatrice had taken to wearing fashionable clothes, tight-sleeved dresses with epaulettes and elaborately gored skirts, and in the evening flowered dresses with the neck cut square and very low. She had her hair done differently, with a center parting, and made no pretense of wearing mourning for her mother.

Her activities caused a concern that approached scandal, and at least two people tried to check them, Dr. Porterfield and Augustus. The doctor had remained silent about the fact that two deaths he had certified as being due to gastric fever and ptomaine poisoning had in fact been caused by arsenic, but there was no diminution in his practice, perhaps in part because his patients hoped for some tidbits of gossip. Those who had such hopes were disappointed, for the doctor gave them to understand that although he could say tremendous things if he wished, in particular about the way in which the postmortems had been conducted, he must stay silent until he had given evidence in court. When news of Beatrice's musical and card evenings came to his ears, however (his daughters had accepted invitations to some of them), he paid her a visit.

She received him in the gallery, wearing a particularly outrageous creation in peacock blue. He took her hands.

"My dear Beatrice, this is a grievous time. Believe me, although I have not come to see you, you have been in my thoughts. What you have experienced must have been very hard to bear."

She disengaged her hands. "Thank you for your sympathy. I am quite well."

"You have been taking the pills I prescribed? And you are sleeping properly?" He repossessed himself of one hand. "The pulse is a little rapid."

"I assure you, Doctor, there is nothing wrong with me. What is it, Hales?"

Hales was long, thin and deferential. "It is simply a matter of when you would like refreshments to be served this evening, madam."

"I think nine o'clock. And perhaps we might have the potted tongue as well as ham and beef. The usual puddings. And if it is possible to provide a savory . . ."

"I thought of angels on horseback. They are very popular with the gentlemen."

"That will do very well, Hales. A few people are coming this evening for whist," she explained to Porterfield, who made a humming noise and waited for Hales to withdraw. Then he asked if he might sit, and did so. The perfection of his white spats was revealed.

"As an old friend of the family, I hope I may be—ahem—permitted to speak frankly. The truth is, Beatrice, that your conduct is giving offense."

The words were no sooner spoken than he regretted them, but he was not to be spared. Beatrice's eye flashed. She looked and sounded much like her mother.

"My conduct, Doctor? Do you say that *my* conduct is giving offense?" Desperately he raised his hand to check the onslaught he foresaw. "In these last weeks I have learned that my husband did not die a natural death, as you told me, and that he had taken my sister-in-law as his lover. Yet you say that my conduct—Oh, I cannot believe that you are serious."

"I beg your pardon." The doctor, red about the gills, tried again. "I know what you suffered, what you must still be suffering. But to fill this house with people, to play cards until all hours, to have music and singing so soon after your mother's death—this is truly not what should be."

"Ah." She rose and went to one of the windows looking out on the ruined garden, spoke with her back turned. "Very well, Doctor, you have given your opinion. I will not trouble you to do so again."

It is never easy to grasp what somebody whose back is turned is saying, and Dr. Porterfield was a little hard of hearing. "I beg your pardon."

She turned. "I will be as plain as you. You are no longer my doctor, so there will be no need for you to pay further visits."

He was appalled. "But I have been your family physician—and your dear mother's—for years."

"And you made wrong diagnoses of her illness and of my husband's. Did you suppose that I should require your services after that?" She crossed the room, tugged the bell pull, and told the maid to show Dr. Porterfield out.

Augustus made a more dexterous approach, by way of an invitation to dinner. His daughters were there, with two or three of their current admirers, and everything went smoothly, as it always did at Dulwich. Afterward Augustus rose and said, "Now, you young things can do what you like, but I am going to carry Beatrice off. Beatrice, come along."

He took her into the study, where he had asked George to state his intentions about Isabel. The heads of moose and elk looked down at them. Augustus offered a glass of port, which Beatrice declined. He poured one himself and lighted a cigar.

"Now, my dear, I want to talk about this whole ghastly business. We never have spoken about it, have we, but in the end it can't be avoided. Get things out in the open, is my motto. You've not been to see Isabel, I can understand that, but still . . . You couldn't bring yourself to it, I suppose?"

"No, Augustus, I could not."

"I quite understand. She's keeping up pretty well, poor girl, though it's a scandal they should keep her in that place. That villain of a butler was blackmailing her, y'know. Don't know why the police haven't arrested him." Beatrice did not reply. His gaze moved from her bodice, which was showing a good deal of bosom, to the gaudy fan-shaped handbag that rested on her lap. "Russell's the best man you can get, they tell me. He seems to think everything will be all right, or would be if it weren't for those damn letters—if you'll excuse me, Beatrice. Thank God the trial comes on early in the new year, so we'll have her out again then. What a time they take, though, these lawyer fellows."

"Is there something particular you want to talk about?"

"Yes. I want to say I understand your difficulties. I don't excuse Isabel, y'know; don't excuse Roger, for that matter. But we've got to face facts, see things as they are. Keep a stiff upper lip. Don't walk away from the sound of gunfire." Beatrice said nothing, and Augustus began to feel that he was dealing with a deuced uncooperative woman. "It's not easy for me either, I can tell you. People don't say anything, but you can tell what they're thinking. And what about the girls? There was a chap looking after Eleanor, partner in a firm of brokers in Leadenhall Street, decent family with land up in Yorkshire. Haven't seen hide nor hair of him since this affair. These fellows here this evening, nice enough boys, but young Travis hasn't two pennies to rub together, and although Clyde Manners has what might be called expectations, they're on the horizon." He became aware that he was losing track of what he had meant to say. "Point is, it's not easy for anybody."

"And we mustn't walk away from the sound of gunfire."

"You're pulling an old man's leg." Augustus poured himself another glass of port. "Point is, there are things you do, and things you don't do. If I took notice of all the things people are saying about me behind my back—friends of mine, mind you—I'd be cutting some men in the street, telling others they were scoundrels, and I don't know what else. Can't be done. You've got to smile and nod and look as if you didn't care."

"That is exactly what I have been doing, Augustus."

"*You* have? Ah, well, now—"

"You brought me in here, among all these animals you shot in Africa or India or wherever it was, to tell me I shouldn't give parties, and to say that if I didn't wear mourning for my husband I should wear it for my mother, isn't that so?"

"Shouldn't presume to tell you anything, m'dear. You're your mother's daughter, independent as she was. Always admired her. But independence is one thing, whist parties and singsongs is another. You shouldn't do it. People don't like it; looks bad."

"They'll say I don't care. Isn't that what you were advising?"

"Yes. But what you're doing, that just ain't right."

"Then they must think it wrong. Is that all you have to say?"

"Oh, dear me, I've offended you. Didn't mean to, you know that." He took her hand, and she did not draw it away as she had done from Dr. Porterfield.

"I know that. But you see, Augustus, if I didn't try to put a good face on things, I don't know what would happen. Do you know what I think about more than anything else? My babies."

Beatrice had no babies. He stared at her.

"Oh, I know you're thinking crazy Beatrice, what's she talking about, it's another of her fads. But those little children I carried were real to me. They were so near to being born; one of them was seven months old, did you know that?"

"Distressing, very." Augustus did not care for such talk. If women spoke about these things at all, it should be to each other.

"The body was perfectly formed. It was a little boy, a little man. And I think, if those children had lived, if even one of them had lived, Roger would not have behaved as he did. None of this would have happened."

What was the woman talking about? Augustus felt profoundly uncomfortable. But he had brought her here to say something, and he was not going to be stopped. "Beatrice, m'dear, I think you should go away."

"Go away? What for?"

"Take Charlotte with you, get away to some little watering place, forget about all this."

"Go to the sea? At this time of year!"

"Oh, I don't care where it is. Go to some spa, Bath or Cheltenham. Or across the Channel—Dieppe, Ostend."

"Two English ladies together—do you think that would be proper?"

Augustus lost his temper. "Dammit, woman, can't you see what I'm saying? It'll be better for everybody in the family, yourself included, if you're out of London for a while. The way you're carrying on, anybody might think you were celebrating seeing your mother in the grave and Isabel in prison."

"Are you going to say that my conduct gives offense? I have been told that once already this week." She rose. "Thank you for your concern, but I am not going away and I shall not stop giving my little evening entertainments. They take my mind off other things, and do nobody any harm."

She kept her word. Christmas dinner was held at the villa that year instead of at Albert House. There was an enormous Christmas tree blazing with candles and weighed down with presents, and the servants were occupied for the better part of two days in putting up decorations. All the family came to dinner, and Augustus brought his family too. You had to admit, as he said to a friend afterward, that she was a filly with plenty of pluck. So they ate their goose and cracked nuts and drank port and pulled crackers and played games almost as if nothing had happened, and as if they could disregard the fact that two members of the family were dead and a third lay in Brixton Prison awaiting trial.

5

It was on the day, early in the new year, when Paul learned that he would be required to give evidence at Isabel's trial, that he went on the drinking bout which in the end was to provide for him a revelation. When he told the police about seeing Hilda collect the letter and about his talk with Jenkins, he had not understood that he would be asked to say all this in court. The man from the Treasury Solicitor's office, however, left him in no doubt of it. He was a puffy little fellow who found it hard to catch his breath and so wheezed occasionally, like an engine needing lubrication.

"Don't understand you, Mr. Vandervent. You made your deposition, swore it was true; just asking you to repeat it. Quite straightforward, no problems."

"I don't wish to give evidence."

"Don't *wish* to?" Wheeze wheeze. "But you must."

"If I gave evidence at all it would be for the defense."

The little man wheezed so much that it would have been hard to tell whether he was indignant, amused, or about to have a fit. His office was small, dark and very high, and they were close together. The little man smelled of strong cheese and peppermint. "So that's the way the wind blows. Couldn't advise it, young man. Might have to treat you as a hostile witness."

"What does that mean?"

"What it says." Wheeze wheeze. "Means you told us one thing and now you want to say something else. So Mr. Makepeace, he'll be the Treasury Counsel—Mr. Makepeace, *Q.C.*, you understand: he's a Queen's Counsel—he doesn't examine you, he *cross*-examines you. He's a terror at cross-examination, is Mr. Makepeace."

"Then I shan't give evidence at all."

"Can't do that." Wheeze wheeze. The wheezes were evidently laughter. "You've made your statement, got to stick to it. Otherwise Mr. Justice Hawkins—he'll be trying the case—might say that you were mute of malice, and you wouldn't like that. Very severe is Hawkins J., and very hot on the law. You don't want to fall foul of Hawkins J., or get the wrong side of Mr. Makepeace, for that matter."

Paul returned to the office so upset that he foolishly confided in the Caterpillar. There had not been much conversation between them since Harriet's death, and almost none since the arrest of Isabel, when Bertie had said that fornication and taking human life were equally deadly sins, and had implied that one led to the other. Now he listened to Paul's account of his interview, and then said, "You must know where your duty lies. You must stand up and tell the truth, in the Lord's name. I have done so myself."

"*You* have?"

"In your father's desk I found after his death women's garments. I told Aunt Harriet, feeling that cousin Beatrice would be distressed if I spoke to her. When Aunt Harriet died I knew that it was my duty to inform the police."

"In my father's desk . . . What sort of garments are you talking about?" Bertie's eyes gleamed as he described them in detail. "But they couldn't have been—" Paul stopped himself from saying that such clothes could not have been bought for Isabel because she would never have worn them. "I don't believe my father had anything to do with them."

"Possibly not." Bertie had been watching Paul with the interest of a boy who after pinning a fly sees it wriggling. "I believe the police officers have discovered that they were bought by your uncle George. They asked me whether I had known anything about what they called a bit of fluff that he might have tucked away somewhere. I could not help them, although if I had known anything I should have thought it my duty to tell them. Lechery is a sin in the eyes of the law, and the house in which you lived was a bed of it. Your sister-in-law, your uncle, your father—"

"Be quiet about my father." Paul came round the desk with his fist raised.

"If you wish to strike me for telling the truth, you may." Bertie stood with his hands limp at his sides. Paul strode out and slammed the door. He went to see Dangerfield, and asked to be moved to another room.

"Can't get on with Bertie, eh? It's your job to get on with him when you're working together. Don't say I blame you, though; can't stick him myself. What's the upset?"

"It was about my father," Paul said, and wondered whether after all Bertie had not simply been telling the truth. "I don't want to discuss it. If I can't get away from him I must leave."

"Don't want that, do we? Can't get rid of Bertie, though, or at least an outsider like myself can't. He's one of the family. What Mortimer and Collard needs is a good shaking up, but that's easier said than done. In the last year or two we've been using capital to pay some of the partners' salaries. That's bad business."

"What does Uncle George say?"

"Nothing at all; doesn't seem to know what he's about half the time. I could do with some help, my boy, help to get the place moving again. The works down below doesn't pay for itself. I'm not sure it pays for us to make our own toys. There'll have to be changes. What d'you say—are you on my side?" Paul said that he supposed he was, and Dangerfield clapped him on the shoulder. "I'll see what I can do about a move. What would you say to a job on the sales side? Just stick it out for another few weeks, and I think you'll see some changes."

Paul left with the feeling that something had been promised him, although he could not have said what it was. He felt that he could not bear to sit opposite the Caterpillar, to see those red-rimmed eyes shift quickly away whenever Paul looked up. He went down the stairs into the works, nodded to Hexham and spoke to a couple of the men on the machines with whom he had talked about labor problems, then walked out into the street. He felt a sense of liberation in doing so, even though he was only an hour early in leaving.

It was a fine night, but bitterly cold. He walked, without thought of where he was going, through some of the alleys that were wrapped in a spider coil around the offices, instead of making at once for the Strand. These alleys were dark and the district was said to be dangerous once dusk had fallen, but he felt in the mood for action, and would have welcomed the chance of a fight. He met nothing worse than a blind beggar who stood with his dog and whined for alms where four alleys met. Paul dropped a coin into his tin, passed him, and came out into a narrow street. There was a pub at one end. He went into it, ordered a pint of ale, which he took into a corner, and there thought about standing up in court and giving evidence which perhaps would damage Isabel's chances. He closed his eyes and saw Mr. Makepeace, Q.C., a little smarmy man rather like the Caterpillar, asking questions with a perpetual sneer on his lips, in a voice thick as treacle. Or he refused to give evidence and was treated as a hostile witness, with awful insinuations made by treacly Makepeace about the relationship between Isabel and his father. A shudder shook his body as he heard Makepeace's voice, that very treacly whine.

"A copper, can you spare a copper for a poor man as lost his savings and his sight with it when his home was glimmed ten years ago so that all he has to depend on is faithful Fido?"

He opened his eyes. It was the beggar with his dog, a brown-and-white terrier.

"I've spared a copper already."

"Why so you have, sir, I recognize you from the voice. You're a real gent, I can tell that." The beggar sat down on the bench beside Paul. He was tall and thin, and wore a jacket composed of different-colored patches of material, with dingy nankeen trousers. He had no overcoat. "You couldn't manage a drop of something to keep the weather out now, could you?"

Before Paul could answer, a voice said, "Fred, my old friend, how goes it? Still on the lurking game, are you?" The voice belonged to a bristly ginger-haired man who wore a checked cap and a loud checked coat and trousers. "You want to watch out for Fred; he was a real gonof before he lost his peepers. I'll buy him a pint for old times' sakes. No reason why you should put yourself out."

Paul did not fancy being left alone with the beggar. He went up to the bar with the ginger man, who introduced himself as Billy Purley. "I can see the name don't mean anything to you. Ergo, you're not one of the sporting fraternity. I've put on a little weight, but it's not so far back that there wasn't nobody could take on Billy Purley and come off best. You'll know the Ring, I take it, the Ring at Blackfriars?"

"I've heard of it."

"You ask any of the gentlemen at the Ring—they was real gentlemen, dooks and earls, some of them, and I've fought in front of royalty—you ask 'em who was the gamest middleweight they ever see, and they'll tell you Billy Purley. Good luck." He raised his glass, and Paul saw that a pint of beer was in front of him. "And what d'you want with Fred?"

"Nothing. He came up and spoke to me. I'd dropped a copper in his tin outside."

"Like I say, you want to watch out for Fred. Pardon me just half a mo." He took another pint over to the beggar, and returned. "When Fred had his peepers he could go through your pockets so you didn't know he'd touched you. He worked with a little dollymop who pushed up against you and asked you to mind where you were going, then he was into your garret and had your watch and vallybles while you were saying you was sorry and giving her the eye. Then he lost his peepers—"

"That was when his house burned down."

"Did he tell you that? Ah, Fred's a good un. I'll tell you how it was. Fred was one for the girls and he had two or three around. This little dollymop he worked with, Pauline her name was, only as high as my top waistcoat button but a regular little spitfire—well, Pauline rumbles what's going on. One day she finds Fred under the sheets with one of these birds, both of 'em in the land of nod, so she boils a big saucepan of water and throws it all over 'em. Fred was unlucky, copped it right in the face. He lost his peepers and that was finish for him as a gonof. Though mind you, if you was unwise enough to let him get real close to you, he's still got fingers light as feathers."

The beer was thick, dark and strong, and by the time Paul had drunk another pint his feet felt remarkably light, and the ground seemed as soft as if he were walking on cushions. When Billy Purley asked if he'd be interested in a bit of real sport the like of which you didn't see much nowadays, he said that he would. They left Fred in the pub talking to a man wearing a stovepipe hat and a dark suit, who was, Billy said, the local undertaker. The ginger man led the way through small streets and alleys in the direction of Seven Dials, and Paul felt a twinge of uncertainty when his companion asked: "How are you fixed for the ready? Billy Purley's a sportsman, nobody can say different. You're a sportsman too, I can see that, but a bit of the ready will come in handy. Can you manage a couple of quid?" Paul said that he could. In fact, he had a whole month's money with him. "Right, then, we're in, and you won't be sorry. You'll see a bit of good sport. Here we are."

They had stopped before a mean-looking house with chinks of light showing through shuttered windows. Purley knocked on the door three times, looking up and down the street as he did so, a precaution that seemed unnecessary since there was nobody in sight. The door was opened an inch or two, and then wider.

"I brought a friend. Young, but he wants to see a bit of sport."

Billy held a whispered colloquy with the man at the door, and then they were inside. The place smelled of animals, together with some other smell which Paul could not identify. At a muttered word from Billy he handed over two pound notes, and the ginger man gave one of them to the doorkeeper, who was revealed in the light of the passage as a beatle-browed figure with the flattened nose of the ex-boxer. He led them into a back room,

which had been made into a bar. The animal smell came
from this bar. Twenty men were in here talking and
drinking, and almost half of them had dogs with them,
some in their arms and some on leashes. They were
mostly smallish, bulldogs and terriers, although there was
a retriever and also a large spotted dog, of a breed unknown to Paul, who growled continually. Their owners
were mostly dressed in clothes like those of Billy Purley,
although there were a couple of soldiers, and one young
man wearing evening dress and a silk scarf, who was
obviously very drunk.

Beer appeared in front of them, and Paul paid for it.
He asked what had happened to the second pound.

"My commission. For introducing you. No need to look
like that; there's no taste in nothing now, is there?"

"What's going to happen, a dogfight?"

"A dogfight—oh, dear me." He nudged the man next
to him. "My young friend was asking if we was going
to watch a dogfight—what d'you think of that?"

The man was holding on the leash a panting white
bulldog with sore-looking eyes. He laughed, showing a
few rotten teeth. "A bit green, ain't he?"

"This is—" Billy began, but there was a shout from
below them of "Ready," and the company, drinks in their
hands, moved to a door which led to the basement. As
they were descending the steep stone stairs Paul recognized the other smell he had noticed as that of blood.

The basement was large, and a circular pit about ten
feet in diameter had been made in the middle of it. The
walls of the pit had a high wooden rim, and not far above
this hung an incongruous-looking candelabra which
brightly illuminated the scene. There were tethering
posts for the dogs, which were now yelping wildly. Paul
was about to ask what was going to happen, when there

was a concerted cheer as the bruiser who had let them in came down the stairs carrying a big wire cage. The cage was full of rats.

He put the cage into the pit to cries of "Going to pull 'em out, are you, Jem?" and "Those ain't rats—more like mice they look." Jem opened the door of the cage and lifted it so that the rats, perhaps thirty of them tumbled out. They moved around in the pit, sniffing and smelling each other, looking up at the strange light. The man who had been serving drinks was sitting at a table on a platform built to one side of the room, and now he banged it for their attention.

"Gennlemen and sportsmen, these rats here were caught a couple of days ago and they ain't been fed since, so Jem had to watch out for hisself. These are not tame animals, gennlemen, they are real fighting rats."

Somebody shouted, "Let's get on with it."

"I quite agree. We got some fine matches, so let's get on with 'em. And the first is between Jumbo, oo you all know is a real good ratter, and Rover, what's a new dog to us but 'is owner, Mr. Rudd, says 'e can break a rat's neck just with one snap of 'is jaw. Just bring the dogs forward if you please, so as we can see 'em, and then back your fancy. As for me, I'm willing to bet two to one on Jumbo, and I'll take anything up to a pony."

"What are they betting on?" Paul asked.

"They each have five minutes in the ring, and it's which kills most rats."

"But ratting is against the law."

Billy Purley looked at him and grinned. "You got a oncer?"

"What?"

"A quid, a oncer, a bar. Come on, come on." Paul had taken out his wallet and Purley snatched it from his hand, extracted a pound note and shouted, "This says that Rover takes 'im—what odds about Rover?" He engaged in what seemed to be furious argument with Jumbo's owner, and came back satisfied. "He gave me threes. Fifty-fifty on the winnings, right?"

Paul began to protest, and then stopped himself. What was the use? He tried to move away, but could not do so for the press of bodies beside him. There was silence except for the yelping of dogs. Jumbo had just been put into the pit.

The bulldog rushed at the rats, who clustered together in fear. He dived into the mound of them, came out with one in his mouth, crunched its neck, left it lying on the floor and went for another. He had killed a dozen within a couple of minutes. Then a desperate rat attached itself to his neck and clung on, although Jumbo dashed it against the sides of the pit. Round and round they went, while the men shouted encouragement. Just before the timekeeper beat a gong the rat dropped off dead, its body a squashed mass. Jumbo had a great wound in his neck where he had been bitten. The timekeeper counted up the dead rats and shouted, "Eighteen." There was a hum of surprise, evidently at the lowness of the score.

The smell of the blood, the pitiful terror of the rats as they scurried around looking for a way out, the brutish eagerness for more blood and more killing on the faces around him, were all more than Paul could bear. Before Rover could be put into the pit he shouldered his way out of the place, up the stairs and into the street. Once outside the house, he took several deep breaths and began to walk with his head down, not knowing where he was going but eager only to get away from the grimy horror of the scene. When he found himself outside a pub he went in, asked for a double whisky, drank it in two gulps and felt a little better. It was not until he was in the street again that he felt that delicious sensation of walking on cushions to be much accentuated, and noticed that the street lights had taken on a strange uncustomary delicacy, so that now they shimmered vaguely like some paintings by modern Frenchmen that he had seen.

He could not have said afterward where he had been, how many pubs he had entered, or how much time had passed, when he found himself in Leicester Square and outside the cigar divan called the Caravanserai. Nor could he have said what impulse made him enter. Thoughts of Uncle George swam confusedly in his mind with lines of poetry about Isabel and lost love, and memories of his father, and all these were blended with the strange softness and vagueness of the light and a general consciousness of being enclosed within—what was it some poet had said?—a dream within a dream. This awareness of dream stayed with him during what followed, as though a cushioning softness were interposed between himself and the world.

It was in the dream that he entered the cigar divan, bought a packet of Abdullah cigarettes from one of the grave Oriental attendants and sat down on a sofa to smoke—which he had done only a dozen times before in his life—and to read the *Pall Mall Gazette*. Or to try to read it, for the type danced unfamiliarly, and the words had the strangest way of blurring into each other. In the dream, too, he was conscious of men entering the divan and speaking to the attendants, and then passing sometimes not out into the square again, but through a curtain at the back of the store. He closed his eyes and there came into his mind a verse from the *Rubáiyát:*

> Think, in this battered Caravanserai
> Whose portals are alternate Night and Day,
>   How Sultan after Sultan with his pomp
> Abode his destined hour, and went his way.

Night and day, he said in the dream without moving his lips, yet the words echoed distinctly in the air. Could that be so, could he have heard the words without uttering them? He looked across to see another figure pass beyond the curtain, and at the same time was aware of an attendant standing beside him and murmuring something about coffee. He spoke, listening carefully to the words.

"Night and day," he said.

The attendant bowed his head and made a flowing gesture toward the curtain. When Paul rose and moved in that direction, however, a gentle hand checked him, a gentle voice murmured something about sesame. Gently, gently, he was led toward the counter and the other Oriental, and understood that the words that he had heard as "Enter sesame" were really "entrance fee." He paid another pound. Everything seemed to cost a pound tonight. Then the curtain was drawn aside for him, and he encountered blackness. Had he closed his eyes again without knowing it? But there was simply another curtain, thin and silky but impenetrable. Behind it was the sound of music. He pushed aside this second curtain.

The light was dim, and it was not provided by gas lamps but came from fittings with designs of dragons, griffins and unicorns on them, fittings that seemed part of the walls. The carpet on which he trod was thick and soft as moss. Around on either side were mounds of cushions piled on the floor outside semicircular tents made from some kind of rich brocade. From the end of the room a figure advanced to meet him. It was a woman, cheeks red with rouge and eyelids heavy with mascara. She wore what he supposed to be Indian dress, loose, flowing robes in dark colors. Her voice was low and pleasant.

"Welcome to the Caravanserai. Are you a novice?" When he did not reply, she said, "Is this your first visit? It is? Then come with me to the Meeting Place." She took his hand in one that was unexpectedly hard and firm, and they walked past the tents, one or two of which had the curtains drawn in front of them. When Paul asked their purpose, she replied, "They are the Wilderness. Do you understand me?"

"No."

"The Wilderness that is Paradise, if you remember your *Rubáiyát*."

They came to yet another curtain, beyond which was a winding staircase. Here it was so dark that Paul might have stumbled but for the hand of his guide. The staircase opened directly into a large room. It was almost as dark as the one below and lighted in the same way, with thick curtains drawn over to conceal the existence of windows. There was a smell that he guessed to be incense, and everything in the room had been devised to avoid angularity. There were low sofas curved like scimitars, round low tables, and again cushions on the floor. Even the curtains concealing the walls were shaped so that they should not anywhere present a straight line. There was the sound of tinkling music.

His guide led him to a sofa, and told him to sit. There was another young man on the sofa, fair-haired and wearing full evening dress. He looked at Paul with an uncertain gaze. "Very jolly place, don't y'think? Meet some good company. Like Eve."

"Eve?"

"Just brought you in. Comes from the—the—you know, Garden of Eden, not from old Omar. No women in old Omar." He giggled. "I'm waiting for Claretta; been here half an hour."

Eve returned and gave Paul a drink in a round, delicate tumbler. The liquid was warm, sweet and faintly spicy. The fair-haired young man complained again that he had been waiting half an hour for Claretta.

"You must be patient. Why do you not dance with Faustina? Give me your hand and I will take you to her."

The young man allowed himself to be led away to where three or four women sat together. One of them rose and moved into the young man's arms. They did not exactly dance, and indeed there was no music except the background tinkling, but they stood together very close, swaying a little. Then they sat down for a few moments on cushions and after that went out together toward the Wilderness, or Paradise.

Paul saw this while he sipped the spicy drink. He congratulated himself on the fact that he understood perfectly what was happening. He was in a brothel, one of the many around Haymarket, Leicester Square and Covent Garden. He had heard that some of these places practiced the most elaborate make-believe, so that in one the decorations represented the court of Louis XV, and in another a school where all the women were dressed like children. It was said that there were even brothels which contained only children—there had been a case not long ago when a man had bought a child so that he could reveal the scandal.

He knew all this, and knew also that he should leave. He had never performed the sexual act, and did not wish to begin with a prostitute. But when he tried to stand, he found that his legs were unready to support him. Was it the beer and whisky, or the sweet, spicy drink? Dreamily he began to raise the glass to his lips, but the distance seemed endless. Was he unable to raise the glass, had some spell been placed upon him? Then the glass was taken away, and Eve's soft voice said:

"And lately, by the Tavern Door agape,
Came stealing through the dusk an Angel Shape

> Bearing a vessel on his shoulder; and
> He bid me taste of it, and 'twas—the Grape!

I think you have had enough of the Grape. It is time for the Wilderness and for Paradise. Come."

Again he allowed himself to be led by the hand—it seemed that he could do nothing else, that his own will was paralyzed—across the room to the place where the women waited. They sat together, and he was told that their names were Dolores, Georgina and Maria. As Eve named them, each rose and turned in front of him, revealing her charms. Dolores was tall and elegant. She carried a fan with which she made play, and wore a black dress that fitted as if it had been skin. Georgina was brawny, with thick arms and plump hands covered with rings, and had on a dress in garish purples and yellows. Maria was small, with a tip-tilted nose and a mass of fair hair that cascaded down to her bare shoulders. A scent of powder came from them, and their faces were covered thickly with paint, but even in the dim light he realized that none of them was young.

"No," he cried, and one of them, Georgina, turned away from him with a shrug of displeasure. Some ridiculous feeling that he should not injure their feelings made him give an excuse. "I have no money, I can't pay."

"What a naughty boy." Dolores tapped him lightly on the cheek with her fan. "But you're so young—isn't he just the youngest you've ever seen?—that it needn't matter. Eve, love, I'll arrange it with you afterward. Come along now, darling. I promise you a *lovely* time." She came close to him and moved one hand down his jacket and trousers until she touched his penis. "Oh, what *have* you got there?" she cried in a falsetto voice.

The touch, the undesired intimacy, broke the spell. He pulled away from Eve, who still held his hand, turned and stumbled across the room, down the stairs, past the Wilderness, out through the curtains. He ran from the cigar divan, where the two Orientals saw his departure without the least sign of surprise, and into Leicester Square. There he sat on a bench for several minutes in a daze. Then he walked the eight miles home to Blackheath.

6

Mr. Justice Hawkins, more generally known to the public as 'Enery 'Awkins or 'Anging 'Awkins, sat in his robing room at the Old Bailey, and thought how much he detested cold weather. He protected himself against it by wearing especially warm underclothes and also mittens from October until March. In court he insisted that no window should ever be opened. But still he was cold. There was a fire in the robing room, although it was not much of a fire. He sat in front of it now and rubbed his mittened hands, although what good would warming his hands do? It would give him chilblains, that was all. Every sensible man, Sir Henry thought, should live out of England in the winter, but it was not possible to take his own good advice if he wished to remain one of Her Majesty's judges. And he did so wish, there was no doubt about that. He was in his middle seventies, but nobody had suggested that his powers were in decline. He was still unmatched in his capacity for absorbing every detail of a case and then presenting it lucidly to a jury, and Mr. Justice Hawkins did not feel himself that his judgments were severe. He was strongly opposed to flogging, and no one felt more tenderly toward children who were unlucky enough to find themselves in court. There were certain things, however, about which he had no doubt.

If a man stole anything he must be sent to prison, or you would have everybody stealing. If one person killed another by intent, he should certainly be hanged.

He became aware that Roberts had come in. The valet took down the black robe with white fur edgings that the judge had designed himself—in another man this might have been thought to show a touch of vanity—and Mr. Justice Hawkins slipped his arms into it.

"You have my sandwiches?" He had sandwiches packed for him every day he was in court, and ate them with a glass of water rather than wine, so that his mind should be clear and his attention unflagging the whole day.

"Yes, Sir Henry."

"It's cold, Roberts, very cold. See if you can do something about this fire. It may be an illusion of warmth, but I should like to see flames roaring up the chimney when I have my lunch."

"I'll use the bellows, Sir Henry."

The judge nodded, took out his watch, and nodded again in appreciation of Roberts's good timekeeping. There was a tap at the door. That would be Champ, the usher, who had come to precede him into court, and to order that everybody should be upstanding until he was seated. Mr. Justice Hawkins felt that this was as it should be. The act of respect to him was an act of respect to the Crown and to the law. It was part of the natural order of things. And Champ, who now walked in front of him, was in every way a good fellow. He laughed at the judge's jokes, looked solemn when counsel were being rebuked, and was positively distressed on the rare occasions when a reproof was being administered to the public in the gallery. Champ, too, was part of the natural order of things.

At this time Mr. Justice Hawkins had not once thought about the case he was to try. He knew, of course, that two people had died of poison, and that a lady was accused of administering it to one of them, because he read the newspapers, but beyond that he had remained deliberately ignorant. It was a matter of principle with him that he should come freshly to each case he tried, making his mind a blank page upon which the opposing counsel and their witnesses should write.

7

No sooner had the jury been sworn and taken their places than they were sent out of court again, as Sir Charles Russell rose and said that he had an objection to certain evidence that he understood his honorable friend might well desire to mention in his opening. Mr. Justice Hawkins metaphorically rubbed his hands. A legal argument of this kind was something he relished. Few things gave him greater pleasure than making decisions on points of law, and he was unperturbed by those critics who suggested that he was not a particularly good lawyer. He settled back in his chair with as much enjoyment as if he were at the play.

There were, it seemed, certain letters that the accused had written to her brother-in-law Roger Vandervent. These letters were of a compromising nature, but they had nothing directly to do with the charge on which the defendant was standing trial. They should not, therefore, be introduced as evidence. So far Sir Charles.

"You object to any quotations from these letters?"

"I find it difficult to see how my learned friend can quote from them without introducing material which is strongly prejudicial to my client, even though it is irrelevant to the charge."

The judge bowed his head. "Very well, Sir Charles. Mr. Makepeace?"

Mr. Makepeace stood up. He looked always a little wan,

but his pallor was increased to an almost deathly cast when he wore a wig. Yet his voice was strong, and his eye even sparkled slightly.

"My lord, I think my learned friend's account of these letters is hardly complete. They are—"

Russell was on his feet, his face red. "Are you suggesting that I was endeavoring to mislead his lordship?"

"Nothing of the kind." Makepeace did not give way. Hawkins was delighted. He suggested that further explanation might be helpful, and Russell reluctantly sat down.

"These letters—there are ten of them—describe in terms that I should not think it proper to use in court the guilty passion of the accused for her brother-in-law. The last of the letters was written in answer to what was evidently his suggestion that their association should be broken off. I rely upon this letter in particular, and the others in general, as evidence of motive."

The judge put his small, handsome head a little to one side. "Would it not be sufficient to mention the existence of the letters? Is it necessary to quote passages?"

"That would be necessary. The tone of the letters is almost as important as their content."

"And you are strongly opposed to direct quotation, Sir Charles?"

"That is so, my lord."

The judge glanced just once at the prisoner in the dock, delicate and frail in appearance. "I am rather in the dark here. I wish you would give me a sample of the kind of thing you object to."

Russell bowed his head. His voice was powerful, almost hectoring, the voice of a man driven to despair by the unreasonableness of those with whom he was dealing. In part this attitude was genuine, and in part assumed. Russell felt that the introduction of the letters was unjust, but he was also striking an attitude that he hoped would make his point effectively. He bent down now to consult with his junior, who was marking two or three passages in the copies in front of him. He straightened up and seemed to consider for a moment.

"Some of the letters contain intimate detail. Is it your wish that I should read one of these?"

Again Hawkins glanced at the prisoner. "If you please."

She looked down in front of her as Russell read a passage in a loud, clear voice. " 'When you kiss my breasts it gives me feelings I have never known. When I put my hand round your John Thomas—what a funny word that is you've taught me—I long to feel him inside me. Oh, my darling, I cannot wait until we are together again.' I should not wish that passage read, my lord. There are similar passages. They would be prejudicial, and they have nothing to do with the charge."

"What do you say to that, Mr. Makepeace?"

As Makepeace bobbed up Russell bobbed down again, as though they were Punch and Judy. "I said, my lord, that there were terms in the letters I should not think it proper to use in court. Those details are not relevant or necessary, but the general tone of the letters is an essential part of my case. These letters are evidence of motive, and I propose to use them as such. I shall confine myself to that."

Mr. Justice Hawkins considered, and then spoke. His voice was as heavy as Russell's, but had a richness and fluency that the other man's lacked. "It is a difficult question. I shall admit these letters as evidence of motive, and counsel for the prosecution may use them for that purpose. At the same time they should not be used simply to show a guilty relationship between the accused and her brother-in-law. Objections may be taken to them as they come up, Sir Charles, and no doubt if you find it necessary to object you will do so. That is my decision."

Both counsel bowed to the judge and sat down. Russell had lost not a battle but the first round. He said, in a voice loud enough to be heard by Makepeace but perhaps not by the judge: "The last letter would have done as well."

A moment later the jury filed back, looking around as they took their seats. Had things changed in their absence? What had been happening? Nothing gave a clue. The accused woman was still in the dock, looking for the most part straight ahead, with the faintest suggestion of a smile on her lips. Mr. Makepeace, Harold Makepeace, Q.C., inclined his head and began to speak.

Makepeace was aware of some difficulties in presenting his case, the prime one being that in English law it is possible to make an indictment for murder upon only one count. So nearly forty years earlier Palmer had been accused only of poisoning his friend Cook, although the police knew that he had at least half a dozen other victims. The question of whether proceedings should be taken in the case of Roger Vandervent or that of Harriet Collard had caused long and agonized deliberation. The decision had gone in favor of Vandervent because it was felt that the letters could most easily be introduced in relation to his death. It was also true, as Makepeace, who could be jovially cynical in a way that belied his desiccated air, had pointed out, that jurymen were human beings. They saw the papers, would have read about Mrs. Collard's death from arsenical poisoning, and would not forget its link with the present charge. At the same time Makepeace knew that he would have to tread carefully, and that Russell would be ready to object the instant his foot strayed outside the accepted guidelines. And so Makepeace opened quietly.

"May it please you, my lord, gentlemen of the jury. The prisoner Isabel Mary Collard stands charged before

you with the willful murder of Roger James Vandervent
by the administration of arsenic. It is right that I should
tell you immediately that the case will demand your particular attention because, as the Crown admits, it is based
upon circumstantial evidence and not upon direct proof
of the administration of the poison. It is of course characteristic of many poisoning cases that the actual vehicle
of poison and the moment of its administration cannot
be named, as we can often name it in an affair involving
stabbing or shooting. What we shall hope to demonstrate
is that the prisoner had an overwhelmingly strong motive,
that she purchased arsenic shortly before the death, and
that she had ample opportunity for administering the
poison.

"And now let me sketch for you the story and the char-
acters. This is a tale of two families living, apparently
on the friendliest terms, in the salubrious suburb of Blackheath. Albert House, upon the edge of the heath, was
the home of Mrs. Collard, a widow lady in her early sixties.
This was the family home, where she had lived since
childhood, and Mrs. Collard was much respected in the
neighborhood. At nearby Belmont Hill, in Victoria Villa,
lived her son, George, and his wife, Isabel, her daughter
Beatrice with her husband, Roger Vandervent . . ."

Makepeace was without a doubt among the half dozen
most eminent advocates in the country, yet it would have
been difficult to say in just what his eminence consisted.
Certainly not in the passion of rhetoric, for his tone was
dry, his manner uncolorful. He was less effective in cross-
examination than the ferocious Russell, the urbane Ed-
ward Clarke and several others. He was in a technical
sense a very good lawyer, but there were better ones
wearing silk or even in stuff gowns. Perhaps his outstand-
ing skill lay in presenting a case, which he could do with
an order and clarity that made complexities seem simple

and closed off the blind alleys of other possibilities to show a clear route along which the jury could travel to reach the verdict he desired. He took his time now, as always, but he made sure that every member of the jury knew about Albert House and Victoria Villa, and the people who lived in them.

To the jury, three of whom were tradesmen, six merchants of one sort or another, and three gentlemen of independent means, the proceedings were deeply impressive. The little judge on high in his pretty robe, Champ standing stiff as a waxwork, the learned men in wigs, the hushed, heavy air—they understood that these things were necessary for the administration of justice. Some of them looked quickly at the figure in the dock, who seemed tiny in these surroundings, and then glanced away again just as quickly. Isabel was wearing a dark-blue dress. She did not look at the jury nor at her counsel, but for the most part sat staring straight ahead.

Now Makepeace raised his voice above its usual monotone, only a little but enough to be effective in capturing the jury's special attention. They knew that there were scandalous details to be revealed about the affair, and now here they were.

"The establishment at Victoria Villa was not what it seemed. Mr. Vandervent was a prosperous man of business. Mrs. Isabel Collard was a wife with an attentive husband. But these two people, Roger Vandervent and Isabel Collard, formed an attachment to each other of a kind that can only be called disgraceful. Their relationship should have precluded anything but sisterly and brotherly feelings, but it did not. They lusted after each other, and so that this lust might be indulged easily, and that the wronged husband and wife might be kept in ignorance, Roger Vandervent took a set of rooms near Charing Cross. He had rented these rooms for several months, and was still renting them when he died. There the guilty couple met.

"That these facts are not in dispute is because of one particular and extraordinary circumstance. The prisoner saw Roger Vandervent every day at home, and met him secretly once or twice a week, but this was not enough for her. So besotted was she that she wrote him letters to these rented rooms, letters expressing what she called her love for him, and describing in detail the base desires that were fulfilled when they met." Makepeace's long, solemn face became somehow longer, and his voice took on a funereal tone as he continued. "Gentlemen of the jury, much in these letters is of such a character that it is impossible to read them aloud in court. These are letters such as Messalina might have written to one of her lovers—"

Russell was on his feet. "My lord, I must object. To characterize the letters in this way is highly prejudicial."

"Would you prefer that they should be read in full, Sir Charles?" Hawkins asked sweetly.

"No, my lord." Russell knew that he was being teased. He deliberately took a pinch of snuff before continuing. "With respect, it is grossly improper for my learned friend to speak of the letters in this way, when they have no connection with Roger Vandervent's death. He has established that they are love letters. Further details are not necessary."

Hawkins nodded. "I take your point. Mr. Makepeace, please refrain from any further description."

Makepeace bowed, but Russell should have intervened sooner. An impression had been conveyed that the letters were truly appalling in character, and it was an impression that could not be erased.

"Very well, my lord. I will add only that there were ten of these letters."

Makepeace paused and hitched up his gown. Two or three of the jury took the chance of looking again at the prisoner, who continued to stare straight ahead, her chin slightly raised. Makepeace resumed, his voice lowered just a note or two as though he were ashamed of his purple patch.

"Now, as his lordship or my learned friend would quickly point out if I failed to do so, infidelity is one thing and murder is another. But what these letters show is that the accused is a woman of unbridled passions. What she wanted she was determined to get, and to satisfy her lust she was prepared to wreck the happiness of two families. Roger Vandervent was as guilty as she, but he was evidently capable of better feelings, of remorse. It seems that he must have told her that the affair should be broken off, and the last letter is apparently a reply to this suggestion. I propose to quote just three sentences from it." He looked across for a possible objection, but Russell's head was buried in papers. "Here are the sentences. 'I cannot live without you, cannot endure it. If I can never be in bed with you again, my darling, what is life worth? I cannot believe that you would end things like this unless there was somebody else.' Those sentences will give you an indication of her feelings. And what feelings they were! I say again to you, gentlemen of the jury, and I shall have cause to repeat it, that Isabel Collard is on trial here on a charge of murder and not because of her infidelity, yet what kind of woman is it who can use such words as these? 'If I can never be in bed with you again, my darling, what is life worth?'" Mr. Makepeace paused to let these words sink in, then gave a just perceptible sigh acknowledging that there was no limit to human folly and wickedness.

"Whatever you think about it, there is no doubt that she thought herself scorned, ill used. She had the man, and did not want to let him go. It is the contention of the prosecution, gentlemen, that this was the motive for the murder of Roger Vandervent." And now, with the central theme of Isabel's wickedness established, he outlined the rest of the case. She had killed her lover in a fit of jealous passion. As they would learn, she had bought arsenic less than a week before his death. They would hear the evidence of a maid that she had given Roger Vandervent a drink from a whisky bottle which had then mysteriously vanished, and that soon after taking this drink he had suffered the last spasm of illness. Makepeace wound up to a conclusion.

"I began by warning you that the evidence in this case is circumstantial, but it is right that I should end by saying that it is in my view very strong. We cannot show you the moment when the arsenic was administered, but we can tell you the likely vehicle and we can show you the prisoner buying arsenic. Why did she do so at all, and why did she buy it in a district two or three miles from her home? Well, that is something for you to bear in mind. But I must tell you finally that it is for the Crown to make out its case. Suspicion will not do, probability will not do. You must put out of mind anything you may have seen or heard about the case outside this court. You should consider only the evidence given here. You must weigh that evidence, dispassionately and candidly, and you must not find the accused guilty unless it brings home to your minds the conviction of guilt beyond any reasonable doubt which would influence your minds in the ordinary affairs of life."

Mr. Justice Hawkins stifled a yawn. Makepeace's tone was a little light, and Hawkins's own manner as an advocate had always been thrusting. The opening did not seem to him impressive. He looked now with a kind of affectionate amusement at Russell below him, and thought how differently, and how much better, he would have done it.

The effect of a prosecution can often depend very much upon the order in which the points are presented. If Makepeace's opening had been quiet, this was in part because his personality was the reverse of flamboyant, but also because he thought that a quiet presentation would point up the lurid facts most powerfully for a jury. He had got the letters in, and hoped to get a little more of them in, and they were the most important single feature of the case. So far as he was concerned, the story should be told simply and straightforwardly. It would be up to Russell to provide any fireworks.

First, then, the doctors, to show the death and its cause. And first among the doctors Porterfield, immensely on his dignity, coat and trousers beautifully pressed, gold chain conspicuous across his waistcoat, shoes shining like a full moon on a summer night, on his hands gray gloves, which he carefully took off and placed beside him when he took the oath. He was taken through the course of Roger's illness, and described symptoms in detail. Then came the unavoidable embarrassment of the last visit.

"Your colleague Dr. Hassall was present on that occasion."

"He was."

"Did he make any suggestion afterwards about the cause of death?"

"He thought that a post-mortem should be carried out."

"But that was not your opinion?"

"It was my view that Mr. Vandervent had died of gastric fever. I gave a certificate to that effect." The doctor's assurance was magnificent.

"Even though his condition had deteriorated so suddenly."

"I have seen many similar cases. You must remember

that my experience greatly exceeds Dr. Hassall's." He spoke the words with fine solemnity. It seemed hardly possible that such a man could have been wrong.

"You were present at the autopsy after the body was exhumed?"

"I was."

"And you agree that Dr. Mulhall found a quantity of arsenic in the stomach and intestines, a quantity more than sufficient to cause death?"

"I can confirm that that was the case," Dr. Porterfield said in a tone suggesting that without his agreement the whole prosecution case might have collapsed.

Makepeace sat down. Russell left the cross-examination to his junior Molesey, who briskly ran through the length of time Porterfield had been the family doctor.

"You knew them all well?"

"I knew them very well."

"Did you ever see any sign of marital discord in either the Vandervent or Collard families?"

"Not the faintest sign of such a thing."

With that Dr. Porterfield was released. He bowed to Mr. Justice Hawkins, to counsel, to the jury, and retired with his dignity unimpaired, his prestige somehow even enhanced. He was followed by Dr. Mulhall, a brisk, no-nonsense kind of man, who said that he had discovered 2.5 grains of arsenic in stomach, intestines and liver. This would correspond to a much larger quantity actually taken into the system. How much? It was difficult to say without knowing how much had been expelled by the body, but probably fifteen to twenty grains.

"What is the smallest quantity known to have caused death in humans?"

"According to Taylor, two and a half grains. That would be comparatively rare."

"But fifteen grains would cause death?"

"Fifteen grains would certainly cause death."

There was no cross-examination.

Next in the box was Hilda, looking young and pretty, but nervous. This nervousness disappeared, however, under the gentle and as it seemed almost uninterested questions of Mr. Makepeace. Quietly he led her through what she had done in the bedroom on the day that Roger Vandervent had his final illness. Yes, she had been sitting beside the bed during part of the morning and part of the afternoon. She had been told to give him a drink of arrowroot or beef tea if he wanted it, and to call Mrs. Vandervent if the master asked for anything else. At about three o'clock, although she could not be sure of the exact time, the master had woken up and seemed much brighter.

"Did he ask you for something?"

"Yes, sir. He said he wanted a tot of whisky, it would do him good. He seemed so much better, sir, and you see, he had such a way with him."

"Just tell us what happened."

"Why, he asked me to lean over the bed, and then he whispered to me. 'You be a good girl, Hilda, and give me a tot of whisky.' So then I said something about the mistress saying he should have the arrowroot. 'Bother that,' he says. 'There's nothing like a drop of whisky for getting your strength up.' Then he says, quite like his old self, 'Now, my girl, you just go over to the washstand and take a glass from the top of it. Then you open the cupboard underneath and you'll find a bottle of whisky. You pour me a good tot and bring it over here.' So I did that, although my hand was shaking while I did it."

"And Mr. Vandervent drank it?"

"He drank it in two big gulps, yes, sir."

"And then?"

"Then he gave back the glass and said I should wash

it up so nobody would know, and put it back. So that's what I did."

"What happened after that?"

"He took a little of the arrowroot so that the doctor shouldn't smell whisky on his breath, although he didn't like it."

"Did you stay with him after he drank the whisky?"

"Not exactly, sir. He seemed so much better, and he said there was no need for me to sit there, I could go about my business, so I did. I had things to do in the other bedrooms, and I was popping in and out. Then I heard a sort of a cry, and I went in and he called out something about the pain and getting the doctor."

"And then?"

"Then I ran out and just outside I met Jenkins."

"That is, the butler."

"Yes, sir. And he said he'd tell the mistress." Hilda had become quite flushed with excitement in telling her story.

"Now, you said nothing about this drink of whisky at the time. Why was that?" She hesitated. "You may speak freely."

"I was afraid, sir."

"Because you suspected there might have been something wrong with the whisky?"

"Oh, no, sir. Just that I knew I'd done something wrong."

"And is this the first time you have told the story?"

"No, sir. I told it to Mr. Paul."

"That is, Mr. Paul Vandervent."

"That's right, sir. I told it to him two or three weeks afterwards, when he remembered—"

Makepeace held up a hand frail as a leaf. "We shall hear from Mr. Paul Vandervent himself what he noticed." He looked at his notes. "Ah, yes. Did you know that the bottle of whisky was kept in that cupboard?"

"Yes, sir, I did."

"So that would have been fairly common knowledge, would it?"

"Yes, sir. Sometimes Mr. Roger would have a nightcap, and then he would leave the glass on the washstand. That was how I knew."

"Do you remember if there were any other bottles in the cupboard when you got the whisky?"

"Yes, sir. There was a bottle of brandy and a bottle of port."

"Both of them open?"

"That's right. They were about half full."

"Two or three weeks after Mr. Vandervent's death all of these bottles had disappeared. You do not know what happened to them?"

"No."

Mr. Makepeace subsided gently, and Russell was on his feet. It was a fine sight, one of his contemporaries said, to see him rise to cross-examine. "His very appearance was often a shock to the witness—the manly, defiant bearing, the noble brow, the haughty look, the remorseless mouth, those deep-set eyes, widely opened, and that searching glance which pierced the very soul." And indeed as she confronted Russell, the jauntiness that Hilda had acquired during her examination dropped from her as though she were sloughing off a skin, leaving beneath the raw, defenseless flesh. Yet his first questions were almost jocular.

"Those bottles in the cupboard. Did you ever have a little nip from them, now, thinking it might not be noticed?"

"Oh, no, sir."

"Nor any of the other servants, as far as you know? Your friend Jenkins, perhaps?"

"Not that I know of. We wouldn't do a thing like that." Hilda's color rose. She sensed that she had made a mistake.

"Oh, wouldn't you, now?" She shook her head, staring at him. The characteristic Russell effect upon witnesses, as of a cobra upon a rabbit, had already been achieved. His next words were still quiet.

"Jenkins, who was the butler, is a friend of yours, is he not?" She stared at him dumbly. "Are you now living with him as man and wife? Answer me, please."

There was a long pause before she whispered, "Yes."

"The two of you together have been blackmailing the prisoner on account of these letters we have heard about?"

Mr. Makepeace was on his feet. "I must object to this line of questioning. What may have happened to the letters is nothing to do with the charge against the prisoner."

"My lord, the question is aimed at showing the lack of credibility of the witness."

Hawkins looked from one to the other of them. "You may continue, Sir Charles, but please confine yourself to establishing the point relating to the credibility of the witness."

"I shall do my best, my lord. Perhaps no more than two or three questions may be necessary." He fixed Hilda with the deadly Russell eye. "Is it correct that you were dismissed from service at Victoria Villa some weeks after Mr. Vandervent's death?"

"Yes."

"Will you tell the jury the circumstances?"

She looked from her tormentor to Mr. Makepeace, who was gazing studiously at the table in front of him, and then at the judge, who stared back at her impassively. "I—I cannot—"

"You cannot answer? Very well, let me put a suggestion

to you and see if you agree with it. Your partner Jenkins had possession of the letters we have heard about, and asked Mrs. Collard for money, which she sent by post. Your part was to collect the letters and give them to Jenkins. Do you agree with that?" She did not reply and Russell repeated, thundering out the words, "Do you agree with that?"

"You must answer the question," Hawkins said, and she whispered her agreement.

"Very well," Russell said, and his tone was different, so that she looked up like a child told that punishment is over. "Now tell me this. You were by the bedside part of the morning and part of the afternoon?"

"Yes."

"Nobody could have come into the room unknown to you at those times?"

"No."

"This was on the Monday. Now let us go back to Sunday. That was the day on which Mr. Vandervent was taken ill. You have said that when he took a drink the glass would be left on the washstand. How did you know when a glass had been used?"

"By the smell. And there was often a little drink left in it."

"Would it generally be whisky?"

"Mostly, sir. He didn't often touch the port or brandy."

"And it was drunk as a nightcap, so that you found the glass there in the morning, is that right? Very good. Now, can you remember if there was a used glass on Tuesday morning?"

She hesitated, then shook her head. "I don't remember."

Russell said quite kindly, "Do you understand why I am asking these questions?"

"No, sir."

"Because if the whisky was poisoned and caused his illness, Mr. Vandervent must have taken it at some time on the Sunday when he was first ill, so that the glass might have been there on the following morning. But let us leave that. You said that after drinking the whisky he took some arrowroot."

"Yes, so that the doctor—"

"Shouldn't know. Quite so. How much of it did he drink?"

"Not much; only a few sips."

"And he commented that he disliked it."

"He said it was horrible. But I think—" She paused, fearful of offending this terrible man, then went on. "It was just that he didn't like arrowroot."

Russell nodded. "Now, you said that the fact that these bottles were kept in the cupboard was fairly common knowledge. You meant to the servants, yourself and Jenkins and so on."

"Yes, sir."

"Other members of the household would not have been likely to know about the bottles?"

"I couldn't say. Mrs. Vandervent, I suppose she might."

"Mrs. Vandervent, yes. Now, just one more thing. You were often on this floor of the house doing the bedrooms, were you not? How often did you see Mrs. Collard enter Mr. Vandervent's room?"

"Why, sir, I don't think I ever did,"

"So that it is very unlikely she knew about these famous bottles?"

"I suppose it is, sir."

"And while Mr. Vandervent was ill, was Mrs. Collard ever in the room alone with him, to your knowledge?"

"Not to my knowledge, no."

And with that Hilda left the witness box. There were those who said afterward that Russell had rather compromised his own case by that attack on her credibility, and that he would have done better to concentrate on showing that it would have been difficult for Isabel to doctor the whisky. By discrediting Hilda, he made it less likely that the jury would believe anything she said. But Russell was not one for finespun subtleties, and he was satisfied with what he had done.

8

Paul had sat for the whole morning in the witnesses' waiting room, which was high and narrow, and like much of the Old Bailey, dark. There was a bench on either side, as though it were a railway waiting room. Hilda had been on it for an hour in the morning until she was called, but she sat at the other end from him, and did not speak. There were half a dozen other people in the room when he first entered it, and he thought that they were witnesses in the trial, but of course they were for other courts. They were called by an usher, went away, were replaced by others. One old fellow complained that he ought not to have been asked to come there because he had a bad leg. "Can't hardly walk on her, you see. Up here, that's where she gets me," he said, rubbing his thigh. "If they knew what she was like they'd never have called me. Fair gives me gyp, she does." Paul had brought a collection of poems with him, but found it impossible to read them. He sank into a reverie in which the memory of his father lying white-faced in bed blended with thoughts of Isabel and the nightmare recollection of the creatures at the Caravanserai, the woman who had plucked greedily at his trousers and the other, whose fat fingers were covered with rings. The usher had to call his name twice.

When he entered the witness box his first impressions were of the extreme quietness, and of the court being crowded with people. Then it seemed to him that Isabel was not there. As Mr. Makepeace led him through the opening questions about his name and where he lived— quietly, as quietly as if they were in church—he looked around and eventually saw Isabel, much nearer than he had imagined, and unchanged. What change had he expected? He did not know.

What was it Makepeace had been asking? "I beg your pardon," he said. "Would you repeat that?"

"Why did you think that your father might have had something to drink other than arrowroot or beef tea?"

"I remembered that the last time I saw him there was the print of a glass on the table by his bed."

Mr. Makepeace nodded and was prepared to go on, but the judge intervened. "You mean that you saw this in your mind's eye like Horatio"—there was a ripple of amusement in court—"some weeks after your father's death?" Paul said yes. Mr. Justice Hawkins made a note, and continued.

"Are you quite certain of this three- or four-week-old memory?"

"Yes."

"You are telling the court that, if I may put it in that way, it was imprinted on your mind like a photograph?"

His tone was skeptical, but Paul said yes again.

Mr. Makepeace went on. "What did you do?"

"I spoke to my stepmother, and asked her whether Father had had anything else to drink on the day he died. She did not know of anything. Then I remembered that Hilda had been beside the bed for part of the time, and asked her."

"And what did she say?"

"She began to cry. Then she said she had given him a drink of whisky."

"Did she say where it had come from?"

"From the cupboard below the washstand."

"Did you make any further investigation?"

"Yes. Father's room was locked, but I got the key and looked in the cupboard. The whisky was not there, and the other bottles she had mentioned were not there either."

Makepeace was about to sit down, when the judge spoke again. His voice was heavy and sounded sarcastic even when, as now, the words were straightforward.

"Can you tell the court the reason for this detective investigation on your part?"

"Yes, my lord. I thought there was something strange about Father's death. He had seemed so much better, and then he died so suddenly."

"Was this feeling shared by others in the household?"

"Not so far as I know."

Again Mr. Justice Hawkins made a note. What was he writing? But now Sir Charles Russell was on his feet, his manner benevolent, almost paternal.

"Mr. Vandervent, I shall not keep you long. I am sure the court has been as much impressed as his lordship by your detective work. I want now to move to another example of it. Did the defendant approach you at some time in August in relation to some letters she had written?"

Paul launched into the story of his visit to Camberwell and his interrogation of Hilda. Mr. Justice Hawkins intervened with questions, and in the end asked whether he had read the stories of M. Gaboriau. Paul said he had not.

"I thought perhaps you were emulating the methods

of Monsieur Lecoq." Again the ripple of amusement. The judge looked around, smiling. Sir Charles took snuff. Mr. Makepeace flung back his head and regarded the ceiling. All of them, Paul thought, were like actors in a play.

"Just one or two more questions and I have done. You are a member of the household. Did you ever witness any serious quarrel between the two couples living there?"

"No."

"Would it be fair to say that it was a very harmonious household?"

"It would."

And that was all. He stepped down from the witness box and walked out of the court. Outside, in the bitter air of that January day, he could hardly believe that the ordeal which he had regarded with such fear was over. His part had after all been almost negligible. He had been needed to fill out Hilda's story, that was all. Nothing he had said would make any difference to the question of whether, at the end of the play, the little judge with the liking for feeble jokes had the black cap placed on his head or not. How could Isabel's fate, how could anybody's fate, be decided by such playactors?

He thought about all this as he went home to Blackheath, and he thought also of the judge's obvious skepticism about the glass beside the bed. It truly had been imprinted on his mind like the print on a picture. He tried, quite consciously, to create a series of photographs of the Caravanserai in the same way, and at a certain moment on the return journey, as the train rumbled over points between New Cross and Lewisham, he succeeded. And having done so he knew, without fully understanding it, the astonishing truth.

9

Harold Makepeace was in the ordinary affairs of life a scrupulously honest man, but his tactics as an advocate were often devious. He had no doubt that Isabel Collard was guilty, but also realized that whether or not the jury found her so depended very much on the letters. The more they were introduced, the greater was the likelihood of conviction. It was with this in mind that he called Jenkins into the box. He would be subject to severe cross-examination, but what did it matter if he was shown to be what he undoubtedly was, a disgusting creature?

So Jenkins gave his evidence. To provide an inducement for him to do so, it had been necessary to agree that he would not be prosecuted by the police on a blackmail charge. This was a delicate matter, in the sense that nothing could be committed to paper, but Jenkins had said that he quite understood, and that a gentleman's word was good enough for him. Makepeace had had no personal contact with this distasteful matter, nor had he previously seen Jenkins. The man did not look agreeable, but he gave his evidence clearly. In the matter of the bottles, he said that he knew they were in the cupboard, but could not account for their disappearance. He found the letters when cleaning out one of the drawers and, yes, he had read them.

"I started to read one in case it was something important—"

"There is no need to give a reason. You read all the letters?"

"Yes, sir."

"I am going to read a few phrases from the letters, and shall ask what you made of them. This is from the third letter. 'I long to be with you all the time, not just snatching two or three hours of bliss. To sleep together in the same bed, to lie all night in each other's arms—oh, when can we do that? May it be soon.' That is letter three, and letter five returns to the same theme in different terms. 'We want to be together always, darling, don't we? What should I do with John Thomas if I had him all day and every day—' "

Makepeace stopped in apparent confusion. Russell was on his feet, protesting furiously. The judge said severely, "Mr. Makepeace, I must ask you to be more careful. What is the point of reading that passage?"

"My lord, I must apologize. I am doing my best, but the letters are of such a character that it is difficult for me."

"No doubt. But I am at a loss to understand the point you wish to make."

"The fact that the defendant seems to have envisaged a time when she would be free to live with the deceased. This passage ends: 'You say that you would never do anything, but I *could* and *would* do something. What use would it be, though, if you were not free?' "

"You wish to put that passage to the witness? I do not see what he can have to say about it."

"There is a further passage—"

"Is it of the same character?"

"Very much so, my lord."

"Then I cannot allow it. You have established that the defendant looked forward to the possibility of life with the deceased."

"With respect, my lord, I am trying to determine the means by which this was to be achieved."

"And does your further quotation bear upon this directly?"

Mr. Makepeace said reluctantly, "Not directly, my lord."

"Then I cannot allow further quotation." Mr. Justice Hawkins sat back, suppressing the sigh of pleasure that he always felt at winning an argument with counsel.

Mr. Makepeace bowed slightly. He did not much mind being deprived of the further quotation, since his point had already been made. To Jenkins, who had been following the exchange with bewilderment, he said, "What did you make of passages like those I have been reading?"

"Beg pardon?"

"These passages in the letters, about being together always—what did you think they meant?"

"I don't rightly know."

Makepeace turned again to the little man on high. "My lord, I should like to read one more passage, just a few words at the end of the very last letter. I regard them as important."

The judge sighed quite audibly. "Very well, Mr. Makepeace. A few words, you said."

"No more than a sentence. The last words of the last letter are: 'I would do anything—*anything*—rather than give you up.'" He had been looking at the jury, but now turned back to Jenkins. "What did you think those words meant?"

"Well." Jenkins hesitated. "Didn't want to give him up, did she?"

"Did you have no further thought, a thought that made you feel with confidence that you could ask for money?"

"Oh, I tumble to it," Jenkins said, with the air of one upon whom a light has suddenly burst. "I thought maybe, well, she might have done away with him."

"So you took these letters, and asked the defendant for money."

"Right. If she'd had her fun, why shouldn't she pay for it?"

"And she paid you without question, sending money to the address you gave."

"That's right. Mind you, I never asked for too much."

Another question or two, and Makepeace sat down. Russell rose, huge, terrifying, flashing-eyed, and put his first question. "There is a name for what you were doing. Do you know what it is?" When Jenkins was mute, he thundered, "The name is blackmail."

Makepeace sat back and closed his eyes. Sir Charles would destroy Jenkins, crush him under foot for the loathsome cockroach he was, but that did not matter. The important parts of the letters were in, and so was the suggestion that Jenkins had assumed that Isabel Collard had done away with her husband. Makepeace only half listened during the two hours in which the wretched Jenkins was knocked down, and then picked up to be knocked down again, by Sir Charles. The courtroom was stiflingly close even on this January day, thanks to Sir Henry's insistence that every window be closed, and he catnapped for a good half hour.

10

It was a general legal opinion afterward that the case has shown Russell at something well below his best, and that his activities had been less leonine (an adjective his admirers often applied) than like those of a bull in a china shop. Yet he had one triumph, in the cross-examination of Jacob Morley the chemist. Russell rose to question him with suavity, friendliness even.

"Mr. Morley, I understand you're an old soldier."

"Right, sir. In the army from a boy, and loved it."

"But you had to leave when you had the accident to your eye."

"No accident. That was done by a blackamoor."

"Indeed. I can see you're a man Her Majesty was unlucky to lose. But I'm sure you've brought a soldierly neatness into keeping your shop. And this book." He ruffled the pages of the poisons book. "Beautifully kept."

"Much obliged."

"And you have no doubt that you sold a quantity of arsenic on the eighteenth of May to a lady who signed herself Isabel Collard?"

"That's the name, Sir Charles."

"But you can't tell us that the lady really was Mrs. Collard, can you? You described your customer as fairly tall. Will you stand up, Mrs. Collard." Isabel stood. "Can you be sure that this is the lady you saw?"

"No, sir, I can't. She wore a veil in my shop."

"I understand. Her face was hidden. And then you said 'fairly tall.' Does Mrs. Collard look to you fairly tall?"

"Why, I don't rightly know."

"She is just under five feet three inches in height, which I suppose is an average height for a woman. Then you said also that her coat and skirt were tight around the hips. Just look at Mrs. Collard now, and tell me whether you think anything would be likely to be tight around her hips." Isabel's waist and hips were beautifully slender.

"Why, again, sir, I don't rightly know. Not being, as you might say, an expert on ladies' fashions."

"Perhaps I may put it a little differently. Would you agree that the defendant is thin?"

"Certainly would, no doubt about it."

"But from your description, the visitor to your shop was on the plump side."

"Putting it that way, sir, I'd have to agree with you."

"Very handsome of you, Mr. Morley. Now, would you mind reading this?" He held up a piece of white card on which "I can read this" had been printed in large letters. The judge, who was sitting at about the same distance from Russell as the witness, could read it easily, but Morley put a hand over his eyepatch, half closed his other eye, and then shook his head.

"That's a darnation foolish thing—always put a hand over the peeper that isn't there when I can't see something, as though that'd help. I can't quite make it out."

Russell took a couple of steps toward him. "Can you read it now?"

"Still can't manage it. Sight ain't good, is that what you're trying to say, Sir Charles? Because there's no argument. Should have gig lamps by rights; tried two or three pair but never could get along with them."

"Just tell me when I'm at the right distance." He was about four feet from Morley when the chemist laughed heartily.

"No trouble now. 'I can read this.' Yes, very good."

"You're a good-natured man, Mr. Morley. Now, when this lady came in, it was a fine day."

"If you say so, Sir Charles."

"At any rate, it was May, and you wouldn't have had the lights on."

"That's correct."

"But your shop is very dark, I understand."

"Again, bound to agree. Some corners in it are so dark I can't find my own stock." The chemist laughed again.

"Thank you. Now, I suggest that all you can tell us of the person who bought poison from you is that she was fairly tall, on the stout side, wore a hat that concealed her hair, white shoes, and a blue coat and skirt."

"I quite agree."

"In fact, she looked—as far as you could see her—quite unlike Mrs. Collard?"

"Putting it that way, I suppose you're perfectly right."

So that was a triumph, or at least a success. Yet it left

the obvious question: why should another woman have deliberately signed Isabel Collard's name in the poisons book?

11

There were few defense witnesses, for after all what could they say? Russell called George and Beatrice to say that it would have been difficult for Isabel to gain access to the bedroom during Roger's illness for long enough to doctor the whisky, but of course it could not be said to have been impossible. George was very nervous while giving evidence, Beatrice perfectly composed. She agreed that she knew of the presence of the bottles in the cupboard beneath the wash basin, but she had never looked for them after Roger's death. Neither was subject to much cross-examination, Makepeace feeling that his case was clearly made out.

Russell was basically an optimistic man, and he felt confident of a verdict, as he told Molesey when they talked after all the evidence had been given, and nothing remained but the final speeches and the summing up.

"What does it amount to, after all? They've been very strong about the whisky; too strong for their own good, if you ask me. What chance did she have of putting poison into it? Very little; practically none. And then we pretty well scotched the identification by the chemist. What else is there in the case?"

"There are the letters."

"Damn it, man, all those letters say is that she was upset at the end of the relationship."

"But what the other side managed to get in . . ." Molesey felt that his senior should have been more alert in checking Makepeace, but he knew that Russell did not care for adverse criticism. He ended rather lamely, "We all know what juries are."

They were talking in the changing room, and Russell glared when Mr. Humperdinck put his head around the door. "Yes?" he said. "What do you want?"

The solicitor said apologetically, "Mrs. Collard—I think you should see her."

"Why?"

"She wants—she would like—" So awful was the look in Russell's eye that Humperdinck found it hard to utter the simple words he had to say. "She would like to make a statement."

Molesey groaned aloud, which was perhaps a mistake, because he seemed to be preempting Russell's decision. He, too, came in for one of the great man's glares. Then Russell said that he would see her immediately, before she was returned to Brixton. Humperdinck incautiously went on. "But, Sir Charles, a statement. Can that be wise?"

"I have said that I will see her."

When he did so, a few minutes later, his manner was gentle, as he asked what she wanted to say.

Her hands had been trembling a little, but now she put them together and they were steady. "I may say something if I wish, isn't that so?"

"Who told you that? Humperdinck, I suppose."

"He answered my questions, yes. It is terrible to sit there and listen to people saying they think I did this and that, and that I put poison into the whisky. I never even knew whisky was kept in that cupboard, yet I am not allowed to say so. I may not give evidence, I may not tell my own story."

"You may not. That is the English law."

"So I wish to say those things. I knew nothing of the whisky, and I could not have bought the poison because

I was in a railway train on the way to London when it was sold. That is what I wish to say."

"Was anybody with you in the railway carriage? Some companion, I mean."

"No."

"And why were you going to London?"

"I was going to see Roger."

Russell considered. A statement made from the dock was unsworn, and could not be made the subject of cross-examination. In his experience it rarely impressed juries. The things Isabel Collard wanted to say could be said as well or better by her counsel. And yet—and yet she might be a she-devil, but she looked more like an angel. She was not only an attractive woman, but one with a look of innocence about her as well. He was inclined to think that a statement by her could do no harm and might, just might, impress the jury favorably.

"Very well. If you are sure that it is your wish."

"I am sure."

"Have you written a statement?"

"No. I should like simply to speak, to explain things. I do not feel that I need anything written."

Did this come from the heart, or was it coolly calculated? Before Russell left she asked him how the case was going, and he said well.

"And you are confident I shall be acquitted?"

He used words that he had spoken before. "We must put our trust in God. We are safe also in putting our trust in an English jury. I have faith in them, and you may have faith too."

12

On that evening Paul moved out of Victoria Villa. Before he did so he saw Beatrice. She was occupied in planning a card party for the weekend, and the informal supper that would go with it. She did not seem surprised, but then nothing appeared to surprise her nowadays.

"So you are going to strike out for yourself. Perhaps it is for the best. Where are you going?"

"I have found rooms in Guilford Street near Russell Square, which will do for the time being. I shall look around. Beatrice." He rarely used her name, and she looked at him keenly. "I don't want you to think that I am leaving because of you. I can't stay here any more, that's all. I think you should leave too. I think the house should be sold."

"Leave? I had not thought of it. Perhaps I shall leave one day, but not yet."

"Have you considered at all what it will be like when Isabel comes back?"

"Comes back? She will never come back. She is guilty. She poisoned your father and my mother."

"I don't believe it."

"She robbed me of your father and then she poisoned him. She will not come back here. I don't wish her name to be mentioned in my hearing."

"I am sorry."

"Never mind." She kissed him on the forehead. "It's a pity we didn't get to know each other better. You never forgave your father for marrying me."

So he left the villa. His clothes and the best of his books went comfortably into a couple of suitcases, and a hansom took him up to Guilford Street. There he had a couple of attic rooms, clean and spacious. There was an old oak wardrobe for his clothes, and shelves on which he carefully arranged his books. Then he sat at the window and looked out at the smoky streets around him and at the just visible glimpse of Russell Square. He wondered whether Isabel would be found guilty, and what he should do.

The final speeches came on the following day. He went to court to hear them.

13

"My lord," Russell said. "Mrs. Collard has told me that she wishes to make a statement. I have asked her whether it was written, and she said no."

Hawkins's lips tightened in displeasure. Statements from the dock had an emotional and sensational quality of which he disapproved. Isabel Collard stood up and faced him. She put a hand to her throat, and Russell feared that she might break down. Then she seemed to gather confidence. Her voice was low but clear. Paul, who had queued for an hour to get a seat in the gallery, saw that she had the complete attention of the jury. One red-faced pork-butcherish-looking man listened to her with his mouth wide open.

"My lord," she said, "I wish to say that I am completely innocent of the charge made against me, and to refer in particular to the suggestion that I purchased arsenic from Mr. Morley's shop, and then put it into a bottle of whisky. I wish to say that I never visited Mr. Morley's shop at any time in my life, and do not even know where it is. At the time he sold the arsenic, in the afternoon of May the eighteenth, I was in a railway train on my way to London. I was going to see Roger Vandervent, and I spent the rest of the afternoon with him. I swear that this is true.

"With reference to the whisky, I did not know that it was kept in that cupboard. I did not even know that it existed. Again, I swear that this is true. My lord, it was my endeavor to keep my love affair secret, and it was for this reason that I met Mr. Vandervent in London.

It would have been very foolish of me to enter his bedroom, with the risk that I might be seen. I never did any such thing."

She paused as though about to add something further, and then sat down. There was a sense of anticlimax. The red-faced juryman closed his mouth as though he were snapping a fly. Mr. Justice Hawkins reflected that although the statement had been, as he expected, irrelevant, it had been mercifully short. Russell was left frowning. There was of course no way of proving anything she said, and the last two or three sentences had too much an air of calculation. The frown was still on his forehead as he rose to make the closing speech for the defense.

It was agreed later that neither Russell nor Makepeace was seen at his best in these closing speeches. Russell used the argument that access to the whisky was difficult and that the whisky was in any case only one possible vehicle for poison, and he stressed that Morley's identification was worthless, but he was disturbed throughout by the feeling that it had been a mistake to let Isabel make a statement at all. In relation to the identification, Makepeace replied that somebody had bought poison and signed Isabel Collard's name, and that it would have been natural for her to conceal her identity as nearly as possible. As for her access to the whisky, did they really suppose that a woman with the feelings she entertained toward the deceased would hesitate to take the "risk," as she called it in her statement, of entering his bedroom? But Makepeace did not display any particular passion— that was not his manner—nor did he go out of his way to say that only one verdict was possible. The jury might very well be swayed, as many a jury had been in the past, by Mr. Justice Hawkins.

The judge began his summing up immediately after

lunch, which for him had consisted of four tiny egg sandwiches and a bottle of Perrier water. Then he followed Champ, who was no less aware than the judge that this was a solemn occasion, into court. Champ beat three times with his gavel, and Mr. Justice Hawkins began to sum up in the case of the Crown versus Collard.

Henry Hawkins had some contempt for those who thought that a judge's function was merely to preside, take notes and be dispassionate. He always, he said once, took the greatest care to study every fact in a case, but when he had reached a conclusion it was his duty to see that the jury did not go wrong. A judge, he said in one of his many aphorisms, does not sit to perform the mechanical work of an automaton, but to see that justice is done. Quite early in this case he had decided that Isabel Collard was guilty, and in summing up he aimed to lead the jury to that conclusion.

Within a few minutes of his opening it was plain, not from any distortion of the evidence but from the tone used, what Mr. Justice Hawkins thought the verdict should be. He dealt briskly and harshly with Isabel's statement. "This was a statement that the accused woman made, knowing that she could not be cross-examined upon it. And what did she say? That she knew nothing of the whisky bottle, and had no chance of entering the bedroom alone. But this is mere assertion, and you may think there is force in the prosecution's contention that a woman of such strong passions as those revealed in her letters would have been prepared to risk anything to achieve her ends. And then she tells us that at the time when arsenic was bought from Mr. Morley she was in a railway train, but again this is assertion and not evidence. It is difficult to see why her statement was made, except that it showed the winsome quality of the accused woman's appearance and personality."

He moved to the letters, and was severer still. Hawkins

believed, even more strongly than most of those who listened to him, in the sanctity of the marriage vow. He had been deeply shocked not only by the situation revealed in the letters but by their language, and he made this clear. "What do you think of these letters, gentlemen of the jury? Counsel for the defense has said with force and eloquence that they are evidence of adultery, not of murder. That is perfectly true, yet it is right that you should consider what such letters must imply in relation to the person who wrote them.

"Only fragments of the letters have been read in court—you have been spared the rest—but those fragments show a filthy and unbridled sensuality on this woman's part. She writes in the language of the gutter, and the desires she expresses are not much different from those of a common prostitute. Counsel for the defense has said that the letters provide no evidence of motive. It is for you to decide, but you may feel that there could hardly be a stronger motive than that provided by the suggested breaking off of this relationship by the man who, however belatedly, had some decent feelings left. What does she say? 'I would do anything—anything—rather than give you up,' and in other letters she was saying that she could and would do something, even though the man did nothing himself. What do such passages mean? Some of them may suggest only a desire for separation from the marriage partners, but consider that passage about doing anything rather than give up her lover. What can it be except a threat of suicide or murder? Well, it is for you to make another interpretation, if you think one is appropriate."

At this point Paul rose, stumbled out of the gallery and left the court, unable to bear the words to which he had to listen. So he was not there to hear the judge say that Morley's identification was worth nothing, but that somebody had signed the accused woman's name in the poisons book, and they must consider whether this was an odd kind of joke, a piece of malice—or whether it had really been Isabel Collard. Nor did he hear the judge's final warning that what they thought of the character of the accused was not in itself to the point. She was not being charged with moral turpitude, and if they found there was a reasonable doubt of her guilt they must acquit her. When those words were spoken Paul was back in his rooms, staring out the window. When the jury retired he was out walking, down busy Holborn, into Gray's Inn Road, and then through regions he hardly knew, Islington and Clerkenwell, long streets of gray, quiet houses. It was less than an hour before the jury returned, and the open-mouthed, pork-butcher-ish man, who was the foreman, stood up and announced the verdict.

Champ carefully smoothed the square of black silk and placed it upon the judge's head. Mr. Justice Hawkins, 'Anging 'Awkins, said that she had had a fair trial, complimented counsel upon both sides, and sentenced the accused woman to be hanged by the neck until she was dead. And Isabel Collard, who had listened to all that had been said apparently unmoved, crumpled to the ground in a faint.

By that time Paul Vandervent had come to a decision.

14

It was a Wednesday evening when the verdict was given. On the following night, a wet one with rain driving across the heath, George Collard paid a visit to Albert House. He stood, rubbing his hands, by the fire which brightened part of the Great Hall but never warmed it. His face was pale.

"I've come from Isabel." He paused, but neither Charlotte nor Robert Dangerfield said anything. "She's bearing up. Of course, there may be a reprieve, there must be a reprieve." Still they said nothing. "She asked after you both. You particularly, Charlotte."

"You mean she asked when I was coming to see her." George gave an indecisive wave of the hand. "I am not going. I do not wish to see her again. Robert feels as I do."

Robert twirled his mustache. "The verdict's been given now. We ought to accept it, put the whole thing behind us. Charlotte and I plan to get married in March, no point in waiting any longer. We shall live here, we've decided on that."

"So that you'll inherit the house."

"Yes. If you or Beatrice, or both of you, wish to live here too, of course it could be arranged."

"Speaking for myself, no, thanks. It's not a happy house, I always hated it. I can't say what Bee will feel, but I think her answer will be the same as mine." George looked around at the dim recesses of the great Hall, then up at the gallery. Steam rose from his damp clothing. "I shall take my share of the rest, such as it is."

"What about me?" Bertie had come in, unnoticed.

Charlotte looked at her lover. Robert Dangerfield said, "Happy for you to stay for the time being. Later on you might find it convenient to make another arrangement."

"You mean you want to turn me out. Aunt Harriet was the only one who liked me; perhaps that's why she was poisoned." Bertie's eyes blinked rapidly; he glared venomously from one to the other of them.

"No need for that sort of talk," Dangerfield said. "Least said soonest mended. This whole thing's been a nightmare, but it's over now. We must all put it behind us. Nobody can say you didn't stand by your wife, George, but I think now you should accept the verdict."

"I don't know why you let him talk like that; he's not even a member of the family. What right has he got to say what happens?" Bertie's voice had risen almost to a screech. "I want to stay here."

Dangerfield gave him a disdainful glance. George moved away from the fire, passed a hand over his face. "Humperdinck thought the summing up was unfair." His voice died away. He dropped into a chair.

"Charlotte, I want to stay here. Why can't I?" Bertie asked.

"We'll talk about it at some other time. Won't we, Robert?"

Dangerfield shrugged. "If you like. But I thought we'd agreed on a course of action. Things must be settled, about the house, about everything."

"George, I'm sorry, but I can't see Isabel again. I hope you understand," Charlotte said.

George had been abstracted, and seemed not to have heard. He said, "Robert, can we have a private word?"

They had the word in the library. "You've heard about young Paul?" George asked as soon as they were inside the room. "He's leaving the firm. Some rubbish about going into journalism." His hands twisted and intertwined.

"Leaving! He said nothing to me."

"Came to see me this afternoon. You were out somewhere or other. You know he's left the villa, gone into rooms."

"Yes, I knew that. I'm surprised, I must admit. I spoke to him the other day and he asked for a move inside the firm. I was going to mention it to you when this awful affair was over. He can't get on with Bertie. Can't say I blame him."

George's pudgy face was set in lines of despair. "Might

as well give the damn firm up, don't you think? Sell it as a going concern. Nobody in the family's interested any more."

"Nonsense." Dangerfield slapped him on the shoulder. "Just need a little more effort from all concerned, that's all. I'll have a word with young Paul tomorrow, see if he'll change his mind."

"He won't."

"We'll see. But if he doesn't, cheer up, old man. It isn't the end of the world."

When Dangerfield spoke to Paul he found that George had been right. The young man was determined to leave.

"You're being a fool, d'you know that? If you stay you should be a partner in a year or two. Have you got a job?"

"No. But I shall get one."

"What are you going to live on in the meantime?"

"I have some money." The boy's mouth was firmly set.

"You've made up your mind, I can see that. Look here, young Paul, I'm not one of the family yet, but I'm going to be. Is this to do with Isabel? You feel you've got to get away from home; you've done that. Now you're cutting yourself off from the family firm. I understand it, but believe me, you'll be sorry. I've known tragedy in my own life—you've heard about it, I daresay. Only thing is to face it head on. Don't flinch from 'em; face 'em and see if they like a taste of cold steel." He coughed. "In a manner of speaking. But the thing is, face it out."

"I don't know what you mean."

"Accept it. That's what Charlotte and I have done. Isabel must have been mad but she did it, poisoned them both. She's guilty."

The boy stared at him, and Dangerfield noticed the dark shadows under his eyes. "And in less than three weeks she'll be hanged," he said.

(269)

(5)

The Last Death

Evening News, January 22

ANOTHER DEATH IN COLLARD FAMILY

Mr. George Collard died suddenly at his home in Blackheath today. It is understood that Dr. Porterfield, the family physician, has requested that a post-mortem should take place.

Mr. Collard was the husband of Isabel Collard, who at the Old Bailey last week was found guilty of murdering her brother-in-law Roger Vandervent, and sentenced to death.

Daily Mail, January 25

AMAZING THIRD BLACKHEATH DEATH: MR. COLLARD AND POISONED SWEETS— POLICE INVESTIGATE WHO SENT THEM

By Our Special Crime Reporter Digby Stevens

A mystery as strange and sinister as any tale of the Borgias unfolded today as the police confirmed that the death of Mr. George Collard of Victoria Villa, Blackheath, was caused by poison.

The poison, which is believed to be arsenic in powder form, was contained in a box of sweets sent to Mr. Collard through the post. It is believed that Mr. Collard ate three or four of the sweets, and collapsed within a very short time.

Within a few months three members of this unhappy family have died from poison. Mr. Collard's brother-in-law, Roger Vandervent, died last May, and his mother, Mrs. Harriet Collard, in September. Now George Collard is dead. *Who is the poisoner?*

I was granted an interview with Superintendent Titmus, who is in charge of the case. He told me that the sweets, a box of French crystallized fruits, were received by post on the morning of the 22nd. They were addressed to Mr. Collard in block printing. By lucky chance the wrapping paper in which they came was preserved, and the Superintendent hinted that important clues may be found in this, and in a message that was enclosed with the sweets. When I asked if the message was handwritten, he declined to give further information.

"We are following up clues connected with the package," the Superintendent said. "It is impossible to give more details at present."

I put to him the vital question, the question that must occur to anybody who has followed this fascinating human drama of poison and mystery.

"A few days ago at the Old Bailey Mrs. Collard was found guilty of administering poison to her brother-in-law. Is this latest appalling crime linked with the other deaths, in your opinion?"

The Superintendent replied that there must be a strong presumption of the crimes being linked. He added quite properly that it would not be right for him to make conjectures about Mrs. Collard's position. "That must be a matter for the legal experts."

Nor would he say what lines of investigation are being pursued by the police, but it seems reasonable to suppose that the box of fruits, the wrap-

ping paper and the place of posting will be subjects of special interest.

Daily Mail, January 28

THE BLACKHEATH POISONINGS
EXCLUSIVE INTERVIEW WITH
THE BEREAVED FAMILY

By Our Special Crime Reporter Digby Stevens

I was given the privilege today of an interview
with surviving members of the Collard family,
who have suffered three tragic losses in the space
of a few months. I was received in the magnificent
gallery of Victoria Villa, designed some fifty years
ago on the finest Palladian models by the grandfa-
ther of Mrs. Vandervent, whose husband was the
first of the poisoner's victims. The gallery's splendid windows look out onto the gardens, which
were also designed on the Italian model to show
various ingenious perspectives, although modifications have been made to these.

Mrs. Vandervent was wearing a dark flowered
dress with what, for the benefit of our lady read-
ers, is I believe known as a gored skirt. She regards
the wearing of mourning as hypocritical. She was
accompanied by her sister, Charlotte Collard, and
by Mr. Robert Dangerfield, who is engaged to
marry Miss Collard. Mr. Dangerfield explained
that they had granted this interview in the hope,
as he said, of quieting rumors and getting a little
peace. It is a fact that even as I left, several reporters and photographers were clustered round the
entrance colonnade. Mrs. Vandervent told me
of the circumstances surrounding her brother's
death.

The package came in the post on the morning
of Saturday the 22nd, was taken in by one of the
maids and left in the hall. I spoke to the girl afterward, and she confirmed that the rectangular
package was addressed in printing to Mr. George

Collard, and marked "personal." Mr. Collard must have taken it upstairs with him, and the first Mrs. Vandervent knew was when she heard a cry from his room just before midday.

She found him lying on the floor. The box of fruits, of which three had been eaten, stood on a table. With them she remembers that there was a printed notice saying something to the effect that this was a manufacturer's sample. Mrs. Vandervent got her brother onto his bed with the maid's help, and called the doctor immediately.

Mr. Collard spoke only a few words, but they may prove highly significant. "I have been poisoned," he said. The significance is that he suspected poison immediately.

When Dr. Porterfield arrived, the sick man was beyond help. He died in little more than an hour.

The doctor said that he could not possibly sign a death certificate, and ordered a post-mortem. The result of this has still not been announced officially, but I understand that a number of the fruits had been coated with arsenic. The sweetness of the fruits would have effectively concealed the arsenic, which has very little taste.

I asked Mrs. Vandervent whether she could think of any reason for the deaths.

"I cannot tell you," she replied. "It is as though an enemy is conducting a vendetta, determined to wipe out our whole family." She clasped her hands together as though in prayer. "I have tried to stay here because this is my family home," she cried. "But I can do so no longer." She will move away from what is to her now a house of sorrow, and will live outside London.

Mr. Dangerfield has a theory of his own. He thinks that there may be a madman in the district with a long-standing grievance against the Collard family. I asked if he had mentioned this idea to the police, and he said that they were aware of it.

In the meantime, Mrs. Isabel Collard remains

in Brixton Prison. I understand that Sir Charles Russell, her counsel, will have a discussion with the Crown's legal authorities early next week.

The Times, January 30 (Editorial)

A CASE FOR ACTION

The recent development in what are popularly called the Blackheath Poisonings is disturbing in more ways than one. A week ago Mr. George Collard died after being sent some poisoned crystallized fruits. This is the third death in his family, and in two of the cases there seems to have been no obvious motive. The apparently far-fetched idea that a maniac is at work, somebody with a real or imaginary grudge against the whole Collard family, must be considered. The police authorities are no doubt examining this theory now, together with others, and we must hope that their investigations are brought to a speedy and successful conclusion.

But there is another aspect of the matter that calls for speedy action to be taken. In the early part of this month Isabel Collard, wife of the George Collard who has just died, was found guilty of administering poison to her brother-in-law. She is now in prison, lying under sentence of death. We have in this country no court of appeal from a jury's verdict, and this affair must strengthen the case of those who think that such a court should be brought into being.* The Blackheath Poisonings form a pattern in the sense that the poison has been the same in each case, and that the victims were all members of a family, and it is crystal clear that Mrs. Collard can have had no connection with the third death. When the fatal package was posted to her husband, she was languishing in prison.

---

* The Court of Appeal in England was established after the passage of the Criminal Appeals Act in 1907.

It is an old philosophical observation that a negative cannot be proved, and the innocence of Mrs. Collard in relation to this latest crime has no direct connection with the case in which she was found guilty. Yet the doubts of her guilt raised by it must be overwhelming. To put the matter simply, it is quite certain that if she were put on trial now, an acquittal would be inevitable. Even at the time voices were not lacking to say that she had been the victim of a natural reprehension of her admitted immorality. It is no criticism of the fairness of the trial to say that the verdict in it should not be allowed to stand. The situation is one without precedent in our criminal annals, and it calls for immediate action by the authorities concerned.

2

Mr. Makepeace put down the *Times* editorial on the table quietly, as he did everything. The Home Secretary looked at him, but Makepeace made no comment. The two of them sat for a moment as though fixed, the Home Secretary behind his desk with eyebrows raised waiting for a comment, and Makepeace in front of it on the right-hand side, looking blankly at the folded newspaper.

Their silence was broken by Sir Charles Russell, the third person in the room. Russell had been impatiently swinging one leg to and fro, and now he got up and stood beside the mantelpiece as though he were in his own office.

"There's no doubt at all that they're right," he said. "She must be released."

The Home Secretary was a tall man without a chin. He had a reputation for never committing himself to a decision that could not be attributed to somebody else in the event of trouble. He said in a thin, fluting voice,

"It is not quite so easily settled. What do you say, Mr. Makepeace?"

"You've spoken to Sir Henry?"

"Naturally." And it was indeed natural that the judge should be the first person consulted upon such a matter. The Home Secretary frowned at the memory. The discussion with Hawkins had not been agreeable, and in the end the Home Secretary had been forced into committing himself to a point of view.

"Sir Henry has of course the most immense respect for the traditional processes of law. As have we all," he added hastily.

"You mean he won't admit that a jury's verdict could have been wrong," Russell said.

The Home Secretary coughed. "Perhaps there is a little of that feeling. But in the end he said that if you gentlemen consented to the woman's release he would make no objection."

"I am not entirely happy," Makepeace said pensively, and with an air of abstraction. "I should like to know the result of the police investigation, or at least the present position."

The Home Secretary shuffled papers. "The position is that they are still trying to trace the origins of the wrapping paper and the form enclosed with the fruits."

"What about the purchase of the fruits themselves? They are not the kind of things sold in large quantities after Christmas."

"They have been traced. They were bought at—ah—Harrods." His voice went up a note. "I'm afraid I haven't the full details, but I gather nothing useful was learned about the purchase. The investigation is likely to be long-drawn-out. We must, I need hardly remind you, come to a decision quickly."

"With respect, I can't see that all this matters," Russell

said. He strode across the room, plumped up a cushion on a sofa and flung himself down on it. "The woman is going to be hanged in a few days. If she is to be released it should be done now, with no shilly-shallying." He looked at the Home Secretary, whose glance drifted away. "What did you have in mind, Harold?"

Still pensively, Makepeace murmured, "If it were possible to reach a conclusion, to make an arrest, that would give reassurance to the public."

Russell got up. "Very commendable, to reassure the public, but that isn't the point. I must tell you, gentlemen, that whatever may be the result of the police investigation, it is my strong opinion that Isabel Collard ought never to have been convicted, and that her present imprisonment is an injustice which should promptly be ended. I make no complaint about the conduct of the trial, but I do say that the verdict was against the evidence. I may have made a mistake in agreeing that she should make a statement. In any case, her crime was adultery, and because of her adultery she was convicted of murder."

The Home Secretary nodded. Russell was inclined to talk to people as if he were addressing a public meeting, but still sentiments strongly expressed helped to take matters out of the Home Secretary's hands, something for which he was always grateful.

Now Russell had reached the mantelpiece again, and he was still talking. "Whatever the result of the inquiry into Collard's death, it is my view that his wife should be released. Until she is set free I shall continue, with all the force at my disposal, to give my support to any newspaper asking that she should be set free. I have a letter drafted to *The Times*, but I delayed sending it until I knew the result of this meeting."

Again the Home Secretary raised his eyebrows, and

this time Makepeace responded. Stroking his chin, and with the faintest suggestion of a sigh, he said, "I hope, Sir Charles, you have no complaint to make about the conduct of the prosecution?"

"None at all."

"Nor—I think I should speak for him since he is not here—about Sir Henry's summing up?"

"I make no imputations of any kind."

Again with that half sigh, Mr. Makepeace said, "In that case I don't think I should resist your suggestion."

The Home Secretary was a man who liked every *i* dotted and every *t* crossed. "You are in agreement with Sir Charles that Mrs. Collard should be released?"

There was a fractional hestiation. "That is so. But I should wish the form of words to be chosen with care."

"Oh, the form of words," Russell said impatiently.

"It must not be said that the jury's verdict was wrong, not said nor even implied. I am sure, Home Secretary, you see the importance of that." The Home Secretary said that he did. "I think what we should do now is to look for a phrase that will say what we wish to convey. Sir Charles, perhaps you would like to draw up a chair. . . ."

3

The paragraph in the paper was headed: MRS. COLLARD TO BE RELEASED. It read:

> The Home Secretary made known today his decision in the case of Mrs. Collard, who last month was found guilty of poisoning Roger Vandervent with arsenic. The Home Secretary's statement says that because of the doubts raised by recent developments in the case, he has recommended

that Her Majesty should grant a free pardon to
Mrs. Collard. Mr. Vandervent's death was the first
of three poisonings in the same family, the third
of which took place while Mrs. Collard was in
prison.

It is understood that she will be released in the
course of the next few days. Police inquiries into
all three cases are continuing.

Police inquiries are continuing, Titmus thought. It
would be truer to say that they had come to a dead stop.
The clues that had appeared so promising had all turned
into broken threads. There were three of them in particular. First, the box of fruits, which was labeled "Fruits
Confits Exquise," and was obviously expensive. Second,
the wrapping paper and label. And third, a printed slip
found inside the box, which said: "This free sample comes
to you with the compliments of the manufacturers. They
will be glad to have your opinion of the goods." There
was a fourth possibility, that of tracing the arsenic. The
fruits consisted of apricots, pears, figs and plums. There
were twenty of them in the box, and all had been coated
with white arsenic, which adhered to the sticky fruits.

What had happened to the four leads? The box of fruits
had seemed particularly promising, especially when they
discovered that it was a make imported only to the order
of Harrods. Sales after Christmas had been few, and an
assistant remembered one which seemed unusual. Two
street urchins, around eight or nine years old, had somehow slipped in past the doorman and reached the sweets
department. One of them said that he wanted a box of
"vose fings," and pointed to the fruits.

The clerk was a middle-aged woman. "Run along,
sonny," she said.

"I want vose fings. They're the ones, ain't they, Jack?"
he said to his companion, who agreed that they were
the ones.

"I daresay you want them, but you can't have them. Run along."

"But I got the money, see." And he produced a guinea, which was the price of the box. When the clerk asked how he had got so much money, he said that a gentleman had given it to him, asked him to buy a box of the fruits, and said that he would get a shilling when he brought them back. It seemed an odd tale but the money was real enough, and the clerk sold the ragamuffin the box of fruits. She could not remember anything about the boys except that they were typical street urchins, and they had not said what the gentleman looked like. Inquiries in the area had failed to discover the boys. End of first clue.

The brown wrapping paper and the label on it proved to be of a common kind, sold at many stores. The writing on the label was in rather laboriously printed capitals, and there was not enough of it to be of use to handwriting experts. The parcel had been posted in the Charing Cross area on January 21, and in this particular search for a needle in a haystack no needle was found. End of second clue.

Attempts to find out where the arsenic had been bought proved useless. In this and in some other aspects of the inquiry Titmus had assistance from Scotland Yard detectives, assistance which he often felt he could have done without, in view of their distinctly lofty approach. The two Bills were also active, although both of them thought that they had found the arsenic already, in what they had turned up at the villa and at Albert House.

"Stands to reason, I mean," one of them said to Charlie Davis. "What he did was keep a bit out of the tins we found, for what you might call future use. Shouldn't be surprised if he's still got a few ounces by him. You want to look out when you down that pint of ale, doesn't he, Bill?"

"That's right. They tell me a couple of grains in a pint does wonders for the complexion, isn't that so, Bill?"

Their laughter was unseemly, but as Charlie had said to the superintendent, there was some force in what they said. There was so much arsenic easily available that it seemed almost pointless to make the round of chemists when they had no idea of the person they were looking for, except that he was male. The rounds were made, however, without result.

The printed slip did provide some information, but of a baffling kind. It had not, of course, been put in by the makers of the fruits, but had been inserted afterward. Scotland Yard did actually prove of use here. By analyzing the paper and making comparisons of the printing type used, they discovered that a Yorkshire printing house named Battersby had done the work. Battersby's were able to trace the order, which had been carried out for a firm of toymakers named York and Hudson. The toymakers agreed that they had sent out the slips with a new line in toy soldiers which had movable arms and legs. Because the soldiers were expensive, they had made only a few dozen boxes, one of which had been sent to Mortimer and Collard. And what had happened to the box when it arrived at the firm, a few days before George Collard's death? It had been given to him for his opinion on whether this was a line that should be stocked. Charlie Davis found the soldiers on the desk in Collard's office, but the slip was missing.

"What this means," Titmus said to him, underlining the obvious, "is that somebody at the firm must have sent that box of fruits. But you say any of them could have got hold of the slip."

"Collard wasn't in his office all the time. Anybody could have gone in there and taken it."

"They'd have had to know it was there."

Davis shook his head. "I couldn't find that anybody, any of the family, would have known that. The box went straight up to Collard after it had been opened."

"Of course, he might have taken it in to Dangerfield and asked his opinion of it. Dangerfield says, 'Leave it with me,' spots the label and realizes he can use it, returns the box to Collard's room later. That's possible."

"I suppose so," Charlie said unenthusiastically. The affair had become too much for him.

"Or there's another possibility we haven't even considered. George Collard may have taken the slip out of the box himself."

"But that's crazy."

"It may sound crazy, Charlie, but then there seems a good chance that we're dealing with a madman. You know the question I'd like to have answered?" His subordinate shook his head like a punch-drunk boxer. "Who will be next?"

4

In order to avoid publicity, Isabel was released from Brixton very early in the morning. It was still almost dark—a heavy, damp fog obscured everything—and for a moment she thought that nobody had come to meet her. Then the portly figure of her father emerged from the mist. Augustus folded her in his arms, picked up her case and led her to the waiting hansom.

On the way back to Dulwich she asked about her mother and sisters, but said nothing about Blackheath. Nor did she do so later, after she had embraced and been embraced, and had been installed in her old room. Her mother went up to have a talk, on Augustus's instructions, but came down after half an hour, saying that it was impossible to get the girl to say anything.

"She isn't a girl; she's a married woman," Augustus said. "I mean a widow. And what d'you mean, won't say anything? Of course she must say something about what she's going to do."

"Just leave it a little while, Augustus. Let her settle in."

Augustus responded with a snort, but he went to the office and "left it" until the evening. During the day, Isabel, he learned, had been composed and cheerful, talking to her mother and sisters as though the events of the past months had never happened. It was more than Augustus could stand, and after dinner he spoke to her.

"We're all glad to have you home, my love, you know that. Stay here as long as you like."

"Thank you, Father."

"You must have been thinking in these last weeks, thinking about the future and what you were going to do."

She gave him a small, chilly smile. "After I was sentenced, I tried not to think about the future."

"Of course, of course." Augustus was conscious of having put it badly, and aware, too, that the discussion was not going to be easy. "But you must have thought—well, to put it bluntly, do you want to go back to the villa? I don't know if it's possible, but—"

"I shall never go back there. I shall never return to Blackheath."

"Ha." He brooded on this. "It's as I suggested—you've given some thought to it. Naturally you'll have plans. All I want to say is that if I can help I will. Perhaps a little holiday out of London—Cheltenham or Bath—

might be a good thing. Your mother would go with you, I'm sure." He remembered suddenly that he had made a similar suggestion to Beatrice.

"Father, I am not ill. I don't think you are facing the reality of what has happened. I have been at the center of a trial for murder. No doubt some people still think I am guilty even though I have been pardoned for something I did not do. I am notorious; I shall be recognized. If mother and I went to Bath, it would not be very pleasant for her, to say nothing of myself. It will not be comfortable for any of you while I am at Dulwich, and I shall not stay here long."

All this might be true, but it was not what he had expected. He found it difficult to talk to her when, after what she had experienced, she was so cool and so hard. And somewhere in the back of his mind he felt, no doubt about it, a sense of relief that she wouldn't be with them too long. He had a duty as a father, he told himself, to the other girls as well as Isabel, and her presence in the household would not make it easier to find them husbands.

"What do you propose to do?"

"I am not sure. But you need not worry. I shan't be a burden to you."

"I don't know what George will cut up for, but I can easily find out. Not a great deal, I'm afraid. Dangerfield and Charlotte are going to live in Albert House, and Beatrice is selling the villa. You know that, I expect."

"In my situation, how do you suppose that I know anything?" There was a pause. "And Paul?"

"He's not living at home; got rooms somewhere. Left the firm too. I understand he's got some potty little job as a journalist." His tone was censorious. He did not approve of journalists. She made no comment.

Mrs. Payne was not a malicious woman, but she could

not refrain from asking, that night in bed, whether he had found it easy to talk to their daughter. Augustus said it had been devilish difficult, but that at least it was settled that she would not stay long at Dulwich.

"You didn't say that she must go?"

"Of course not; what do you take me for? She said it herself. Indeed, she says everything herself; she don't care about anything. She's our daughter, but I'm afraid she's got no morals of any sort."

"Oh, Augustus."

"It's true. I can't think what's to become of her."

But such forebodings were belied by what happened. On the following night an acquaintance of Augustus's named Solly Smith came to dinner. He lived in Johannesburg, where he had a rapidly expanding business supplying all kinds of clothing to the men working the gold mines of The Rand. Augustus acted as his English agent, and had the vague idea that Solly might be interested in one of his daughters. Solly's name had originally been Solomon Schmidt, and he was a Jew who had come from Germany to South Africa a few years earlier without a penny in his pocket; but he had plenty of money now, and as Augustus said to his wife, they had to move with the times. He had done business with Jews and found them no more dishonest than Gentiles, and it was not so long since Britain had had a Jewish Prime Minister. If Solly should fancy one of the girls, and if they were able to contemplate living in Jo'burg . . .

That was not the way it turned out. From the first evening Solly Smith had eyes for nobody but Isabel. He took her out almost every night, to theaters and concerts and to Buffalo Bill's Wild West Show, which had recently come to London. In the afternoons he accompanied her to exhibitions of new paintings by Millais, Corot and Herkomer, for which Augustus was sure he didn't care a fig.

When he went up to Lancashire to talk to cotton manufacturers, he wrote to her almost every day, and on his return
he told Augustus that he had proposed marriage and been
accepted. Augustus was pleased in one way, shocked in
another. He felt that he had to mention Isabel's past.

"Bless you, Gus, all that I know about. Isabel she herself
tell me." Solly's heavily accented English was intelligible
but erratic, with words sometimes oddly placed. "In
South Africa we do not think about this kind of thing
so much. One of my best friends, Izzy Williams, last year
he shoots a man in a poker game."

Augustus did not care for the shortening of his name,
but somehow Solly seemed unable to understand his objection, and went on using the abbreviation. Augustus
was unable to resist asking what had happened to Izzy
Williams.

"Hunnerd pound fine he paid. The other man, his
sleeve of aces is full. What do you say?"

"About Isabel? I'm delighted, but it isn't for me to say
anything. I just wanted to make sure you knew what
had happened. And I ought to say that she's got very
little money."

"I have enough for two. Big house, of servants plenty."
Solly's nose was bent and sharp as a bird's beak. "And
no more Rogers. If I find she looks at another man, I
beat her. Eh?"

So it was settled. Less than six weeks after leaving
prison she was joined in marriage to Solomon Smith at
a registry office. Augustus and his family were there, and
afterward Solly gave a small party, to which he invited
some of his business associates. A couple of paragraphs,
no more, appeared in the papers. Very soon after the
wedding the couple left for South Africa.

"You see," Isabel said to her father just before she left.
"I said that I shouldn't be a burden."

"But do you love him?"

"I don't know about that. I loved somebody once, and it brought me no luck. Solly and I have an arrangement. I think it will work very well."

There were several things Augustus wanted to say— that you should not love somebody who was not your husband, that marriage should be a bond and not an arrangement, that she was going to a violent and barbarous city, so filled with Jews that people called it Jewburg— but what was the use? Nothing he said could possibly influence her.

He said that he hoped she would be happy. At that she smiled. "Solly has a lot of money. That isn't everything, but it helps."

5

The question that Titmus had asked of Charlie Davis— "Who will be next?"—was never answered, for nobody else died. Investigations into the case continued for weeks, even for months, but nothing further that seemed relevant happened, nothing new was discovered.

There were, certainly, things to report about the activities of the Collard family. At the end of March Robert Dangerfield and Charlotte were married, and thereafter they lived at Albert House. Most of the staff were dismissed, and new ones engaged. By this time Dangerfield had taken over the running of the firm, and was supposed to have made extensive changes there too. He certainly brought in the son of a retired major general whom he had known in India. He had also dispensed with the services of Bertie Williams, who had become the assistant secretary of the London Temperance society, and was living with several other temperance supporters in a house owned by the society. Beatrice had left Victoria Villa, which was now standing empty. She had gone on a round of visits to friends in the Midlands, and the house was up for sale. Paul Vandervent was working as a journalist on the *Evening Gazette,* and was still living in his Guilford Street rooms.

All this, six months after the death of George Collard, was known to Titmus, and about this time active inquiries into what had happened were given up. A view of the case formed itself in the superintendent's mind, however, and it was one that he never saw reason to change. He believed that Isabel Collard had in fact poisoned both Roger Vandervent and Harriet Collard. According to this theory, she had confessed guilt to her husband, and he had forgiven her. When she had been sentenced to death George had taken the only way he knew to save her. He had poisoned himself, and made the death look like murder. This explained the use of the label, George having put it in with the box of fruits which he had then posted to himself. He had taken a particularly large dose so that he should not have long to suffer. This was Titmus's explantion, which Charlie Davis thought far-fetched.

The file on the case was never closed. It gathered dust over the years, since there was nothing to add to it. The Blackheath Poisonings were never explained.

Epilogue

From Paul Vandervent's Journal

June 15, 1930   The empire of the O'Brien newspaper group, of which the Evening Gazette is a luminary, is far-flung. One of its smaller twinkling stars is the Johannesburg Rand Weekly Gazette, a gossipy affair which picks up bits of news often ignored by the more staid South African daily papers. I look through it occasionally, and was doing so today when I saw a short notice.

DEATH OF MRS. SOLLY SMITH—
ECHO OF FAMOUS MURDER TRIAL

The death has occurred at her home in Johannesburg of Isabel, wife of Solly Smith, head of the well-known firm of merchant bankers. Mrs. Smith had been in poor health for some time, and had recently come out of hospital after an operation for the removal of a tumor. Before her illness, Mrs. Smith was one of the most celebrated of the city's hostesses, famous for the lavishness of her parties. She was in her sixty-third year.

Few of the visitors who partook of the fabulous Smith hospitality knew that many years ago Mrs. Smith was the central figure in a sensational murder trial. In the last decade of the nineteenth century she was tried and found guilty on a charge of poisoning her brother-in-law. The verdict was later upset, and she was granted a free pardon. She put the past completely behind her in South Africa, and did not care to be reminded of it, or even to see people from the old country. "Isabel was the best wife a man could have, and I shall miss her deeply" Solly, now a hale and hearty eighty, said after the funeral. She is survived by a son and a daughter, Gordon and Miriam.

I put down the paper, and at that instant one of the subs came into the room to ask about changing the front page in the next edition. I was blinded by tears, and had to turn away to the window to compose myself. When I spoke, my voice was still choked, not my own. How terrible is the past when it comes back like this, with the force of a tidal wave. I remembered it all: life at the folly and Sunday lunch at the church, Isabel sitting in the long gallery like a queen, my adoration and my vision of her as a being removed from the stress of ordinary daily life, the pressure of her nails on my palm when we left the poetry recital, Father's illness and death, and the awful things that followed. . . . There they were, all back with me as they had not been for years.

Somerset Maugham says somewhere that Victorians felt about women as though they had no back passages, and that is the way I felt about Isabel. How innocent I was then, how foolish, how young. You would think that thirty-odd years at the Gazette as journalist, at first anonymous and then with a by-line, then editorial writer and at last deputy editor, would have shown me what the world was like. And so it has, but how do you forget your own youth?

It is because of Isabel, or so I feel, that I have never

*married, and I shall never marry now. I am in my middle
fifties, my flat in Great Russell Street is convenient and
comfortable and will no doubt see me out, Mrs. Rowe
who comes in and does for me keeps the place clean and
tidy. If I want to give a dinner party she is a very fair
cook, and her daughter comes in to wait at table. What
more could one want? A very great deal, would be a
truthful answer: a wife to keep the bed warm and children to soften the cheerless advance of old age. But although there have been women whom I have dined and
wined and danced, and sometimes brought back here
to bed, there has never been one whom I would have
wished to marry. At any hint that my partner in an alli-
ance which had been continued for a week—or in a couple
of cases for several weeks—thought that it might be permanent, I was off like a shot, saying, politely of course,
No, thanks. Was this because of Isabel? I think so. Certainly she is the only woman about whom I could ever
think of using the word "love." Is this to admit that my
life has been a failure? I really don't know. Certainly
it contains unfulfilled hopes and ambitions, but isn't that
true of every life? To have made a reasonable success
as a journalist—is that success or failure? Don't know,
don't know.*

*If I look sideways I can see the British Museum from
the window of the room which I call the library because
it contains a lot of books. This evening when I got home
I took out a file labeled "Ancient History" and extracted
from it the last letter Isabel wrote me. What am I talking
about? I should say the only letter she wrote me. It was
written while she was on the boat to South Africa after
her marriage, and posted in Cape Town. The paper, now
very faded, is thick, with a deckle edge, the writing nervous, with an upward slant, as though the writer were*

eager to get the letter done with. I used to know it by heart.

Dear Paul,

There is nobody else in England to whom I feel I need to write a letter, but you are on my mind. I worry about you, I think I behaved wrongly to you, I took advantage of your youth, the calf love you felt for me, your readiness to do anything that might help me. I should never have involved you in my affairs. Believe me, I am deeply sorry. When I saw you in the witness box looking so much like Roger, it wrung my heart. I think I should never have spoken to you about my affairs if you had not reminded me so often of Roger.

That terrible judge would say that a woman like me has no heart to be wrung. I know that even Russell thought I was despicable, and he was my own counsel. I am writing in part so that you may understand, or at least won't think too badly of me.

I never loved George. Our relations—our marriage relations, I mean—were always grotesque or nonexistent. I cannot tell you the ridiculous things he proposed to me. Within a month of marrying him I knew that I had made an awful mistake. And within a week of meeting Roger I loved him. I should never have stayed at the villa, should have told George I couldn't live there, made some excuse. . . . Oh, I could go on and on, but it would be useless. You can never understand my feelings, or at least not yet. Perhaps you will someday.

But really I am writing to say that you must forget me. I shall never regret loving Roger. I regret nothing, nothing—except that I involved you in my trouble. That was dreadfully wrong.

I do not know, shall never know, what happened, but I had nothing to do with it. It is all a mystery to me. How could anybody think that I would have killed Roger? I loved him. I shall never love anybody else. The man I have married seems kind and generous, but he knows I do not love him. So far as love is concerned, my life is over. Yours is only beginning. Do not let this terrible experience affect you. Forget me.

Isabel

I have copied the letter here, because it seems to me that there can be no harm now in writing the full story. All those who played a part in it are dead, all except me. Augustus died just before the century was out, collapsing while he was making a speech at a City luncheon asking for volunteers to go out to South Africa and fight against the Boers. He had managed to marry off all but one of his daughters, and left his family well provided for. Beatrice died two or three years later, when she was taking the cure at Baden-Baden. She never had a permanent home again after the tragedies, and I suppose you might say that her life was shattered by them.

Bertie, the Caterpillar Bertie Williams—how I loathed him—deserves a paragraph to himself. He rose to a high position in the temperance movement, and was well known as a speaker. During the Great War he journeyed round the country addressing meetings, because it was thought that this was the time when a drive should be made to convert the whole of Britain into one great temperance society, with the closure of all pubs. Bertie caught influenza while addressing an open-air meeting in Huddersfield, and it developed into pneumonia, which carried him off. He was given an obituary in The Times, which surprised and infuriated me. An obituary for the Caterpillar! It hardly seemed possible.

Dangerfield outlasted them by some years. He died a few years back, I can't remember just how many, having expanded Dangerfield, Mortimer and Collard into a very successful firm that sold all kinds of sporting goods. Charlotte survived him only a short time. I used to see them occasionally—not at the church, because I could never bear to go back there, but we would have dinner at a restaurant in London, and once or twice they came here. There is no doubt that Charlotte loved him, but did he love her or did he just want the money and position which he certainly got? I don't know. They had no children.

And now Isabel is gone, the last link with my youth broken. The houses have gone too, both the folly and the church. The folly remained empty and unsold for several years. Children had fun breaking its windows, the stucco peeled, vandals wrecked what was left of the garden. I passed it once or twice, and was saddened by what I saw. When at last the place was sold, the villa was demolished and two modern houses built upon the site, hideous creations of red brick with mock-Tudor embellishments. I suppose the folly was mock too, but at least it was an imitation with some grandeur about it, a certain style. The Dangerfields lived in the church for more than the prescribed fifteen years, but of course it was an absurdly large house for a couple without children, and in the end they sold it and moved to Kensington. The church also remained unsold for a year or two, but then it was bought by a man who turned it into a school for young children. The school lasted for a while, and then the house was empty again until it was bought by a property firm, who transformed its appearance inside and out, putting in a new front and twenty new windows, splitting up the Great Hall and destroying the gallery. The whole thing made a small apartment block.

So it has all gone, my youth and the people I shared it with. They are as distant as Germinations, the tiny pamphlet of imitative verses that I published (at my own expense, of course) with money I had saved from my first year or so on the paper, in the days when I thought

I might be a poet. I sent a copy of it to Isabel in Johannesburg, but she never acknowledged it. Perhaps it was better so.

I stopped writing for an hour or so after the last paragraph. I walked round this apartment, trying to look at it as though I were outside it all, completely detached, examining what I have made of things, wondering whether I might have done something different. Idle thoughts, all idle. The shape of my life was ordered by what happened nearly forty years ago. When I came back here to the library I opened the French windows that lead out to the stone balcony overlooking Great Russell Street. It is nearly three in the morning. The air is warm, the street quiet, the lamps glitter, the bulk of the British Museum is reassuring. Things are not so bad.

And now I go on to the end.

The ability to see a past incident or person visually is one that I have had since childhood. I have told how I recalled by its means that damp print of a glass ring on my father's bedside table. I had of course no proof that my vision was truthful, yet I knew that this was so. A similar vision of something at the Caravanserai told me the truth about the Blackheath Poisonings. If I had not been so drunk, if I had not in my drunkenness used the words "night and day," which were needed as an admission phrase, everything would have been different. There in the Caravanserai I met Dolores, Georgina and Maria. I refused Dolores's advances and ran away.

That was what happened. But something in that scene lingered in my memory, although for days I could not tell what it was. I went over it again and again, separating one fragment from another as though I were looking (as we would say now) at each frame of a cinema film. Going in there, talking to Eve, the introduction to the women,

Dolores's fan, Georgina's ring-covered hands, Maria's thick fair hair, Dolores's attempt to seduce me . . . And when I had run through the film a hundred times I knew what I had seen. It was Georgina's hands, those pudgy hands covered with rings, hands that twisted and untwisted before she turned away from me. I knew those hands. They were the hands of Uncle George.

It might be thought that I would have considered this idea only to reject it, but that would be to underestimate the clarity and certainty of my vision. As soon as this had come to my mind I knew it to be true. I could not prove it, but I knew that my genial burbling Uncle George and the Georgina who had turned away from me abruptly in the Caravanserai were the same person. If I had not been so young and so innocent, I should have understood almost at once that the Caravanserai was a meeting place for transvestites and not a brothel in the ordinary sense. I should have know what the fair-haired young man was implying when he said that there were no women in old Omar, and would have realized that prostitutes did not, as Dolores did, say that the client needn't pay. This was a club, one of several around Haymarket and Covent Garden at that time, in which if any payment at all was made it came from the mostly middle-aged men who tried to fulfill their natures by dressing up as women, and not from those who visited them.

If the stranger wore a uniform, so much the better. The greatest prize for most of these transvestites must have been a young guardsman. And I knew the meaning also of the women's clothes found in Father's desk, which the Caterpillar had told me that the police had traced to Uncle George. He had said, as I learned later, that he had bought them for a mistress, and had got some prostitute to confirm this. But of course he had not bought them for a woman. He meant to wear them himself, and in some way or another Father must have found them and realized that.

But although I understood all this, and understood the nature of the clubs that George had visited when he came home so late, I had no proof of it. I was as sure that George had given poison to Father and to Step-grand as if I had seen him doing it, sure also that it was he in women's clothing who had bought arsenic and signed the register in Isabel's name; but what could I do about it? I spent a night or two in anguish, and then resolved that I would wait until the end of the trial. I refused to believe that Isabel could be found guilty.

At the same time I felt that I could no longer have any contact with Uncle George. I moved out of the villa.

Then came the guilty verdict. On the following morning I went in to see George in his office. He was sitting at his desk, engaged in looking at samples on his desk, one a fire engine and the other a box of soldiers, a couple of which were out on the table.

"Paul," he said, "just look at this." He showed me that the fire engine had a ladder that raised itself and also a hose that squirted water, and that the soldiers had movable legs so that you could actually march them along. He was beaming with that characteristic Uncle George jollity.

"Uncle George," I said. "Georgina."

His head went up. He dropped the soldier. As he looked up at me, his lower lip quivered as though he were about to cry.

"Father found out, didn't he? You quarreled. And he was going to do something about it."

He gulped as though he were swallowing medicine, and then the words poured out. "Roger found me one day trying on some new clothes, something I'd got that was, well, rather fast, cut like this." The pudgy hands sketched an outline low on his chest. "I told him that it was for a fancy-dress party, and he seemed to accept it. But then he found some things I'd bought—a corset, gloves and so on. They were delivered here to the office, some stupid boy put them on his desk by mistake and he opened the parcel. That's what he said, but I believe he was determined to ruin me.

"He showed me the things and accused me. He said, 'You're one of those fellows who like to dress as a woman,' and he took the things with him. I fought, I scratched him, but he went off with them. He said I must resign from the firm, and he told me he'd advise Isabel to leave me, that she had had enough of what he called my goings-on. It was a game, you know; I wanted her to pretend that we were both girls, that was all. But she would never do it. I warned Roger then; I said, 'I shan't endure this, I am not going to suffer it, I won't have my life destroyed.' And he said—oh, he could be so hateful, your father— 'What do you think you can do about it?' So I showed him."

There was something horrible about the way he said all this. He sat there in his respectable formal suit with its high collar and sober necktie, but the voice in which he spoke had feminine intonations and there was something coy, almost flirtatious, in his manner.

"So you poisoned him," I said. "You wore your woman's clothing, bought the poison and signed for it in Isabel's name. And then you put it in the whisky."

"Oh, Isabel," he said pettishly. "I didn't see why I should have any regard for Isabel. She would never, never play with me." He put his hand up to his hair, stroked it and smiled. "But it was just a game to sign her name in the book; I didn't think it would go any further. I could hardly sign my own name, after all, could I? And Porterfield was all right. Everything would have been all right if there weren't so many busybodies about."

"And Harriet," I said. "She was your mother."

He flung himself back in his chair. "It was all her fault, don't you see? When I was little she used to dress me in the most lovely frocks. After I had to put on knee breeches I cried and cried, they were so rough. And then I'm sure she knew. About my little games, I mean. She showed me the corset and other things and said she knew I'd bought them, and asked who they were for. I said a friend. She gave me one of those looks of hers—they always frightened me, those looks—and said nothing like it must happen again. Oh, it was really frightening."

"It was the medicine, I suppose? After we got back from the theater."

"Yes, I'd put just a tiny bit in once or twice before. Just to see what happened, you know; it was interesting. But when she was so frightening, I knew I had to do something. I took the bottle away with me afterwards, and nobody noticed. Things were particularly difficult just then." He gave a brief high giggle, like a hiccup, quite unlike any sound made by the Uncle George I knew.

"What do you mean?"

"I have a number of expenses," he said coyly. "Some of my friends are awfully extravagant." It occurred to me afterward that he perhaps meant that he, too, was paying blackmail. "I expected that Mother would have money to leave. I was the eldest; she should have left the estate to the eldest. But she cheated me, as she always did."

"What are you going to do now?"

He stared. "Do? What should I do?"

"Isabel is innocent. She has been sentenced to death."

"I've told you already, I don't see that I need have any regard for Isabel. Think of the things she was doing with your father, the filthy letters she wrote to him. If I'd known about them—"

"You didn't know?"

"*Of course not. Do you think I should have put up with such goings-on for five minutes? What do you take me for?*"

We looked at each other, and as I stared at his indignant yet slightly smirking face I knew that he was insane. Then, as though a light had been taken away, he was again the Uncle George I had known. He said quietly, "I'm fond of you, Paul. I hope you don't have any foolish ideas about using my little games to hurt me. You couldn't do that, you know. What I've said to you is just between the two of us. I should never repeat a word of it to anybody else."

I suppose I had gone to see him with some vague hope that he would back down, say that he was ready to confess his guilt to the police, but of course that was a pipe dream. I think now that he would not have spoken as he did unless he had been strongly attracted by me, but that thought did not cross my mind at the time. Yet in spite of my youth I was not altogether foolish. I had known what his answer was likely to be, and I knew also what I must do.

The last sight of Uncle George behind his desk is scored on my mind as though with an etching tool. I saw at the same time the box of soldiers on the desk below me— I had remained standing while we talked—with that printed slip on top of it. Something in my unconscious mind must have understood the usefulness of the slip, and made me pick it up. We gave each other a long look. He said, "You do understand?"

I said that I understood, and walked out.

There is not much more to put down. Writing now, long, long after it all happened, I should like to be able to say that I had wrestled with my conscience, had considered telling the police what I knew, or contemplated going back to the Caravanserai and trying to obtain evi-

dence of George's activities there. I doubt if the police would have paid me any attention, but the truth is that at the time I did not think of doing any such thing. Isabel had only three weeks to live, and I knew that she was innocent. I saw only one way in which she could be saved.

The poison was a white arsenic used at the house as a weed-killer, named WeKillIt. I had often seen tins of it around, and I bought some in a shop. I went into Harrods, looked at the crystallized fruits, noted a box likely to appeal particularly to George, and sent the boys in to buy it. Then I dusted all of them with arsenic, taking them out of the box and replacing each one carefully. I put in the label. There was no need in those days to worry about fingerprints as there would be today, and no fear, either, that George would offer the fruits to anybody else. Indeed, there was nobody to whom he could offer them except Beatrice, who disliked sweet things.

And then, with no feeling of any kind, I posted the package.

At the time I did not think that I was doing anything wrong. My action seemed inevitable. Even today I doubt if I could have done anything else that would have saved Isabel. But in fact the action marked me for life. I killed another person, killed him deliberately, and this is something I have never been able to forget. Is that why I have never married? I suppose a psychologist might be able to tell me, but I have never been inclined to consult one. For a long time there were nights when I saw Father in dreams, lying in bed as he was at the end, trying desperately to say something that I knew to be vitally important. I leaned toward him in an attempt to grasp what it was, but although his lips moved I could never understand what he said. Then I would wake with a voice in my ears, and know that the voice was my own, and what word I had spoken.

Those nightmares are less frequent now, but my life has been marked always by this shadow in the past, as well as by the memory of Isabel. I see no way in which I could have saved her without doing what I did, yet I have suffered ever since an overwhelming feeling of guilt. The knowledge that I deliberately took another life will stay with me forever.

I have written almost all night, and now the dawn is showing palely over the rooftops. A single pair of footsteps sound in the street, and I catch my breath as they approach. They reach this block, seem to hesitate—and pass on. I know very well that they are the steps of a man going to work or returning home after a night out. Yet whenever the street is quiet and I hear footsteps outside, I wait with senses taut, nerves stretched like elastic, for those feet to ascend the stairs and enter the apartment. I do not know who the visitor will be—he is faceless and bodiless, a phantom—but I know he will whisper the word that I speak in dreams and wake to find ringing in my ears: Murderer.

FOR THE BEST IN MYSTERY, LOOK FOR THE

☐ **THE PENGUIN COMPLETE FATHER BROWN**
G.K. Chesterton

Here, in one volume, are forty-nine sensational cases investigated by the high priest of detective fiction, Father Brown, whose cherubic face and unworldly simplicity disguise an uncanny understanding of the criminal mind.
718 pages   ISBN: 0-14-009766-X

☐ **BRIARPATCH**
Ross Thomas

This Edgar Award-winning thriller is the story of Benjamin Dill, who returns to the Sunbelt city of his youth to attend his sister's funeral—and find her killer.
384 pages   ISBN: 0-14-010581-6

☐ **APPLEBY AND THE OSPREYS**
Michael Innes

When Lord Osprey is murdered in Clusters, his ancestral home, with an Oriental dagger, it falls to Sir John Appleby and Lord Osprey's faithful butler, Bagot, to pick out the clever killer from an assortment of the lord's eccentric house guests.
184 pages   ISBN: 0-14-011092-5

☐ **GOLD BY GEMINI**
Jonathan Gash

Lovejoy, the antiques dealer whom the *Chicago Sun-Times* calls "one of the most likable rogues in mystery history," searches for Roman gold coins and greedy bird-killers on the Isle of Man.
224 pages   ISBN: 0-451-82185-8

☐ **REILLY: ACE OF SPIES**
Robin Bruce Lockhart

This is the incredible true story of superspy Sidney Reilly, said to be the inspiration for James Bond. Robin Bruce Lockhart's book tells the thrilling story of the British Secret Service agent's shadowy Russian past and near-legendary exploits in espionage and in love.
192 pages   ISBN: 0-14-006895-3

☐ **STRANGERS ON A TRAIN**
Patricia Highsmith

Almost against his will, Guy Haines is trapped in a nightmare of shared guilt when he agrees to kill the father of the man who will kill Guy's wife. The basis for the unforgettable Hitchcock thriller.
256 pages   ISBN: 0-14-003796-9

☐ **THE THIN WOMAN**
Dorothy Cannell

An interior designer who is also a passionate eater, her rented companion who writes trashy novels, and a rich dead uncle with a conditional will are the principals in this delicious thriller.   *242 pages   ISBN: 0-14-007947-5*

FOR THE BEST IN MYSTERY, LOOK FOR THE